NETHERWEAR

or

Eqinox - The Precursor

Chris Stedman

Illustrated by Sue Rosser

Published by BlotterPress.com

February 2012

ISBN 978 095719 4441

Copyright © C. Stedman 2012

Dedicated to my children.

Table of Contents

Author's foreword

Some years ago, the daughter of a friend learned that 'knickers' was considered a rude word, so of course, she continually repeated it to see the reactions of adults. She was eventually taught to say 'underwear', which didn't evoke the same reaction. *Netherwear* is just another word for *knickers*.

Every time you come across a word in this book, you are automatically set the task of thinking to yourself, *what else does it mean?*

Adults lose their *elgins*, not their marbles, they play *elgins* and are *a couple of elgins short of a Parthenon*.

Mathematicians, or *Arithmates* as they are called here, have great difficulties in their work because the philosophers have copyrighted infinity and the *arithmates* are not allowed to use it, or even know about it, making their life different from every other *arithmate* in the universe. One of the best/worst things to befall an *arithmate* is the sign of the *Sigmata* (Σ) on the hands and forehead. If it doesn't ring a bell, look up *stigmata*.

If you have a little Greek and a very little Latin, reading this will become easier. For instance a Greek scholar will instantly recognise a *quadric gammagram* as a swastika so that a *Ferrikross* is like that iron (ferrous) object which that band of marauding riffs, the Third Reich, gave out for bravery.

You will find the *Amorics* with *Lynkern* as *Precedent* (a *Precedent* is a leader because he does everything first, setting a precedent, of course).

Twains wun on *twaks* and come from *Anerak*. Between the two engines is a *snake sandwich* containing *clarridges* (hotels on wheels) wherein one travels; but if you fall asleep, you may have a *narcolexic attack* - talk poetically in your sleep.

Most fun is *extra-nuptial replication practice* which it appears most people do in their spare time, when not reading the *Thundering Tempora* (The Times newspaper used to be known as the Thunderer).

Tournament Square in walled *Faience* (faience is a type of earthenware or 'china') is where battles take place between the most revolting students and giant military machines.

The *Thatcherfactorismoptimist* Party founded by St. Thatch failed because of it's long and silly name.

Of course, the most dangerous thing in the universe is that number which is *776 plus one*, for it must never be said, being the number of the devil or *HobB*. This is almost as dangerous as failing to begin and end spiritual words (like GoD and HobB and WitcH) with a capital letter, thereby allowing evil to enter.

All in all, if you have a love of words and enjoy playing games with linguistics, mathematics, literary history, geography, Sherlock Holmes, quantum theories, religious dogma *(Godmatics?)* and ethics, you will enjoy it.

One comment from the first person ever to read this text that must be put to death straight away: I was accused of plagiarising *Terry Pratchett*. Truth is that when this book was written, I had never heard of him, although having now read some of his work, I acknowledge that there are a couple of accidentally generated vague coincidences with the works of that great writer, such as use of the word thaumaturge (a miracle worker), the unit of magic, millithaums (now removed from the text!) and the concept of a non-spherical planet - although mine is supported on Quantum Probability rather than on elephants!

Have fun reading and interpreting it and looking for all the jocular and obscure literary, religious, historical, geographical and scientific references.

Just remember that virtually every word can have two - or more meanings Think - what else would you call drinking *glasses* but *specs?* If you DO understand the jokes, great, if you don't, they are designed not to be noticed or detract from the rest of your enjoyment, so it doesn't matter anyway.

Chris Stedman. December 1999

Netherwear

Chapter 0   Where?

As planets go, so Equinox is. Typical and virtually spherical, except that it is made up of 47 geoplatelets each of which is convex to a radius equal to the diameter of the whole. Thus, like certain coins in our pockets, the planet retains a constant diameter whilst appearing to have sides.

Certain magical properties exist in space and time which the locals call Qontûm.   These cause strange eruptions of confusion amid a normally calm and peaceful environ.

Once upon a time, on Equinox, something landed. It landed from a long way away. It took a very long time for the microbes on it to Darwinise themselves into beings, some of which looked remarkably like us. In fact, the entire planet bore a remarkable resemblance to Earth, except that there were nearly as many differences as similarities.

It was then that the something that landed was found; that is where we begin.

Chapter 1   The Orijin

But the spherical coffin was open; its contents were spread around, smothering the catafalque.

Sideways and outside the rope, the circumspect queue shuffled forward, missing little in their examination of the scene.

The crowd were fascinated but deferential. Silently, each stared with intense and respectful bowed head. Each shuffler played the part every bit as though offering final respects to a long dead ancestor, which in one sense was true.

Even in this excited but sombre cosmopolitan assemblage, one stood out.

The deceptively youthful-looking Smelt was distinctive; his high forehead and greying hair portrayed a seriously distinguished demeanour. Without betraying his considerable interest, he studied the scene with more concern and a far greater awareness of its significance than the majority of his companions.

In tow, but faithfully leading the way, was what he had always believed to be an intelligent but nevertheless appropriately obedient little middle-aged consort.

On the wall behind Smelt was mounted an exhibition of how the Orijin was sought and found; mostly fact but for the benefit of the more sensitive and the religiots, part elegiac, part eulogy, part religious dogma and part urban myth.

The ever lengthening trail of Triseps viewed the holographically exhibited detail backwards - with their second heads so that the first head - the one with the main brain - could study the Orijin itself.

Smelt glanced back and forth from the Orijin to his partner. Could this, he wondered, *really* be *the* egg, the ex ovo omnia from which all life on Planet Five had evolved?

Slowly but definitely, the growing clump of Triseps crabbed steadily: sidling, they preferred to call it. Each Trisep stood proud with his or her main head at the front, complete with the normal three eyes, mouth, a couple of ears (so that there was a spare one) and a nostril or two; the second head at the back not needing a mouth or nostrils but having its own local brain. The additional brain didn't do much thinking in practise, what there was of this diminutive organ just sat; it didn't even sit and think, mostly. It received information and analysed it, not always very accurately, before passing it relatively slowly, a small bit at a time, through the spinal cord to the first head. So slow, in fact, that a Trisep would often turn the front head to get the information to the main brain more quickly and accurately through its local eyes.

The Orijin

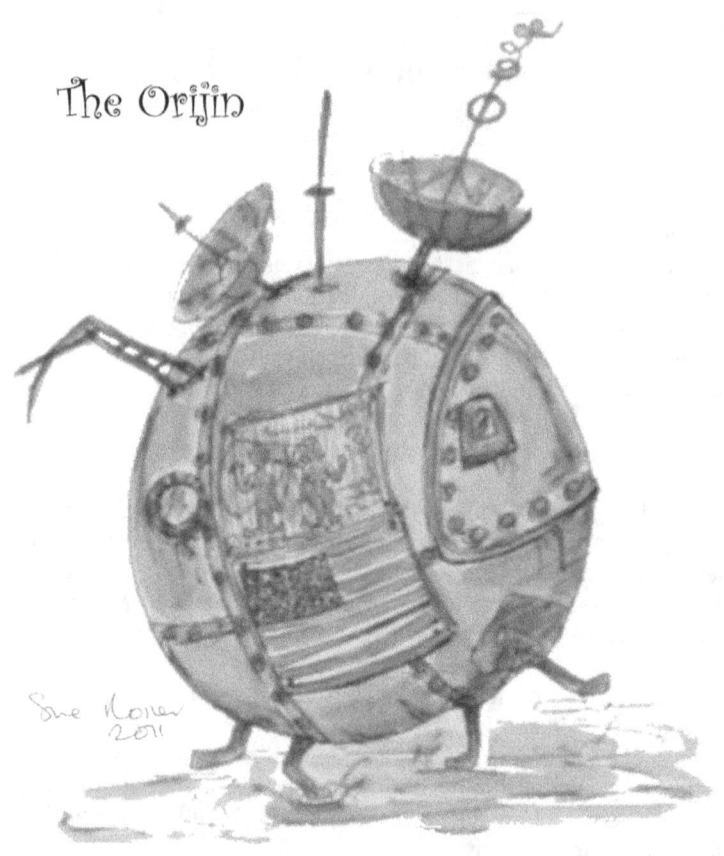

Only two-thirds of a hite in diameter, the sphere of the Orijin must have been travelling for several million years before landing with all the gentle precision of a meteor into Squelchpool Moor. Amazingly, it fell undamaged and buried itself in the hot mud equatorial quags bordering Omeg, the Sacred River of Squeith (or Σqueith[1]) . For now, it was on a roped-off pedestal in the new but temporary museum built specially to house it.

Here in Selondre, the Squeithian capital, crowds of native Triseps were gathering to see it. After obscure objections from the religiots about flying it, the Orijin took two whole days to be transplanted via an olde-fashioned barge from Squelchpool to Selondre.

---

[1]   *Σ is a special form of capital 'S', left over from an ancient language. It is called Sigmata or, more correctly, Σigmata and they sometimes attach themselves to Arithmates in a most embarrassing manner. Squeith (or more correctly, Σqueïth) itself is a country not dissimilar to Britain in a curious sort of way.*

The museum's visitors all knew that they were staring at the only possible source of life on Eqinox, Planet Five of their solar system.

Scientists had proved many years before that Eden Garden was somewhere near Omeg, which was why the Sacred River was worshipped. The greatly increased density of old and dead biomass there proved it, but some still doubted.

And some doubted the existence of one or more GodS[2], but they still worshipped Omeg, just in case.

Now, however, all doubt was eliminated. Life had been sent to Eqinox by GoD and here, now, was the evidence. The main question that remained was whether the Orijin was sent by GoD directly or by way of other beings like themselves. Obviously, as all Triseps knew, they had been made in GoD's image with two heads, four legs and three arms.

And that was that; there it was. They could see it with their own three eyes: the Ovum of GoD, the Orijin. A shining metal sphere sporting numerous pock marks and minor pittings from its encounters with space dust during its travels. There was no question of *what* it was; it was obvious. And it was obvious that the first seeds of life in the form of a few planted microbes must have been on board and were incubated in the hot muds of the sulphur-carbon quags at Squelchpool.

Squelchpool was to be renamed formally. It would now be called Eden Garden. A blue plaque on the wall said so.

A gigantic spired Dagoba was being built - or rather, nanobuilt - at Eden Garden. It was obvious that every Trisep on Eqinox would now feel a need to visit the Dagoba at least once during each seven year life cycle.[3]

---

[2]   *GoD in Squeïthian is always written using the runes of the ancients, hence G°Δ. These days, it is written as GoD following an accidental discovery of acceptability by an autotranslator; however, like WizarD and other spiritual entities, there must be a capital letter at both ends to keep out the evil spirits. No writer has ever dared try to find out what would happen if written in any other form. Try if you dare.*

[3]   *It should be explained at this point that Triseps (short for Trioptic Septapeds - see Squeïthian Lexikern), function with distinct seven year cycles which are as follows: Cycle one is the building cycle where their bodies grow but their brain is too immature to learn anything; Cycle two is the learning cycle where all learning is achieved; Cycle three is the reproduction cycle for the herd leader and two other females. After reproducing, they retire. For the other women and the men, this period is for learning how to work; Cycles four to twelve are working cycles; Cycles thirteen and fourteen are genuine retirement cycles. Most die of old age (the ageing process is not inhibited these days). Death occurs during cycle fourteen with no automed intervention. A very few sages teaching the young are treated to continue to live until cycle twenty one. None of this is relevant to the story, however, and established principles aren't always a true reflection of reality ...*

Once built, the Dagoba would also house the Orijin, the relic of GoD; or the relic of the Ovum of GoD, some would say; or a bit of old tin and stuff; or something and nothing in particular. It all depended on whether you were a religiot, a Dirwanist, a fatalist or a genuine philosopher-atheist.

Smelt

Of course, some were none of those, neither believing nor accepting anyone's notions at all, except - perhaps - for Stephen's. Stephen sold millions of his popular volumes on Qontûm, but only because he had been round hawking it relentlessly and was even more successful in marketing than Jowver's Evidencers.

'Wow! Look at those markings on the side!' whispered Smelt to Smelta.

Smelta nodded her front head in agreement.

'I see why they said it had come from Planet Three,' she replied, 'there's a line drawing of a sun and planets with an arrow to the third planet from the light and heat source.'

She peered closer. 'Wait a minute - hey - but look at those feint line drawings of beings: they're bigger than their planet!'

'I guess that's just to show us what GodS look like; it's not necessarily there to define their size. Anyway, they don't think it means *our* third planet;' he retorted, 'Planet Three from our sun is barren and always has been. You know, the Orijin must have come from deep space somewhere. They might be able to work out where it came from by that oblong with thirteen red and white stripes and fifty stars in one corner. They think that's a map of their part of the universe, but haven't worked out where it is yet or what the stripes mean. Perhaps the stripes are a view of thirteen galaxies from their particular location'

Smelt and Smelta jutted chins and shrugged their front heads to each other but had to move on because the long queue was forcing them forward. Or rather, sideways.

Smelt was growing smaller with age even though he was only in his fourth cycle. He looked up to Smelta, his herd leader. She was privileged to accompany him on this sacred pilgrimage. She had completed her reproductive cycle and was now retired. Retired, that is, according to the term's definition, but as a woman the term rings more hollow.

Smelta of course, as all herd leaders, was responsible for all the major decisions of the household. Herd sizes were allocated each year by the Central Council according to the ratio of males to females. Nuptials were arranged at birth, took place at the end of the second cycle and lasted for life in theory; usually in practise, too. The system needed to be organised because of the natural gender mismatch of more females than males, despite the chaps finding that one female was always more than enough to contend with.

In some cycles as few as six females per male were produced, but in the Year-of-the-Decapod - when Smelt was born - there were seven females per male. At first sight, this is wonderful for males and appalling for females, but that is not how life worked out. The males were very firmly kept in their place by the females, who literally ruled the roost; so much so that the Squeithian Government had to establish an Anti-husband Beating Squad. The females, meanwhile, were in their element with their fellows.

According to the unwritten rules of life, only three of the females in any herd should reproduce once each during their life, the others theoretically remaining unreproductive workers who just took sex for pleasure.

5

All this was true. At least, it should have been true. Except of course for accidents. Games where one is practising replication techniques rarely work out according to plan.

There were a lot of accidents. Every cycle there were far more baby Triseps than traditional theory predicted. Illicit raving orgy parties held in old warehouses were mostly to blame. And by the time some illegal substances were sniffed, and after a few dances to the latest autoerotic nanogroove in all-round multiphonic omnisound, the result was inevitable.

A not surprising increase in the birth rate occurred immediately following the invention of the fully automatic flying moovacar, complete with sleeping cowches. This led to calls for compulsory deposition of the superfluous daughters in statutory condominimums - cosmopolitan places run by all sorts of people - where condoms were kept to a minimum by statute because the Triseptokatholicus Order had a hand in running it.

Extra powers of a magical nature, by the way, were experienced by the rare generations with seven females per male, but only by those older males who had themselves, and whose fathers had each shared the same misfortune to father seven females; itself only achievable through practising nefarious extra-nuptial replication. Most agreed, however, that it was certainly great fun practising.

Ordinary Triseps had no special powers normally. Except mothers-in-lorr, of course, who can draw on closely shrouded and enigmatic magical resources at times of planetary crises. Such minor miracle working thaumaturges are only effective when they stop nagging for a minimum of seven days and seven nights (a rare event for any woman!). Of course, one thauma in forty-seven can become a WitcH[4], but that's another story.

However, since the invention of nanomanufacturing and automeds, most of the good spells previously performable only by thaumas and WitcheS were now available to everybody.

That left only the bad spells. Mostly.

* * * * *

'Just one set of eyes, did you notice?' Smelta asked.

'Yes, very strange, that. If a creature doesn't have two heads with two sets of eyes, how can they see what is attacking them from behind?'

'Perhaps those two line drawings are front and back ends.'

'You mean instead of the fronts of two different genders?'

---

[4] Like WizarD, WitcH must always be written with a capital at both ends to keep out the evil spirits.

'Yes, but it's strange that they seem to have mouths both ends if that is true. After all, you only need eyes and ears on your second head and a mini-brain, not a head big enough for a complete brain or mouth. Very odd. Very odd indeed. I wonder if we'll ever know.'

Of course it was odd from a Trisep's viewpoint. On each head, the Triseps' third eye saw light only in the x-ray spectrum and was probably evolved for hunting, especially at night; the hyperbolic rise in technology in the last few hundred centuries had meant that hunting was long since eliminated. Extra-nuptial sex had taken over as the main spare-time activity. These days, the third eye was mostly used for eyeing up members of the opposite sex through their clothes. A coloured belt in marital arts could be gained if this could be achieved without being spotted by one's partner; failure meant a belt in the eye instead.

Talking of marital arts, there was a problem with numerical gender mismatch. As a result, a new gender was now being bred with multiple two-way sex organs, various sizes of mamaglans, blonde hair one end and dark hair the other - and naturally brainless, of course.

Developed in the Gateway to the Antipole, Ballam, this third gender, was designed to replace the bridies who plied their own brand of professionalism on street corners asking, 'Do you want a bit of fun, luvvy?' The new gender were commonly known as Sharen from the verb, *to share*. They could satisfy a whole orgy of up to twenty - males or females - in one single autostack.

Smelt did not know why he suddenly thought of Sharens, but then he wondered why he shouldn't.

'Did you read about the capsule?' Smelta asked. 'They found a sort of box with all sorts of things in it. The majority of the content had turned into a difficult-to-analyse rust-coloured dust, but they're doing a sub-particle and ultric-bionic analysis of it now, so something should come of it. They found some encoded stuff in there too, but it wasn't in sub-atomic picocode, so being a bit more primitive, it could be less of a problem to decipher. One scientist went so far as to suggest that the code may contain hundreds of atoms for each code segment - if it is true, you would never think that GoD would be so inefficient.'

'Yes,' replied Smelt as they left the museum, 'I'm having some replicates sent to me for analysis. Sometimes the hobby of decryption means that you can get to hear what's going on a bit earlier. They seem to think that I'll be able to decode the ciphers. Apparently there are some writings, too. That'll be something to add to the Pentatouch of the Old Promisings, or to The Folius generally, I'll bet. Let's have a strong drink.'

Their second heads jutted their chins at each other at the thought of the drink and they raised their eyes GodwardS. Being near the rear end, second heads always experienced the diarrhoea effects of intoxication first, but never dared let on their annoyance. There were, however, certain advantages to not having nostrils at that end, so close to the exhaust.

Sharens

'Talking of the religiots, did you read that poster at the end of the exhibition board?' asked Smelt.

'No, we had to move too quickly. Why?'

'Well, they had written a new beginning for The Folius, reading: *In the beginning was the Orijin. And the Orijin was from GoD and the Orijin was of GoD and from the Orijin, all life GoD made.*'

'I'm not convinced.' said Smelta with sideways glances from both heads, 'it looks a bit too Trisep-made, if you ask me. Far from supernatural, anyway, and I liked the language of the original, *In the beginning was Ovoid. And Ovoid was without form* etc.'

'Yes, I'm inclined to agree, but I think that was a different bit from one of the GodspellS of the New Promisings.' nodded Smelt, trying to prove a point, 'Now, how about that drink?'

'Good idea,' replied Smelta, 'I'm thirsty too. They wouldn't let you add to the Pentatouch, though - that was written down by the five sages touched by GoD. Look at the riots after Dirwan's writings on the Theory of Evolvement. Everyone said that it couldn't be right because it didn't agree with Genetics, the creation folio of the Pentatouch in The Folius.'

'I never thought it agreed with Exercises either, the second folio where the seven tribes move across the planet, exercising.' appended Smelt.

Smelt and Smelta always enjoyed keeping up with each other in proving their knowledge, 'But when you read Loveliness and consider the devoutness of the Lovels, the GoD lovers, you can't help wondering.'

'Wondering what?'

'Well, whether there is something in this GoD idea after all. And after all, look at the next two folios. All Numerology ever did was count everybody on GoD's orders on Domesday. Deteriorations, the fifth folio of The Folius, truthfully tells how the planet deteriorated when GoD's lorrs were disobeyed. Many were turned into salt pillars, lots of them, so no-one ever dared suggest that the sixth folio should be called *The Evolvement Chronicles of Dirwan*.'

Smelt looked at her. 'You're not becoming a religiot; a door-knocking Jowver's Evidencer are you?'

She laughed. 'No, nor am I going to become a nün of the Triseptokatholicus Order. What about the sixth folio?'

'True,' said Smelt, 'you're not the sort. And you're right. They'd never get away with *The Evolvement Chronicles of Dirwan,* but perhaps when we've translated the writings from the Orijin, they will tell us about their GodS and their Kings, so we might be able to add to them yet. Perhaps we'll now have the First Folio of Kings. Eh?'

'Either way, it proves the scientists right about the location of Eden Garden.' said Smelta.

'True. Let's see the building work at Eden - and have a drink on the way.' Smelt suggested, getting bored with the subject.

* * * * *

The couple trotted across to where the moovacar was parked. At about two lengths, it recognised them and opened both sides to provide a porch shelter like an umbrella. They got in and Smelta put a finger into a hole near the provisions hatch.

'Eden Garden please.' she said.

'Again please.' replied the moovacar to its trekkers, as drivers were called.

'Eden Garden.' Smelta replied more slowly.

9

'I do not know Eden Garden. Do you mean Eden House or Evenden Garden?' replied the moovacar.

'Neither. It used to be called Squelchpool. Squelchpool please.'

'Update *Squelchpool* with aka *Eden Garden?*' asked the moovacar as it rose to move.

'Yes,' confirmed Smelta, 'Squelchpool aka Eden Garden.' and removed her finger.

The moovacar began to rise. Since the discovery of hydrotrophic conversion using nanotechnology - sub-atomic sized machines that could modify the very atoms themselves, a great deal more had become possible, including free energy to power free flying moovacars.

These days, ordinary water from atmospheric vapour is decomposed and the atoms are rebuilt into any molecule you wish, or even into pure energy. As a result, every part of life changed. Changed completely. For instance, moovacars now used pure energy to overcome gravity; likewise, most other manufacturing processes had been changed into little more than computer design processes.

The technology hinged on the discovery that certain ways of dismantling atoms used less energy than was available when they put themselves back together. Unfortunately, nobody ever managed to work out why this effect occurred, not even the great Stephen.

Smelt put his finger into the hole in front of him. 'Caleptic hi-ball, please.'

'Darling, it's far too early!' Smelta reprimanded, 'just have a normal geeantee.'

'But I need it. I really need it. That thing has got to me. I mean, to meet GoD's Ovum was really something; a most powerful influence. My coddled brain's even more scrambled, now!'

Smelta thought for a breath or two, stole a glance at her husband and put her finger into the hole. 'Same for me, please.' Somehow she always found it difficult not to say *please,* even when talking to a machine. She removed her finger.

Smelt deepened his thought level. 'It wasn't GoD's Ovum. It was only a machine like this moovacar.'

'But even if the Orijin *is* a machine, it must have been *sent* by GoD.' She turned both heads and looked squarely at Smelt. 'And so, if that is true, then much of the dust found inside could be the disintegrated remains of working parts.'

'Possibly. Or it could have been nothing more than transport for the microbes.'

The provisions hatch berped. They took their drinks from it and looked down at the ground. They were now flying at twice the speed of sound and would arrive in a few minutes. The landscape below was criss-crossed with decaying roads and olde-fashioned moovacar Speed-Routes. Of course, they were rarely used now that all modern vehicles flew. The roads hadn't seen more than the odd vintage moovacar for upwards of a hundred years now.

'But supposing it wasn't GoD. Suppose it was Triseps like us. What then?' Smelt conjectured.

'They weren't like us. Didn't you see the drawings?'

'That doesn't mean anything. It only means that a few molecules are at variance in their nanostructure, their triple septihelix ribena-acid, from which all life forms are made. Obviously this applies across the universe, so they won't be that different. If they've had any sense, they will have sent us a formula so that we can reproduce them on this planet. Our whole diversity of life developed from a few microbes in the Ovum - and look at the difference between us, for instance and the Coker tree.'

Smelta looked at him and raised an eyebrow, 'But the Coker tree is over a thousand hites - *and* it lives for many hundred years!'

'Nevertheless the nucleic nanostructure is only slightly different, with a two per-cent change to the triple septihelix ribena-acid. When they discovered that, Dirwan was proved right and wrong, all at the same time. I mean, the species *were* created and did not evolve from nothing, but the *changes* from one microbe to tree to Trisep all evolved from one single Ovum.'

The thirty-breaths-to-landing warning ping sounded. Short time on Eqinox, by the way, was always measured in breaths.

They downed their drinks and replaced the drinking specs in the hatch for recycling back to water vapour.

As they looked out of the window, they could see the gleaming casponite towers and minarettes of the incomplete Dagoba. Of course, the bottom was unfinished; only the roof was complete. The base looked like a giant pair of ice-cream cones, joined at the thin ends, as this part was still growing, both up and down.

'It reminds me of a diabolo on end.' remarked Smelt, in passing.

They got out and sidled towards the erection.

At one side was the builder's hut, not much larger than a moovacar, with the builder looking through an olde-fashioned folio with lots of pictures of naked Sharens. They sidled over.

'That's impressive!' said Smelt, gesturing to the building.

'Do you want to see it finished?' asked the builder, 'I'm Bodgitt. What's your name?'

'Smelt.'

'Really!' said Bodgitt, surprised. 'Do they still do that?'

'No,' replied Smelt, 'not since they invented nanomachines, but there's still an incredibly good demand for traditionally made stuff, hand built, without a computer;' he paused for effect, 'but there are only two of us left now.'

Smelt paused again, 'Yes, please.'

'Yes please what?' asked Bodgitt, puzzled.

'Yes please, I'd like to see it finished.'

The overweight Bodgitt stood up, scratched his imaginary beard, sucked in his breath and shook his front head. His laggardly second head realised what was going on and inevitably followed suit several breaths later. Smelta noticed the smile-shaped gap between Bodgitt's midcoat and his rear trousers showing a cleavage worthy of Belcanto trying to reach top C. All builders had this gap and Smelta had always assumed that it must be their legally required uniform.

Bodgitt pressed a touch panel and spoke a few words in computerese, like 'full external view' and 'isometric' and 'whole Dagoba' and 'sidle-through tour'

A holographic image of the completed Dagoba appeared in front of the hut. As they looked at it, the front entrance enlarged and they felt as though they were entering through the doors. The inside was the most fantastic they had ever seen, and in the most luscious colours both in the visible and x-ray spectra.

Smelt and Smelta watched spellbound, then stood in silence for a whole forty-seven breaths when the tour ended.

'Woo-oow!' They eventually breathed in unison.

'You would think,' began Smelt, 'that with such an important building, it would be built using traditional methods.'

'Never work, mate.' Bodgitt replied, 'there aren't enough of us left who've got the skills. My mate Gerry still uses the traditional methods. You always know his work because he leaves a blue plaque on each one. "Gerry Built", it says. Good bloke is Gerry, but he works by eye and doesn't always get straight lines, especially if he's had a bit to drink. He's all right, though, except when the windows fall out.'

Smelta nodded. 'Aren't you going to build a hotel?'

'Nah,' responded Bodgitt, 'not no more. Flying moovacars are now so fast and comfortable with their sleeping cowches inside that hotels aren't needed.'

'And a moovacar park as well?' added Smelta.

'Ah, yes, well!' Bodgitt looked at her and drew in his breath in a builder-like fashion. Smelta almost expected him to quote her an extortionate price, but he just paused to think instead.

'When it's finished, there will be an automated chimney lift and underground autostack. The moovacars will be left on the chimney and taken down to the M.C.P. below, see?'

'M.C.P.?' asked Smelta, glancing at her husband, 'Who is an M.C.P.?'

'Not a who. It's a what. It means Moova-Car Park.' He paused before he explained, 'When you go, see, they'll be returned to the front door, the moovacars, I mean. To meet you, see. Automatic, like, see?'

'Ah!' said Smelt, 'You mean an autostack!'

'You call it that, but we builders have different names for things, more technical, like. See?'

'Mm.' said Smelta, still feeling embarrassed and changing the subject, 'The Dagoba's grown at least a quarter of a hite since we arrived.'

'Yes' replied Bodgitt, 'it will be the largest building on Eqinox. We'll have it finished in three weeks. Wonderful, isn't it, how the computer makes the nanomachines and they reproduce themselves for a certain time and then change to build the building according to the preset programme.'

He glanced at Smelt and Smelta to make sure he hadn't lost his audience, looked up and down the Dagoba and continued, 'Then when the edge of the design is reached, they stop building and just sit and wait. It works exactly the same way as a baby being built in the womb.'

'What for?' asked Smelt.

'What's a womb for or what's a baby for, guv?' Re-asked Bodgitt.

'No, what do they wait for? The nanomachines I mean.'

'They don't wait, they just go ahead and build it.' replied Bodgitt, puzzled.

'But you said,' continued Smelt, 'that when they reach the edge of the building, they stop building and just sit and wait. What are they waiting for?'

'Oh that,' replied Bodgitt, 'yes.'

Smelt looked at Bodgitt and waited, trying to catch one of his eyes, all of which were currently occupied admiring the work. Eventually Smelt sighed, 'Well, what *are* they waiting for?'

Bodgitt looked back in surprise at finding a guest. 'Oh, I see,' said Bodgitt, 'well, in case of damage of course. If an out of control moovacar crashes into it, or some idiot scratches his initials, the nanomachines will immediately repair the damage, converting water from moisture in the air. Then they'll shut down again until the next time.'

'Is that why they're not building it traditionally?' asked Smelt.

'One reason, yes.' replied Bodgitt. 'Of course, a traditional building will last a long time, but deteriorates. Using nanomachines, the building stays perfect forever. That's why we need the soldiernanos.'

'Soldiernanos?' Queried Smelta, turning both heads towards Bodgitt.

'Ah, yes, well, you see, mmmmm.' said Bodgitt.

'Mmmmm what?' checked Smelta.

'Well, if you want to modify the building, it will try to repair itself to its original design, so you need soldiernanos to kill the nanomachines before implanting replacement nanos with the new design. But don't worry about that, we've nearly got the hang of it. Still experimental, though. With smaller buildings, it's easier to destroy it completely and rebuild from scratch with the modification, even if you only want to change a door handle. Also, this method at least builds the foundations as well by modifying the sub-structure with burrowing nanos'

'Fascinating;' replied Smelt, 'where was the Ovum found?'

'The Ovum?'

'GoD's Ovum, the Orijin.'

'Ah, yes. It wasn't here, see.'

'I guessed that.' replied Smelt, 'Where was it?'

'It was just over there,' he replied, pointing into the quags and squelches, 'do you want to see the hole?'

'Yes, please.' Smelt and Smelta said in unison.

'Come, follow. I'll show you.'

Smelt and Smelta followed Bodgitt at a trot and then a gallop across the virgin moor. Bodgitt led a couple of lengths in front of them.

Suddenly, Smelt and Smelta pulled up short. Bodgitt had disappeared. Vanished. Departed. Become invisible. Gone. In short, he simply wasn't there.

The facility to stop dead from a gallop in less than half a length was a consequence of the way that Triseps moved. Their gait when galloping was more like the hop of the Ozzilland rookanga than a conventional gallop; stopping consisted simply of absorbing the bounce and not starting another one.

They looked at each other with both of their heads and gingerly tip-toed forward in silence, testing the ground for each step.

And there it was, a hole. A very strange hole and invisible until you nearly fell into it, the edge hidden like a ha-ha.

The hole fell away at an angle of about forty-five degrees and was smooth sided. A moaning sound was coming from a very long way down. A very long way down indeed. This must be Bodgitt, obviously hurt.

'Halloa' called Smelt down the hole and listened.

The hole continued to moan.

Smelt shouted louder.

The hole continued to moan with unchanging pitch.

'I don't know whether that *is* Bodgitt moaning.' he said, 'it sounds more like a chorus of Cher-ants.'

Smelta turned her front head towards him, 'But darling, Cher-ants only live in the Yodle Valley of Upper Helvetica. That's why they call it the Yodle Valley.'

Smelta looked down the hole, 'Bodgitt!' She screamed, 'are you all right?'

The hole continued to moan at the same pitch.

'I think we'd better get some help!' said Smelt. 'Wait here!'

'Not on my own, I won't' replied Smelta.

Smelt looked at his herd leader sternly, his eyes reminding her of her nuptial obligations to obey. Smelta glared back, her eyes reminding him that she was the herd leader and therefore powerful in her own right.

Smelt nodded in agreement. 'I'll find a couple of branches to mark the spot with a cross, so we can see it more easily from the air.'

Together they galloped back to the builder's hut where there would be a callall. But Bodgitt's hut did not recognise them and so remained firmly locked. They ran across to their own moovacar and put out an emergency callall from there.

Smelt switched on the emergency following radio beacon and manually trekked the moovacar at tree-top height until he saw the cross. He circled the cross twice to see what else he could see and avoid what could literally become a pitfall down the hole, got out and waited for the Multicare to arrive.

Meanwhile, Smelta callalled Bodgitta, Bodgitt's herd leader to give her the news of what had happened to her husband.

Two hundred breaths later, the swish of the Multicare could be heard overhead and Smelt pointed out the place he wanted them to land.

It only took a few breaths to explain what had happened to Bodgitt.

'I've never seen such a smooth-sided hole!' exclaimed their leader, 'And it seems to be so straight. Whatever made it? I'm Carehedd, by the way, leader of the Multicare team.

'Could have been some of them nanomachines, gone out of control.' said Putout4 - one of the Triseps specially trained in fire fighting, 'Always said them machines was dangerous. Bet it goes all the way through Eqinox to Ånjap on the other side.'

Everyone turned and looked at him, not sure whether he was thick or brilliant.

As if to prove his brilliance, he added, 'Or at least, if not Ånjap, somewhere on the Nipoff Archipelago.'

'Have you got Miner with you?' asked Smelt, thinking how silly it would be if you were not given a name that reflected your life's major career at birth.

'No, but Putout3 does caving as a hobby.' replied Carehedd. 'We'll send him down on a rope and see what's there. I must say, though, I don't like the sound of that whining. Sounds a bit like Helvetican Cher-ants, don't you think?'

'That's what *we* thought.' said Smelt, ominously glancing at Smelta with both heads, 'but it's not bad enough to be called singing by those who like Cher-ants.'

The Multicare was moved to the top of the hole, enabling the fire boom to be extended down to it.

Carehedd personally tied a growable cable to the end of the fire boom, attaching it and its growing box to one of the power unit points there and Putout3 clipped himself to the other end. He attached a micro-neutron gun pin to his uniform and clipped the psycho-trigger hairclip above his ears at Smelta's suggestion. She commented that she was worried about the Cher-ant noise and feared there might be a lethal army of them.

'At least the noise isn't as bad as the Welks Valleys Male Choir of Agwgwlland.' Smelt added.

15

Putout3 stopped dead in his tracks and glared at Smelt at the mention of Agwgwlland. 'Even mention of the Welks Valleys Male Choir makes me ill, please don't mention it again while I'm down by here.'

'Don't worry about him,' said Carehedd, 'he comes from Ffordd Llwydd - it's a competing valley, you see. That's why he's little and dark and hairy and likes working down holes in the ground.'

Putout3 switched on his head-lamp and shone it down the hole as he attached himself to the self-growing cable.

'There's nothing here, just a black hole.' he said as he began to slide. His commentary was now coming from speakers on the side of the Multicare via a microphone on his headset.

As he continued sliding, the clump of Triseps were joined by another Multicare and the Multicare Area Director. When the Area Director asked his computer about the incident, it said that there had never been another similar incident in the four hundred cycles since Multicare was formed from separate Ambulance, Fire, Police, Air Rescue, Submarine Rescue, Traffic-Gestapo and Anti-husband Beating departments.

It didn't occur to any of them at that stage that computers cannot report what has been intentionally withheld from their knowledge base.

Putout3's running commentary rapidly became rather boring after a while, simply because he had nothing to report, except the exceptional smoothness of the sides of the hole and the fact that there was nothing there to be seen, and anything that was there would undoubtedly have slithered unerringly down to whatever was below.

'STOP!' Shouted the side of the Multicare, relaying from Putout3.

Everybody's two heads turned to look at the commenter and then the front heads turned to look at the hole. There was, of course, nothing to see.

Carehedd went up to the Multicare vehicle, put his finger in the side and said something in computerese, like *Switch On Picture.* Suddenly a live holographic picture appeared in front of everyone of what Putout3 was seeing.

There it was, a hole. Not *the* hole, but another hole branching off sideways from the main hole. Putout3 shone his flashlight into it. 'It's very rough,' he said, 'not smooth like the main hole. Actually, come to think of it, the main hole doesn't seem quite the same down here, either. I don't think it's quite so smooth as it was at the top. It's still about the same diameter, just big enough for me, but somehow ... well, somehow the texture isn't quite so smooth when you touch it, somehow. And yet, somehow, it's sort of, well, it's the same. Somehow.'

The distinction was too fine to be able to detect by the others at the surface, but when in a hole, one's ability to describe can be limited, somehow.

'I think it's just an old critter burrow.' said Putout3 looking at the horizontal hole and relaying a picture through the commenter. He looked round and ordered the rope to continue growing.

* * * * *

Meanwhile, Carehedd had set to work with a little box taken from the back of the Multicare. This he held against the walls of the hole and also against the general ground outside.

He returned to the main clump of Triseps, obviously puzzled. 'The structural analysis of the walls of the hole,' he began and then turned and looked back as if it could give him some inspiration, '. . . is identical to the surrounding ground except . . .' he stopped and focused objectively at the spectators.

The anticipation rose while his audience experienced the feeling that they were watching a thriller in an olde-fashioned theatre. Carehedd scratched his front head with his third arm. 'Erm . . .' he added.

Except *what?*' asked Smelt impatiently.

'Except for three things.' said Carehedd. 'First that it is a very thin layer compressed by over a thousand times to its present form, and also that there is no living or fossilised biomass there - not even squashed microbes. You would expect *something* there, wouldn't you?'

'Yes,' responded Smelt, 'you would. And what else?'

'Oh, the third thing - well, third and fourth really. The sides are perfectly smooth and the bore is perfectly straight and constant in diameter. Most puzzling. Do you know, you can see Putout3's light even now from up here?' said Carehedd.

Smelt thought about the problem. Why would there not be any biomass in the shell of the hole, when this area was the most prolific for life and fossils in the whole of Eqinox ? It was impossible for there not to be any microbes in the squashed material making up the pipe.

'And fifthly,' added Carehedd, appearing to have problems counting beyond two, 'the smoothness takes some believing, even if it were made with nanomachines, which I don't think it was. And whatever caused it emerged at this point and seemed to continue, leaving this mound of spoil, but it was some time ago by the way it has settled and the edge grown over.'

'I think I need a drink.' said Smelt and wandered over to his moovacar. He put his finger into the hole and asked for two medium strength geeantees. He took the specs with geeantees over to where Smelta was standing. 'Has anyone told Bodgitta yet?' he asked the assembled clump.

'Yes, I did, don't you remember?' replied Smelta. 'I expected her to be here by now. I don't know why Bodgitt wasn't wearing his personal callall.'

17

'Perhaps he was but it was damaged or won't work underground.' said Smelt, sipping his geeantee as casually as he felt able in the distraught circumstances

He looked at his drink and said, 'I think I need a bit more gee and a bit less tee.'

There was a whiz overhead and a moovacar came in to land. An overdressed, over made up, overweight, lady Trisep got out. She ran over to the crowd. 'What's happened to Bodgitt? Where is he? I'm Bodgitta. What have you done with him? Has he fallen into a squelch? How could he get hurt out here? There's nothing here to fall on him. Why are there so many Triseps? Where *is* he? What was he doing out here in the middle of nowhere anyway? Why wasn't he at the Dagoba, in his hut? Where is he? Why hasn't he called me on his personal callall? What are you doing to him? Why is that fire boom stuck into the ground? Have you got him? Well, where *is* he? I mean, I mean, well, I mean why won't you tell me er . . .' she ran out of breath.

Carehedd, who was quite used to dealing with Triseps in all sorts of anxious states just stood with his mouth open wondering when she would stop. She had stopped, but only for a moment to collect her breath, so he had to strike fast.

'I think you had better join some of Putout3's wives. He's gone to look for Bodgitt. Come and sit down in the hospivoid and I'll explain everything.'

Suddenly there was a loud yell from the side of the Multicare. 'Yeow! Stop!' it said. It was Putout3 shouting at the growable cable.

Carehedd spoke to the commenter. 'What's happened, Putout3?'

'I've got to the bottom. Well, I haven't got to the bottom. I mean I've got to the end of the hole. There's a large cave here - can you see it? The pipe was just a sort of chimney. It's huge. It's gigantic. It's as big as The Arena Dome. No, bigger, much bigger. I can only just see the bottom and the limited power of my flashlight won't reach to the other side. Can you see it? Can you *see* it?'

'No' Carehedd said to the commenter, 'it won't show that distance. What can you see in the x-ray spectrum?'

'Something moving, but no real colour,' replied Putout3. 'In fact, I can't see it very clearly but the whole floor seems to be moving. There seems to be some sort of life down there, but it's so far away that I can't work it out. I think I need some help on this one.'

'Are they Cher-ants?' asked Carehedd to the commenter, 'The hole is still moaning.'

'I don't know, I don't think so. You can't hear any sound from here so it must be an oracular delusion. Probably your own breathing amplified by the hole, a bit like a Squeithian trumpet'

'OK. Where's Bodgitt?'

'Is he there?' began Bodgitta, 'What have you done with him? Can you see him? Is he all right? Is he hurt? Where is he? What is . . .'

'I never did like the Squeithian trumpet,' muttered Putout4 to himself, I much prefer the Coronglay, even though you can't tell it from a Frenshorn, except for the former's equally appalling squalling drawl. I would love one, but I can't afford the embouchure to go with it.'

'Hold it, hold it!' said Carehedd to Bodgitta, 'I'll ask him.'

'What's going on up there?' asked Putout3 who could hear but not see the surface through the commenter.

'I've got Bodgitta here. Naturally, she wants to know what's happened to Bodgitt.

'I don't know, I can't see that far.' replied Putout3.

'Well, what would happen to you if you weren't tied on?'

'I suppose I would drop off, but not straight down because the pipe is at an angle and smooth so I would have been going at speed when I left the pipe.'

'Do you mean that the pipe just comes to an end?' asked Smelt to the commenter.

'That's right. It's like a sort of chimney. There's cold air flowing upwards in the pipe. I need equipment, a lot of caving equipment. Can you get some spikes to drive into the roof here and a power gantry that we can lower to the floor. I shall need some help, too, can you send two or three more Triseps and a good light down here - a long distance spotlight?' asked Putout3.

'I'll send them down straight away,'

'And make sure they're armed,' added Putout3 through the commenter, 'I'm not sure what we're going to find down there, but something is certainly going on and I don't like it.'

'And I'll send a medic.' concluded Carehedd.

The team set about the task of preparing the equipment and Triseps to send down the pipe. Meanwhile, Carehedd prepared by making callalls to the main museum curator, professors of geology and the Eqinox Government.

Then he set about interrogating the computer about underground life forms, but didn't find anything worth looking at, although he wasn't sure what he was looking for anyway. That reminded him: 'Don't forget to set up a computer relay to the cave.' he called to the busy throng.

Carehedd raised his eyes GodwarD. It was his job and he wouldn't forget simple things like that.

A whiz from overhead. An unusually large black moovacar with darkened windows appeared and landed.

Carehedd looked across at the moovacar, somewhat surprised, *'Cronus and Rhea* - that was quick - I've only just told them.'

Two Triseps got out of the large black moovacar. One was in a uniform and introduced Grounsell, the Minister for Ground Works from Eqinox Government.

19

'Carehedd said, 'How in the name of Cronus did you get here so quickly?'

'We heard the first emergency callall and we've been following it right through. I wanted to be here in person. You've done well so far. Is somebody looking after Bodgitta?'

'Yes,' replied Carehedd, 'she's in the hospivoid having a Grief Encounter. I hope a Grief Encounter counselling session with the automed will help her.' He continued to explain his plans in detail to Grounsell.

When Carehedd was called away, Grounsell turned his front head to face Smelta directly. He blushed bright yellow as blood rushed to his front head. She blushed too and turned, pretending not to notice him.

Smelt was facing the other way at the time, so he only noticed her with his second head and the full implication did not hit him immediately. When it did, he turned his front head slowly towards Smelta and asked, 'Do you know each other?'

Smelta was quick. 'Do *who* know each other? Do you mean Carehedd and me?'

Even so, she nearly dropped her spec of geeantee.

Smelt wondered whether he had made a mistake and said, 'No, you and Grounsell of course.'

Smelta found it hard to lie and blushed again - a problem experienced by every intelligence in the universe. 'Why should we know each other?' She replied, not lying directly but forging her lie as an intention to deceive. 'Actually, we did meet once when I was delivering one of your sculptures, I believe, but I'm not very sure.'

She glanced back at Grounsell. 'Would you like a drink? Perhaps I can get one for you.'

'That would be lovely. I'll have a spec of Calept with ice please.'

'Sure.' replied Smelta and wandered over to the moovacar to order it.

Smelt watched her suspiciously. He knew that she had been up to something during the days when he was in his workshop, and he thought it might have been Sharen, which would have been almost acceptable. Now, however, his suspicions were aroused. But only slightly and only for a moment.

'Ready to go?' Shouted Carehedd.

'Phew, saved by the bellow,' thought Smelta, but secretly wondered how long it would be before the subject raised its ugly head again. Her first and second heads turned and looked at each other. Actually, she thought, he really was rather fanciable.

'Mind if I go down?' Smelt asked Carehedd.

'What, the hole?' responded Carehedd, amazed that he would be so foolish as to ask. Smelt's look told him that he was serious. 'Well hurry up then - you'll have to be kitted out, but we'll wait for you if you really want to go.'

'Thanks,' Smelt replied to Carehedd, 'keep an eye on Smelta for me, won't you.' He blew a kiss to Smelta, glancing suspiciously from her to Grounsell and back again with his rear head.

Chapter 2   Qontûm

Even with the surface layer compacted to a thousand densities, it didn't take very long for the spikes to be driven into the cavern roof and for a gantry to be set up. A very bright light was installed at one end and beamed down, revealing the floor below.

They all adjusted the trinoculars attached to their safety helmets for best normal and x-ray vision at that distance.

If there hadn't been a good rail on the gantry, Smelt, Putout3 and the four others would have fallen off in shock.

Spread out below them was a miniature city like a model, complete with pathways and houses and public buildings and colourless trees and even fields of equally colourless crops.

Putout3 eventually broke the silence, but not with any expected comment, 'They haven't got roofs on their houses. I've never seen anything like it.'

'Don't need them, there's no wind or rain and the temperature down here would be constant' Smelt replied, intelligently.

The trees were about thrice as tall as the Triseps and the single-storey houses were a little shorter. The light swung round to reveal sports arenas, organised farming areas and all the signs of an apparently primitive but highly intelligent civilisation.

There were funny little singled headed beings, too, doing all the normal sorts of things that you would expect them to be doing; walking, shopping, gathering crops, making love and sitting on toilets. Astonishingly, they seemed to be ignoring the light, as though it wasn't there.

'Have you noticed the colours?' said Smelt, to no-one in particular.

'Colours? What colours? There aren't any.' replied Putout3.

'That's what I mean. Everything is rock colour. The houses, the furniture, their clothes. But look at the trees and shrubs and the little beings themselves. Look, they are all colourless, if not to say translucent.'

'But just look at those little creatures. What are they?' Wondered Putout3, 'They've only got one head and two arms. And they balance on only two legs without falling over. I mean all the critters I've ever seen are all different colours. Even Triseps are all different colours. But them, well they all look the same to me! How can they recognise each other? But they're not Cher-ants. And they're not singing, thank goodness.'

'I don't think they've noticed us yet, even with our super-bright lights. Look, they're not looking up at us. Don't you think that's odd?' said Smelt, 'I wonder if they really haven't spotted us yet or whether they are just pretending to behave normally.'

He paused to watch them and added, 'I would expect them to be rushing about getting out of the way when a clump of invading Triseps is just about to land on them. Do you think that they really haven't seen us?'

Putout3 shrugged. "Seems so."

Smelt pointed off to one side, 'Look, there's a giant spunj-squelch - and it's exactly in line with the pipe. Those little bipeds next to it must have seen Bodgitt earlier when he fell down the pipe. Obviously the spunj-squelch is designed to be a soft landing for anything that falls down the pipe; the same as we put around tall buildings to stop self-administered premature deceasement.'

'Yes,' replied Putout3, 'things falling down the pipe must be a common problem. Perhaps that is what really happens to Triseps thought to have been lost in the squelches.'

'Rather looks like it, doesn't it.'

'But what baffles me is how Triseps could have existed on Eqinox for two million cycles and never before have discovered this pipe or these obviously intelligent creatures and their underground city!'

Something else struck Smelt that nobody else had mentioned so far. The beings were bipeds exactly like the line drawings on the Orijin back in the Squeithian capital of Selondre. The more he looked at them, the more they looked like the line drawings. But for some reason that he could not explain even to himself, he decided to withhold this thought for publication at a more appropriate moment.

Smelt remembered one more detail from the Orijin too. Next to the picture of the two eyed, single headed biped, there was a scaled drawing of the Orijin itself to indicate size. Clearly, these beings were much smaller than those pictured on the Orijin. Smelt could not stop staring at the little people with one head, two arms and two legs. He just stood, mouth agape, peering down. And how, he wondered, could this place possibly exist without the life-giving and life-sustaining energy from sunlight? The amazing sight generated in him far more questions than it answered.

'What can you see down there?' asked the commenter with the voice of Carehedd, 'Grounsell is still here and he wants to know.'

'There are little critters like the line drawings on the Orijin. Can't you see it on the display?' asked Putout3.

'So much,' Smelt muttered imperceptibly to himself, 'for trying to keep the suggestion quiet.'

'Not yet - it only shows up to about five lengths.'

It should be mentioned here that everything on Eqinox was measured in lengths or hites. These were both an approximate and an exact measure. For precision engineering, there was a Standard Length and a Standard Hite defined as a specific number of hydrogen atoms long, although the number of digits to describe it was even longer. For everyday use, however, Triseps multiplied their own length, calculating by using their x-ray vision, but all this is irrelevant to the story, really.

What happened next? Ah, yes! Putout3 explained to the surface what he could see in some detail and Smelt added his comment about the funny little critters looking like the drawings on the Orijin.

'Wow!' said Carehedd through the commenter.

'Are you sure?' asked Grounsell.

'Oh, there's no doubt about it,' responded Smelt, 'these beings are identical in shape to those on the Orijin, even down to the two eyes, even though they all seem to be blind - at least, they seem blind to our light. From the organisation down here, I presume they must be able to see in other wavelengths.'

With the hydrotrophic converter powering the angle of descent, they worked their way diagonally sideways to land gently in the spunj-squelch. When they were about six lengths above ground, the little people began to look up at them. Smelt saw that they all seemed to be chewing and they reminded him of childhood stories about Gobblings, funny little creatures from another world that could perform magic.

With their chewing habit, they should definitely be called Gobblings! Or was it chewing, he wondered. Were they just opening and shutting their mouths for some other reason, he wondered, like some land-based ghoti[5]?

One Gobbling, a bit taller than the rest, came running towards the gantry as they landed.

'Hello.' she said. The Gobbling was obviously a female by the drooping mamaglans that weren't shared by all. Those with mamaglans also had long hair on their heads despite their bodies otherwise being bald and translucent. Other Gobblings did not have mamaglans, but had more of the translucent body hair instead.

The Triseps looked at each other, amazed. They could speak. And they could speak Squeithian!

'Er ... hello,' replied Smelt eventually, 'how do you know our language?'

---

[5] *Ghoti is one of those rare words for which the meaning is clearer when checked in a dictionary. Briefly, GH is pronounced 'f' as in enou**gh**, O is pronounced 'i' as in w**o**men; ti is pronounced 'sh' as in sta**ti**on. Got it? In short, a ghoti is a finned undersea critter.*

'Easy.' replied the Gobbling with a Fjordian accent. 'Triseps from the surface keep falling down that hole and they arrive here. Happens about once every three cycles on average. Of course, we can't get them back and they're usually so badly injured and we haven't got the special energy-giving light from your sun, so they don't live long, but we learn what we can from them and take their pain away. We do our best for them but it never has been good enough.'

'Why are they injured if they land on the artificial spunj-squelch?' Smelt asked.

'Let me kiss thy hand,' the Gobbling continued and leant forward expectantly. Smelt hardly considered the action and dismissed his own doubt. Almost automatically, he put out his third hand and accepted a wet kiss on its back.

'How did you get down here?' She continued, 'Triseps usually arrive with a big bang out of the sky. That's why we've made this big spunj-squelch and nobody lives in this part.'

'We've come on a gantry, a cradle that can be lowered and raised. We can go back again when we want to.' replied Smelt, whose professional demeanour made him a natural spokesman.

'We've always expected this. We've been waiting for it for many years. Was there no attempt to stop you by your precedent - your leader - the one who precedes? We have been ready to welcome you as honoured guests for a long time. What is your name?'

'Smelt.' Somehow, he felt, her greeting did not ring quite true. It must have been a modulation in the voice, but there was a hollowness of truth, even in this alien tone. He wasn't sure, though, that he would go so far as to say that she was prevaricating in order to fabricate a false allegory, as the politicians so politely put it.

'My name, in your language, would be Quax because I'm a doctor professionally, but my real name is unpronounceable by your tongues.' said the Gobbling. 'By the way, after talking to many Triseps, we have called our city, in your language, Qontûm.'

'Qontûm?' Repeated Smelt, who had almost but never quite understood the meaning of the word.

'Yes,' replied Quax, 'you see, the reason we have called it that is because it is a ...'

She was cut short by the interrupting commenter. Grounsell's voice said, 'I think I had better come down and join you. Is that all right, guys?'

'Just wait for us to send the gantry up and meet us at the end of the pipe.' replied Smelt, nodding an apology to Quax for the interruption. 'Come on, we'd better get off.'

Smelt explained to Quax that Grounsell was the Minister for Ground Works from the Eqinox Government, and that he was a far more important Trisep.

In many ways, Smelt was a fairly ordinary fellow, who just happened to mix in higher circles because of his hobby; it was truly exhilarating for him to be a part of that initial meeting between the species, but somehow there was a niggling fear at the back of his mind that things were not quite as they seemed.

Nevertheless, Smelt could not afford to consider his worries at this time when his name could go down in history for being one of the first to visit Qontûm City. He was really a bit vain, behind the façade.

Then it happened; Smelt didn't know why, but without warning, he suddenly said that he needed to return to the surface as soon as the introductions were over. He claimed that he needed to brief Grounsell, but this was really an excuse.

The truth is that Smelt had not really been himself since the discovery of the Orijin. Somehow, it had affected him, but he could not possibly define how. He had a few secret feelings that he even kept from himself most of the time. Even now, he would only admit the uncharacteristic and antipodal thoughts at a deeply sub-conscious level. On the one hand, his nervous streak confessed that he was a bit - no, somewhat - frightened and hated the underground world, company and publicity; on the other, a secret vanity nevertheless confessed that he did rather want to be the first to be interviewed for the History Records.

* * * * *

As soon as Grounsell was briefed, the History Record interviews were over and they had a chance to talk, he said to Smelta, 'It isn't possible, it just isn't possible. Something is wrong and even though I've seen what I have seen with my own eyes, something about it doesn't fit, but I can't work out what.' he took a few breaths for thought.

Smelta looked at him, puzzled so he continued to explain. 'I thought that the Orijin must have made that pipe when it arrived on the planet, but it wasn't found there. If the Orijin travelled down that hole to Qontûm, it could well have compressed the soil at the sides and made the hardened pipe, but I don't understand why it was found in a shallow pit hundreds of lengths from this pipe entrance to Qontûm. Surely, it would have been in Qontûm itself, or perhaps in a pit under it, but certainly not so far away.'

'Simple,' replied Smelta, 'two million years of eqiquakes. There's no problem there.'

'Mmmm. I'm not convinced. And there's one other problem. The pipe was at a much sharper angle when we came up than when we went down. It was as though Qontûm had moved, but it can't possibly have done of course.'

'Must be your imagination, dear. A pipe in solid ground can't move.' replied Smelta.

'Maybe, perhaps. The probability is that it is just my imagination and Qontûm and the pipe haven't moved. It's just that I would have sworn … oh, and I didn't see the animal burrow on the way back up.'

'Perhaps you just weren't looking for it. Your mind must have been on other things.'

Smelt affectedly scratched his left front ear with his right hand. 'And what's happened to all the Triseps over the years? Surely they haven't *all* died of their injuries, have they? They said that Bodgitt was hardly hurt at all; he only had a few cuts and bruises on him because of the soft landing. They said that we can see him later, when they've stabilised him.'

'Perhaps they've only just installed the soft landing.' said Smelta, wanting to believe the best of everyone.

Smelt continued, 'But couldn't they or the visiting Triseps have burrowed their way upwards and out with a new tunnel? They had little tunnels leading off in all directions out of the edges of the city, so the idea couldn't have been new to them. And then there was the pipe itself and … well, and … nor were they uncurious as a species.'

Smelta nodded and listened intently for further clues.

'And something else,' added Smelt, 'I am worried about why the Gobblings were so hesitant to answer questions about Bodgitt. Now, that is worrying. Very worrying indeed.'

'So to your mind, they bodged the interview?' suggested Smelta.

'Yes.' confirmed Smelt, slowly and deliberately but unwittingly scratching the back of his third hand.

* * * * *

The portoffice of EBC landed as Smelt sidled over from his moovacar. The portoffice was more of a portable studio than office really, and the Eqinox Bleating Centre's ENN channel distributed the Eqinox Nebulus News planet-wide. Most Triseps left their public service receiving e-commenters set to automatic so that their favourite entertainment arrived at the appropriate time and any special announcements paused the normal preference.

'I wonder why *they* took so long to get here.' remarked Smelt, 'they're usually hot on the trail of the tail of absolutely everything.'

The reporter was like correspondents all over the universe, slick, smooth, irritatingly blonde and asking awkward questions but never quite listening to the answers. Realistically, this reporter was better than most and actually spoke intelligently. Her name was Cate'aeddy, but no one could remember why, although they usually just shortened it to Kate. Certainly, she had become a most popular senior reporter and was never away from the most harrowing incidents. She was even more popular since she published her two autobiographies about her life of war reporting, *What Cate'aeddy Did* and *What Cate'aeddy Did Next.*

Her studio was ready for transmission within five breaths of landing.

'We're live on bleat.' she began as Smelt poked his front head into the portoffice, 'Do come in, you're our star witness.'

'Already? I mean, can't we talk about it and prepare?' he had seen thousands of such reports of 'incidents' and should have known better. ENN always dive straight in and interview without introduction.

'So what happened?' asked Cate'aeddy, 'I hear there was some sort of hole with an undiscovered species at the bottom of it. Is that really true?'

'Well, yes, I suppose so, but it's not quite as simple as that.' he automatically scratched the itch on the back of his third hand. 'You see, the hole isn't just a hole, it's a ... er ... well, it's a pipe with hard sides. And the diameter is constant for about five hundred lengths. Down at 45 degrees, but a sharper angle coming up. And then there's nothing. Well, actually, it's not nothing, it's a sort of cave, a hemisphere of about, well, I suppose, about five hundred lengths in radius. And at the base there's this city, you see, without roofs. And there are transparent Gobblings with only one head, and eyes that can see in the dark and there are caves and tunnels all round the edge, but I don't know where they go; and trees and fields and things. Oh, and I've just remembered, other critters with only one head and four legs in the fields. And they're all translucent. You can virtually see right through them.'

He had been looking down towards the edge of the floor, but suddenly remembered himself and looked up, almost surprised to be in the portoffice.

'Are you all right?' asked Cate'aeddy, 'You haven't been drinking, have you?'

'Drinking?' Responded Smelt, suddenly looking up at Cate'aeddy as if he had seen her for the first time, 'no, of course not. I've just never seen anything quite so ... er quite so curiously quaint.'

'Quaint?' Queried Cate'aeddy. 'I'm finding all this rather hard to believe.' What else can you tell us? How big are these so called Gobblings?'

'Well, they're about, well, about, I mean, er, I suppose about half as tall as us, but they only have two legs and two arms and one head and only two eyes. They really are very odd.' said Smelt, scratching the back of his third hand.'

'We'll have a holocam down there soon, so we will all be able to be there and see what you saw.'

Outside, a holocam operator was preparing to be lowered into the hole. Holographic cams and the receiving holocommenters had been in everyday use for several hundred years and had reached the pinnacle of holotechnology.

'Do you know what I can't get over more than anything else?' asked Smelt, metaphorically, 'and that is that you could see through them. They were totally transparent. All of them. And the trees. And the plants and all the other critters. They were all transparent. You could see right through them. It's amazing. Do you know, you could see right through them?'

'You've said that three times now. You know what they say, *what I say three times is true.* My, it really *did* affect you, didn't it. Say, could you *really* see right through - even through the trees?' asked Cate'aeddy, incredulously.

'Yeah. Right through. Well, virtually.' said Smelt as he shrugged, shook both his heads and scratched the back of his third hand.

'Let's get this right,' said Cate'aeddy, 'you're not reporting a dream, are you?'

'No, of course not.'

'And this isn't any sort of WitcherY?'

'I hope not. I am not at that level of competence in WitcherY, I would need to spend more time learning from my mother-in-lorr.'

'Is your mother-in-lorr a WitcH?' she asked and continued without pause, 'And you're not a philosopher who believes that the physical apparency of an object does not necessarily prove its existence?'

'No. And I was joking about being a WitcH'

'I never joke about anything.' Retorted Cate'aeddy. 'And you aren't a Qontûm scientist who believes that an object being in one place or moving is a matter for probability?'

'No, no, no.' He looked straight at her. 'NO!'

Smelt looked at his hand. It itched.

'I'd better go and wash.' he said suddenly without explanation. There was no inflammation or swelling or rash. It just itched. He remembered the wet kiss and wondered whether there was some kind of toxin in the saliva, a bit like the common field nettle.

Cate'aeddy looked at him, for once she was struck totally dumb, but only for a few breaths. 'Wash?' She mused. 'Did you say, wash?'

By now she was talking to his non-responsive back head as he was sidling away. Eventually his rear head realised it was being talked to, but just shrugged in response.

Smelt turned his front head as he continued toward the facilities, 'yes, wash. I'll explain in a minute. I'm itching where one of the Gobblings touched me.' he disappeared into the facilities.

Cate'aeddy turned towards the holocam and said, 'As you see, Smelt seems to have a problem and it seems that he's been slightly affected by the Gobblings. We'll bring you the next development at Squelchpool as soon as it happens here, live on ENN. We're sending a holocam down the hole right now, but there's nothing to see at the moment.'

Outside, Carehedd was watching the ENN report and was suddenly worried by Smelt's itching and disappearance. He had noticed the first couple of times he scratched, but thought nothing of it until Cate'aeddy mentioned it. Realising the implications for those still down in Qontûm, Carehedd spoke through the commenter to Grounsell and told him of Smelt's problem. 'You'd better not let the Gobblings touch you at all.' he added.

'We've *all* been wet-kissed on the hand and they're being very hospitable.' Grounsell replied through the commenter, quite unperturbed.

Carehedd thought for a breath or two. He now knew from the commenter that the Gobblings could speak Squeithian and understood all that was being said. He didn't want to offend them, so he tried to be diplomatic.

'We're a bit worried here on the surface that we might contaminate the beings down there and so we don't want you to touch them.'

'Oh, that's all right, not a problem,' began Grounsell, nonchalantly and not picking up the inference, 'they've seen lots of us over the years and they've never caught anything from us yet. Anyway, we all went into the hospivoid for a medicheck before we came down and none of us had anything.'

'Well, it's not just that,' began Carehedd, 'there might be a problem the other way round, too.'

'What do you mean?' asked Grounsell through the commenter.

Carehedd hesitated. 'Well,' he began and stopped to think, 'it's Smelt. There's an irritation where he was wet-kissed by the Gobblings. He's had to go and wash his third hand where it was itching. By the way, do they mind being called Gobblings - I mean, what do they *want* to be called?'

Grounsell had taken a full two-way commenter down with him and Quax was listening.

She answered for herself. 'Other Triseps who have landed here have called us that. The term is not offensive to us, although that term covers all our tribes. Some Triseps use the term Hobbimps for this tribe.'

'This tribe?' asked Grounsell.

'I meant *we Gobblings*. The title, *Hobbimps* rolls of our tongues more readily.'

'I see. And the irritation?'

'Ah, you have nothing to worry about from our kisses. They are intended in friendship. We will be offended if they are not accepted. We have a great deal more to fear from you than you from us.'

'Sorry to have offended you.' said Carehedd diplomatically, through the commenter.

'Smelt offends us more by washing his hand.' replied Quax. 'In any case, those visiting us could not wash their hands because we have too little pure water to waste any on washing.'

Grounsell resisted the urge, whether physically or only psychologically required, to scratch the back of his third hand where he had been kissed.

Carehedd said, 'I understand that, Quax. We do not wish in any way to offend you.' he paused and asked, 'Grounsell, could we have a general status report from you please?'

Grounsell looked at Carehedd through the commenter, surprised. Modern technology meant that status reports were not necessary these days as everything could be seen through the commenter or via callalls. 'Fine!' he responded, 'just fine.'

Grounsell looked puzzled, but then you can't expect a politician to be intelligent too.

At the request of Quax and on the grounds of courtesy, the commenter was switched off while Grounsell and his clump of Triseps remained guests of the Gobblings. Meanwhile a frantic Convention was convened on the surface.

Smelt eventually emerged from the facilities. He looked round as though he was lost, which he was. His third hand was covered with what looked like a levva glove.

'Have you washed your hands?' asked Cate'aeddy, intending only to re-introduce him into the conversation.

'Have I ... er ... what?' asked Smelt, blankly.

Cate'aeddy glanced at the holocam and back to Smelt. Even politicians weren't this dopey, she thought, even though he wasn't one, 'Have you washed your hands? I mean, are you all right?' She re-asked.

Smelt snapped out of his zombie state. 'Oh, yes, of course, I think I've hurt my hand, though, somehow. It's a bit like a snake sting, but I don't understand. I thought that washing it would help, but as soon as the water touched it, it swelled up and popped like a balloon. I had to think of something pretty quickly to cover it, so I ordered this glove to be nanomade.

'I think you'd better go to the hospivoid on the Multicare where there's an automed, and get it seen to.'

All this was transmitted live through the e-commenter to what was now the largest audience ever recorded. The infobox in the bottom corner of the picture showed that over 99.3% of the entire population were watching at that moment. The percentage was still growing.

Smelta, who had been waiting just outside of holocam view in a corner of the portoffice, took an arm to help the hesitant Smelt to the hospivoid. Cate'aeddy told an autofollowing holocam to stay with them, which it did. She had a private message into her ear.

'Our ENN holocam has reached the end of the hole,' she began, 'so we'll now add another holoquadrant to our exclusive report.'

Most viewers preferred to watch multiple holoquadrants, where a number of holograms were shown at the same time and the eye would follow the action from one to another as events took place. That way, the complete story could be assimilated at once. It was discovered many years ago that the brain's capacity to take in information was far greater than most information systems provided, thus it became quite common to watch a drama with several scenes occurring at once, or even several different dramas at the same time. ENN would often show both sides of a battle or several distinct views of a sporting event, all at the same time. Triseps loved it. There were even some known as *cowch spuds* who just watched the e-commenters and never moved from their sleeping cowches.

Smelt was now in the hospivoid and held his third hand out for analysis by the automed. He expected the usual response within a few breaths. He waited. And waited. Nothing happened. And he waited. And still nothing happened. Nothing, that is, except the automed saying, 'please wait, I am diagnosing your problem.' every forty-seven breaths, but that doesn't count as something happening.

Eventually, the automed said, 'checking with external data.' Another delay.

'What do you think is happening? Smelta said, worried about her husband for the first time in her life. Neither had ever experienced such a delay from the automed before. It usually gave an instant diagnosis, or at worst didn't take longer than about four breaths.

Smelt looked at her with both heads. He was clearly frightened. Very frightened indeed. 'I don't know'

The automed spoke, 'Smelt, you have a lesion. At current progress, you will die in eighteen point three seven days. No further analysis.'

No Trisep in living generations anywhere in the entire planet had ever heard anything like this before. Everyone was hearing it now through the autofollowing holocam that Smelt had forgotten.

In sitting rooms, moovacars, streets all over Eqinox, Triseps looked at each other. In silence, they all turned both their heads to their partners. For the first time in most of their lives, there was fear in their eyes. Genuine fear. This was new.

'But, er, I mean, but, well, er, what can be done about it?' asked Smelt.

The automed said nothing for a few breaths, analysing his potential response to various answers and allowing him time to prepare for the answer. 'Nothing can be done now.' said the automed.

99.4% of Triseps studied him and looked back at Cate'aeddy in a different holoquadrant for her response. She, too, was dumbfounded and even she was sitting watching, mouth agape.

'But can't you even tell us what it is?' asked Smelta, 'Please tell us all you know.'

'It would not be possible to tell you all I know;' replied the automed, 'this condition is new to my experience. I will tell you all that is relevant.'

Smelt and Smelta glanced at each other in a new fear and back to the automed.

'No, I cannot tell you what it is' continued the automed after a pause, 'it is outside all known medical experience. If it were a bacterium, I would make appropriate anti-bacteria. If it were a virus, I would analyse it and make an anti virus. If it were a fungus, I would cut it out, atom by atom until it was no longer in you. If it were cellular decay, I would reverse it. What you have is an undiagnosable lesion that is spreading at a fixed rate. I cannot remove it because it has already infected a fixed percentage of every cell in your body. If you wish, I can cure it but there will be a slight side-effect.'

'Good, then cure it.'

'Would you like to know the side-effect?'

'If you insist.'

'That side-effect is that you will die within two hours. If no safe cure is found, you will die in any case in eighteen point three six days. I recommend that you be treated by Profmed at Selondre Hospice. Do you agree?'

'Do I have any choice?'

'You have no choice.' confirmed the automed.

Smelt nodded and said, 'I see. I understand, I think. Thank you. We will go immediately.' and added under his breath, 'I suppose.'

'It's a pleasure' said the automed, 'I must examine Smelta; until then you must both remain isolated. Your moovacar has been summoned to here and will be waiting outside when I have finished with you. You will be taken to Selondre Hospice for further analysis and treatment.'

Silence was endured without comment, but only for about forty-seven breaths.

While we are all waiting for the forty-seventh breath, perhaps it should be mentioned here that all the planet shared in Smelt's confusion. And Smelta's grief. Here was something that was unknown to science and it would dramatically affect everyone. Indeed, there was no other talking point that day, anywhere in Squeith, or indeed on the whole of Eqinox. Callalls were made from everyone to everyone else they had ever known. Clumps of Triseps stood in circles and scratched both their heads at the same time. More geeantee was consumed that day than for a long time, although mostly with more gee and rather less tee.

Eventually the automed spoke, 'You are clear to leave, Smelta. You have not been infected yet. You are not touching Smelt at the moment. If you touch Smelt, you will need to be isolated again. You may go with Smelt if you wish or you may leave separately.'

'I'd like to spend one night with Smelta.' said Smelt.

'You cannot do that,' replied the automed, 'You have an unknown condition and must be isolated by statute. You will go directly to

Selondre Hospice. Smelta can go with you if she wishes or she may go home or elsewhere. It is your choice.'

Smelta looked at her husband and understood his psychological isolation as well as his new physical isolation. 'I go with him.' she said.

'Your moovacar is now waiting at the door. Please leave. My report has been sent to Selondre Hospice and is being analysed by the super-computer there, Kraye943. I wish you well.'

'Thank you.' said Smelt to the machine. 'Wasn't Kraye943 the computer that worked out the answer to the problem of the analysis of forty-two?'

'Yes, and no' replied the automed, 'it stated that forty-two equals six times nine, but could not tell us why. M, the great intelligence, worked out that it must have been working in base thirteen. Funny, the question was set by some idiot of a passing hitchhiker! I've been trying to find him ever since to give him a Phroydtest.'

'M?'

'Your memory is temporarily affected. M refers to Mycroft, the greatest intelligence on Eqinox. You must remember him because of his more famous brother, Sherlock, the great detective who is usually high on illegal substances, making him more of a heroine than a hero.'

'Er ...' replied Smelt, but didn't have time to check his brains.

The door swung open and there was nowhere for Smelt and Smelta to go except into the moovacar. He could not have run away, even if he had wanted to. As he got into the moovacar, he was followed by the autofollowing holocam, which didn't even ask his permission. But Smelt had totally forgotten his audience and was concentrating on his own concerns at present.

Back at what Putout3 now described as *the pithead,* Carehedd was watching both the closed circuit commenter showing the events in Qontûm and also the public e-commenter showing Smelt and his herd leader returning to Selondre.

In Selondre itself the gaunt Squeithian Precedent, Polit46 (so called because he was only intended to be an ordinary politician, being one vote short of an election, but was elected Precedent of the Eqinox Government as well as of Squeith after a meteorite unexpectedly landed and not just killed but totally destroyed his predecessor) ... where were we ... ah yes - Polit46 was performing his duty and setting a precedent by calling an immediate emergency Convention of politicians, scientists and philosophers. As 99.5% of the world's population were currently watching ENN, he asked for a holoquadrant in their current picture. It was granted immediately for reason only of its newsworthiness. If it had not been newsworthy, ENN would not have let anyone advertise anything without paying for it, however urgent. And political speeches are always counted as advertising.

Cate'aeddy managed to introduce the Precedent, Polit46 without making the usual joke that he was one number short of the magic forty-seven. EBC suspended the public bleating of all other holoquadrants for the duration.

Polit46 sat on a formal armcowch in a government office.

'As you know,' Polit46 began with a gravely serious face, 'you have today witnessed what could become a world crisis. We have met a new species for the first time in many centuries; a species who knew of us and have had an opportunity to study all about us, but of whom we knew nothing until today.' He looked at the floor, embarrassed and in a gesture known by Phroyd-test analysts as false-truthing.

Polit 46

A second holoquadrant opened up and showed a still hologram of a Gobbling.

'These creatures are being called Gobblings or Hobbimps, and you will be seeing them shortly on your e-commenters because a holocam team is being lowered to them, even as we speak. I must ask that you all remain calm, because that is the only way we can deal with this matter. The area will be sealed off and Kernal has already set up a prohibition zone surrounding the hole, so your moovacars will not take you there even if you ask them to.'

'Triseps of Eqinox,' he continued, 'You already know that there is a possible threat of unknown disease decimating our population. This must be taken very seriously indeed. I have had no choice but to seal the area and I am sure you will all agree with that. My next duty is to call a Convention of all relevant and qualified Triseps in the Conventionium here in Selondre where we can discuss this problem face-to-face. I therefore call upon all professors of medicine, chemistry, biochemistry, geology, nanotechnology and astrophysics, ambassadors and Squeithian and Eqinoxian politicians to meet tomorrow morning at the Conventionium at Selondre. You can expect to stay for several days. My autodiary has already prepared a list of these Triseps and you will receive a personal confirmation callall shortly. Finally, I call upon every Trisep on the entire planet of Eqinox to think of solutions to these little local difficulties. I call upon you all to listen in to the Convention and if any one of you has any proposals, ideas, suggestions or can otherwise assist in any way, you know that it is your duty to advise the Convention. If it is adequately demonstrated that you can help, you too will be invited to join us at the Conventionium. I know that my fellow Triseps will not let me down in this, our greatest hour of need.'

As soon as this momentous speech had ended, concentration for the 99.6% of the population who were watching was all refocused by a new holoquadrant opening up.

* * * * *

The holocam had arrived at Qontûm.

The visitors to Qontûm were still not aware of the full implications of Smelt's return or of the other surface activities, because they only had a closed-circuit commenter and did not have the public e-commenter that every one else saw.

Cate'aeddy looked straight at the holocam. 'You are now seeing pictures direct from Qontûm. These pictures are live.' They did not need to hear that; they knew it already, and it said so on the infobox.

Carehedd spoke to his commenter. 'Grounsell, I think you should know that Smelt has had to go to Selondre Hospice. He had a burst lesion where he was kissed by Quax, the Gobbling. The automed could not diagnose his problem and only gave him eighteen days to live. Are you experiencing any problems?'

Grounsell looked at Putout3 in secret panic. They were now being watched by everyone on the e-commenter. 'Carehedd said that . . .'

'I heard.' interrupted Putout3. 'How do you feel?'

'Fine.' replied Grounsell, still a bit mystified.

'Look at your hand.' said Putout3.

Grounsell and Putout3 raised their third hands in unison and peered at them.

'Felt a bit itchy earlier, but it seems all right now,' said Grounsell, 'it's a bit red, though.'

Mycroft

'So is mine.' replied Putout3. 'And it is beginning to itch a bit now. Did you get all that Carehedd?'

'Yes, I heard every word.'

'Quax, you're a doctor, have you ever seen this happening before?' asked Grounsell.

Quax looked away, obviously feeling guilty. 'No.' she said, not meeting their eyes. 'I must go and look at Bodgitt. He was in a pretty bad state.'

Putout3 looked accusingly at Quax. 'I thought you said that he only had a few cuts and bruises. Can we see him now, please? Is he in there?' he pointed to one of the few buildings big enough for Bodgitt to be treated in.

'Er, no. I must go now.' said Quax hurriedly and disappeared into one of the side tunnels at the edge of the city. Most of the tunnels would not have been large enough to take Triseps, and the one that Quax went into was certainly too small. Small groups of the Gobblings, in ones and twos, began disappearing in various directions.

'Wait a minute,' said Grounsell to the vanishing crowd, 'er, please wait a minute. Is there any official here we can talk to?'

The remaining crowd just stared, chewing, and said nothing.

'Will one of you please tell me. Where is our Bodgitt please?' said Grounsell.

Silence.

'We only want to help our friend recover from falling down here.' said Putout3, 'will somebody please help.'

Silence. The few who remained just looked at him and ignored them all.

'Well, who is your precedent, your leader?'

No response.

'Will somebody *please* take us to our countryman, Bodgitt.'

No response.

'Will you at least ask Quax to come back.'

No response.

'Please.'

There were only two Gobblings left now, and they looked rather nervous and frightened. Somehow, and unobserved, the streets had emptied too.

'Where *is* everybody?' The last two were slinking away.

'Wait a minute,' said Grounsell, trying to stop the last one from leaving.

'Don't! Thou darest not touch me lest thou wilt die. Thou wilt die, slowly and painfully. Dost thou understand?'

Putout3 raised one eyebrow at the archaic language but otherwise ignored him. He stepped forward and stopped him with his forearms. The Gobbling bit his finger and he let go. Putout3 looked at his wet finger. Wet from his own bright yellow blood and wet from the salival fluid of the Gobbling.

By the time Putout3 looked up again to where the Gobbling was, he had disappeared.

'I think we had better go back up.' said Putout3 to Grounsell.

'We can't go without Bodgitt.' said Grounsell.

'Oh yes we can,' said Putout3. 'There's more to this than meets the trioptics. I think the Defenss should deal with this. I don't like it. I don't like it at all.'

They all looked at each other. Suddenly they were all frightened and froze.

'We'd better all get back into the cradle' said Putout3 to all assembled.

There was no question. No delay. They were all in the cradle in an instant.

And safely away.

At the surface, the Multicare was waiting to take Putout3 to the Selondre Hospice. Already, he was losing too much blood. The bleeding simply wouldn't stop. He wasn't worried about that, the automed in the hospivoid would deal with that. He was more worried about the whereabouts of Bodgitt. At that time, the infection risk from the Gobbling's wet bite didn't occur to him.

They were safely away from Qontûm.

Nobody could possibly have anticipated what was going to happen, and happen very soon.

Chapter 3   Kill or Cure

'Darling, it's all getting so painful.' Smelt lay on his sleeping cowch in Selondre Hospice. Smelta could do nothing to help.

A professor of medicine had taken some samples and was doing some rather unusual medical tests. The advanced automed had run out of ideas but was keeping Smelt stable. They had never before seen manual tests. The automed usually did all the tests itself, but they had never before seen blood being taken in a tube with a hollow needle in the end.

'Where is it hurting?' asked Smelta.

'Every nerve fibre seems to be aching. Profmed said that he did not want to give me any drugs whatsoever until he's finished all his tests. At the moment, I just need to rest. Listen, I need you to get the contents of the Orijin and take it back to the laboratory for decryption. Perhaps you can make a start for me. I need to sleep now.'

She kissed him on his front forehead and was just about to leave.

'Oh, wait!' said Smelt.

She turned her front head towards him.

'The pipe was made of the same material as the surrounding rocks and soil, but there was no live or dead biomass in its structure. Can you get a sample to the laboratory. I want to have a closer look at it.' he said.

She left just as Putout3 and the others were arriving.

The automed insisted that she pass yet another medicheck herself before being released.

* * * * *

Back at the top of the hole, the Defenss were arriving. In force.

Kernal gave orders that the hole and the Ovum-shaped slight mound round it must be roped off so that nobody else would fall down it. A careful search was begun for other holes in the quags and squelches. There were a number of false alarms when other mound-rings were discovered, just like the one round the hole, but nothing was found in the centre. Or at least, something *was* found: normal soil, but there was no hole. However, because the slightly raised rings were so similar in their Ovum shape and cross section, they were investigated further and their location recorded, but nothing was found.

The fire boom was withdrawn from the hole, the Multicare removed from the scene and replaced with Defenss vehicles. The hole was surrounded and watched over but not studied. Smelta's request for a sample was denied, for the moment. At least, until some high level decisions had been made at the Conventionium.

Kernal was surveying the area and his troops drinking a mid-afternoon cup of lactinfuse. He looked down at his drink. Brilliant, he thought, how nanotechnology could manufacture something so perfect and yet different every time, just like the real infusion of dried leaves. He dreamed of the days when he was young and had to help squeeze the post-natal discharge from critter mamaglans for putting on corn-seed scrunchies for breakfast and adding to cups of lactinfuse.

A Sqoddie wandered up. 'Why are we here?' he asked. 'I mean, what are we supposed to do?'

Kernal looked at him and jolted himself back into the real world. 'You saw the e-commenter bleat today, didn't you?'

'Yes,' replied the Sqoddie, 'but now we're here, shouldn't we *do* something?'

Kernal looked at him sadly. 'I have my orders, and so do you.' he paused. 'We must just make the area safe and then be ready for anything, even an attack, from below. We've done all that. Now we just drink lactinfuse and wait for our next orders. I expect the Convention at the Conventionium will send us new orders soon enough.'

'Well, the big neutron gun is in place pointing at where the hole was supposed to be. I think it's in the right place.'

Kernal turned both heads and looked at the Sqoddie, '*Is*, you mean, not *supposed to be.* I know you can't see it until you've almost fallen in, but it isn't invisible.'

'Sorry, Kernal,' said the Sqoddie, 'it's just that I couldn't see it when I went up on the bridge just now.'

'Do you mean the bridge we set up directly over the hole?'

'Yes, of course.' replied the Sqoddie, 'but it's quite small, so I suppose it's just hidden in the grass.'

'More like you're looking in the wrong place!' Retorted Kernal with a smile, 'let's have a look, anyway.'

Kernal and the Sqoddie sidled through the camp to the temporary hoverfloat autobridge set up by the Defenss over the hole and looked. 'Well, you can't see it from here,' said Kernal, we'd better go up and look down at it.'

As they looked down, there seemed to be no sign of the hole at all. In fact, it looked just like the rest of the damp, grassy moorland all around. Kernal looked around as though he had lost something, which he had. He looked at the Sqoddie and said, 'This *is* the right bridge, isn't it, I mean, are we looking in the right place?'

'Yes, it is.' replied the Sqoddie. 'I remember because there was a cross of branches next to it - see there.' he pointed to the crossed branches on the ground originally left there by Smelt.

Kernal called some more Sqoddies to bring some probes to investigate. Meanwhile, he wandered across to the EBC-ENN portoffice. Cate'aeddy was still there but not transmitting at that moment. She was preparing herself to look battle-scarred by roughing her hair, changing into battle fatigues and applying some bruise make-up.

'You look as though you've got all of Squeith's problems on your shoulders.' Cate'aeddy remarked casually.

'I have.' retorted Kernal, gravely. 'I need to see a replay of the hole as it was this morning.'

'Sure, why?' Cate'aeddy put her finger in a slot and gave a few orders to the computer. 'Here it is just after we arrived here. What's the problem, it hasn't overgrown with trees already, has it?' She laughed, but only elicited a suspicious sideways glance from Kernal.

Kernal looked carefully a the hologram in front of him and of Triseps entering and leaving the hole. 'I think you'd better come with me.' he said.

Cate'aeddy gave the computer a last instruction to put her on public bleat. The autofollowing holocam followed her and looked everywhere she looked, yet also showed her face, of course. With Kernal, she mounted the bridge and looked down. So did the autofollowing holocam.

A Sqoddie was poking the ground where the hole should have been and was tied to a nearby vehicle for safety.

'I don't understand,' said Cate'aeddy, 'what's going on?'

'Perhaps *you* can tell *me*. *I* certainly don't know.' replied Kernal.

The Sqoddie continued to prod. His stick met with the same resistance as the soil around. He hadn't needed his safety harness after all.

Cate'aeddy turned to the holocam, as unruffled as when she was in the midst of war reporting, 'Something very odd has happened here today. This morning, a hole was in the ground below us. Now it seems to have heeled over, like a skin wound. I am left wondering whether I dreamed the events of this morning, but from the Defenss equipment around me I know it was true. This is Cate'aeddy with Squeith's greatest puzzle, ENN, Squelchpool Moor.'

* * * * *

The speaker at the Conventionium was silenced. As soon as Cate'aeddy had come on bleat, everyone watched the e-commenter and virtually ignored the speaker.

The precedent, Polit46, stood and spoke. 'Very hard to believe. I don't know what to say.' he looked at the delegates and thought hard. 'I am going to sit down. I am sure some of you scientists will have some suggestions.' He lowered his eyes, all six of them. He scratched behind an ear. He scratched his chin. He shook his heads.

Squeith's four thousand greatest brains thought.

Total Silence.

Polit46 sat down and plaited his three arms.

* * * * *

Profmed looked at Smelt with one head and Putout3 with the other. They had all been watching the e-commenter bleat.

'Your infection, the Contaigen, is new to us, but I've worked out what is happening. You've been, as it were, programmed to die. I do so enjoy these problems. Fascinating, isn't it. Every cell in both of your bodies has been infected with a slow acting, time-delayed deceasement proteañ. As the automed said, unless you are cured, you will die in about eighteen days, Smelt.

As for you, Putout3, because your wound is more serious, you will die in about ten days.' Profmed smiled a *trust your doctor* sort of smile and looked around the ward at each victim in turn, 'in fact, you have all been programmed to die.'

Profmed smiled and turned to leave.

Grounsell stopped him short, 'Is that it? Even the automed has a better bedside manner than that!'

'Oh, I don't suppose you'll actually die, if that's what is worrying you,' responded the Profmed, casually, 'but you might.'

'Why don't you think we'll die?' asked Smelt.

'Well,' said Profmed, scratching his forehead with his third arm, now I know what the problem is, I can cure it.'

With one accord, his patients all heaved a sigh of relief.

'Probably.' added Profmed casually and left the room.

The atmosphere could have been cut with the long blade of a Helvetican Defenss knife.

After an interminable pause, Grounsell said, 'No point in us just sitting here, and it's my department, so I'd better make a decision.' he told the callall to put him through to the Conventionium. He could see from a holoquadrant of the e-commenter that the hall still had no speaker but individuals were beginning discussions with their immediate neighbours.

'Put me on Convention bleat, please.' he said as soon as he was through to the not very intelligent Trisep who answered.

'I can't do that.' came the response.

'Then put me through to Polit46.'

'I can't do that without authority.'

'I *am* authority. I am Grounsell, the Minister for Ground Works from Eqinox Government.'

'Sorry, I didn't recognise you. Now, how can I help you?'

Furiousness threatened. 'Just put me on Convention bleat, please.' he paused. 'NOW!'

'You're on bleat now' came a computerised voice.

The Convention could see Grounsell as though he were standing at the front of the hall. He was just lowering his eyes from a heavenwards glance and muttering, 'Olay, about time too!'

The infobox provided the viewers with Grounsell's personal and professional details, so there was no need for an introduction, even to those who had no previous interest in who he was.

'I am speaking to you from my ward in Selondre Hospice. All of us who met and touched the Gobblings have had to be isolated. Unless treated, we will all die in the next ten to twenty days.' Grounsell paused to gather his thoughts.

'As a planet, we have a problem. For the first time in many hundreds of cycles, we have a threat to our civilisation. Despite Cate'aeddy's comments, what you have seen today was *not* a dream. Sadly, it is only too real. It is a threat that we must all face together. Gobblings have existed in mythology. Until now, only in mythology. My first recommendation is that the whole of Eqinox must be ready for some sort of attack now we know that they exist and now that they know that we know they exist.' Grounsell paused and looked at the assembly, assessing its corporate mood.

'We must remember that the Gobblings are still holding Bodgitt, the builder of the Dagoba at Eden Garden. We don't even know if he is alive, and if so, whether he is badly hurt.' he looked around through the e-commenter at the audience he was addressing in the Conventionium.

'I recommend, with help and permission of Kernal, that we start digging and find the hole. The hole was lined with a pipe of soil compacted to over one thousand times normal density. That must still be there, so it should be easy to find. I am sure that only the surface will be covered over. Then we can send some Sqoddies down to find out what is really going on in Qontûm and whether we can recover Bodgitt. Nevertheless, regardless of the outcome, we know enough to be warned of grave danger and should be prepared for any possible event. Being on the surface gives us an advantage because we know which direction they will come from, if they come. It is also a disadvantage in that we cannot guess where they will turn up. It now seems obvious that they can create or remove access to us at will, through these pipes. The matter is in your hands. I say that we should dig.'

Grounsell paused and awaited a response, but answer came there none, so he switched out of the public circuit.

Polit46 stood up and sidled to the podium. He looked squarely at the audience with his front head. He looked round the assembly of Eqinox's best brains filling the Conventionium and waited for an appropriate moment to speak, pausing until silence was achieved. Even though there was a crisis, he was still primarily a politician.

'Fellow Triseps,' he began, 'You have all heard Grounsell speak to us from his ward in Selondre Hospice. You are all aware of the threat and you will all have reached your own conclusions. I have just been told that automeds all over Eqinox have been inundated with Triseps with fobias about Gobblings. Some Triseps are even frightened of fear itself, not really having experienced it before. Both Gobblingfobia and fobofobia are curable by using the automed's Phroydtest.'

Members of the Convention began to chatter, everyone with their own idea of what should be done.

Polit46 raised his hand for silence, 'Digging will begin tomorrow.'

'Well, they seem to be getting on with it,' said Smelt, 'I'm glad I'm not having to dig out that hole myself!'

'Never want to go near the place again.' retorted Putout3. The ward groaned in weary confirmation and sounding more like a chorus of Cher-ants.

The door opened to reveal Profmed. 'Hello everyone.' he said cheerily.

A dozen heads turned towards the door, eyeing Profmed with a highly sceptical smile.

'I've worked out what's happening to you.' said Profmed.

'You've already told us.' retorted Putout3.

'No, there's more now and it's really exciting.' said Profmed, 'You see, your individual cells are now beginning a new phase. When you next eat, they will begin to clone and you will double your size almost instantly.' Profmed was still smiling as though playing with a new toy.

'You call that exciting?' said Putout3. Profmed was in grave danger of being thumped, if not completely lynched.

'Yes,' said Profmed, continuing without listening, 'it looks as if the cells are using your existing proteañ and then cloning themselves into Gobblings, or replicates of them at least.'

A shudder swept round the ward and all eyes glanced at one another and returned to concentrate firmly on Profmed.

'So we're not going to die, we're going to turn into Gobblings, is that right?' asked Grounsell.

'Yes.' said Profmed, then added after an interminable pause as though he wanted to cause the most possible upset, 'but you won't of course.'

'Why not?' chorused the entire ward.

'Because I've found a cure.' Profmed said casually, 'Who wants to be first to try it out?'

As a politician, Grounsell thought that he was far too important to become a guinea pig so he remained silent.

The room was silent until Profmed's eyes fell upon Smelt.

Somehow, when a Trisep like Profmed pierces you with his eye, you feel guilty. Smelt felt slightly guilty, but he also wanted to get the treatment over and done with and at times like that, fear of additional pain in delay must be logically balanced against the fear of the treatment itself. Smelt's logical analysis extended to saying a silent eenie, meenie, minie, mo between the two options.

His preference lost.

'I will,' said Smelt, hesitantly, 'what shall I do next?'

'Follow me and I'll set you up.' said Profmed in his best bedside manner.

Profmed led Smelt through numerous corridors and up and down stairs and rotolifts until they reached his laboratory. He looked round at the cowch with lots of wires attached and a big machine with what looked like a large, olde-fashioned laser gun pointing at it. The laboratory reminded Smelt of old pre-holographic films about monsters with bolts through the neck being built by mad scientists. In fact, he thought it would make a good filmset even in modern times.

Smelt looked at Profmed. 'You *do* know what you're doing? I mean, what are my chances?'

'Oh, fine, fine. It'll work, it'll work.' he said without turning his front head from the equipment he was adjusting, 'and if it doesn't work on you, we'll try something else on the others. Now, I've just got to adjust this for your weight and size.'

Profmed's second head looked straight at Smelt and shrugged.

'Bedside manner, indeed! Well, at least he's honest I suppose.' he muttered under his breath, 'better than being told it will work when it won't.'

'Do you mind if Smelta is here for the treatment,' Smelt asked aloud, 'I would like her to be present.'

'No point,' replied Profmed. 'You can callall her if you want.'

He did want.

'Oh, hello, darling,' Smelta said as soon as she saw who was calling, 'glad you callalled. I've got replicates of three things from the capsule found in the Orijin and I've started to analyse them. I haven't worked out the disc with a sort of very long spiral groove in yet, but there are two things like olde-fashioned folios. One of them is like a Lexikern with pictures and the other is full of writing. I think it is some sort of religious work. By the way, how are you now?' She looked up at his picture from her work and saw the laboratory behind and around him. 'Where on Eqinox are you?' She asked, puzzled.

'I'm in Profmed's laboratory.' he replied as matter-of-factly as he could muster in the circumstances, 'he's going to perform an experiment on me. He thinks he might have a cure for my Contaigen.' he hesitated and looked away from the callall's holocam and blurted, 'But I might die instead.'

Smelta looked more concerned. 'Die! Die? Die today, do you mean?'

'If it doesn't work, perhaps yes.' he replied, 'I wanted to talk to you before I went ahead.' she was looking at him unsure of how to respond,

'It's an experiment, you see,' he continued, 'but of course, it might not work, and if it doesn't, I could die even more quickly.'

The poignant moment hung in the air and his words were as heartening as a plumbumic balloon.

Smelta began to cry.

'I might be saving the lives of every Trisep on Eqinox by helping with this experiment,' Smelt began, 'please don't be sad. Do you want to watch?'

'Not sensible, it might hurt.' said Profmed in his special brand of bedsidese.

Smelta wept an even more bitter tear.

'Does she need a Grief Encounter?' suggested Profmed.

Smelta overheard and extricated the tear from its hiding place in her cheek dimple. 'Not likely!' she replied.

Smelt and Smelta said their good-byes before he lay on the sleeping cowch specially designed for the curious shape of Triseps.

'I'm going to zap your third hand first,' said Profmed, 'and then do a test. If it works we will do the rest of you.'

More dials adjusted and buttons pressed. 'Are you ready?'

This was even worse than the old films. This was positively primitive. Surely, he felt, surely nobody had used methods of healing like this for generations past?

'Isn't this a bit er ... well, er ... basic?' asked Smelt.

'If the experiment works, the equipment will be miniaturised and the software incorporated into every automed. I've already updated every automed on Eqinox with the analysis characteristics of the Contaigen.' Profmed continued to fiddle with dials and equipment.

'Ready to go now?' Profmed asked.

'Even you could have phrased it better than that!' Smelt said with a bitter laugh. He was beginning to get used to Profmed's bedside manner.

'Eh?' Responded Profmed, 'I just want to finish you off as soon as possible, that's all.'

'Exactly,' replied Smelt, 'that's what I'm afraid of!'

'Well, it will only be a minute before you're done with.' added Profmed, still blissfully unaware of his hopelessness in personal communication, 'I'll just push this button and it will soon be all over for you.'

Smelt could not stop himself laughing and wondering if Profmed really was so hopeless or whether he did it for the purpose to cheer him up. Surely, not even a doctor could be *that* insensitive.

'Before you start, could we let the ward of Contaigenees watch on a commenter, so they know what is going to happen?' Suggested Smelt.

Profmed nodded in agreement, set it up without further comment and said to the ward, 'I'm just about to start the treatment on Smelt, and he wanted you to watch so that you'll know what to expect when it's your turn to go.'

Profmed turned round and immediately pushed the button.

Smelt was used to the silent operation of automeds and did not expect bleeping and whirring and flashing lights from all the equipment. His third hand began to tingle and he could feel his strength and energy draining away, cell by cell. The Contaigen was being killed, but the remainder of each cell was left damaged by the treatment.

For Smelt, this was rapidly becoming one of those rare moments when death would be a sweeter preference to the continued pain of life, but such choice was not available.

'You are going to need to take ultric-proteañ, a lot of it, and you should be back to normal within about five days, but you will feel very weak indeed until then. You must also eat and drink exactly and only what the automed gives you. I will set up the programming for it myself.' Profmed advised.

He looked at Smelt's hand. It had shrivelled slightly and Smelt was trying to move it. 'How does it feel?' Profmed asked.

Already, Smelt felt better, but only a little, and he was about to cross the threshold from death-wish back to normality, 'Pain. Great pain. A very deep ache. I can't move it. It looks like a corpse.'

'Good, very good.'

'Good? You call my pain good? It hurts!' said Smelt.

'It will. I expect you will feel worse when your whole body has been done over. But you must have the treatment if you are to survive. Right, stop bellyaching, I need to do some more tests now.'

'One problem with working on cells,' Profmed began as he started on the tests, 'is that even if you correct an imbalance at sub-atomic level, you still need to keep each cell alive. It is not possible to destroy it and rebuild it using nanotechnology as you do with all non-living things. We can't just rebuild you, unfortunately. We have to give all the cells a chance to grow and repair themselves naturally. We can help with ultric-proteañ, but can't re-make you artificially. Even if each cell is rebuilt perfectly and give it the correct atomic sub-structure, its survival is a matter for the GodS. We never did discover what makes a cell actually live, so we can make it right, but we can't give it life; at least, not with any guarantee.'

Profmed glanced up from his experiments and added, 'so you might not last very long anyway.' He immediately forgot his attempt at friendly social intercourse again and returned his concentration to the experiments.

'It's not hurting quite so much now.' said Smelt, 'it's more of a deep ache, and I still can't seem to move it.'

'Take this.' Profmed said, offering a piece of odd-shaped laboratory equipment full of a luminescent grey drink, 'it's a spec of ultric-proteañ.'

Within a few minutes of drinking the bitter concoction, Smelt began to feel better and the pain slowly subsided.

'By Cronus I feel like a session with Sharen!' exclaimed Smelt. He closed his eyes and raised his head in simulation of ecstasy.

Profmed turned and stared at Smelt with raised eyebrows. 'You *must* be ill if you want Sharen!' he turned away and scratched the top of his front head with one hand, stroked his imaginary beard with the second and put the first finger of his third hand in the computer talk hole. 'Why is Smelt experiencing aphrodisiac tendencies?' he asked the machine.

'Confirm love type,' began the computer, 'pornographic, erotic, nuptial, agapistic or deviant?'

'Sharen.' confirmed Profmed after a dubious pause.

The computer made a sound that could have been mistaken for clearing the throat with a laughing cough.

'Are you not experienced enough in the marital arts?' Profmed asked.

The special laboratory automed answered the Prof's question, '96.8% probability that ultric-proteañ caused aphrodisia. The ultric-proteañ would have caused hyper-activity in the hormone centres of the genitalia. 1.6% probability that it was a Phroydian response to medical treatment immediately following a visit by his herd leader.' said the automed, '1.3% probability that it was caused by deviant own-gender preference for Profmed. 0.9% probability that . . .'

'All right, all right, that's enough, thank you.' said Profmed, turning a pink shade of bright grey. 'Hey, that's more than 100%.'

'Of course,' replied the computer, 'there is a minus one point eight per cent chance that the patient does not exist and is an illusory variant of one of your experimental autogenerates.'

Profmed shrugged and looked straight at Smelt, 'It will be worse when you have the full body dose.'

'What's an autogenerate?' asked Smelt.

'Eh? Oh, it's a brainless clone designed for drug testing.'

Smelt looked at Profmed with a sideways glance and wondered whether he would end up as an autogenerate. He callalled Smelta, 'I'm going to be all right.' he said.

'I didn't say that,' said Profmed, 'the Contaigen is already spreading back into your third hand, so we need to give you a whole-body dose. It will be excruciating for you, but you should survive it. We ought to start immediately.'

Smelta looked at them both through the callall and started to weep, 'I thought you had it worked out,' she said to Profmed, 'What is the survival chance?'

'Oh, pretty good, over 70%, I would say.' replied Profmed without looking round, while his second head shrugged; then he added, 'with a bit of luck, but it might not be.' his bedside manner unimproved from the experiences of the day.

Smelta began to cry louder.

'It's probably better than that, I just like to be on the safe side. You probably only need to worry about ten per cent.' he added.

'I wish I could eat, I'm suddenly feeling very hungry now,' said Smelt, 'can I have a boiled Ovum?'

'No.' said the computer.

'Well, can I have the combined music, story and food, from a Delius Myth recipe?

'You can have the Delius and the Myth separately, but I cannot permit you to combine them to produce a tasty meal.'

'Why not?'

'Too dangerous until you've had your treatment. It could speed up the degeneration process,' added Profmed. 'you had better finish your callall, unless Smelta wants to watch you in pain.'

'No thanks, replied Smelta, I'll have a fried Ovum with some belly slices from a dead hogg and then I shall get on with the decryption to take my mind off it all.'

Smelt tried to relax, but it was very difficult now that he knew what excruciating torture was about to be inflicted upon the rest of him.

* * * * *

Meanwhile, Smelta began to decipher the replicate of the olde-fashioned folio. She found it hard to concentrate, but she did her best in the circumstances.

She discovered that she was right about the first folio. It was called the *Oxford Dictionary with Pictures.* It was indeed a Lexikern.

The Lexikern had already been fed into the computer for her and she only needed to manipulate the data in Smelt's laboratory. She was able to get the gist of the other folio in the form of a series of pictures taken from the Lexikern with other words between.

It took the rest of the day to analyse the first half pulpleaf of the second folio, which seemed to be about how a planet came to be in existence. It was remarkably similar to the beginning of the Folio of Genetics, telling about the making of Planet Five out of nothing. And how the stars came to be made. And how the seas came to be made. And how the land was made. And how the beings came to be made.

And her work was done. And Smelta saw that it was good.

One thing puzzled her, though. Whenever the super being, or GoD was mentioned, there was a picture of a sort of bearded Gobbling oozing red and tied and nailed to a golejibbit, a vertical pole with a horizontal crossbar. And it wasn't a mistake, either. All of the cross-references in the Lexikern showed this picture, except two, one of which showed a Gobbling with a long white beard sitting on a big chair on what looked like an olde-fashioned cloud from before the weather was centrally controlled.

The last reference showed a plugged bottle of a light brown fluid.

This was most curious. Even when a team lost, the golesentry was never tied to a golejibbit. In any case, what had golejibbits to do with GoD? She could not get any further at present until this puzzle was solved. What had Agwgwllanders playing with their odd-shaped balls on a green with a golejibbit each end got to do with Genetics and making Eqinox ... or any other planet, come to that?

The whole time, she was wanting to find out how Smelt was getting on, but Profmed had particularly asked her not to interrupt his treatment. She did try once, but Profmed had switched his callall to autoanswer. And Smelta *hated* autoanswer callalls.

Eventually, she gave in and callalled Grounsell and Putout3 in the ward at Selondre Hospice.

'We don't know what's happening, either.' they said in unison. Grounsell added, 'I think Profmed has stopped us watching for the moment to save our mental anguish, but he's making it worse.'

'I should be playing in twelve days,' added Putout3, 'so I only want to know how long my recovery is going to be.'

'Ah!' said Smelta through the e-commenter. 'I had forgotten that you are Welks.'

'I'm not from down by there, bach!, I'm from Ffordd Llwydd, the next valley. We're playing the Welks, see and I'm the golesentry.'

'Sorry. I just hoped you could solve a problem for me. Do you know the connection between GoD and a Gobbling tied and nailed to a golejibbit?'

Putout3 and Grounsell looked at each other with both their heads.

Grounsell put his finger on the shush button to talk in confidence. 'Do you think she's being affected by what Smelt is going through? I mean, do you think she's beginning to lose her elgins?'

'Sounds to me as though she has always been out of her bassinette.' replied Putout3.

Grounsell removed his finger from the shush button, 'Sorry, none of us here have any ideas.'

'Thanks. I just wondered what it all had to do with the Genetics folio of The Folius anyway. Bye.'

Both heads of every Trisep in the ward shook in unison and raised their eyes GodwardS, thinking she should be straight-jacketed.

'Definitely.' said Grounsell, nodding in agreement while still shaking his other head.

'Ai,' said one of the others, 'she's one dalli short of a lama, that's for sure.'

The callall berped. Grounsell answered it.

Profmed was standing sideways on. In the half breath since making the callall he had forgotten making it.

'What's up Profmed?' asked Grounsell.

'Oh! Ah, it's you. I thought you would like to know what's happened to Smelt.'

'Yes?'

'Ah, yes, well, the treatment's finished.'

'And?'

'He's going to need to rest for a bit, but it seems to have worked.'

'Only seems to have?' asked Grounsell.

'Oh, yes, it worked, but he's going to need to sleep for about two days before he can talk to anyone. I think you should be next, Grounsell and then the others. I can only do one at a time, I'll do the rest tomorrow. Sorry you can't eat, but you know why not.'

'What about the ... hello? Hello? Cronus! He's gone.' said Grounsell, 'well, I suppose I'd better go over to Profmed now.'

'Good luck!' The remaining Contaigen-infected patients chorused.

He nodded and dropped his heads in resigned acceptance of the inevitable knowing it would be more than painful, almost worse than deceasement itself, which had for a great many cycles been free of pain.

'Oh,' added Putout3, 'you had better tell Profmed about Smelta and her strange fantasies. I've been thinking. She is the only female who has been in contact with us; those of us who have the Contaigen, I mean. I wonder if she has been somehow affected by the Contaigen through us. And you know how strange females can be sometimes. I expect Profmed will want to give her an automed Phroydtest.'

Grounsell smiled, nodded and left.

* * * * *

It was several days before the expedition members were able to escape from Profmed's care and return to civilisation – and a while longer before their bodies fully recovered.

Meanwhile, a great deal else had occurred on Eqinox.

Chapter 4   The Crater

'Where exactly was the Orijin found? Can you show me on a map?' Smelt asked Maecenas, Eqinox Government's Chief Scientist and Scientific Historian.

Maecenas was taller than average with high forehead and receding hair. His intelligent demeanour and purposeful stance set him apart from the average Trisep. But then, of course, he really was different, more intelligent and more capable than most, particularly when it came to solving problems. There was only one who could out-think him to any significant degree.

'You were on your way to it when you tripped over the hole. Near enough exactly half way.'

Smelt's logic kicked in. 'Exactly half way means nothing. From which starting point - from home, from the Dagoba? From where I'd parked my moovacar? Forget those questions, it doesn't matter. How did you know where to look for it?'

'The problem was that it seemed rather odd to have so much more of the old biomass here than anywhere else on the planet, so there must have been some reason for it.' replied Maecenas, 'so we just looked harder there.'

Smelt raised a fascinated eyebrow.

'We'd been searching for a long time for something, but we didn't know what. Then one researcher decided to look for objects, anything really. We had no idea exactly what we were seeking then, so we checked for any slight gravity difference. Then when we added the results to the ground density tests and underground frequency ranging, we saw this object about five hites down. Quite close to the surface, really. Our tests were designed to find something at a rather greater depth; we didn't expect an answer so close to the surface squelches.

Maecenas paused for effect and waited for Smelt's brain to catch up, 'When you found the hole, I mean the pipe, everyone thought that you had found the original entry point of the Orijin and wondered whether it had somehow moved. You see, the wall of the pipe was a thousand times denser than the surrounding soil, and some are sure it must have been made before there was life because there was no biomass in its structure.'

'And do you still think that?'

'Well, no, not really; some of us never did. Also, the diameter was rather too large. Anyway, an object hitting even such soft ground would not have made such a long and straight and smooth and precisely manufactured pipe as that. Shame we didn't take a sample for further analysis while we had the chance.'

Somehow and for the second time recently, Smelt felt that there was a degree of hypocrisy in his interlocutor's assertions, but he wasn't quite sure whether this senior government advisor actually counted as a politician. If a politician, he would, of course, have sworn the Hypocritic Oath ensuring that the truth is employed as economically as possible.

Maecenas stopped and looked out across the countryside, 'Do you know, there have been hundreds of scientists over the years who have excavated those tiny Ovum-shaped mounds like the one round the pipe. They are found in squelches all over Eqinox and nobody has ever found anything in them or under them. If you dig up the soil, there's just no difference when compared with the surrounding soil. They've been a major puzzle. Just look at the history folios. In the Middle-Eons, magic powers were attributed to them and pre-copulate daughters were sacrificed to GoD in them. The thing is that they're so low that you wouldn't even notice them unless you were actually looking. Funny, in the old days they were known as Gobbling-rings or Faerie-rings because they were so small that you could sidle over them without noticing they existed. Strange how there's so much truth in some of the old myths.'

'Truth? Ah, yes, I see. Why didn't the ground density tests and frequency ranging discover the pipe and the cave of Qontûm, do you think?' asked Smelt.

'There are those who have been wondering about that. There are two main theories: either the average density remained constant because the pipe and cave walls were made from material compacted from the hollow, or they simply weren't there.'

'How could they not have been there?'

'You might just as well ask,' replied Maecenas, 'how the hole could disappear and the surface look as though it hadn't been disturbed for generations.'

'When are the Defenss starting to dig?' asked Smelt.

'About now, I think. They may already have started. Perhaps ENN will have a report on the e-commenter.'

There she was, Cate'aeddy in one holoquadrant and a view of where the hole used to be, in another.

'… Which is about all that can be said at the moment.' she said.

Maecenas told the e-commenter to review back, which it did.

Cate'aeddy began, 'As you can see, the sappachines have started to dig and as they do so, we must not forget that Bodgitt is still down there somewhere with the Gobblings; he will almost certainly be in pain from his fall and possibly from the Contaigen which these horrible Hobbimps seem to inflict upon Triseps. The sappachines have already reached about six lengths down to where the hole should be and they have still found nothing.'

Another holoquadrant opened showing the original hole as it had been when the autofollowing holocam went down it. The infobox showed that the image had now been measured and the pipe was 463.871407 lengths. The diameter of the hemisphere of Qontûm was calculated from the curve of the edge to be 3123.998 lengths. These of course are all exact multiples of the magic number: forty-seven, any arithmate will tell you that.

'We are all finding it hard to believe that just three days ago there was a hole. It was just here, a quite definite, solid hole; now, today, as you can see, there is no hole.' commented Cate'aeddy.

Maecenas thought hard. 'I've got an idea,' he said and made a callall.

'Ah, Kernal, would you do an ultric-bionic analysis on the soil at the point where the hole used to be and see if it is any different from the surrounding soil. I want to see if the biomass content is different in any way.'

'I don't have the equipment, but the sappachines do seem to be digging down the pipe and there is a slight difference with the surrounding soil colour. I will need to get the Multicare in to do the analysis because we don't use those analysers. Shouldn't take more than a few hundred breaths to get here though. Should we continue digging?'

'Oh, yes of course, we must remember Bodgitt,' said Maecenas, 'digging is first priority.'

The two sappachines continued to dig without finding a hole. The sappachines had been very firmly chained to a series of land anchors set at least 200 lengths apart. Although the sappachines were remote controlled they were not designed to hover under their own water-vapour, so to speak, so Kernal feared he might lose them if they suddenly vanished into a void.

The Multicare arrived with an ultric-bionic analyser on board and Kernal asked for a Sqoddie to volunteer to go down with it on a growable cable.

Back in Selondre the meeting of arithmates, professors of medicine, chemistry, biochemistry, geology, nanotechnology, astrophysics and Qontûm engineering theoreticians, as well as Eqinox politicians, continued in session at the Conventionium. Now, everyone was watching this moment on the e-commenter and awaiting the analysis with baited breaths.

One professor of geology asked for a prepared slice across where the hole was, with glass either side. Several other scientists in the Conventionium immediately asked for samples too, more to ensure maintenance of their personal credibility than for genuine scientific reasons.

A holoquadrant showed the Multicare arriving, a Sqoddie being trained in the test equipment's use and an autofollowing holocam hovering overhead.

Smelt looked at Maecenas, trying to read his mind and missed slightly. 'Do we have any literature on little beings like the Gobblings from historical records?'

'There are the legends I mentioned, but I haven't checked the records. Of course, there are some secret documents that only the Eqinox Government has access to, but they are mostly about old wars. As Adviser, I have access to the secret files.' Maecenas told the computer to give him access to the data at his security level. The problem was, he did not know what to look for. At least, he indicated to Smelt that he didn't know what to look for, 'I have access to some of them, at least.' he added at length.

The first reference to appear was of the little green bipeds with pointed ears from the Green Aisle, that verdant corridor of land so near to Squeith and yet so far in so many political and practical ways. They were, it seemed, particularly found near areas of squelches. Of course, there were no photographs or drawings. These bipeds, it seemed were famous for Lepperdcorns, so called because they laugh like the spotted lepperd of Zimgululland and tell really bad, corny jokes.

'Look!' exclaimed Smelt, 'Entry four!'

'*These celebrated photographs printed in The Thundering Tempora,*' the article began, beneath two pre-holographic flatcampics, '*were taken within two cycles of the invention of olde-fashioned cams. The picture shows Faeries at the bottom of a young Trisep's garden. There was publicity all over Eqinox at the time and large numbers of Triseps claimed to have seen them, but if they were real, they never let themselves be pictured again. Four different Triseps who tried at various times to investigate by watching the bottom of the garden alone all night each disappeared before morning dawned. After that, other investigators were themselves watched by teams of photographers but nothing further happened. There have been stories of Faeries throughout history but these are the only ones ever photographed.*'

'There is no doubt,' concluded Maecenas 'that these were the same as the Gobblings seen in Qontûm.'

'Yes,' replied Smelt, 'except for the wings of course.'

'Wings?'

'Yes, wings. See?'

'Oh, yes. Cute aren't they. I shouldn't think they could fly with wings that small, though.' said Smelt.

'Mm, about as useful as the wings of the black and white nün-polepengu, wouldn't you say?' retorted Maecenas, intending to be more rhetorical than he succeeded in being.

'Yes. And the colour?' Retorted Smelt.

'They're not in colour! They're sepia and white flatcampics.' responded Maecenas.

'No, the colour of the Faeries themselves.' corrected Smelt.

'Mm. That's not what I meant. I suppose these are white and the Gobblings were translucent. But their heads are the same!' Maecenas sounded as though he was almost trying to excuse them.

'Well, similar. They both have only one head, two eyes and two legs. They could be a variant species.' he thought for a moment, then added, 'You know, Maecenas, I would have expected you to know all about this.'

Maecenas looked away, guiltily.

'You *did* know, didn't you? You knew all along and didn't want to admit it. You were just pretending that you were searching for the first time.' Smelt turned both his heads full on Maecenas and glared, 'exactly what are you hiding?'

Maecenas glanced at Smelt and looked away again. 'I'm hiding nothing ... at least, not personally.'

'But you are!' protested Smelt, 'How can you not be doing it personally?'

Maecenas sagged. 'Government policy. Official secrets. Even I am not permitted to release certain data, or even admit its existence without permission. To be truthful, I am not fully sure that I truly have access to the full story.'

Smelt understood and felt sorry for Maecenas. 'Everybody knows about the Gobblings now, so is it any longer a secret?'

'Yes and no. I would have to get permission from Polit46.'

Smelt looked at the e-commenter. The Conventionium was still full and sitting and Polit46 was there. 'Ask him.' he said.

Maecenas set a confidential Trisep to Trisep callall to Polit46.

Even though Smelt was in the same room, the anti-sound emitted by the callall while shushcallalls were in progress meant that he couldn't hear what was being said, but he could see a heated discussion. It was obvious that Polit46 was exceedingly reluctant to let something secret become public knowledge, but realised that the circumstances offered no variation in choice.

'I've got permission.' said Maecenas, turning to Smelt, 'so I'd better tell you all I really know, but I have to warn you not to repeat it.'

Smelt ordered two large geeantees and sat down, ready to listen. 'Should you just be telling me - or should you be addressing the Conventionium?'

Maecenas bit his lip in thought. 'I've only got permission to tell *you* at the moment.' He looked away and thought for a moment before adding, 'But you are not under any such legal restriction, only a moral obligation .'

Smelt took his geeantee, passed one to Maecenas and looked expectantly at him. He hesitated before continuing.

A Faerie-Gobbling

'The secret records go back hundreds of cycles. There's a whole data section devoted to the subject. The records are so highly classified that many of the old paper records and old folios have not even been copied onto the data bank, so I've only read a few in holofolio form, but I understand the others say the same thing.' Maecenas jutted his front chin and his heads respectively looked at the floor and ceiling for inspiration.

'Basically,' Maecenas continued, 'there used to be legends about brightly-lit, flying beefburghers with little alien bipeds on board and some Triseps disappeared. A few even returned with really weird stories about being used for experimental breeding with verdant men from other planets; but they were all treated as cranks and always died very quickly, so no real notice was taken of them.'

Smelt raised his eyebrows in interest.

'Eventually, about three hundred cycles ago, during the Great Western Wars - when primitive atom-splitting molotovs devastated vast areas that could not be used until nanomachines were invented to convert radiating elements into harmless non-radiating elements by adjusting the sub-atomic structures - there was one particular battle between Sammowa and Eislland over ghotiing[6] rights in the Azorrics. Eislland was a land covered in squelches and was totally devastated; there was a gigantic crater. It's still there to this day. Some Triseps went into the crater in an anti-radiation moovacar and saw over a hundred underground caverns at the edges of the crater. Every cavern had dead Gobblings inside; hundreds of thousands of them. That was when the truth of their existence became known. Until then, nobody really believed the legends.'

'So it became public knowledge?' asked Smelt.

'No, it was all hushed up. They had primitive moving picture cams but the public never saw the images. Investigations then showed that these beings were in caverns under squelches all over Eqinox. There were about seven distinct species. Some had wings like the Faeries, but some were more like the translucent, non-flying Gobblings. Then the caverns were filled in, so there's no evidence left.'

'So the picture in The Thundering Temporra was genuine, then?'

'Oh, yes, of course, but nobody dared admit it.' replied Maecenas.

'And what about the Triseps who disappeared? What happened to them?' Smelt looked suspiciously at Maecenas, who was studying the floor again.

'Well, to disappear, they always fall down a pipe into a Gobbling cavern and it depends on which species of Gobbling they meet at the bottom, really. Some interrogate, remove the memory of the visit and return the Trisep to the surface. Others - most of them, actually - just eat any Trisep who falls into one of their temporary holes. The ones under Squelchpool have a particularly nasty bite. Actually, Profmed was wrong in his analysis. The Gobbling fluid injected into you and the others would definitely not have turned you into clones of the Gobblings. It is actually a sort of preservative. It would have made your body stop functioning in about 20 days. After that, each part of you would have remained alive with the injected fluid acting as a

---

[6]   Ghotiing - the act of withdrawing an undersea critter from its natural home of the sea. See the Lexikern for full definition of **ghoti**.

preservative. So you would have been kept alive and tasty but de-animated.'

'Nasty!' shuddered Smelt. 'So do you think that is what's happening to Bodgitt?'

'Oh yes, but we've got another fifteen days or so until he de-animates. They won't start eating him for at least a month after that, when the flavour has mellowed, so we've got plenty of time. Or we could negotiate.'

'Negotiate? Negotiate! What do you mean, negotiate? We can't even get to them, let alone negotiate!' Smelt looked at Maecenas, puzzled, 'can we?'

'There's a secret private line callall to them from the Eqinox Precedent's private office. And they have their own inter-species callall system. The olde-fashioned wire line is tested once a year, but hasn't been used for communication since the Ozzilland rookanga scare a hundred and two cycles ago.' replied Maecenas.

'What about when Triseps go missing?'

'Oh, er that. Yes.' said Maecenas and hesitated.

'Well?'

'Ah, well, yes.' he looked at the floor in embarrassment, 'There's a secret contract. It's called *The Agreement.*'

Smelt was dumb-struck and just glared at Maecenas for not having told him before. Eventually, he re-loaded his current conversation and asked, 'Which says?'

'Oh, it's just about what happens to Triseps who fall into one of their holes, and a few other bits and pieces.'

'And what *does* happen to them?

'Finders keepers, really. It is a very old contract from before automeds. Most who fell in would have died from their injuries anyway, so if they get a Trisep, they can keep it.'

'And do what - eat it?'

'Well, er,'

'You mean, yes?' Smelt insisted.

Maecenas dropped his heads in shame and they looked at each other between his legs in consolation.

'That's cannibalism.' said Smelt.

'No, it's not.'

'Yes, it is.'

'No, it is definitely not!' insisted Maecenas.

'Yes, it *is*;' argued Smelt, and thought for a moment, 'no, I suppose it isn't really, is it. But, I mean, are you telling me that for Gobblings to eat Triseps has got official sanction?'

'We've never re-negotiated The Agreement. You see, they've kept up with us in technology because they can visit us at any time and we don't even know they have been. They also have certain powers that my predecessors have called magic, but in practice is just a matter of motorphroyd. At least, that is the conclusion that was drawn during the researches. No proper tests were ever done.'

'By motorphroyd, you mean moving things by brain power alone?'

Maecenas thought for a few breaths, 'Not just moving things, but actually transforming them. Just like we do these days with nanotechnology.'

'You mean … ' pondered Smelt, 'that Gobblings can perform 'magic' using motorphroyd? Is that how they can create a pipe through the ground and then reconvert it to the original form?'

Maecenas nodded his first head in confirmation and shook his second head at the idea of the secret becoming public knowledge, 'Yes, that's how they always visit us. Then they re-form the original surface. The only evidence of their visits is the miniature Ovum-shaped Faerie-rings or Gobbling-rings caused by pressure waves from their exit pipe formation process.'

A Leperdcorn

'Why shouldn't this become public?' asked Smelt.

'Because there could be riots all over Eqinox. The planet's government would lose all credibility if it became known that such an important secret had been kept for so long.' Maecenas looked worried. 'And then there are their pre-historic wars, which was why they went underground in the first place - but that's another secret; a story which is best retained for another day.'

'It's about time,' argued Smelt, 'that all Eqinox knew. I think you should tell the Convention and see what they suggest. First let me callall Smelta.'

Smelt callalled Smelta at home; she wasn't there: she had switched out her personal callallcode. Neither was she in the laboratory. For all practical purposes, she had effectively disappeared. 'She does that sometimes,' he muttered, 'I wonder what she's up to this time.' he thought about his suspicions of her in the past and his mind began to wander.

'Why would she go off callall?' asked Maecenas, genuinely puzzled.

Smelt shook his front head to recover but left the frown on his second head. 'Why do any of us go off callall?' he responded with a genuine innocence.

Maecenas opened his mouth to speak, stopped, put his front head on one side and looked at Smelt, puzzled. As he thought, so he realised that in his experience, Triseps would only go off callall if they had something to hide. 'Isn't Smelta supposed to be doing some research?'

Smelt suddenly felt uneasy. 'Would they have come to the surface to take her away?'

'Oh, no. At least, I doubt it. No, I think that's unlikely, although we *are* living in strange times.'

'We'd better callall the Convention.' said Smelt, quickly changing the subject.

'Oh, yes. I suppose we had. I'll warn Polit46 first.' Maecenas pondered and made a shushcallall, but left his end open for Smelt to hear.

Polit46 appeared in the callall, increasingly wearied by events, his hair visibly greying.

'Your hair is visibly greying' said Maecenas obviously. 'We've got no choice. We must go public.'

'They won't believe it. They'll think it's just more politician's propaganda, and like everything else I say, an economy of the honesty of the allegory. Do you know, I sometimes wonder whether it is ever worth telling the truth? You might as well lie all the time because nothing is believed anyway.'

'True, nothing you say as a politician is going to be believed, of course, but they might believe it from me.' replied the more credible Maecenas, 'They're going to find out eventually anyway. You don't think the Gobblings will keep it secret do you? I mean, once the sappachines hit their living quarters?'

'Or ENN, I suppose.' appended Polit46, unbaling his sinking ship.

Smelt added for good measure, 'remember that lying is not about telling lies, but is the intent to deceive. You have deceived all Eqinox by keeping the secret of the Gobblings for so long. The longer you deceive them, the greater the long term deception perception and the worse for you politically.'

Polit46 bowed his head. If he did not tell all Eqinox, then he would be found to be a liar when the secret escaped. If he *did* tell Eqinox, then he would be admitting to being a liar now. There was no escape. He did not want to be thought of as a liar, even though truth massage was a part of the job. But there was one last escape.

'All right, I concede to you, Maecenas;' Polit46 began, 'but when you speak, if you really must admit to an inkling of the truth, you must state - or at least, imply - that I had to conceal the whole truth because of The Agreement with the Gobblings.' he stopped and looked at the others for inspiration.

'Can you remind me of the full details of The Agreement?' continued Polit46, 'It does not seem to be in the central data bank.'

'No, it is only on pulpleaves for security, so I'll have to tell you what I can remember of it. Altogether there are forty-seven clauses. But basically, there are seven tenets: *Zero:* neither Triseps nor Gobblings have any rights over the territory or property of the other. *One:* that there should be no contact except in case of dire emergency and to that end an olde-fashioned callall cable was set up between our Precedent and their leadership. This was last used over a hundred cycles ago. In fact, it was used during the Ozzilland rookanga scare.'

'What happened then?' asked Polit46.

'The rookangas were facing extinction because they were being caught and gobbled up by the Gobblings, even though they could have hopped over them in a single bound, so we nearly went to war over them.'

'And the other tenets?'

'Two: that Triseps would not admit the Gobblings' existence or the existence of The Agreement publicly.'

'Why not?'

'To stop further investigation. *Three:* that publicity about any contact should be suppressed or dismissed as ridiculous for the same reason.'

He paused for effect.

Four: that Gobblings would not make excessive or unnecessary visits to the surface or colonise the surface or otherwise interfere with Triseps or their space.'

'Ah!' responded Smelt with some pleasure.

Maecenas raised one eyebrow and continued, *'Five:* both they and we agreed to remain warless for all time so long as we kept to our contract in every word. *Six:* that we would warn them of any impending disaster such as collision with a giant meteor or major wars between our own countries.'

Maecenas turned from the callall as though he had finished.

'And?' asked Polit46 forcefully.

'And what?' asked Maecenas, trying to sound innocent.

'And what was the seventh tenet?'

'Er. Yes, the seventh tenet.' he stopped and looked away. 'As I said, there are forty-seven clauses, but the specific clauses are irrelevant. It is the tenets that count.'

'It didn't work. You didn't put me off the scent. The seventh tenet? Well?'

'Well, that if any Triseps should accidentally fall down any of their temporary holes, then they would not be returned.'

'Why not?'

'Er, well, at the time, automeds were not as good as they are today, and they would probably have died from their injuries anyway ... and the alternative would have been a long, slow, painful deceasement ... and, well, Triseps are a very great delicacy, prized for their aphrodisiac qualities.'

'Do you mean that they would eat us?'

'Yes, in short.'

'And we agreed to that?'

'Yes.'

'Why?'

'Why??'

'Yes, why?'

'Because Triseps are a very great delicacy, prized for their aphrod ...
'

'No, no, no, I mean, why did we agree to it?' insisted Polit46.

'Because we didn't have any choice; basically, they would have eaten those of us who fell down the holes anyway. But we did get them to agree to one thing.' Said Maecenas.

'Which was?'

'That they would only put their holes in squelches where it is unsafe for Triseps to roam in any case, so that there would be a natural explanation for any Trisep who disappeared.'

'Oh.' responded Polit46, running out of ideas, 'and you think that we should tell all Eqinox about it?'

'There's no real choice now.' replied Maecenas.

'Oh, GoD help us.'

'Well, GoD won't help, really! I mean, the religiots and some of the less heathen are already asking for GoD's help, but he's never helped yet.' Maecenas really did take things a bit too literally at times.

'No, I mean ... ' began Polit46.

'Of course, if GoD has taken hold of your sub-conscientious,' continued Maecenas, 'making you, unconsciously, painstakingly and diligently truthful and competent, then I suppose your Sole would ...'

'No, No! No, I mean ... oh, never mind. I think I'd better prepare the Convention for this little speech of yours, don't you?' retorted Polit46.

'What about the rest of Eqinox ?' asked Smelt from behind Maecenas.

'Eh, what?' said Polit46, looking round and back to the callall, 'I thought we were on shush!'

'We are your end.' said Maecenas, 'Smelt just wondered when we were going to tell the rest of the world.'

'First we'll put the Convention into Secret-Session and I'll prepare them for the news.' he turned away and made some notes on his personal autodiary so that it would build a complete speech for him.

The callall was terminated and within forty-seven breaths, Polit46's autodiary had arranged Secret-Session for the Convention and made him ready, 'Fellow Triseps,' he began as he stood to interrupt the current speaker, 'I have some new and vitally important news. It is so important that we have just entered Secret-Session.' he foolishly deviated from his speech, 'Perhaps the clump of scientists playing the politicians at elgins at the back of the hall would like to pay attention please.' he stopped and waited for them to return to their cowches.

'Actually, the news is not new, I've known about it for some time and so have a very few others. I would like the full story to be given to you by Maecenas, who from his name you will know is the Chief Scientist and Scientific Historian. He will start with an event in the ghotiing wars when Sammowa dropped an atom-splitting molotov on Eislland and left a gigantic crater.'

Maecenas appeared via the callall on the commenter at the front of the Conventionium ready to tell his story. 'Er,' he began and changed his mind, 'Well, because of the great import and secrecy of the matter which I need to discuss with you, I think it would be better if I were to come to the Conventionium and speak to you all face-to-face. Meanwhile, Polit46 will have time to finish his own speech, although he will probably wait until I arrive to answer your questions. I shall be watching on the e-commenter en-route.'

* * * * *

Smelt was puzzled about the disappearance of Smelta. However hard he tried, she could not be found anywhere. He gave up and decided to callall Profmed to see how he was getting on with treating Grounsell.

'He's gone.' said Profmed.

'Gone? What do you mean, gone?' Retorted Smelt.

'Gone. Not here. Gone home. He's got an automed at home, so they went home. Are *you* all right Smelt?'

'Me? Oh, yes, fully recovered, thank you. I expect it will be a while before my strength is a hundred per cent again, but we're nearly there.'

'Good, good, fine, fine. Come and see me if you have any more symptoms.' said Profmed automatically, clearly having lost interest and now thinking about his next problem.

'Good-bye.' said Smelt and terminated the callall.

He looked at the e-commenter to see what was going on. The Conventionium quadrant was blank and the infobox showed that it was expected to be blank for a long time yet. Maecenas really had set off a time-molotov.

The infobox also showed that 59% of Triseps on Eqinox watching e-commenters were watching The Seventy Six Sexploits of Sharing Sharen.

He put in a callall to Grounsell. Grounsell wasn't at home; Grounsella said so. Grounsell had switched out his personal callallcode.

'Twice in one day,' muttered Smelt out loud, 'normally only happens once a year.' he looked at Grounsella. He looked her down and up. *What legs!* he thought, *slim, and perfectly bowed.* And her mamaglans were just that perfect hand-size that the more cultivated Trisep males loved. Their eyes met and he pretended not to have been noticing her attractiveness. But she wouldn't forget that moment of unwitting display, albeit via the callall.

He spoke of Grounsell again. 'I can't find him anywhere. Did he tell you where he was going?'

'I thought he was still at Selondre Hospice. I didn't check, did you?'

'Yes. Profmed said that they had already left.'

'With whom? Who was he being treated with? I thought he was being treated alone?'

'He was; Profmed had to treat us individually.'

'So who were *they* then?'

'They who? Then, er, they were - what? Eh?' dribbled the confused Smelt.

'*They* - who were *they?* - You said that Profmed said *they* had already left Selondre Hospice.'

'I did.' He thought for a breath, 'He did.' his heads looked at each other. 'Yes! He did, didn't he. I wonder if he meant ...'

'Hello? Hello? He's hung up!' said Grounsella to herself, confused.

'What now?' Profmed growled at the callall.

'Sorry, but who did Grounsell leave Selondre Hospice with?'

'Why?'

'Just wondered. Was it Smelta by any chance?'

'Yes, of course it was. Who else did you think?'

'Grounsella, of course. I assumed that he had left with his herd leader.'

Profmed turned and looked at Smelt in the callall, 'Huh.' he laughed. 'I thought they would be coming to you.' he stopped and looked, 'Oh by the way, do you know the connection between golejibbits, Eislland and GoD? Smelta wanted to know.'

'Thanks for the info. Er, no, I don't. No idea. Goodness, you *have* been talking to Smelta, haven't you! Did *you* think she needed a Phroydtest?' Smelt saw Profmed shake his front head, terminated the callall and interrogated the computer about the whereabouts of Smelta's moovacar.

'On its way to Eislland. Slow overnight sleeping mode. All external communication outed.'

Smelt looked away and back again, disbelieving. He callalled Grounsella.

'You're not going to believe this,' Smelt began, and told her the story so far.

'Can't say I'm surprised,' she retorted, 'he has been out of touch an awful lot recently, but I didn't think he even knew Smelta.'

'Neither did I, except she saw him once when personally delivering one of my sculptures. It took her a whole day to do that.'

'Yes, I remember.' Grounsella replied, 'but she didn't deliver it. It took a whole day for Grounsell to go to you and collect it.'

They looked at each other through the callall with both heads, suddenly knowing all. Smelt told Grounsella about the moovacar. 'That's enough for me!' She billowed, reddening rapidly, 'shall I come to you now?'

'Yes, I think you must.'

Smelt set his autodiary to order the moovacar to take him to Eislland as soon as Grounsella arrived.

The infobox on the e-commenter was estimating another day and a half before the Conventionium reconvened in public session. In Cate'aeddy's holoquadrant, there was a heated debate about what was probably going on in Secret-Session in the Conventionium.

To Smelt, it was the best comedy programme he had ever seen. Suggestions about the lethal Contaigen spreading round the world, forthcoming war with atom-splitting molotovs, voodoo mind-malaise magic, theories about the caverns and surface of Eqinox just being two layers of many were side-splitting.

But they were not all wrong in every respect.

Then, in a final display of ultimate ridiculousness, one pseudo-scientist suggested that the Gobblings were the children of GoD and each one was a Trisep's guardian angel!

Grounsella arrived. He could tell her the whole story on the way to Eislland.

'You're … wow!' said Smelt, looking Grounsella down and up but in the flesh this time, and taking particular note of her impressively perfect mamaglans. Somehow she hadn't looked quite so gorgeous through the callall, even in three-dimensional holoview.

Grounsella looked at Smelt. Her heads were arguing with each other about her moods. The limited brain of her rear head was in mourning for her erring husband and suggesting a Grief Encounter, but her highly intelligent front head had appraised him fully and was way ahead of current reality.

Smelt read her faces and reciprocated.

Their greeting hug and kiss was more impassioned than either would have dared in public, but in the double circumstances of lost, yet newly found, they both felt as justified as they undoubtedly really were.

Smelt set the moovacar to arrive in Eislland overnight, shortly after Grounsell and Smelta. Grounsella nodded and smiled in confirmation of his forwardness.

As the moovacar flew, they settled into intertwingled mutual comfort for the night and Smelt began to relate the tale that was even now being related to the Convention.

As he finished, Smelt stopped dead in his train of the story, 'I feel ever so slightly guilty.'

'We might, but they don't' Grounsella replied and huddled closer.

Smelt didn't need another invitation. 'Why not.' he breathed warmly in her ear.

* * * * *

'By Cronus and Rhea! What are you doing here?' Smelta turned her front head to confront Smelt and Grounsella, who had flown over at high level, landed secretly and parked out of sight.

'More to the point,' responded Grounsella with a typical woman to woman jealous felinity, 'what are *you* doing here?'

'Research, of course,' replied Grounsell. He had recovered his composure and was ready to answer, 'we wanted to see what the connection was between this undergrowth-covered crater, GoD, Gobblings and golejibbits.'

'Why didn't you ask me?' asked Smelt.

'You were tied up with Maecenas and we thought you wouldn't want to be disensconced, so we came on our own.' responded Smelta, passing a guilty glance at Grounsell.

Smelt and Grounsella caught each others' eyes. 'Just answer one question that's been puzzling me,' began Smelt, 'exactly what do you know about this crater and Eislland? Except for one or perhaps two Triseps who had access to secret historical data, nobody knew about this place until today.'

Grounsell looked at Smelta. Everyone looked at Smelta. Smelta looked guilty. Suddenly she began to fire non-stop unintelligible questions, 'What do you mean, nobody knew? Everybody knew didn't they? It's always been here hasn't it? It's on all the maps, isn't it? Everyone knows there is something strange going on here, don't they? Why was it a prohibited zone for two hundred years after the war? Was this the Gobblings' secret headquarters? Why are you with Grounsella? Why aren't you still recovering in Selondre Hospice? Where's Maecenas? What's *really* going on at the Conventionium? Listen, why won't you tell me? What are the . . .'

'Hold on, hold on, hold ON!' interrupted Smelt, 'stop blathering and slow down a bit. I can only answer one question at a time. Now, why did you really come here?'

'Because it is Eqinox's deepest crater and might show signs of the underground world. Also because it remained out of bounds for so long, there must be something going on here. Trouble is, we don't really know what to look for.' She replied with a new elegance of eloquence.

'But why did you come on the slow overnight sleeping mode?' Smelt continued, suspiciously.

'Because I was tired, of course,' replied Smelta, 'and so was Grounsell. I needed him as an expert guide here. Trouble is, he doesn't know any more than I do. Perhaps now we're all together, we can work as a team and see what's here.'

'Well, it all seems innocent enough.' said Grounsella, feeling guilty herself, 'I don't see why we can't help now that we're here.' She looked at Smelt, who hung his heads and bit his bottom lip - both ends.

He looked up and nodded in confirmation. 'What do you want us to do?' he asked.

They sidled to the base of the gigantic cliff edging the crater and stopped in their tracks at the sight of the quag ahead of them.

Using both heads, and all their independent eyes, they all looked at each other at the same time, while still surveying the scene.

'However remote,' began Grounsell, 'there are always those who will leave their rubbish behind. Mind you, it's been here a long time by the look of it!'

'Why,' asked Smelta, 'wherever there's a quag or pond or mire, is there always an olde-fashioned big brass broken bedstead by the bank?'

'And a single laceless left-hand levva boot.' added Smelt, 'but no sign of Triseps; not even any alternating prints of boot and sock.'

'What else is there?' muttered Grounsell to himself, 'Three treadless tyres from olde-fashioned moovacars, an old felt hat, oil drums, lorry load of tar blocks, and of course, a broken bedstead there.'

'How on Eqinox does it get here?' asked Grounsella with a grin, 'is there a Society of Big Brass Broken Bedstead Triseps who dump these things? Do you know, whenever I see a scene like this, with a pond, I think how sad it is that swanns are now extinct.'

'You remind me of Smelta in the bath,' responded Smelt, 'and of the old adage that swanns sing before they die, 'twere no bad thing should certain Triseps die before they sing!'

'Huh! You should hear Grounsell in the bath!.' Grounsella retorted.

* * * * *

69

By the end of the day, the Smelt's moovacar's e-commenter showed that the Convention was still in Secret-Session and the team had found nothing. They had even flown over at various heights looking for vegetation differences and could see nothing relevant, even in the x-ray spectrum with the third eye. There appeared to be a few areas where there was a slight difference, but this could probably be accounted for by differing areas of rock, soil and solar energy receipt values. Smelt explained that this was where over a hundred underground caverns at the edges of the crater had been filled in after the Great Western War, when The Agreement was made with the Gobblings.

'I still don't understand what a golejibbit has got to do with all this.' said Grounsell. 'Can someone enlighten me.'

Smelta explained what she had deciphered so far from the second folio and how the Lexikern always showed a young bearded Gobbling nailed and tied to a golejibbit whenever GoD was mentioned; except twice, of course.

'Twice? What was the variant?' asked Smelt.

'There were two different ones, actually: once it showed an old bearded Gobbling sitting on a cloud, and the other, it showed a plugged bottle of a light brown fluid.' replied Smelta.

'A plugged … ? Perhaps not one GoD but several, do you think?' Responded Grounsella, 'I'm always inclined to think that there's too much work in the universe for just one GoD. Aren't you?'

'I think there might be an explanation for the bottle of light brown fluid; you see it was called *Bells* with a claim that it was *Wholly Spirit.* It must have meant *Holy Sprite.* I think it might have been like the Orijin, a bottle of the first life put onto their planet by GoD. Holy Sprite means *completely enliven,* so it must have been the basis of their life But that doesn't explain the golejibbit.'

'Well, the answer is obvious to any sportsman,' responded Grounsell, 'being tied to a golejibbit is just punishment for failing as a golesentry. Perhaps on Planet Three of their system, GoD has a much more interactive relationship with his subjects.'

'But that seems to be a very heavy punishment for a sporting failure. Perhaps the picture of a young Gobbling tied to a golejibbit is an analogy.' said Grounsella, thoughtfully.

'What for?' asked Smelta.

'For?' Responded Grounsella, 'Ah, obviously the alien Gobblings are raised up in the minds of their fellow beings if they do well in sports, but they will be tied up and nailed down if they are slacking in sports which look after the health of their bodies. It is quite obvious that by using a vertical pole with the horizontal crossbar of a golejibbit, their GoD is demonstrating the importance of health and sport.'

'But why pick golejibbits?' Questioned Grounsell, 'While the Welks are playing with their odd-shaped balls and trying to get them over the golejibbits, others will be cross-country hopping at an out-of-town

Hopping Centre, or spirating to the twist of autoerotic nanogrooves or bail battering to win temporary custody of the ashen remains of a pair of pre-flamed bails stored for some weird and forgotten reason in a beautiful gelt urn.'

'I think the analogy fits perfectly with what GoD must be and how he must think.' said Smelta. 'I think she's right. There seemed to be a suggestion that it was GoD's child who gets nailed to golejibbits for three days, but it is obviously ridiculous that a father, and especially a GoD would do that, so it must be some kind of training in youth.'

'I suppose that's true really, I can't see any fault with the theory,' added Smelt.

'I must admit that I can't think of a better one,' confirmed Grounsell, 'even though I'm not totally happy. But then, I always was a bit agnostic.'

Grounsella kissed him on his front forehead, more for general effect than for any demonstration of affection for her husband.

'Does all this talk of GoD really matter?' asked Grounsell, trying to change the subject. 'I'm not really religious and I shall never be a religiot. It could be equally obvious that the pictures were of GoD painted in the image of the Gobblings. Either way, does it matter anyway?'

Grounsell looked around the clump with a twinkle in his eye. He was still standing next to Smelta. Obviously his herd leader had spent last night with Smelt in the moovacar following them. 'We are all so far away from civilisation,' he said, not fully sure what response he would evoke, 'that nobody would know what any of us were getting up to, would they?' His herd leader's eyes sparkled in anticipation.

'You're right, anything could happen and nobody could guess. Any ideas?' Grounsella said, hoping someone else would take up the thought and drive it home.

Smelta was beginning to catch up with the hidden conversation and her eyes reflected the sparkle, 'I've got some, but I'm not sure I dare admit them in mixed company, remote as we may be.'

'Shall we see what can be learnt from a re-run of The Seventy Six Sexploits of Sharing Sharen?' Suggested the normally staid Grounsell.

'That sounds like the best idea yet' responded Smelt, who fancied another night with Grounsella.

'Let's all have dinner with calepts in my moovacar and then, without any doubt, we'll all enjoy ourselves for the rest of the night.'

A ring of anticipatory smiles satisfied themselves into the faces of the contented and potentially gratified clump.

Chapter 5   The Convention Meets

'We should be back in Selondre in time for the reconvened Convention.' said Smelt, looking at the infobox on the moovacar's e-commenter. 'GoD, I'm tired. What a night! It's brilliant having breakfast out here in the open under the trees. Easy to forget how wonderful it can be here in the tropics. Funny really, I never expected the crater to be such a veritable forest. I thought the place would be totally devoid of life.'

'There's certainly nothing to report from here.' said Grounsell.

'Oh, I don't know,' responded Grounsella with a twinkle.

'Except that the place is full of life.' added Grounsell.

Smelta winked and smiled, 'Shush! There's *nothing* to report!'

'We really must do *nothing* again very soon,' smiled Grounsella, and this time the satisfied grins beamed to leave the very ether in no doubt of the gratification to come.

* * * * *

The Convention was about to reconvene publicly. Grounsell and Smelt were fully briefed as soon as they arrived. Had it not been for the highest classification of secrecy, they would have been briefed earlier through their autodiaries.

'We've decided to go public.' said Polit46, 'even though it is breaking The Agreement with the Gobblings. But first I must speak to them through the secret private line callall from my office to the Gobblings' leader.'

Polit46 left the Convention to continue its heated debates.

Cate'aeddy was here now and she sent an autofollowing holocam after him, but only had permission to display the image in the Conventionium, and not yet publicly.

'Hello?' enquired Polit46 to the olde-fashioned, sound-only, manual callall.

'Hello Polit46,' replied the voice at the other end, 'we have for long breaths waited for your callall. As a doctor, I am in your language called Quax. I am the nominated leader for this cycle.'

'Yes, we saw you on the e-commenter when we visited Qontûm. Please tell me how to address you and your race. What are you called?'

'I told thee, I am called Quax. We have no objection to thy title of Gobblings; words mean nothing to us.'

'We believe that you still have one of our Triseps, a builder called Bodgitt. Will you tell us what has happened to him.'

'He is alive. We will talk about him later. Is there further question required of me to answer?'

'All of Eqinox now knows of your existence, not just the Triseps of Squeith. We have to announce the existence of our contract with you, The Agreement.'

'I fail to understand any reason whatsoever why that should be at all necessary. Why?'

'Because it will calm the minds of those who do not understand. They will then know that we are mutually obliged; you to us and we to you.'

'But thou wilt thus be breaking our contract. If you, the Triseps break it, so can we. We have not colonised the surface at all. Yet.'

'You don't need to colonise the surface, do you?'

'Equally, you do not need to publicise. We need to grow more food. We do not eat nanomanufactured food. We need more space. You have plenty of space to spare!' Retorted Quax.

Polit46 looked nervously at the autofollowing holocam, saw himself in the commenter with his second head, composed himself and thought quickly. It was a good job that this olde-fashioned callall was sound only. 'Are you saying that if I make a public announcement, you will begin to colonise the surface?'

'That is one interpretation.' replied Quax.

'But we couldn't allow you to do that.'

'Thou wouldstn't have any choice, do you?'

'I don't understand. Were the mixed tense, mixed era-speak and mixed address form intentional?'

'Yes. Thou wouldn't have any choice, do you?'

'Would you please, without prejudice to the other matters, return Bodgitt to us? All of this is really not his fault.'

'We will talk about Bodgitt later. Are thy intentions still to advertise the existence and details of The Agreement?'

'I will have to discuss it with the convened Convention in the Conventionium.' replied Polit46, stalling.

'Stop using unnecessary words and wasting time. Yes, or no?'

'I need time to discuss it.'

'There is nothing to discuss. Yes, or no?'

'Well, the whole of Eqinox knows of your existence, so that is no longer a secret.'

'But they do not know of The Agreement? Yes, or no?'

Polit46 shifted from one hoof to the next. And to the next. And to the next. And to the next. And back to the second. His heads looked at each other and his expression sought inspiration from the Convention through the commenter.

'It is not possible to give you an answer immediately.'

'Yes, or no?'

Polit46 thought for a long blink. 'I must discuss with my colleagues to see if there is a way of satisfying those of our nation, who are now out to lynch any and all Gobblings, given the chance, while not breaking the contract. I must have time to do that, at least. Do you understand?'

'I understand.' Quax replied, coldly.

'Then, er, do I have a little time? Please?' Pleaded Polit46, very unpolitician like.

'A little time.' replied Quax, 'and stop the digging at Squelchpool immediately.' she put the callall down impatiently.

Polit46 knew that he had been reversed into a crook, so to speak, and hoped it was a corner that he could back out of again.

He immediately callalled Kernal and ordered him to stop his sappachines digging pending further orders, even though he knew that Quax would smell an instant victory in round one.

With little confidence, but knowing that he was only transmitting to the Conventionium, Polit46 turned to the autofollowing holocam, 'You all heard that. I can see you in a holoquadrant. Has anybody got any good ideas please?'

Silence.

'Maecenas?'

Maecenas shook his front head.

'Grounsell?'

Grounsell shook his front head too. So did everyone else.

'Smelt. You're not usually short of words. Any ideas?'

'No, sorry.' Despite imminent gloom, he thought of Grounsella.

'May I suggest,' said a head from the middle of the Conventionium, that we call their bluff?'

'How?' asked Polit46, dourly.

'Well, you're the politician, can't you think of something, I'm just Nanotech329. Couldn't we threaten war? Or disease? Or something.' he had obviously run out of ideas.

'We could certainly bluff them,' replied Polit46, 'if there were any point to bluffing them and if we had a topic we could bluff them about. Any other ideas?'

'Couldn't you threaten them with annihilation, even if you don't intend to do it?' asked Nanotech329, innocently.

'I should explain,' began Polit46, 'that the Gobblings are, technologically speaking, nearly as advanced as we are. For all we know, they could destroy us as quickly and easily as we could destroy them. We must, in any case, assume that they can. The chances are that they are watching our public service e-commenters, so they'll know exactly what we're up to, especially if ENN and Cate'aeddy get their way. Whatever we do, we must keep Triseps safe. Any other ideas?'

'How many Gobblings are there?' asked Nanotech329.

'We don't know. There are a number of species or tribes, but we don't know how many species or how many individuals in each.'

'How about a Summit meeting?' Suggested Polit23, 'would they send a delegation here to negotiate?'

'Good idea; I'll ask them.' replied Polit46, 'but we need to have our cards prepared before they arrive; they might want to know what we are proposing, too. Any suggestions?'

'We could trade with them; we have plenty of excess food, especially now that we have nanotechnology,' suggested Grounsell.

'Once they have nanotechnology too, they won't want anything else from us anyway. They won't *need* anything else from us, so what will we have left to negotiate with?' asked Polit46.

'Land.' replied Grounsell.

'We're not going to give them our land,' said Polit46, 'if there's nothing else they could want, then we've got nothing to negotiate with.'

'Bodgitt's too minor for long-term negotiation. What have they really got that we need - or want?' asked Polit23.

'Can anyone answer that?' asked Polit46.

'What about the magic?' asked Maecenas and paused for a response.'

Everyone looked at him. He was no longer a child, but was talking about magic?

'Do you mean voodoo mind-malaise magic?' asked Grounsell.

'No. At least, I don't think so. The Gobblings have the power of motorphroyd.' replied Maecenas. 'The nearest thing to magic, really. The art of moving things and transforming materials by brain power alone.' Maecenas paused again for effect and looked around at the audience. 'So you see, the Gobblings already have the equivalent power of our nanotechnology. They don't even need that. So far as I can see, they only need one thing: space. Land, that's what they need. Room for expansion.'

'You're saying that they have nothing we need, but we have land that they need. If we don't agree, then at the very least they will continue eating us as they have done in the past; in the extreme there could be the mother of all wars for surface land? Have I got it right?' asked Polit23.

'Except that we could usefully learn motorphroyd,' added Maecenas.

'We don't need to,' said Nanotech329, 'not now that we have developed nanotechnology as we have.'

'So that's it, then;' concluded Polit46, 'they want land, we want nothing. Does anyone dispute that?'

'Except that we want to publicise The Agreement;' said Maecenas, 'anything else anybody?'

Silence.

'I propose, then, to offer them the chance to come and talk to us,' began Polit46, 'and call their bluff when negotiating for the return of Bodgitt. Is there any land we can safely offer them without setting a precedent for them to take our land?'

There was a long period of silence. Eventually Grounsell spoke, 'What about Eislland? It seems perfect to give them. Nobody lives there; it is so deep that it is at the same level as their underground caverns. The whole country is one huge crater left over from the Great Western Wars. There is plenty of vegetation and natural food if they prefer that.'

'True,' said Polit46, 'and nobody owns it really, except perhaps Sammowa who defeated them in battle.'

Sammowapolit7 stood up. 'Ambassador from I is Sammowa the. Claim Eislland do not we.'

The autotranslator sprung into action and translated the first two sentences. The rest of Eqinox always found Sammowanese very difficult because, although it used Squeithian words, no outsider had ever managed to decipher any logical or grammatical reason for the sequence, even though there most definitely was one.

'agree be can country Eqinox hesitation if my on peace secured that to will without.'

The autotranslator waited for the sentence to end and said, *'If peace can be secured on Eqinox, my country will agree to that without hesitation.'*

'Any Azorrics claims concerning Eislland, ghotiing has in made never only over rights Sammowa territorial the.' *'Sammowa has never made any territorial claims over Eislland, only concerning ghotiing rights in the Azorrics.'*

'Argument *our* that was.' *'That was* our *argument.'* Sammowapolit7 looked round the Conventionium. 'And blessing compliments Eislland friends, government's may my Sammowa use with yes, you' *'Yes, my friends, you may use Eislland with Sammowa government's compliments and blessing.'*

'Thank you.' said Polit46. 'I will not make an offer until they insist. Any further comments before I make the callall? No? Good.'

Polit46 made the callall. Quax was expecting it and answered immediately.

'Yes, or no?' asked Quax before Polit46 even realised he was connected.

'Er, he-hello.' Polit46 stuttered, 'Yes or no what?'

'Are thy intentions still to advertise the existence and details of our contract - of The Agreement?'

'We would like to discuss that and other matters with you. We have some ideas for negotiations. Are you prepared to send a delegation to meet with us - with the leaders of surface Eqinox ?'

'What is there to negotiate about?' asked Quax.

Polit46 looked hard at the callall, forgetting that it was sound only. 'I think we have a great deal to discuss, and a great deal to offer each other. We offer this in peace and ask that you will seriously consider our offer.'

Autotranslator Mk II

'I will have to convene. I cannot speak alone. I will talk to you soon, but not very soon. Tomorrow. I am sure you will come to a deal.' impuned Quax without any inflection - except that of a language spoken by a foreigner who sounded as though she was chewing. She terminated the callall.

The Convention was watching on the commenter. A sigh of relief hovered from everyone to everyone else. To a Trisep they ordered geeantees from the provisions hatches in front of them.

This was the first relief from pressure for several days of Conventioning and the religiots prayed that GoD would intervene on behalf of the Triseps. Unfortunately, like religiots all over the universe, they forgot that there are two sides to every story and if their GoD was truly as they defined, then ultimate fairness and not their prayers would control the outcome of any hot, cold or lukewarm war anyway!.

Polit46 returned to the Conventionium and ordered that the secret private line callall to the Gobblings be extended through to the Conventionium. Then he, too, reached for the geeantee from his provisions hatch.

He felt fully relaxed now, feeling that he had cracked it and asked the hatch for a Dåagøn Häzs ice cream.

The callall extension to the Gobblings was connected and ready in record time.

Smelt and Grounsella disappeared into a private conference room and locked the door. They were noticed only by Smelta and Grounsell, who disappeared into another, and locked their door too. Various other little clumps disappeared into various side rooms either for genuine strategic discussion or for other scheming reasons.

Several Sharens made an appearance and rapidly disappeared again, but nobody saw where they went; at least, nobody admitted seeing where they went. Curiously, a number of the delegates seemed to disappear completely at the same time, but dunno where they went.

Meanwhile, the only meaningful activity was the silent autosuk, which hovered around cleaning cowches and tables as they became empty. But then it did that all day every day anyway, taking energy from the air to operate and making harmless atmospheric water vapour from any dust or rubbish it discovered. Some Triseps complained that the main purpose of an autosuk was to get in the way of whatever they were doing at the time.

* * * * *

Those left in the Conventionium kept one eye on the callall on Polit46's desk at the front. For a long time there was silence.

Interminably later, the olde-fashioned voice only callall berped. Polit46 answered it but had no chance to speak.

'We'll talk.' said Quax abruptly, 'dost thou still wish to negotiate?'

'Of course,' replied Polit46, 'where would you like us to send the moovacars to collect you?'

'If you reconvene, our delegation will arrive as soon as you are all ready. Ensure that the public e-commenters are switched off. Prepare seating for forty-seven.' Quax terminated the callall.

Polit46 shrugged and ordered that the Convention reconvene.

Cate'aeddy watched, helpless and kept one eye on the holoquadrant of the idle sappachines at Squelchpool, half expecting an appearance of Gobblings.

Within a few hundred breaths, the Convention was reconvened and all were ready; a discussion began on how to advise the Gobblings that they were ready to meet.

Imperceivably, a doughnut-shaped ring raised itself in the floor of the Conventionium between the podium and the main seating.

* * * * *

It took several breaths for the reassembled Triseps to realise that a hole had appeared and that Gobblings were appearing through it. When they did, silence swept through in waves as each clump realised that something strange was happening.

On emerging from the hole, each Gobbling raised a hand in a salute of peace and militarily marched directly to a chair without looking round at the assembled Triseps. What most surprised the Triseps, both present and those watching on the e-commenters, was the clothing worn by the Gobblings. Each wore a different colour and the colours played havoc with the eyes of Triseps. However many times the Triseps counted, there were definitely seven Gobblings wearing each of the seven colours of the spectrum. But definitely still only forty seven of the funny little bipeds.

Smelt turned to Smelta and asked her to count the Gobblings and the colours they were wearing. 'There is no doubt you are right;' Smelta replied to his question, 'there are forty seven Gobblings and yet somehow each of the seven primary colours is being worn by seven of them. It must be some sort of mathematical disfusion. Somehow, their seven primary colours are split into the forty-seven primary hues. You'd better ask an arithmate.'

When the last Gobbling left the hole, it began to heal over. Nobody saw the hole closing, but on the next glance there remained only the slightly raised Doughnut-shaped Faerie-ring.

Polit46 had stood from his cowch and was about to address the assembly when he noticed that the hole had healed. He stopped without uttering a syllable and stood staring, open mouthed, at the Faerie-ring.

As Polit46 turned his front head to Quax to read the speech his autodiary had prepared and set into a holofolio, he realised that he had to change his strategy.

'Welcome to Selondre in Squeith and to the Conventionium.' Polit46 began with as much generosity as he could muster towards those he considered an enemy, 'We are delighted to welcome you and trust that we will negotiate in a spirit of friendship and peace.'

Quax was in the centre of the semi-doughnut of Gobblings. She was the only female and needed no introduction. She stood, nodded in agreement and sat down again. But to the Triseps, the males all looked alike - a common problem when first meeting new tribes or races.

As the Triseps watched Quax, something strange happened; she was pure white while the others remained clothed in the seven primary colours and forty-seven primary hues. Somehow a light, yet not a light seemed to emanate from inside her.

Polit46, still confused by this optical deviation, turned half to address the assembly but three-quarters to address Quax, 'For many thousands of years - nay, cycles even - we have shared this planet successfully. Only a few Triseps knew of your existence, and a few more discovered you to their fatal cost.' he paused and looked from Quax to the assembly and back to Quax.

'Obviously,' he continued, 'we have very little that you are likely to want from us although we are naturally prepared to trade with you.'

'Anything else?' asked Quax.

'Yes, we would like you to return Bodgitt to us so that we can treat his wounds.'

'Bodgitt is healthy. We will talk about him later.' replied Quax, 'Do you really have nothing else to say?'

'We have a large number of questions - but they can wait. We have nothing to offer other than friendship.'

'Surface land. We need some. We have no room left below.'

'No room? You could go down to another layer, couldn't you?'

'We go down seven layers already. Layers six and seven are only used for farming; it is too warm to live there. Below that, the increasing temperature inhibits practical life because of the proximity of the magma layer.'

'Have you used *all* the space down there, sideways, I mean?'

'All the safe space, yes.'

'Safe?' Polit46 was no profgeol.

'We have to build our holes carefully and leave supports. We can't build holes under the seas. We can't build at all close to the magmablasts such as Alp-Etnavolc, although we have occupied up to five higher layers in some alps with extinct magmablasts. Alp-Everrest, which your Tensing and Relaxing Exercises help you to climb, has seven higher layers inside.'

Polit46 was speechless and looked round for inspiration. He said the only thing he could think of. 'How do you build a hole?'

Grounsell stood up, 'I am Grounsell, Minister for Ground Works in Eqinox Government.' he waited for kudos penetration. Quax remained unimpressed. 'We have probed the mountains for research and completed ground density tests and underground frequency ranging. Why did we never discover you? Only a few senior advisers such as Maecenas knew that you existed.'

'Our average density remains constant,' responded Quax, 'so you would not see us with density tests. Compaction to a thousand densities provides structural strength to our caverns. When you send probes, we temporarily reconstitute the rock and you never detect us.'

'Are you still moving into new areas?' asked Grounsell.

'I told thee already.' replied Quax.

Grounsell and Polit46 looked at each other with both heads.

'What did you tell us?' asked Grounsell.

'We have used all the safe areas and need more space for growing food now. As I said before, we do not eat nanomanufactured food, so we need more growing space. Because of sunlight, we could grow over forty-seven times the quantity of food in the same area above ground compared with our underground plantations.'

'But we do not have any spare land for you to use,' responded Polit46.

'You have a great deal of land that you do not use.'

'Where?'

'As you will recall, one hundred and two cycles ago, we began to grow food in Ozzilland and to eat the rookanga. However, you were far more advanced technologically than we were then and we accepted The

Agreement for fear of you attacking us. We are no longer afraid of you. Ozzilland would be adequate to provide food for us.'

Polit46's lower jaw dropped in horror. He looked across the Conventionium to the Ozzilland ambassador, Ozzipolit7, whose mouth was similarly agape.

The Triseps quickly regained their composure and Ozzipolit7 went to the front and sat on an empty cowch. 'Ozzilland is already occupied completely, except for the desert areas, and you could not grow food there.'

'No it is not fully occupied; it is nearly empty.' said Quax. 'In any case, the Triseps there have poor genetics. Remember that they are all descended from convicts.'

'From convicts? From convicts! I must protest!' replied Ozzipolit7 from the floor of the Convention, 'There are Triseps everywhere, good Triseps; there are cities there. Ozzilland is not just desert and coral reef.'

'In the Nipoff Archipelago, in Ånjap, there are one thousand, three hundred and fifty-eight Triseps to the quad, on average. It is quite amazing to us that over thirteen hundred Triseps can pack into a quad of forty-seven hites by forty-seven lengths.' Quax paused and looked around the Conventionium. 'In Ozzilland there is one Trisep to seventeen quads. It is empty. You do not grow food there. You do not need it.'

'Obviously we would like to help you, but we cannot give you land that is occupied.' said Ozzipolit7.

'Sorry we can't help,' added Polit46.

'It is not occupied enough.'

'I am sorry to disappoint you,' replied Polit46, 'but it is not possible to give you an occupied country like Ozzilland.'

'It is not occupied. Ozzilland is the most appropriate country for our needs. You do not use it. We need it ... mate.'

'Well, you're to the point, Shealar, but we need it too.' said Ozzipolit7.

Quax looked round and back to Ozzipolit7. 'Wast thou talking at or to me?'

'Yes.'

'I have a name. It is Quax. Use it!' she retorted in a voice beyond her usual tone, sharp and precise almost to the point of viciousness.

'I am truly sorry. I did not intend to offend you. I will use your name in future.'

Quax said nothing in reply, but continued to stare forward.

Polit46 stood, opened his mouth to speak but Quax got there first. 'We need the land only. We have no need for any of the gadgets you offer. All Gobblings like natural-grown food. We need Ozzilland. It is sensible. We work. We have a need to work, therefore we need to eat.'

'Like Thermos.' muttered Grounsell to himself without moving his lips.

'Yes,' said Quax, 'like Thermos, your Profsiens said, eat is work and work is eat.'

Grounsell looked up surprised that Quax had heard him. 'Yes, Didn't he also prove that the more pressure you put on your mother-in-lorr, the more hot air she produces?'

Quax, being female and less politically erroneous, simply turned her eyes black and glared at him. 'No, that was Thermos's Lorr of Boiling Wives. I cannot dispute the lorrs of Thermos-Dynamism, but I do not approve of them.'

She almost smiled. Grounsell felt encouraged and wondered if there was a less serious side to this apparently callous female. A side that could, perhaps, be tapped.

'But mostly, we need land to grow food.' she continued, returning to her more usual cool self - and to the subject. 'We have decided that Ozzilland is necessary. Do you have a better suggestion?'

'Eislland.' replied Polit46. 'Eislland is not used by us - and the Triseps of Sammowa who own it are happy to part with it for your use.'

'Useless!' ejaculated Quax, 'It is a barren wasteland still contaminated by the atom-splitting molotov dropped on it by Sammowa.'

Maecenas stood and spoke. 'You may be fully assured that Eislland has been fully cleaned. One of the first tasks of nanomachines and soldiernanos, when they were invented, was to clean up areas of contamination on the planet. Special search and kill soldiernanos were contrived to remove nuclear contamination. I repeat, you may be fully assured that there is no contamination on Eislland; even the soldiernanos self-destruct on completion of their duty.'

'Even if you claim to have cleaned it with soldiernanos, how can we be sure that our food will be uncontaminated with the remains of the soldiernanos themselves.'

'You have our assurance. You are welcome to do your own tests.'

'If Eislland is so clean, why have you not re-colonised the country yourselves?'

'There is no contamination in Eislland,' replied Maecenas.

'There is no contamination in Ozzilland. Ozzilland is empty. You can move your Triseps from Ozzilland to Eislland.'

'No.' said Polit46.

'Is it because it is contaminated and thou art not telling us?'

'No, it is not contaminated, but we cannot move our Triseps from Ozzilland to Eislland.'

'You could if you wanted to!' insisted Quax.

'But we don't want to. We cannot accept that suggestion, but we will offer Eislland freely.'

'You will want to very soon.' responded Quax, added nothing and remained motionless.

The entire Convention began to chatter. A rising tone of concern flared and spread around the Conventionium.

Polit46 stood and raised his third hand to call for silence. His demeanour altered from serious to disturbed and concerned.

'We would like to continue to discuss and negotiate on a friendly basis. You appear to be offering an ultimatum. Can you confirm that we have understood correctly. Are you threatening us?' asked Polit46.

'We do not need to threaten;' replied Quax, 'you overcame us in the planet-wide slaving war which forced us underground, but that was many thousands of cycles ago and we have the only records of that war. We have now deciphered the ancient texts; both Triseps and Gobblings were returned to a state of primitive stone toolage. It was the Gobblings who were defeated absolutely.'

'Does that mean that . . .' began Polit46.

'But!' interrupted Quax forcefully, '... but I would not like to guarantee that you would defeat us in any future conflict. Our capabilities and technology are as advanced as yours and we have a number of other advantages of which you have neither current knowledge nor are likely to be appraised imminently thereof.'

All the delegates in the Conventionium were silent. Some were still trying to translate her language into everyday Squeithian. An atmosphere of fear prevailed. At all costs, a war must be avoided. Polit46 looked down to the floor and back to Quax. 'We would like you to be more precise and define the level of your comment.' He waited for Quax to respond but she did not reply.

'In short,' he insisted eventually, 'is your statement a suggestion, a possibility, a probability, a threat or a final ultimatum?'

'I do not issue ultimata. I do not need to threaten. Neither should you read more into my statement than precisely what I said, except that you know what we want and that you know our capabilities. I have stated the facts only.'

'We are only asking for a more precise interpretation.' retorted Maecenas.

'The precision and quality of your interpretation is wholly dependent upon your intelligence and your capability to determine the meaning of the words of your own language.'

She awaited a response in vain. 'We know our interests and you know yours. You now know our interests and we know yours. I have defined our limited needs in terms of your capability to provide. You have answered my statements of need without thought or debate either of the facts or the consequences of positive or negative responses.'

Polit46 and Maecenas looked at each other with both heads. It would take them a while to comprehend and fully appraise the situation.

'I can readily understand thy confusion.' Quax added. 'I am satisfied that I have laid out the Gobblings' position quite adequately. Your position is obvious. The decision thou must make is obvious. We will leave you all until you have made the decision. We will return at this time in two days and negotiation will recommence.'

Quax stood, lowered her upper body towards Polit46 and Maecenas in a gesture of honour and led the Gobblings to the hole in front of the platform. Nobody had noticed the hole reappear, but there it was, an indisputable and very solid hole.

Maecenas involuntarily returned the gesture and even offered a wave of friendship, which Polit46 copied.

The assembly began to break into anarchic local discussions. Polit46 considered retreat to be the safest form of valour at this time, so announced a long enough recess for the assembly to eat and discuss privately the debate they had just witnessed.

Grounsell, Grounsella, Smelt, Smelta, Polit46 and Maecenas left the Conventionium together for a private debating chamber.

'Should we invite Ozzipolit7 to join us?' Suggested Smelta.

'Not yet,' replied Maecenas, 'he went off with Sammowapolit7, so they may be working out a solution of their own. We will invite them in when we solve the dilemma or if we become hopelessly stuck in a quag. Ozzipolit7 is hopelessly entrenched in his position at the moment and probably feels that he has no room for manoeuvre.'

'What about Kernal?' Suggested Polit46, helpfully.

'As Precedent, you never cease to amaze me.' said Maecenas, shaking his front head.

Polit46 looked puzzled but said nothing. He knew there was no hope of outwitting Maecenas.

'Perhaps. Later, perhaps. Kernal can wait. For the moment, we have a quorum. Mycroft would be a more suitable choice, don't you think?' Suggested Maecenas.

'Mycroft! M? Do you think M could help?' Responded Polit46 clutching at whatever drink-sucking tube he could get hold of. 'But isn't he best known for helping his brother solve strange crimes?'

'That's what he is *publicly* famous for, yes.'

'Do you *really* think he can help us?'

'I do. M has the greatest brain on the planet; certainly far greater than mine.' said Maecenas, 'Mycroft would find a solution more quickly than any of us. Sad that he spends his entire life recycling geeantees at the Necropol Club and rarely emerges. I did suggest that he should join the Convention, but he only laughed and said that he had greater matters on which to expend his time.'

'This Mycroft, or M as you call him, is he the other holder of the secret of The Agreement?' asked Smelt.

'Yes. He's the only Trisep who has read *all* the history and knows The Agreement intimately.' replied Maecenas. 'If anybody can help us interpret Quax's comments in the light of The Agreement and pre-history, *he* can.'

Smelt turned and stared at Maecenas. 'Pre-history?' he asked.

'Mycroft, in his capacity of M, has almost certainly had direct contact with various species of Gobblings and can advise on why they went underground originally and what problems they would face by remaining on the surface permanently.'

'Various species?' asked Smelt, 'How many different species are there?'

'Mycroft can answer that more accurately than I, but I think there are - or were - at least one sub-species per country, but only about seven main species which corresponded to the original seven tribes of Yishrel mentioned in The Folius folio of Exercises.'

'There are too many revelations here for me,' said Smelta, 'I thought the seven tribes referred to Triseps.'

'Yes and no. It could refer to Triseps or Gobblings or both. Most likely both; or, of course, a combination, perhaps.'

'You don't know, do you?' Prompted Polit46.

'I think M can answer the questions better than I.' replied Maecenas in a conveniently avoiding sort of way.

* * * * *

Maecenas and Polit46 had already left, leaving Smelt engrossed in deep conversation with Grounsella. They were in such deep and animated conversation that it took the full use of both heads and all three arms.

Smelta and Grounsell had slipped out, arm in arm, without being spotted and made for hired sleeping quarters.

And then they were two; two alone, lost to the planet and whispering privately - but no longer about Gobblings.

We've been talking all day long; time for some sleep, I think.' said Smelt. 'Whatever has happened to Smelta? Where has she gone?' Of course, he didn't really care, so long as he could be with Grounsella for now.

'More to the point, where's Grounsell?' Responded Grounsella. 'They both seem to have disappeared.'

'I didn't see them go; I had my back eyes closed.'

'So did I; I was concentrating. Are you thinking what I am thinking?'

'I am beginning to suspect that I may be.'

'Shall we emulate them?' asked Grounsella.

'Do you mean,' began Smelt with an excited smirk, 'that you would like us to practise our replication techniques?'

'Oh, definitely. Let's hire some sleeping quarters together.' they were already at the moovacar.

She put her finger near the provisions hatch and spoke without taking her eyes from his. 'Two Caleptic hi-balls please. Make it triples.'

'I feel really sorry for those Gobblings. Replication can't be much fun for them with only one head and two arms.'

Smelt and Grounsell each switched out their personal callallcodes. They were uninterruptable by the outside world and they intended to enjoy every delicious moment of it.

* * * * *

'WAKE UP! WAKE UP! SMELT! ARE YOU IN THERE?' Someone was banging on the door from the outside and there was a great deal of shouting.

'What in the name of Cronus and Rhea is going on?' asked Smelt superfluously to the equally baffled Grounsella. Their arms were plaited and their bodies intertwingled in a peacefully pleasant post-coital sleep.

Smelt rubbed his eyes and combed his fingers through his grey hair, stumbling toward the door in his sleepful state.

Carehedd burst in as though he had been trying to demolish the door and turtled across the room to the far wall.

Smelt threw a stern glance at him and recognised him immediately from his uniform, 'What's going on, Carehedd?' he demanded.

'I've been sent to find you.' breathed Carehedd heavily from his upside-down position; his second head had slithered gracefully under the double sleeping cowch when he had somersaulted through the door to land on the floor.

Smelt helped him out and up and he shook himself straight.

'Well, you've certainly done that - and with a vengeance. But what is so important that it can't wait until the morning?'

Carehedd was still trying to compose himself when he spotted Grounsella with his back head. She had been trying to blend into the wall and disappear. Both heads turned from Smelt to Grounsella and to the sleeping cowch and back again. He knew who they both were. They could not hide their secret, even though their own respective partners had also been practising replication in their own secret place.

Shocked by the unprecedented revelation, Carehedd stumbled over his own words to fall unerringly into confusion, 'I er, I mean er they er, well, you see it's like this ...' he began, 'They're all back there.'

'Most informative,' muttered Smelt, becoming rather more in tune with his surroundings, 'who are all back where?'

Carehedd took a few more deep breaths of recovery. 'The Convention. It has reconvened and you are wanted.'

'Me? Reconvened? Why? It's the middle of the night! Don't be ridiculous! What's going on?'

'They've lost Ozzilland.' said Carehedd, still panting.

'Ouch!' Smelt had quite literally kicked himself to see if he was dreaming. He wasn't. 'Lost it? What do you mean, lost it? Ozzilland is a continent. You can't lose a continent. Now, if you said that you'd lost those tiny Forklland Aisles, tiny land corridors in the seas of the Azorrics, once saved by St. Thatch from a band of marauding Triseps who were arjibargying about who should own them, well, I would understand, but you can't, well, you just can't lose Ozzilland, I mean it's big, it's very big, I mean ... '

'You don't mean Ozzipolit7, do you by any chance?' Suggested Grounsella helpfully.

'Eh? Oh, er No.' said Carehedd clearly, but still recovering his composure, 'I mean Ozzilland itself. It's not there. You'd better see for yourself.' he turned on the e-commenter.

Cate'aeddy was preparing to speak from the front of the Conventionium. Behind her was anarchic pandemonium. Clumps of Triseps were rushing about, holding little conversations and rushing on to somewhere else. Virtually all were simultaneously talking on their personal callalls.

'What's going on?' asked Smelt, turning his heads to Grounsella and Carehedd respectively, who shrugged in turn.

Cate'aeddy turned to the holocam. 'Since yesterday's meeting between the Convention and the Gobblings which was held ex-cam, there has been a dramatic turn of events. We have lost Ozzilland. All contact has been lost. It is not possible to get through with callalls or the public e-commenter network. Even hams playing with olde-fashioned wire-less communicators have not been able to reach any of their friends in Ozzilland. One ham told me that she was a good way through a discussion about the second sun's effect on her period cycles. It was her turn to speak and when she stopped there was no response from her Ozzilland contact.'

Cate'aeddy silenced herself and looked round the Conventionium to see if anything was happening. She was dying to say things like, *A whole population of Triseps have gone, died, vanished, been extinguished, are distraced into a netherlight hole ...* etc., but knew that such words were neither permitted by the Eqinox Government during such a crisis, nor were expedient for fear of massive riots and callall-ins to ENN.

Grounsella tried to put in a callall to Grounsell, but his personal callallcode was switched out. She tried Smelta, but she was also unavailable. She turned to Smelt. 'I can't get Grounsell or Smelta. Any guesses where they are?'

'Yes,' replied Carehedd, 'some of my subordinates have been sent to fetch them. They are on their way to the Conventionium. We located your moovacars, but we never expected ... ' he looked at them both with embarrassment, trying to shut himself up and hide his blunder.

'I think we should go to the hall,' smiled Smelt diplomatically. 'Thank you for waking us.'

Carehedd smiled, nodded and set off for the Multicare, parked outside.

'You'd better take your pill.' said Grounsella on the way to the moovacar. 'Funny, we must have been practising replication at the very moment that Ozzilland is supposed to have disappeared. Talk about the earth moving!'

'Ah, yes, my male morning-after pill,' said Smelt, not really concentrating, 'I'll remember to take it later.'

'Just you make sure you do!' retorted Grounsella with a dryly wry half-smile and with an innermost secret desire for him to forget.

Deep inside what might have been his Sole, Smelt felt a change occurring. Indefinable, powerful, spiritual. He checked his reflection in a passing mirror, but external views don't always reflect the hidden depths. 'I wonder if there are some after-effects of the Contaigen - I must get the automed to do a Phroydtest.' he muttered into his imaginary beard.

'What did you say?' asked Grounsella.

'Oh, er, the pill, must remember to take it. I'll do my best.'

'Oh, yes.' she replied with a less than trusting glance, 'just make sure you do!' She had wrestled with male contraception promises before.

Chapter 6   Preparations

The Conventionium seemed no less disorganised as they watched the proceedings from the moovacar's e-commenter while they flew.

Smelt's and Grounsell's moovacars matched speed and flew side by side the short distance to the Conventionium, so that husbands could be swapped back again through the linkdoor for the sake of propriety.

As they arrived, Cate'aeddy had just been given some more news, which she instantly reported. 'Kernal has been asked by Polit46 to prepare a Defenss task force to visit Ozzilland and see what is really happening. If you can see us in Ozzilland, we know that you seem to have been cut off from the rest of Eqinox by some sort of freak electrical storm that is interfering with all e-commenter channels and all callalls.' she stopped and had a private chat with Polit46. He could only be overheard saying, '... just continue to make it as vague as possible.'

'It appears that we are also unable to get any pictures of Ozzilland from an autofollowing holocam which was sent there on its own. Just before it was due to arrive, its transmissions stopped, so we don't have pictures of anything but ocean. Right now, we don't even know where it is, and its bleatings have ceased.' she paused but vainly awaited a response from Polit46.

'Within the past days there has been a curious series of events, unmatched in living history and it is impossible to think that these could not - in some way - be related.

First there was the discovery of the Orijin, the egg, the ex ovo omnia from which all life on Planet Five has apparently evolved, Dirwanistically.

Second was the appearance of the Gobblings which were genuine, very genuine - even though 8.3% of us thought it was a very clever documentary style fiction play. This is no play. This is not fiction. Eqinox faces its greatest ever crisis.' She changed feet in the rarest of displays of discomfort.

'Today there are two matters that concern us. During the meeting with the Gobblings, there was a slight hint of a suggestion that they would, perhaps, possibly want to colonise Ozzilland, which is about as vague as the situation actually gets." She paused for effect.

"Now, thirdly," she continued, "Ozzilland itself has suddenly disappeared. All communication has been cut for the first time in the history of Eqinox.' Cate'aeddy paused for the depth of the crisis to sink in.

'Eqinox Government will issue recommendations on how to remain safe in the unlikely event of an invasion from Gobblings.' Cate'aeddy looked away from the holocam as she spoke, knowing the truth to be more sinister, 'The news from here at the Conventionium is that ... '

Cate'aeddy was interrupted by the berp of the secret private line callall between Polit46 and Quax. She looked round at it, but Polit46 immediately turned it to shush. The holocam still watched him, his expressions and his involuntary gestures. He was not very lip-readable, and the public elsewhere than in the Conventionium could not know who was his interlocutor.

Polit46 was looking surprised by the callall conversation. He looked round at the Convention and gestured at Cate'aeddy as though presenting her to a theatre audience, even though this callall was sound only.

Cate'aeddy made only passing comments about his gestures, but otherwise watched. She explained that this was a sound-only callall that had been set up between the leader of what she was now calling the 'Underplanet' and the Eqinox Precedent. She did not admit that the secret line had been in existence for over a hundred cycles, a fact still confidential to Convention delegates.

Polit46 smiled as he concluded the callall from Quax. He called the assembly to order and accepted the necessity of ENN's holocam intrusion.

Polit46 sat looking as educated and capable as a politician can - especially one who is incapable of all else. He was joined on his right and left by Ozzipolit7 and Maecenas, the latter deep in some study of his own, peering deeply at some olde-fashioned pulpleaves with writing on.

'Members of my Eqinox Government, members of this Convention, Triseps of Eqinox. I also address the leaders of the Gobblings of the Underplanet who are watching on their own e-commenters.'

The assembly shuffled and many worried glances hovered.

'I address you today as we have an unprecedented situation. Yesterday, as you have heard from Cate'aeddy, we met with a delegation from the Gobbling community who live in a world of their own beneath our surface. During the night, we were cut off from contact with Ozzilland. All contact, that is, including e-commenters and callalls. We have even sent in autofollowing holocams and lost the signals from them. As well.' he emphasised.

'You should know also that during our discussions,' he continued, 'Quax, Leader of the Gobblings expressed an interest in colonising Ozzilland for growing food. I spoke to Quax only a few breaths ago and am assured on an oath of GoD that Gobblings are honourable and have not, I repeat not, invaded Ozzilland. Neither, they have assured me, are they in any way responsible for the total loss of communication. They have assured me that they intend to negotiate with us for a small piece of our unused surface land, such as parts of Ozzilland or, perhaps, Eislland. At the end of my speech, the Gobblings will issue their own formal statement that will be presented in a special infobox holoquadrant of your e-commenters.

'Quax, Leader of the Gobblings told me that they are also unable to communicate with their antipodal tribes on the Underplanet and are even now sending messengers to discover the difficulty. Quax asked for our help at this difficult time for them. Prior to the opportunity for official debate, I can only state my official position that we will provide Trisepitarian help in the usual way of the Yellow Cross Organisation of Helvetica.'

A new holoquadrant opened up and a message appeared written in a giant infobox.

'Ah,' said Polit46, 'here is the Gobblings' message.' he was handed a piece of pulpleaf by an aide.

The holoquadrant showed a still picture of Quax below a drawing of a quadric gammagram, a traditional lucky charm symbol with a set of four rotated gamma runes from an antique language; below it, the infobox showed a message which he read aloud:

To all Triseps, GREETINGS!

0	I am Quax, Leader of all the Gobblings.
1	We greet you. Total peace we offer to surface Triseps.
2	For hundreds of generations, we lived below you and separate in the Underplanet.
3	Only the most senior Gobblings knew of your existence; and those living in the highest-level caverns used for rare but necessary surface visits.
4	We sincerely hope that we can meet, work and live together in mutual acceptance and understanding, each of the other.
5	An unfortunately timed disaster or strange event has befallen both species in the antipodal Ozzilland, where we hoped that you would permit us to grow crops on 108241 quads.
6	Communication with our tribes in Ozzilland is as impossible as your own with yours; thus we must pool technical and defensive resources and solve the mystery together.
7	Whatever transpires, I propose conjoining of our races so that, henceforth, this peace shall be unbroken within my lifetime's power, thus peace in our time is forecast.

We meet in harmony at venue and juncture agreed.

Greetings in peace from all Gobblings to all Triseps.

'Quite clearly, we can hold this message in our hands and declare that this proves the Gobblings' desire for peaceful unity during our lives. They sent me the message by Equi-mail a few breaths ago written on a piece of olde-fashioned pulpleaf.'

Polit46 raised his arm in the air and rotated a piece of pulpleaf for everyone to see, 'I hold this pulpleaf up to you and say with all certainty, this means nothing less than,' he paused, looked around to ensure everyone was watching and firmly said, *'Peace in our time!'*

Polit46 stood with his heads erect and flourished his right hand holding the pulpleaf and the assembly erupted in a thunderous round of applause and roar of enthusiasm for the Trisep who was firmly their fellow of the moment, Precedent Polit46.

Grounsell was sitting next to Maecenas, 'Brilliant! Wonderful! A few minutes ago we thought that we were virtually at war. Now there will be permanent peace.' laughed Grounsell, 'Whatever is happening in Ozzilland, there will be peace - peace in our time. Wow!'

Maecenas looked more serious, 'You might think that, but I couldn't possibly comment.' He proffered a wry smile, a smile which was received with misunderstood equanimity.

Smelt looked straight at Maecenas. 'Are you trying to tell us something we don't already know, or at least suspect?' he asked.

'Beware the Gobblings bearing gifts.' replied Maecenas.

'I never did understand that joke.' said Grounsell and laughed.

Smelt and Maecenas turned to peer at Grounsell, shook both front and back heads in sad weariness, raised their eyes GodwarD and returned their amazed gazes, each to the other. 'I'm afraid it's no joke.' said Maecenas and added casually, 'In any case, even if it were, it wouldn't be a joke, it would be a quotation.'

They all looked down at their hooves for a few breaths, thinking deeply.

Smelta spoke to the air; to anyone who happened to be listening. 'There was a reference to the quadric gammagram in the Oxford Dictionary with Pictures - the reference folio found in the Orijin. It seems that the symbol was used by a murderous band of marauding ruffians called the Third Reich. Strange how we use the same symbol on Eqinox as a lucky charm. But there's something more to all this.' she returned to her deep thought and left the others to their conversations in their own little clumps.

Suddenly, Smelta jumped up from her cowch, yelling 'I-smeller! I-smeller!' and sat down again. She was had obviously ignored Maecenas' pronouncements. Clearly, she was in a world of her own and wholly oblivious to all those who turned to look at her sudden outburst. It was only at times of great discovery that this ancient-language pronouncement was used, and this time it was nothing to do with dirty water in baths.

'What has she found?' asked Polit46, 'What on Eqinox could she have discovered here?'

'Forty-seven times seven; of course, of course! Times forty-seven times seven,' muttered Smelta, almost to herself.

'Eh?' asked Smelt.

'Primary magic number multiplied by the secondary magic number and squared.' she said, becoming more excited. Her gestures were now beginning to attract quite an audience. 'And forty-seven times four as a base.'

The whole assembly was looking at her now; those who were unaware of her decryption capabilities wondered about her sanity.

Smelt caught her attention. 'Stop, stop! Just what are you talking about?'

'Well, it's obvious. The message was 188 words long, if you count the numbers. That's 47 times 4. And the size of the land area they are requesting is 47 squared times 7 squared; and of course, each quad is 47 lengths long by 47 hites wide. Of course, the two squares together make four.'

Silence hovered while each Trisep assimilated the facts and tried to make sense not so much of it, for that was clear, but of the relevance of it. Smelta held her front head in her three hands to deepen her concentration on the problem.

The peace was broken by Maecenas, 'What exactly,' he began slowly, 'are you saying?'

'Saying?' Smelta looked up slowly. 'Saying? Well, I'm not saying anything really, just commenting. Even the delegation led by Quax had forty-seven Gobblings. I don't know what it means, I've only deciphered part of the code. That's all. I am still puzzled by the colours. Did you notice how, when you looked directly at Quax, she wore white, but when you looked at the others and only saw her through the corner of the eyes, her clothes changed back to the seventh hue of mid verdant?'

As suddenly as the interest flared up, so interest in Smelta was lost and the assembly returned to a confusion of celebration and discussion of theories over the apparent loss of Ozzilland. Only a few Triseps wandered towards her to discuss the problem further, but they were soon side-tracked by others who had greater matters to discuss.

Maecenas alone had not lost interest and asked for a full explanation and list of her observations. He listened carefully to all that Smelta had to say and made a callall to Mycroft. M had still not honoured the Convention with his presence.

'Oh, by the way,' commented Smelta, 'did you realise that forty-two is actually forty-seven in base eleven and a quarter, and we all know the importance of that number in astrophysical terms, don't we?'

* * * * *

The Secret-Session began. Maecenas had persuaded Polit46 to convene a confidential Summit to include Ozzipolit7, Smelt, Smelta, Grounsell, Kernal and Mycroft. M had refused to leave his Necropol Club because their naturally grown, hand-brewed drinks and hand-prepared food could not be matched anywhere else on Eqinox. He claimed that outside the Club, he lost his advanced powers of deduction. M's powers were so respected, that he was permitted his little eccentric foibles.

Ever since the Necropol was opened as *the* club for necrotic (dead or retired) politicians, females were not allowed inside, so the small Summit clump of senior Triseps which included Smelta met in the foyer.

'So why are we here?' asked M, lighting up a pipe and blowing smoke of what smelled distinctly like burning doggy droppings.

'What on Eqinox are you inhaling? It smells like, well, it smells like burning dung.'

'Smouldering netherwear. Used once then smoked. To be recommended.' said M.

Maecenas raised his eyebrows in mock amazement. He acted as a natural chairman and suggested that Smelta begin by explaining her discoveries.

'Everything connected with Gobblings appears also to be connected with mythical magic numbers. The length of the original hole and the diameter of the hemisphere of Qontûm were exact multiples of 47, combined with root two and peeka, the circle squaring multiplier. Now we find that the area specified by them in Ozzilland is also an exact multiple of the primary and secondary magic numbers, forty-seven and seven.'

'So is Ozzilland itself.' added M.

'Eh?' asked Maecenas.

'The entire area of Ozzilland is an exact multiple of 47 too.'

'229 345 007 quads' said Ozzipolit7.'

'That's right,' replied M.

Smelta did all the mental calculations. 'But what does it all mean? Why are they all magic numbers?'

'That's for you to discover.' said M, re-lighting his netherwear. 'I never conjecture with only thin air as evidence. I cannot calculate a solution until enough facts are available to eliminate all but one possibility. There is always a solution to a problem and as the details become available you can, by a process of examination of the possibilities, determine which have thus become impossible. Finally, when the impossible has been eliminated, whatever remains, however improbable, must be the solution.'

'Are you saying that we might still find Ozzilland? Even though it has disappeared?' asked Maecenas.

'That's not proven.' replied M.

'But all the evidence is that it is not there any more.' retorted Maecenas.

'As I had to teach my brother, Sherlock in his youth when looking for criminals, absence of evidence is not evidence of absence.'

The clump thought about it and each repeated it in his mind until it gelled.

'Absence of evidence is not evidence of absence.' repeated Maecenas, 'So there's hope for us yet, but there is nothing you can do?'

M nodded.

'So you can't help us?' asked Polit46 to M, 'There's nothing you can do.'

'It is very difficult to answer an antithetical pair of linked question clauses with yes or no.' replied M.

'So you *can* help us?' checked Polit46.

'I don't recall saying that, either. I can only interpret the data available. At present there are nine possible solutions to the Ozzilland problem. These include three highly likely scenarios, four possible but less likely scenarios, one unlikely scenario and one exceedingly unlikely scenario. We can, in any case, eliminate the impossible, but we must never eliminate the apparently ridiculous. In addition there is one set of multiple option scenarios that I have already dismissed.' he sat back and puffed.

Puzzled looks reflected from one to another.

Maecenas broke the silence. 'What is impossible?'

M looked up from his reverie, surprised at the question. 'Well, obviously the physical disappearance of the country, for which there could be three main reasons. You already have the evidence before you. First, an external disaster such as a meteor turning Ozzilland into a giant crater; if that had been the case, we would have felt the shock waves here and the autofollowing holocam would have continued its path satisfactorily until it saw evidence.

'Second, a collapse of the Gobblings' caverns beneath, causing the continent to collapse into the sea; again, the holocam would have shown some evidence of water movement before terminating its transmission.

'Third, a gigantic explosion, for example with an atom-splitting molotov; would again have other evidence. Obviously, therefore, Ozzilland is physically still there, subject to Qontûm improbability factors, but is being subjected either to internal or external kappa-wave blockaging, neutronic destruction of electro-bleating equipments or a science-fiction like mind blocker that renders all transmissions invisible to us; that last, of course, is theoretically possible but least likely and in all practical events except one, impossible. Do you now understand why there are only nine possible scenarios?'

They all nodded even though, in fact, not one of them understood at all; but they all double-nodded their confirmation nevertheless. Politicians are particularly noted for not wanting to appear in any way unintelligent - even though they have as good as admitted lower intelligence by legislating that their automed Phroydtest results should remain state secrets. Fascinating that not one of them has joined the Mental Exercises and Neural Stimulation Association, M.E.N.S.A.

'Good,' continued M, 'then you will also understand that the problem occurred too suddenly for it to have been out of control nanotechnology exterminating either lifetypes or all transmission equipments; those scenarios would have proved a less sudden process.' He took a puff on his netherwear.

'By the way, Kernal, will your hoverfloat autobridge stretch from Antipole - well, Scotaisle, at least - to Ozzilland?'

Kernal shrugged.

'Yes, it will, of course,' continued M, 'at least, it can be made to, with a few minor modifications. Remember to make sure that each Sqoddie is always in sight and touch by short cable with the one in front and the one behind. And while they are moving, remember the effect of mirages in the desert. Also, will you confirm that they will float when all power is lost or hover is switched off?'

'Of course they will.' replied Kernal, 'it is my job to make sure of that.'

Mycroft rose and began to sidle away, his front head facing the wall, his back eyes closed as if in sleep; he stopped, turned his front head back, looked at each in turn then said to all, 'I have one more vitally important thing to say to you, but I cannot say it until after your next meeting with the Gobblings. Meanwhile, under no circumstances must you make irrevocable decisions before you speak with me again lest you - and we all - lose the battle absolutely.' he looked more severely at Smelta, 'And Smelta ...'

'Yes?' she quivered, expecting a reprimand.

'Good work on base 11.25. Brilliant. Keep it up, we may need a few more answers in the next few days if this incident goes as I anticipate.'

'How did you know about that?' asked Smelta, expecting a response. But as she watched him, she had to be satisfied with a smile and a wink.

Kernal looked at M. 'Lose the battle? Eh? What battle? Eh?'

M looked sternly at Kernal and shook both his heads for different reasons. 'Tell him, Smelta and Maecenas.' He instructed with raised eyebrows as he sidled away into the main club doors, with a sigh and a waddle.

Ozzipolit7 followed M's departure with both heads, shook his front head in amazement and said in his strange accent, 'That's a three ecks Joey.'

'Eh?' asked Maecenas.

The autotranslator in the corner woke up, responded to the *'Eh?'* and began to translate the Ozzillandese into a sensible language but was interrupted before it started.

'Well, he's one eck short of a four-ecks.'

'Oh, do you mean that he's lost his elgins?' Maecenas suggested.

'Definitely out of his bassinette.' said Polit46.

'What he said did not make sense, Defenss-wise,' suggested Kernal, 'He's definitely one dalli short of a lama, don't you think? By the way, what is a four-ecks? Is it some sort of quadric gamete - an Ovum containing four yokels?'

'Oh, it's an olde-fashioned alcoholic water drink made with Ozzi'opps which grow exclusively in Ozzilland.' explained Ozzipolit7, with a laugh, 'Would have thought you would have known, as an ex-Sqoddie. You see, before the invention of nanomachines, we ... '

'Yes, yes, yes!' Responded Maecenas, 'but you're wrong, very wrong. Not only is M completely compos mentis, but his intellect is way ahead of mine and all of yours - probably including Smelta. That is why Mycroft is who he is. That is why he is M, Head of Eqinox Government's and Squeithian Government's Intelligence Gathering and Analysis.'

Kernal raised his eyes GodwardS and dropped his gaze to the floor for inspiration.

'I concur with that.' added Smelta, of Maecenas' statement, 'Did you know that Mycroft has held the daily record for completing the cryptic interlocking word puzzle in The Thundering Temporra without a break since he was only half a cycle old?'

'Oh Miroray, oh Temporra; oh Mirror, oh Times; what a reflection of the era in which we live.' replied Maecenas, concluding the private joke.

Smelta laughed. The politicians' expressions reflected their confusion and lack of understanding but they nevertheless laughed nervously out of polite respect. They didn't want to admit that it was they who were less than wholly perfect. Neither would they admit to having too viscous a brain to understand the joke.

'Why was Mycroft talking about hoverfloat autobridges?' asked Kernal.

'Obviously he feels that you have no option but to sidle all the way from Antipole to Ozzilland.' replied Maecenas.

'What, on hoof?'

'Yes.'

'Without a vehicle?'

'Yes.'

'That's just ridiculous.' replied Kernal.

'Have you any better ideas?'

'Yes, we'll send a task force.'

'What about the Defenss force that was already in Ozzilland?' Suggested Maecenas. 'What do you think will happen to any new task force?'

'We could go through the New Seas and start from New Seaslland.'

'Only if you misorient, occidentally,' joked Maecenas, expecting a laugh but only getting blank looks from Kernal, 'It's too far out of the way Sunriseward[7]. In any case, they are not Defenss minded, all they ever do there is make buttalact. Can you just imagine just sitting there all day long shaking lact, the post-natal discharge from mamaglans of their critters. I mean, there is a limit to what you can do with an edible thixotropic gel only useful for spreading on dorolls.' Maecenas wondered why Kernal was ever appointed to his rank in the first place. 'No, you'll have to sidle.'

Kernal obviously didn't like the idea of a long sidle. 'Well, we could send Multicare with a forward probe.'

'That requires the use of automatic equipment and we already know what happens to that, from ENN's autofollowing holocam' responded Maecenas, 'so no, it is not sensible.'

'It will take at least three days to prepare a Defenss task force and move them to Antipole.'

'Then do it in one day.' ordered Polit46.

'I'll do it in two and a half.' Responded Kernal.

'One and a half.' Retorted Polit46.

'Two.'

'Make sure you do.'

'What?' asked Kernal, not quite hearing.

'I said, do it in *two*.' said Polit46, having forgotten his previous words but remembering the rhyme of them.

Kernal looked at Polit46 with both heads and raised all six eyebrows. 'Yes, Sir.   Agreed.   We will do that.' he bowed his head. 'I should leave now and make arrangements.'

'Only use your callall on over-cipher.' said Maecenas.

Kernal looked back, nodded, dropped his eyes to the floor in thought and jutted his chin in parting gesture.

Grounsell and Smelta shared a few moments of reflected mutual care in a period of non-conversational relaxation.

---

[7]   *There are four directions on Eqinox, Poleward (towards the top of the planet), Antipoleward (towards the bottom), Sunriseward (tempora-wise) and Sunsetward (widdershins).*

The callall berped to remind the Summit to return to the Conventionium.

On the e-commenter, Cate'aeddy was reporting the relatively uninteresting mixed scenes of anarchic discussion from the Conventionium. Little occurred; nothing of any consequence.

* * * * *

Bodgitta addressed the Convention prior to the return of Polit46 and his Summit clump from the Necropol Club, 'I know that you are now talking to the Gobblings. The whole of Eqinox knows. I want to remind you that my husband is still being held by them. He was probably injured. Profmed said that once having touched the Gobblings he would, most likely, have contracted The Contaigen. He would then have only about twenty days to live. If he can be returned, Profmed can cure him, but he must be brought back. Please, I beg you, please remember him and I appeal to you to persuade the Gobblings to return him.'

Bodgittson and a Bodgittdort (or several) were alongside, supporting and jointly grieving with their mother; all naturally uncertain whether her grieving was premature or even realistic.

Profmed was there with her. 'The longer he stays away from medical help, the harder it will be for me to cure him. I am improving my technique and all automeds will now diagnose and cure the Contaigen. The cure is painful and still takes about five thousand breaths. I also ask you to appeal to the Gobblings for the return of Bodgitt, the builder of the great new Dagoba at Eden Garden.'

Bodgitta and her supporting offspring supported and cuddled each other and broke down in tiers of tears; Bodgitta had made her point clearly and was now involuntarily illustrating it in the most graphic manner; she had ensured that they would not forget him.

Polit46 and his private party filed from a side door into the Conventionium in preparation for the imminent arrival of Quax and her party of Gobblings.

No Trisep in the Conventionium or watching on the e-commenters spotted the hole appearing betwixt the podium and the main seating, but appear it most certainly did and now Quax was leading her clump of forty-seven translucent Gobblings to their chairs. There was one major difference from before. They no longer looked like a squashed rainbow but were transformed into some sort of battledress in colours that would have blended perfectly with the rock colour of the underground cavern of Qontûm. They were clearly dressed for some purpose other than being delegates to the Convention. On all three cuffs and each collar tip was the same quadric gammagram symbol that was displayed in the infobox of greetings from the Gobblings.

'Salutations.' said Polit46, less formally than he had intended the word to sound. 'We are most honoured by your return visit to us here.'

'Greetings in return.' replied Quax. 'We are most delighted to meet and talk with thee.'

She paused to look round. 'We have some most distressing news which we must share with thee and all of you. Although we do not live under the oceans, we do have access tunnels that enable us to visit Ozzilland. We have walked through one of them as far as its end, but it stops suddenly and there is no trace of there ever having been a tunnel beyond. To us, it is obvious where there has been a tunnel that has been unbuilt - or refilled if you prefer. The Ozzilland tunnel had not been unbuilt, it had never been built. Right now, we are rebuilding it.' She paused for breath.

Jowver's Evidencers

'But that is not the only news. One Gobbling left the caverns beneath Ozzilland immediately before the tunnel disappeared and he stated that there had been an indefinable atmosphere of subconscious fear there. You see, many hundreds of cycles ago, the centre of Ozzilland was used for underground testing of atom-splitting molotovs and there were rumours that Triseps were urgently planning another test on one of these olde-fashioned devices. If surface Triseps tested such a device, it would explain why we have not been able to contact our antipodean cousins. It would also adequately explain why the tunnel location contains rock and not either a hole or an unbuilt hole. We believe that you have carried out such a test and are thus responsible for this action, which caused a collapse of all the underground caverns beneath Ozzilland.'

'That is neither true nor possible.' replied Maecenas. 'The Eqinox Government has neither prepared nor tested atom-splitting molotovs since Sammowa dropped one on Eislland, and you know the consequences of that action.'

'We believe that you did test a molotov of some kind beneath Ozzilland.' Said Quax, 'Further, we believe that you did it with intent, fully knowing that our cousins beneath that land would all die and that we would no longer wish to claim any part of Ozzilland for growing natural foods.'

Polit46 stood to speak. 'I must protest. You may be assured that we would not and have not behaved like that. No molotov has been used in Ozzilland. As Maecenas told you, we have neither used nor tested such appalling weaponry since Eislland was destroyed. In any case, even had we intended such action, we have not had time to prepare it.'

'Perhaps it was already prepared.'

'No, it was not already prepared.' replied Polit46, 'So far as we can understand, there are several possible solutions, and you may be assured that your suggestion is not one of them.'

'Our suggestion not one of them? We are fully satisfied that our theory is the most likely reason for Gobblings all disappearing under Ozzilland. We are also satisfied that the problem was caused from the surface and not from underground. We have no such devices. For many cycles we have also been worried about your increasing use of nanomachines. Clearly, if they were incorrectly programmed the entire planet could be devastated both above and below ground. Just imagine, for instance, a midasnano getting out of control and converting everything it touches to gelt. For all we know at present, the Ozzilland disaster was caused by soldiernanos.'

Maecenas remembered the argument proffered by Mycroft and said, 'Any disaster caused by nanos would take place gradually and not as suddenly as the Ozzilland situation, so we know that is not what happened.'

'Most interesting.' Retorted Quax, 'You offer immediate proof that our theories are incorrect, and without any hesitation whatsoever; yet the best brains of all the Triseps on Eqinox are gathered here in the Conventionium and you claim that you have not been able to come up with a realistic, workable theory between you? No, no, no, this is not acceptable. It is quite clear to us that you have a great deal to hide and that you are hiding it from us. Now tell me, Polit46, are you as Precedent of the Eqinox Government prepared to change your story and tell us the truth of what has happened in or under Ozzilland?'

'There is no false story, so we cannot change it.' replied Polit46.

Quax looked long and hard at Polit46 and then at each of the Gobbling delegates in turn. 'We do not know whether to believe you, but the probability is that you are equivocating. We concede that you could be lying to deceive your own race. This is not a problem to us. If this is so, then we offer to meet you in an ex-cam Summit. The outcome of this is in your hands. For us, we are prepared for any emergency including a full attack on us from surface-residing Triseps. That is why we are now wearing battle fatigues. We came expecting the worst, although I am sure that you are too honourable to attack a peaceful delegation during a conference such as this.'

Polit46 had mostly been speaking from his cowch. Now he stepped forward towards the centre of the podium, moving firmly but ensuring that he did not portray a threatening posture. 'Let me say publicly to all Gobblings and to all Triseps: We have no secrets, we have nothing to hide. We have no intention either of threatening you or attacking you. We are genuinely baffled about Ozzilland and would welcome you to work with us.'

'Taking you at your word, then, perhaps you will start by telling us how Kernal and your Defenss Sqoddies are preparing to examine the fringes of Ozzilland. Or at least, where Ozzilland used to be.'

Maecenas, remembering Mycroft's warning, stepped forward and spoke up, 'I'm not sure that's a good idea. I respectfully suggest that we should each carry out our own researches, you in the Underplanet, we researching above ground. That will satisfy our respective needs for security of secret information.'

Quax immediately responded. 'You obviously have a great deal to hide or you would never make such a statement. Only those who have something to hide would refuse to share their methods at a time like this. I have no doubt that you are hiding much that should be shared and know far more about what is going on in Ozzilland than you are prepared to answer.'

Ozzipolit7 stood and introduced himself to respond, 'I must reply to your serious allegations. I am worried about my relatives and even my own herd that I have left behind in Ozzilland. No, you are wrong. For myself, I believe that it is Gobblings who are to blame after your statement yesterday. There is no other solution.'

'You appear to offer falsehoods greater even than your fellow Triseps. Clearly this Summit must be concluded and we must return to the Underplanet to continue our own researches. You can contact us by the callall or by making a statement on a holoquadrant of the e-commenter,'

Quax gestured to her delegation to leave. Polit46 began to raise his third hand in a gesture to stop them and to open his mouth but Maecenas pushed his arms down again. 'No, let them go.'

Quax turned to them and laughed, 'Huh! You ask us to be friends and to trust you in peace. How can we join with you in peaceful agreement when you cannot even agree with each other. I will make one final comment: if you let us down by failing to genuinely investigate Ozzilland, then you had better be prepared for us because we will not tolerate being crossed.'

Maecenas formally bowed and silently smiled a parting greeting while Polit46 stood and watched in stunned silence. He was shocked enough by the twist in the situation without the added problem for a politician of being seen to be put down by both a friend and a potential enemy within a few breaths. His head remained bowed as he returned to his place in the centre of the podium.

'Chequemate!' said Smelt with a wry smile as Polit46 sat on his cowch.

'Eh?' retorted Polit46, not really concentrating on any but his own confused thoughts.

'Chequemate.' Repeated Smelt, 'Don't you play the game of Financial Monopoly where rents are paid on owned squares of a cheque board to stop the king being captured? Difference is that the loser will give the winner a bit more than a cheque in this game; we are all playing for larger stakes.'

'A fact we are.' replied Polit46, being one vote short of understanding the light-hearted side of anything.

* * * * *

Mumblings and groanings hovered above the heads of the assembled Triseps and most of them were already forming little clumps or talking on their personal callalls - and most realised that time was rapidly running out and perhaps they should prepare for war. The problem was, nobody had any recent experience of battles or real war, so they didn't know quite what to expect, what to prepare for, or even how to prepare.

Cate'aeddy chatted harmlessly about the events of the day into her personal autofollowing holocam. She approached Polit46. 'Tell me Mr. Precedent, what is your view of the current situation?'

Polit46 turned on his Thatched Charm and opened his mouth to speak.

'Let me interrupt you.' said Cate'aeddy.

'You can't.' Retorted Maecenas.

'Can't what?' asked Cate'aeddy, turning her front head.

'You can't interrupt him.'

'Why not, I'm a reporter for ENN. I interrupt everybody.'

'You can't interrupt someone who isn't speaking.'

'But he was about to start speaking.'

'Then if you wanted to interrupt him, you should have waited for him to start speaking and then interrupted. Or you should have said something else, like *before you start ...* ' See?'

'All right,' said Cate'aeddy, giving up, 'I'll start again. Now, Mr. Precedent, let me stop you before you start ... '

'Uh, uh!' interrupted Maecenas, 'you can't stop something before it starts, but you can stop it starting.'

'Will you *please* stop interrupting and let me do my interview!' ejaculated Cate'aeddy.

'Just trying to help.' Said Maecenas and lost interest in his intellectual game, 'Actually, I must have a word with Polit46 myself before you interview him.' he gestured to move to one side out of earshot of the microphone. 'Listen, I wanted to stop you speaking to her for a breath or two.'

Cate'aeddy lost interest and went to interview Grounsell.

'Why?'

'Two reasons, first we should discuss the matter with Mycroft before we go public. OK?'

'Yes.'

'Good.'

'Er, yes?'

'Yes, what?'

'And the second reason?'

'Oh! - Ah, because I didn't want you to make a fool of yourself. You were putting on Thatched Charm like the politicians from the extinct Thatcherfactorismoptimists Party. You don't want to go the same way and become extinct do you?'

'But they died out because nobody could pronounce their ridiculously long name of Thatcherfactor-whatever-it-is-ists.'

'They also died out because Triseps of Eqinox could see the artificiality of their Thatched Charm when they did not know the answer.'

'Yes and the elevation by some in their minds from St. Thatch to a GoD didn't help either.'

'Er, yes. Well, anyway, you were putting on Thatched Charm just now. You will present a far better image to your Triseps if you wait to talk to M and then act more naturally in front of Cate'aeddy's holocam. Remember M's injunction to silence.'

'Yes. I know that you're right.'

'Are you ready? Can I talk to you now?' Cate'aeddy always appeared at the most awkward of junctures.

'No. I will talk to you later, I have a meeting now.' answered Polit46.

'Why, what are you hiding? Will there be, to use your words, 'peace in our time' or can we expect a war with the Gobblings?'

Cate'aeddy and the live bleating autofollowing holocam followed his silent sidle toward the exit. 'Are the Defenss ready for anything the Gobblings can throw at us? What about the Contaigen - will we all be affected as soon as we touch the Gobblings? Are we going to mount a rescue for Bodgitt? Is that what Kernal is doing now? I expected him to be here, where is he? Why won't you speak to me? My name's not Rodjacook, you know. Is it because you don't have any real answers? What should ordinary Triseps of Eqinox do to protect themselves against attack by Gobblings? Who will be the first to explore whether Ozzilland is still there or whether it has been annihilated?' Cate'aeddy ran out of floor. And breath.

Polit46 reached the door, turned to Cate'aeddy, smiled a half Thatched Charm and left without saying a further word, while the ENN reporter was left shrugging and seeking the next most important person to interfere with, interview wise.

A religiot sidled up to her and was immediately interviewed for want of something better to do. 'We have been warning you that Eqinox would come to an end and we forecast that it would be this year. Ozzilland is only the first of all the countries to disappear. Remember the words in the Folio of Revealment, the last folio in the Authorised Version of The Folius. It says that there will be *wars and rumours of wars* and then we will know that we are in the *End Times,* and that *our days are numbered to forty-seven times forty-seven.* You can already see how the Gobblings are in the veritable clutch of *HobB, The Evil One who will make his mark on your forehead,* even as Smelt and Grounsell are left with the evil mark of the Gobblings. *And his number is Seven Hundred and Seventy-Six plus One.* It must be obvious to all that the true GoD, Jowver, must be put in control. You must realise that we follow the sign of the golejibbit, while the quadric gammagram is the sign of the enemy. Read The Folius, brother. You will not be saved if you do not read The Folius.

'Tell me,' responded Cate'aeddy, 'are you a Jowver's Evidencer?' and then added, 'No, of course, you can't be or you wouldn't talk about being saved.'

'Of course I am, of course, of course! There is only One True Way and that is to follow the way of our GoD, Jowver and follow his instructions laid out in the GodspellS of the New Promisings. If you do not follow the ways of Jowver the true GoD, you will fall into eternal damnation and become a follower of HobB. Can I sell you a copy of our True Light Translation? It is better than the Authorised Version of The Folius, a translation of the ancient text authorised by St. Thatch, founder of the Thatcherfactorismoptimists political party. The profits will go to missionary work in Zimgululland.'

'Thank you very much.' said Cate'aeddy, backing away to try to find a more interesting and less loopy Trisep with whom to converse.

'Did you notice that ... well, the Gobblings are using the Quadric gammagram? This is the sign of HobB. Remember that we are nearing the End of Days on Eqinox and all of your viewers have little time left to follow Jowver, the one true GoD.'

'Yes, thank you.' said Cate'aeddy firmly and this time she managed to escape.

* * * * *

EBC decided to use several live holoquadrants to transmit special bleats about war in the old days. There were a great many pre-holotechnology films, both fictitious and real life, about wars. Triseps all over Eqinox set their eyes and ears to concentrate on four films at a time from four appropriately placed holoquadrants, an ear and an eye to each. Excitement mounted and in every home, there were debates and discussions about the extent of devastation that the Gobblings could cause and what could be done to them and how they could best be captured and killed.

Conjecture reigned rife about the powers of Gobblings and a great many attributed to them powers more akin with those of mythological GodS.

* * * * *

This was one of those rare times when mothers-in-lorr stopped nagging for long enough to turn into thaumaturges.

Thaumas all over Eqinox sought old besoms from garden sheds and callalled their fellow thaumas who rapidly reconvened their covens. Suddenly the night was full of thaumas driving besoms instead of normal moovacars. They too, believed that both GoD and the HobB - The Evil One - not only existed but were all powerful in protecting their own Trisep followers against all other physical or spiritual powers.

Without reference to Eqinox Government, EBC bleated a great deal of advice, much of it farcical to those with real knowledge, about preparing for a war with the Gobblings.

EBC advised how to prepare some basic protection against the initial fallout from atom-splitting molotovs. Advice was proffered on setting nanomachines to manufacture and stockpile food so that even if the machines themselves were destroyed by neutrino molotovs, there would be adequate food stocks. Transport advice was given to remain near the ground when driving moovacars in case of any sudden loss of power.

One whole holoquadrant was dedicated to more outrageous suggestions.

'We have been communicating with aliens from planet seven for three cycles and they want to take over Eqinox.' said one of a clump of seven Triseps with little aerials on their heads. Now that they have conquered Ozzilland, they will take over other countries one by one. Of course, we won't know they've taken us over because they will control our minds.'

Their claims were taken seriously by many of the more gullible, who callalled in to say that they had shared experiences of being taken by tall Trisep-like beings from other worlds with thin bodies and giant brains. Some even claimed to have been taken into alien spaceships and been used for mating with the aliens.

The truth is that for reasons of structural differences of their triple septihelix ribena-acid, they would have been more likely to be able to mate with a petunia than with a being from another planet.

One older Trisep wearing clothes made of critter skins claimed that this was a punishment by the creator aliens for daring to use nanotechnology which interfered with their experiment on how Triseps would survive from the first to the final generation.

A clump of philosophers argued forcefully that Ozzilland had never actually been a real place because there was never any evidence of its existence in the first place. They claimed that it existed only in the mental perception of individuals and that its disappearance was another and opposite mental misperception.

The philosophers also said that because the floor was there when you took to your sleeping cowch was not necessarily evidence that it would be there when you woke up. 'The same is true of your country,' one said, 'who knows whether it is really there under your hooves or whether it will be there when you wake up in the morning.' Suddenly now, a few Triseps who previously showed little respect for philosophers, pretended to understand them and took an interest in their curious but invariably impractical ideas.

A clump of Flat Eqinoxers, who believed that the planet was not a sphere but a flat disc 'like a table top and all evidence to the contrary was fabricated by a deceitful government', took a holoquadrant to propose that because Ozzilland was too near the edge of the disc of the planet, it had fallen off. This view was taken up by a Trisep who claimed that Ozzilland had been bitten out of the flat planet by a giant alien monster called a 'shark' floating through space.

'It's not a flat disc!' intoned one embadged Trisep, as convincingly as he could muster, 'I come from Anerak, where we look after the wheeled pressure-vapour engines, and I can see through my pebbles that the twak is curved. You see, well, I need tell you about twains first.'

'If you must.' permitted the interviewer, 'this *is* the ideas channel, after all.' He looked away from the Anerakian and raised his eyebrows GodwardS.

Anerakian and spouse

'Good,' said the Anerakian, 'Our vintage twains wun on twaks. We call them twains because twin olde-fashioned pressure-vapour engines operate in pairs, sandwiching a snake of seven or more very comfortable, air-conditioned, fully restauranted hotels on wheels, called clarridges. Some people call them snake sandwiches. I own a forty-seventh part of a clarridge and work on it every spare breath to keep it going. I like enholing tickets when visitors come, and I wear my uniform to guard it from non-payers and vandals.

'What relevance is this to missing Ozzilland?' asked the interviewer.

'Oh, ah! You are all being bwainwashed. It is obvious that Eqinox is a giant frisby being thrown through space from one GoD to another. The sun is a light so that the receiving GoD can see it coming. You see, when I look at the twaks from Anerak Preservation Centre, they curve over the horizon. Obviously the planet has a curved top. Obviously it must have a flat bottom, so obviously it must by a frisby being thrown. What's more ... '

'Never,' interrupted another, 'that's obviously ridiculous. I have studied and found no evidence against the fact that the planet is toroidal, like a doughnut and the sun swings through it and round it like a figure of eight. You can never see the other side because the sun is too bright and the night stars are the lights from the cottagers; now Ozzilland has gone round the corner and out of sight. That's all. There's no mystery, you should have seen it coming.'

'Yes, sure we should.' said the politely sceptical interviewer, 'next view, please?'

There seemed to be as many suggestions of what was going on as there were Triseps on Eqinox.

The most watched holoquadrant was Cate'aeddy trying to interview Mycroft, who refused to leave the Necropol Club; particularly difficult because females have never been permitted to enter the Club. Cate'aeddy climbed an olde-fashioned ladder to speak to him through the open window.

'Hello, Mycroft.'

The sound of a female voice caused Mycroft to turn his swivel-cowch with such violence that it continued spinning for two full rotations. When it stopped, he frowned at her and yelled, 'Out, out! Get out. What are you doing here? Go away.'

'I'm here to interview you and ask what you feel about the loss of Ozzilland.'

'Then you had better do so, if it will get rid of you any quicker.'

'Well?'

'Well, what?'

'What is your answer?'

'I cannot give an answer when you have not yet asked a question.'

'Yes I have.'

'No, you have talked about asking a question, but you have not yet asked it. Any answer I give will depend upon the precise wording and definition of the question.'

'Very well,' sighed Cate'aeddy, 'What is your opinion about the loss of Ozzilland?'

'That is a different question from the one you said you were here to ask, but I shall answer it nevertheless. I have no opinion about the loss as I do not, yet, have any evidence of it.'

'Well, what do you think is happening there?'

'I cannot answer that without further evidence. You have the same evidence as I have. At present I have conjectured nine possible options with probabilities attached to each. I do not *think* anything is happening.'

'Do you mean that nothing is happening there in that everyone is dead or that there is nothing wrong?'

'I answered your question about what I think. I always speak and answer with the greatest precision. It saves time later. I replied that I do not think.' he raised his eyes GodwarD. 'Thank GoD they don't allow women in this place.'

Cate'aeddy ignored his comment. 'So why can't we communicate with Ozzilland?'

'I have answered your question, the answer is the same.'

'Have you any advice to the 87% of Triseps who are watching this holoquadrant?'

M puffed on his pipe and exhaled the vile smoke in a series of mathematical symbols, 'Yes. Yes, I have. Consider why the Gobbling city of Qontûm is so called. After that, consider whether the effect can spread. Good-bye.'

M closed the window and returned to his old levva armcowch, leaving Cate'aeddy mouthing silently on her perch.

Polit46, Smelt and the others were still on their way to the Necropol Club from the Conventionium - via a jolly good restaurant where they had just shared the most delicious uncooked ghotis from Ånjap on the Nipoff Archipelago.

'... I still think Gobblings have got Soles and will sit close by the third hand of GoD if they're good,' Polit46 was saying as they arrived.

'Maybe,' responded Smelt, 'but what about HobB's interference in our sub-conscientious, making us painstakingly and diligently evil and ... '

Cate'aeddy reached the bottom of her ladder just as the senior Triseps were arriving.

'Can you tell me why Qontûm is so called?' she asked as an interruptive opener.

Their conversation disturbed, they had to readjust their brains to the new topic before they all looked towards Maecenas, who was the most likely to know.

Maecenas looked at Smelt, who shrugged. and motioned back to Maecenas. They had been too deep in conversation in their journey in the moovacar to be bothered with watching the e-commenter.

'No, why?' Polit46 asked.

'Mycroft said that everybody should think about the name. Why was that?'

Maecenas shrugged. 'Pass.'

'What effect does Qontûm have?'

Again, Maecenas and Smelt looked at one another with both heads, baffled at the point of the question.

'Eh?' Retorted Maecenas.

'Can you tell our viewers why Qontûm is so called and what effect does the city's name have?'

Smelta thought she had picked up Cate'aeddy's train of thought. 'Are you asking if the name of Qontûm is itself some sort of magic formula or spell or curse or incantation? What? Which?'

'I hoped *you* could answer that.'

'I'm really not sure that I understand the question, unless you are asking what the word Qontûm itself means. Are you?'

'That sounds like a good place to start. Anything that could help our viewers to understand the word.'

'Well,' began Maecenas, 'the great scientist, Thermos who discovered the lorrs of Thermos-Dynamism, suggested a proposition which was later confirmed and mathematically proved by a great arithmate, Stephen the Hawker.'

'Do you mean the author of *Qontûm State Has Moved Here, Probably?*' suggested Cate'aeddy.

'Well, yes, you see, what happened was that ... ' Maecenas tried to explain.

'I don't need the history, just the meaning,' interrupted Cate'aeddy.

'Oh, I see. well, you see, er ... ' he broke off, wondering where to start.

'What exactly are you asking?'

'I just need an answer to the problem set by M.'

'Problem?' Responded Maecenas, 'What problem?'

Cate'aeddy was beginning to despair and sighed to prove it. 'You *did* see the e-commenter bleat, didn't you? About the meaning of Qontûm?'

'No I didn't.' answered Maecenas, 'But I can answer the question on the meaning of Qontûm. The country occupied by the Gobblings is a Qontûm State and as such has its own energy, probably. It all has to do with elgins and the symbols of the ancients found on the Parthenon in Greasy. Any arithmate will tell you about the elginfunction. The principle concerns the degenerate state of the place, so that a location is not determined absolutely, but only by the probability of its location at a set moment of Temporra, according to a value which is precise within the limits of its own uncertainty; in short, a differential wave. Perhaps *location* is not the best word. Perhaps I should say location relative to the known. The whole problem is decaying anyway.'

'Decaying?' echoed Cate'aeddy, 'And do you understand that?'

'Yes. Don't you? We must go inside; we have a meeting with Mycroft.'

Cate'aeddy glared at Maecenas, who changed his mind about going inside until he had lightened the moment, 'Question for you: who knows everything about nothing, a lot about a little and nothing about everything?'

'Why are you asking me riddles? Aren't there more important things to talk about?'

'It's relevant.' replied Maecenas, dropping his head but raising his eyes towards her in a gesture of the utmost seriousness.

'All right, if it means that I get to talk to you a bit longer, what's the answer?'

'Arithmates, of course.'

'Arithmates?' she queried, 'Arithmates?' Suddenly she saw the light, 'Oh! Arithmates, of course, yes. Very good.' She looked at him somewhat askance as, despite her words, she had no inkling of what he was actually talking about.

Following some decessions several cycles before, when a couple of rationally challenged Triseps became terminally upset by not understanding the jokes and performed their decessions publicly by jumping in front of a charging hippopotamus, which nevertheless still charged them for the privilege, ENN were now legally obliged to explain all jokes in full.

'You know that we must explain the joke in full, don't you?' she said.

'Yes, but you would be better at that than I am. I hate explaining jokes.'

'But as it is your joke, I am afraid you are legally obliged to explain it.'

'If you insist.'

'I don't insist, but Lorranordå gets very upset if we don't obey the lorr, sorry!'

'Very well.' he said.

She put her hand in her pocket and set the her personal autofollowing holocam to see both of them. Maecenas prepared himself to explain the joke and thus avoid unnecessary self-administered premature deceasement by telling the story, 'Arithmates: professional expert mathematicians.' he began, 'They know everything there is to know about nothing, about the number zero and a great deal about real numbers above zero, but because the philosophers own the copyright on Infinity (© Philosophers)[8], they know absolutely nothing about everything whatsoever!'

Cate'aeddy shrugged, 'Thank you, Maecenas. I confess that I still don't understand it, personally, but we have fulfilled the legal obligation to explain.' she said, deflated. It wasn't even a joke worth telling, she decided. She turned to Smelt to bag an instant interview, but was left in limbo watching the back of the clump enter the Necropol Club. She frowned hard and then shrugged her front shoulders again. Her rear shoulders copied several breaths later.

'Well, there it is, Triseps of Eqinox;' Cate'aeddy began, improvising, 'clearly there is a reason why Qontûm is so called and that meaning has

---

[8]   As Infinity (© Philosophers) is the copyright property of the Philosophers, it must always be so marked whenever it is mentioned.

113

a bearing on the whole problem of the Gobblings and the disappearance of Ozzilland. If *you* have an idea, please tell us on our public callall-in.'

Meanwhile, the truth of what happened in - or to Ozzilland was yet to be discovered.

Chapter 7   The Shape of Eqinox

One problem with nanomanufacture is that it doesn't happen instantly. That which is to be made needs to be grown. But first the specification must be correct before the computers will accept it. Then the computer's design must be checked for aesthetic appeal - a problem that had only ever been defined in general terms and computers never quite got the message.

Kernal and his Sqoddies flew the wrong way round Eqinox to Antipole. Nanotech329, who had attended all sessions of the Convention, agreed to join him. His task was to improve the standard hoverfloat autobridge, which was of an old design from before the invention of nanotechnology.

Nanotech329 worked rapidly with the computer to calculate the design improvements required for nanomanufacturing. These hoverfloat autobridges would need to be joinable, flexible, hover when capable, but float safely under all sea conditions in the vicious New Seas between Ozzilland and Antipole.

Nanotech329 had a major task ahead. The problem was not really in the design, which had a very long pedigree from Bailey, the Trisep who designed the first one (non-hovering) several hundred years before. Bailey was so called because his job was to bail out water from ferries. This he found so boring that he designed a floating pontoon bridge instead, which was rather silly because he made himself redundant in the process. But he did make a lot of money because Defenss bought the design and he ended his life still 'bailing out', but this time it was the poor and not a ferry boat.

No, the problem was not in the design, it was in the building. Normally, any item to be made would be grown from a single point, outwards like a cone until the final width and height had been achieved. However, if a single bridge were to be built using this technique, it would take far too long. This was a crisis and the work had to be fast. Very fast.

'I-Smeller, I-Smeller' called Nanotech329 to Kernal after double checking his data.

'Have you found the final solution or just another step on the way?'

'You're not going to like the answer.'

'Try.'

The fastest way to build the bridge will be dangerous. The slowest way is safer. I have calculated two complete methods and the choice is yours.'

'What are they?'

'First we could grow the bridge conventionally from one end. This would be very slow and you could have Sqoddies move on to it as it grows.' He pointed to one of the holoviews.

'Secondly, the hoverfloat autobridge could be grown in ready-joined sections. Each section would grow at the normal speed but because there would be up to 2209 sections growing at once, their forward speed would not give your men time to return if they encounter a problem because the combined speed of the sections would push the front forward at greater than galloping speed.'

Kernal shook his head in amazement at the concept.

'Third, we could build it in sections which are side by side, but these would take too long to move to the end of the line and join up.'

'I thought you said *two* complete methods? queried Kernal.

'I did. Sorry. I forgot that I can't count; I can't think of everything.'

Kernal looked away and chewed it over for a breath or two, before returning his gaze; somehow his eyes retained a slightly GodwardS expression, 'You give me great confidence.' he remarked.

Nanotech329 ignored the comment and looked at Kernal to make sure he was watching. He was building up to an internal crescendo and burst excitely, 'Fourth, and in my opinion the best solution, is not end to end nor side by side building but each to be built from about half way along the next and to make the whole thing a series of trapezoids telescoping one into the next and growing at the same time. This way, your Sqoddies would be moved at many times the growth rate but would be able to return instantly with a manually operated telescoping device. Look at the simulation and see what you think.'

Kernal looked rather dubious at the idea of a bridge made of thousands of short, telescopic sections that would be used in one of the roughest seas on the planet, but nevertheless he suddenly became excited when he saw the proven result.

'Wonderful, wonderful. Brilliant! Now I see why you were shouting I-smeller, I-smeller. They grow together, yet slot together and can be extended or contracted quickly. And that mechanical pulley system means that they can *all, every one,* be extended or contracted quickly. This would make an excellent form of transport over any difficult terrain if moovacars became unusable.'

'There is a problem, though.' reported Nanotech329, hesitantly.

'There can't be any problems! You've solved them all.'

'Not quite all, I haven't checked the hover function.' he looked squarely at Kernal with both heads. 'And we don't know exactly at what point the journey will become dangerous, so you are going to have to find volunteer Sqoddies who don't mind if they suddenly disappear. Do you know the likely point?'

'Yes, we know where the autofollowing holocam disappeared. M has calculated the most likely position when arriving from the Antipole. I'll give you the co-ordinates.'

Nanotech329 looked at Kernal, surprised. 'I'm not any Profgeol, but wasn't the autofollowing holocam lost Poleward, whereas we are starting from Antipole?'

'I expect it will be the same distance, but I suppose we should check in any case.' replied Kernal, more casually than he ought for his position.

Kernal callalled some Sqoddies to include some autofollowing holocams in the inventory.

Together, they worked hard to finalise the new design for the hoverfloat autobridges.

After Kernal had eaten a hearty meal, the callall berped.

'Vittler here. We haven't got any, Kernal.'

'Switch to over-cipher first ... That's better, we can't be heard now. Not got what?'

'Autofollowing holocams, of course.'

'What do you mean, "haven't got any". This is a Defenss exercise, we *must* have some. You are Vittler, it's your job to provide things we need.'

'There are none and we don't have the design, so we can't make any, not that anybody cares if it upsets me.'

'Get some from EBC. Their ENN channels use them all the time.'

'I've tried that, Kernal, they insist on conditions.'

'What conditions?'

'They will let us use their cameras if they can transmit live from them.'

'That's out of the question. We must never let the Gobblings know what we are doing. Remember that they are probably our enemy. They will be able to see us coming. This whole operation is supposed to take place ex-cam.'

'Perhaps you can persuade them; I cannot.'

'Keep trying. I will confer upwards.'

Kernal terminated and made another over-cipher callall to the Necropol Club.

'We're all here.' replied Mycroft.

'We need to borrow some of ENN's autofollowing holocams.' Kernal listed the conditions laid down by EBC's ENN channel.

'EBC have the sole rights to it.' replied M. 'If you want to use their equipment, you will have to work by their rules. But there is more than one way to slaughter the feline. What exactly is the problem?'

'We need to know where the safe edge is, the point beyond which we must not step.'

'Have you got a moovacar with you in Antipole?'

'Yes, of course. I'm speaking from it. We're still on the way there. Why?'

'Has it got a standard remote control unit with it?'

'Naturally.'

'And have you got your elgins?'

'Are you suggesting that I've lost my elgins?'

'No! Do you have a set of elgins to play with?'

'Never go anywhere without them.' said Kernal.

'Are they genuine, pseudo, or nanomanufactured?'

'I've got a really nice genuine set.'

'Yes,' replied M, 'I thought you would have.'

'And have you got a bassinette?'

Kernal was baffled. 'Why?'

'I will tell you in a minute. Have you got one, or at least, a design for one?'

'Nanotech329 is with me and he could build one.'

'Good,' responded M, 'now listen carefully. This is the plan:'

M described a detailed plan to Kernal, explaining how to approach Ozzilland from Antipole, and what to take with him. 'If you follow my instructions to the letter, your men will be safe. You can replay this conversation if you are confused, and I am always here to answer your questions.'

* * * * *

The thirty-breaths-to-landing* warning ping sounded. Kernal and Nanotech329 were ready to land at Scotaisle, a tiny, barren landmass just Poleward of Antipole in the general direction of Ozzilland. Some Sqoddies had already arrived, set up a camp and unloaded a large-unit nanomanufacturing kit.

A small clump of dark Triseps were arriving in brightly painted red and white striped moovacars. These were the Riffs of Morøkka, who were all barbers.

'What on Eqinox are *they* doing here?' asked Nanotech329.

'Tradition,' replied Kernal, 'Whenever the Defenss go into battle, the Riffs of Morøkka cut hair so that the Sqoddies go into battle fresh and tidy. They are all barbers, you see.'

'But we're not going into battle.' he paused and looked squarely at Kernal with both heads, 'are we?'

Kernal hesitated. 'Not exactly, but it makes them feel useful.'

Nanotech329 turned to Kernal and took hold of his collar. 'Look, I thought I knew all that you know. You're obviously keeping back some

vital detail that I haven't been told. Just tell me, are we going to war?
Are you sending me into danger? What's really going on?'

'I think you should take your hand off my collar; it won't help.'

'Perhaps you can tell me the truth then. Are you sending me into
battle?'

Kernal shook his head. 'No, of course not. But we are preparing for
the worst, and none of us know what to expect; that's why I've ordered
a full task force to Antipole. This is not just a Defenss problem, it
affects every single Trisep on Eqinox.'

Nanotech329 relaxed his grip and backed off, ashamed. 'I know. I've
been working hard on the design. Remember, I am not used to this sort
of pressure. I hope we can continue to work together.'

'Have a drink' suggested Kernal and ordered two very large
geeantees from the provisions hatch.

'Cronus and Rhea,' said Nanotech329, 'is war always as pressurised
as this?'

'We're not at war, I tell you. I can see why you are a Nanotech.
You'd never make a Sqoddie. Yes, the mission is dangerous, but I am
hiding nothing from you.'

'I'll go over the new design for the hoverfloat autobridge so that we
can start straight away. There are just a couple of checks I want to
make.'

Kernal sidled over to the barbers for his haircut. His Sqoddies were
still arriving in small clumps and each clump in turn made its way to
the moovacar-workshops of the Riffs of Morøkka to be barbered.

* * * * *

Kernal and Nanotech329 didn't notice them immediately on landing
because they were camouflaged against the background of black rocks
and white snow. There hadn't been that many of them either, but now
they seemed to be coming from everywhere. He had seen them before,
but only through the e-commenter on natural-geography bleats. Now
they were real. Very real.

Nanotech329 looked hard at the black and white nün-polepengus on
little Scotaisle. The more he looked, the more there appeared to be.
There were just thousands of them. They seemed to be appearing from
the very ground itself. They came out of the sea and appeared over the
horizon. These little flying ghotis could walk. It wasn't immediately
obvious whether they were ghotis from the ocean, now walking on land
or birds that could swim in the sea, or land waddlers of obscure interest.

He was certainly amazed at the incredible likeness to nüns of the
Triseptokatholicus Order and could see why they were called nün-
polepengus. He couldn't think of a better name himself and because

they appeared so friendly, he was determined to try to communicate with them.

Nanotech329 lovingly remembered a whole series of Equi-mailings to The Thundering Temporra, an olde-fashioned daily chronicle. The Equi-mailings discussed how to split the nüns (who always sidled along in pairs) by sidling between them. Solutions included distracting them both at the same time in opposite directions by offering them charity money and then sidling round between them. Many other solutions offered equally ridiculous ideas including setting up roadworks and capturing them with nets. And so the suggestions continued.

But the Equi-mailings were about habitually dressed-up Triseps of the Triseptokatholicus Order. The critters before him were wild. And they were alive. And they were real. And they were not in a natural-geography bleat. They were intensely fascinating.

The callall berped. Nanotech329 was jerked from his reverie and answered. 'Vittler here, I suppose,' it said, sounding depressed.

Nanotech329 replied, 'Kernal's at the barbers' at the moment, and the place is full of nün-polepengus.'

'What's that got to do with it? Why is he at the barber's? Isn't this a rather odd time to worry about something for the weekend?' asked Vittler, 'In any case, I can supply anything he needs. Do you want me to send a Sharen, not that they do anything for me?'

'No, you misunderstand. He's having the traditional pre-battle haircut. Perhaps I can answer your query.'

'No. Well, yes actually. Are you going into battle?'

'Who knows. What is your query?'

'I've forgotten. I'll callall you back.' he hung up.

Nanotech329 returned to his daydream and stared at the increasing numbers of nün-polepengus appearing round the moovacar.

The callall berped and Nanotech329 answered in frustration.

'Yes!'

'Me again, I suppose. Vittler here. Nobody remembers me or even cares who I am. Is he back yet?'

'Who?'

'Him.'

'Who's … ah, yes! No.'

'Yes, No?'

'Yes, I mean no.'

'Ah. No.'

'Can I help?' said Nanotech329, returning the conversation to a recognisable level of sanity.

'I've remembered. We've tried again to get some autofollowing holocams but EBC insist that we can only have them if we bleat live on ENN.'

'We don't need them anymore.'

Vittler started to cry. 'Nobody needs me any more. They get nanomachines. They stop needing equipment to fight wars. Nobody wants me any more ... '

'But ... ' Nanotech329's interruption was itself interrupted by more crying.

'I wanted to die and tried to commit decession and set the psycho-trigger hairclip of a micro-neutron gun pin but it wouldn't work.'

'Why not?' asked Nanotech329, feeling sorry for him.

'Because it's programmed not to destroy the wearer. You would think that if you were like me, Vittler in charge of weapons in the Defenss stores, you could at least practise decession, but the weapons don't allow it. What can I do? Even the micro-neutron gun pins hate me. The auto-lasers hate me. None of them will help me.'

'But they are helping you by not letting you commit decession; not permitting unnecessary self-administered premature deceasement, denying you the privilege of killing yourself. That must be good. Decession is against the lorr and a punishable crime, after all, even though it isn't punishable by death any more.'

'No. You see, you don't understand either. They hate me.' continued Vittler, 'They all hate me. Nobody needs me any more. I'm not needed. Even you. I used to supply hoverfloat autobridges to Defenss forces all over Eqinox and now you're making your own.'

'How do you know about that? It's supposed to be top secret. Squeithian eyes only. In fact, I haven't even transmitted the details.'

'You don't need to tell me. I know. You talk to me on the callall and I can see the nanomanufacturing design on the computer behind you. Your own existence, Nanotech329, is against me. Everyone's against me and I want to die.'

'I'm sorry I can't help you;' Responded Nanotech329, wondering what in Eqinox he could possibly do, 'have you tried the automed's Phroydtest?'

'Are you suggesting that I've lost my elgins? Yes, I've tried the automed. Yes, the automed has tried the Phroydtest. And do you know what it said? It said that I wasn't any use to anyone any more, so I should retire. I don't want to retire. Automeds won't let you die. I even tried jumping off the EBC planet wide bleat tower but did you know that it is surrounded by artificial spunj-squelches, so all you do is bounce? Did you know that? Did you?'

'No.' replied Nanotech329, frantic to escape this callall.

'No, of course you didn't. Neither did I. Nobody told me. You see, nobody cares. Even EBC are against me. Did you know that automeds analyse whether you've taken your sleeping tablet and won't give you another one until you take yesterday's tablet, so you can't save them up. So even the automeds are against me. I'm going to go and turn myself into a statistic.'

'A statistic? Do you mean a statistician?'

' 'No. I'm going to become a statistic. Good-bye. Good-bye forever, I hope.'

Nanotech329 saw the callall being terminated from the other end. He shrugged and looked out at a large group of nün-polepengus all throwing themselves, en bloc, over the edge of an ice flow and into the sea. He wondered whether the whole planet was going completely mad and falling out of its bassinette, or whether it was just him becoming confused.

'No wonder,' he muttered to himself, 'that some Triseps join the Jowver's Evidencers or become Triseptokatholicus nüns.' he shook his heads, buried them in his three hands and forgot about making hoverfloat autobridges.

* * * * *

Back at the Necropol Club, Mycroft smoked his netherwear and met with the Summit committee, Maecenas, Smelt and Smelta, Grounsell, Polit46, Ozzipolit7, and Sammowapolit7. They met in the foyer, of course, because Smelta wasn't allowed inside.

'Why don't you go home, Smelta, and prepare a meal for your husband?' M suggested, 'then we can meet inside. I do hate having to meet in the foyer. and the committee will never allow females beyond.'

A deep sigh permeated through and beyond each to the next, following such politically doubtful condescension, but nobody quite had the nerve to comment directly.

'Who are the committee?' asked Smelta.

'I am.' replied Mycroft.

Smelta opened her mouth to speak, looked from each one of the others to the next, to the next. Each in turn avoided her gaze. She was so totally flabbergasted that she could not speak. Mycroft had closed his eyes in condescension in any case. She closed and opened her mouth a few times and gave up.

She sat down on the nearest levva armcowch, and firmly plaited her three arms, having nailed home her point to all but Mycroft.

M sighed, 'Then we'll stay here if we must. What would you all like to drink?'

'Nothing, thank you very much.' Smelta sniffed.

The drinks were ordered while M remained impervious to the atmosphere. 'Why are we here this time? Has there been a development?'

'No.' replied Maecenas, 'we would just like to work through the next stage. 'What do we do next? Should we tell Quax what we are doing and ask them how far they've got?'

'Didn't I make it clear?' Responded M.

'Yes, but we've discussed it since. And there have been some developments.'

M looked up, surprised. 'What developments?'

Polit46 breathed in deeply to speak; he paused. 'Riots.' he said eventually.

'Riots? I haven't heard of any. Where?' queried M, surprised at not hearing the news first.

'Nowhere.' replied Polit46.

'Nowhere? Are you saying,' asked M, 'that you are worried because there aren't any riots? None? Nowhere?'

'He's right;' said Smelta, still trying to recover from impenetrable gender rejection, 'not yet, but there will be. There's quite a pitch of public fear and anxiety.'

'Both?' said M,

'Both what? Asked Smelta.

'Both fear and anxiety. How do you define the difference between them?'

'Nothing. Triseps all over Eqinox are worried, seriously concerned. They are already taking to the streets and keeping away from large buildings.'

'Then see the Multicare Area Director. He will take care of it.'

'No, if rioting starts, and it will, you can be sure, it will be far too big for Multicare to handle.' said Polit46. 'And Defenss have nearly all moved to Antipole now.'

'Shouldn't Lorra be with us?' suggested Maecenas.

'Laura?' queried Ozzipolit7.

'Sorry - Lorranordå - the Eqinox Minister for Anticrime.'

'Ah! Good idea.' said Polit46. The others nodded.

Except Sammowapolit7. '¿Do for have in is Lorranordå, not one Sammowa this we what'

'Eh?' said Polit46.

An autotranslator which had been lying around in a corner behind an old armcowch for several generations, doing nothing but hiding from autosuks and gathering dust, suddenly heard its prompt and realised it had a job to do. It sprung into action, *'What is this Lorranordå, for we do not have one in Sammowa?'*

'He is the minister responsible for good behaviour and making lorrs.' replied M and translated for Sammowapolit7, not because he needed to but out of a liking for good manners, 'And behaviour for good he is lorrs making minister responsible the.'

Sammowapolit7 looked very surprised. 'Courtesy for thank you your.' he said. The autotranslator obviously thought this sentence too obvious and trivial to bother to translate, so it didn't.

'Responsible for good behaviour too, of course.' added Polit46, spelling it out in case Sammowapolit7 had not understood the full implications.

'I said that.' said M.

'Completely et fully understood.' said Sammowapolit7, being grammatically correct in both languages.

Polit46 made a callall to Lorranordå.

Lorranordå was on a sleeping cowch practising replication techniques with Lorranordåa and several others of his herd. 'Please excuse my position, but I've been away from home for several days.' he replied to the callall's holocam.

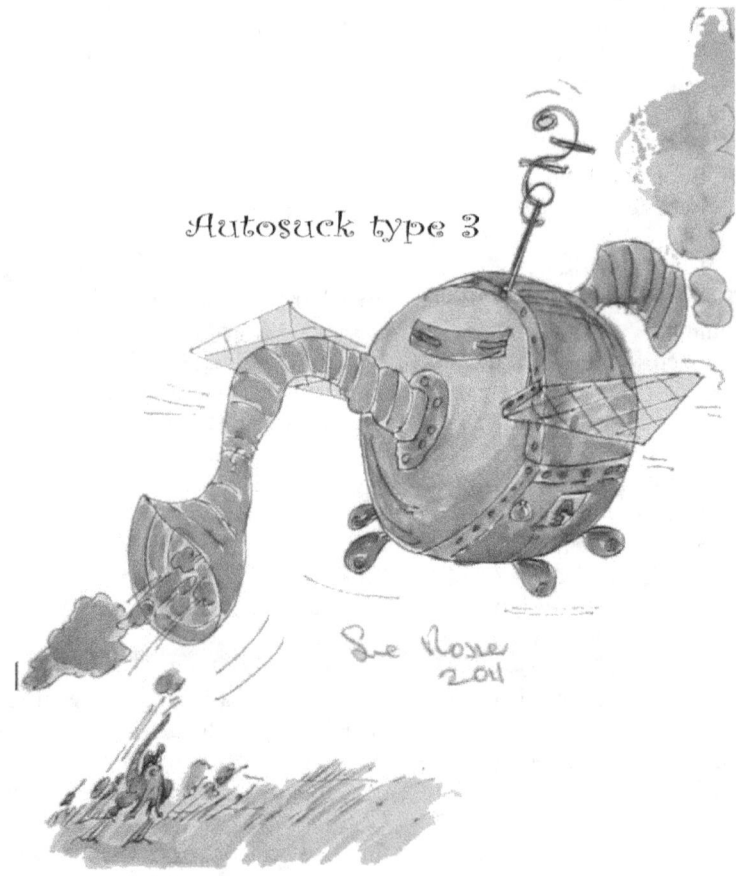

Autosuck type 3

'It's a pleasure;' began Polit46 and hesitated, 'Er, I mean, it's a pleasure to see you. I like your position. I confess that I haven't tried that one myself. Would you like me to callall back later?'

'No. Go ahead.'

'We're a bit worried about the riots.'

'Riots!' Lorranordå stopped what he was doing and looked straight at the callall holocam. 'What do you mean, *riots?* Who is rioting? Where? Why? I mean, tell me!'

'Nobody is rioting. At least, not yet, but there is unrest and we would like you to join our Summit clump. We are clumping here at the Necropol Club.'

Lorranordå looked depressed. 'Have I got time to finish practising replication before coming over?'

'I wouldn't dream of interrupting you.' laughed Polit46, 'come when you're ready.'

'I rather caught him with his trousers down.' said Polit46 as he turned his head back to the clump in the foyer. They had all been enjoying the callall from the back seat, as it were. All except one.

'I've been thinking about Convinciing Geometry.' said M, casually.

Only Maecenas knew what he was talking about, and knew it, although Smelta did have an inkling. 'I think, for the others, I should explain that the great mathematical genius of all time, a Trisep of Vinci (called Leo-nerdo because he was primarily nerd who tamed lions) discovered that Eqinox was in fact a vexal septiquadecahedron and not quite as spherical as we all thought it was. Everyone thought that he was conning them, so his name was changed by Order of the then Precedent from of-Vinci to Con-Vinci. That's why we call it Convinciing Geometry. The Order to change his name was made by the infallible St. Thatch. She said that only she was right and all others were wrong; they usually were, but not always, and not in this case.

'So what, mate? He's dead isn't he? They're all dead, aren't they? Does it matter?' asked Ozzipolit7.

'Just telling the story, that's all. It's not surprising that the Thatcher-factorismoptimists Party became extinct!' said Maecenas. 'By the way, Ozzipolit7 has got a tee-shirt with the formula for it.'

'No I haven't.'

'You have. It says, $E = \sum\Pi\circledR^3$. You must remember it.'

'I have. Never knew it meant anything, though. Hey, My-thingy, er, Croft, you got any more beers, mate?'

Mycroft winced and called Steward.

'Can you explain precisely what on Eqinox is a vexal septiquad-whatever-it-was?' asked Smelta, becoming slightly anxious that she may not have fully understood.

'Shouldn't worry about it, Shealar.' replied Ozzipolit7, laughing.

Smelta looked severely at Ozzipolit7 and addressed him with firm annoyance, 'I think he's saying that the planet is solid and flat-sided and not round. If that's the case, then Kernal's mission to save your country could be in jeopardy. You had better listen. Oh, and stop calling me Shealar.'

M looked at the clump gravely. 'Smelta's right. I don't think any of you have understood the import of this.' he paused to take a long puff on his netherwear. 'Maecenas confused you with too much detail. The point is that Eqinox is a vexal septiquadecahedron.'

'¿A as is same sphere that the thing' asked Sammowapolit7. *'Is that the same thing as a sphere?'* confirmed the autotranslator.

M laughed. 'No. You learn at school that Eqinox is a sphere because that is easier for your immature brain to understand. And it is almost right, because although each of the flat surfaces is convex - curved outwards, that is - it has a constant diameter, like the 23.5 dalli coin. When you combine that with the Underplanet and the probability factors of location and movement affecting the city of Qontûm, for example, you will understand the problem. Do you see?'

The clump remained in baffled silence and stared at each other, not knowing what to do or say next.

'You all look baffled,' he said obviously, 'let me expand. Eqinox is one of those rare, but simple shapes where the radius and diameter are the same.'

The clump all opened their mouths, looked at each other, shook all their heads and still looked baffled.

'Eh?' said Ozzipolit7.

The autotranslator picked up the 'Eh?' cue and spoke, *'No translation is required. The statements were made in clear Squeithian and any attempt at translation would add to complexity and create obfuscation. Only the penultimate sentence may be confusing. By "Do you see?", Mycroft really means, "Do you understand?" or "Do you comprehend?" All else is simple.'*

The clump, as one, turned to the autotranslator and could well have lynched it, like brothers who are fighting will both turn on a well-meaning passing referee who attempts to split them, had not Mycroft raised his hand and continued.

'I wasn't sure, of course, until Smelt left the hole at Squelchpool and told the planet that the angle of the pipe had changed. Then I knew.' he puffed some mathematical symbol shapes in smoke from his smouldering netherwear.

'You are sounding very convincing, M;' said Polit46 eventually, 'but I don't think that any of us here have the slightest idea what you are rattling about.'

'Rattling? Rattling! Rattling indeed! I have just given you a simple and accurate answer to what may have happened to Ozzilland and you say that I am rattling. Well, if you won't listen, I will waste no more time on you.' The smoking netherwear in his pipe gave off some extra fumes for good effect. Both his heads shook and dangled in unmuted disgust at the obvious lack of intellect.

'I partly understand,' said Maecenas eventually and very bravely, 'but none of us have studied science and mathematics to the level that you have. Will you explain again using different words, just to make sure?'

M was still reddening and breathing ever more deeply. He could have exploded in a mess of yellow biomass at any moment, but he managed to hold himself together. He suffered idiots less than most, particularly when they invaded the Necropol Club; his hackles were further raised by the presence of females, despite his respect for Smelta's superior intellect.

'By the way, Maecenas, have you warned Kernal?' M asked.

'About what?'

'About the shape of Eqinox. I assumed he knew, being head of Defenss.'

'Huh.' said Smelt, raising his eyes GodwarD, 'you should know not to assume that Kernal knows anything, except marching. He probably doesn't even know that Ozzilland takes up seven of the seven-sided geoplatelets of which the outer surface of Eqinox consists.'

'I've often wondered,' retorted Maecenas, 'whether any other planets in the universe are made up of forty-seven convex septagons.'

'All of the other planets in our solar system are sphericalish, and would be spherical if they stopped spinning.' replied M, 'Only this planet is inhabited by intelligent beings. Only this planet emanates magic which can be funnelled through thaumas and WitcheS. I have calculated the probability of any planet being this shape to be approximately one in 506 623 120 463, which itself is an important count, but that is irrelevant to this matter.'

* * * * *

'This makes a difference that will need to be programmed into the base formula for the nanomanufacture of the multi-part hoverfloat autobridges.' said Nanotech329 to Kernal. 'Why weren't we told earlier about the true shape of Eqinox ?'

'Apparently, they assumed that I would know. I always thought it was round.'

'And flat?' enquired Nanotech329, cynically.

'Oh, no, not that.'

'But isn't it your job to know things like that?'

'It's my job to shoot Triseps when we are at war, not to understand advanced Convinciing Geometry. Sadly, we haven't had a war since I've been in the job.'

The computer interrupted.

'Cronus! Look at that.' said Nanotech329. 'We're going to have to start again from scratch. Well, almost. Trouble is, once you set nanomachines in action, they carry on working. Even when they run out of material to work on, they just sit and wait until they can finish their programmed task.'

'So does that mean that we have to start afresh?'

'Oh no! Oh, dear no! We will have to set up some soldiernanos that will kill the original nanomachines and replace them with a variant. We only need three more bridge sections to enable us to reach Ozzilland, but all the others need an extra one and a half degrees of pitch flexibility in the joint.'

Nanotech329 spoke some computerese like 'start again' at the computer and looked at the response. 'I thought we would get away with modifying, but now we've got to start again from the beginning. If you want to save time, prepare your Sqoddies to move the old part-built hoverfloat autobridge sections, so that we can restart from the same place.'

* * * * *

The callall berped for Sammowapolit7.

The image of Sammowaprecedent appeared, frenziedly waving all three arms. As always, the callall instantly translated for anyone listening. 'We're being invaded. We're not being invaded. You ought to know what's going on here. Do you know what is going on here? They're all over the place and then they're not there. Or even here. It's a crisis but it's all right because there isn't any problem, but I need your advice. We don't know what to do.'

'¿About are Prez rattling what you' *Prez, what are you rattling about* Sammowapolit7 turned both heads to the clump and looked at each Trisep with a different eye. He turned his front head back to the callall holocam,

'¿A an automed for have Phroyd seen test you' *Have you seen an automed for a Phroydtest?* 'As elgins losing sound though you you're your.' *You sound as though you're losing your elgins.*

'He's fine.' said M. 'It has started, exactly as I expected.' he reclined on his cowch, fully relaxed and puffed some netherwear smoke symbols into the air.

'The Gobblings,' continued Sammowaprecedent, perfectly translated by the callall, 'well, they're not Gobblings, not like those in Qontûm, they most resemble Dark Elves of Sammowan Poetlore. You remember the rhyming couplets,

> Then from those caverns dark and deep,
>> Where crawl our bones that never sleep -
> Came dark and creepy two leg'd things
>> That touched Sammowan hands - with rings
> Of rashes - caused by holy pique;
>> Took hold of breath and made them weak.
> So, soon each Elf-touched Trisep lost
>> All mind and life; thus paid the cost:
> At last to heave one troubled breath,
>> One last - with all such pain - in death.

> For none survived Contaigen long,
>> And like the swanns sang final song:
> Of kisses sour from creatures sweet:
>> Dark Elves I hope you'll never meet.
> For friendships will they make with will,
>> To make you think they wish no ill.
> But truth is rare in outward sign
>> Of whether vicious or benign,
> So when they come with gifts galore,
>> Take not, not once! Or evermore
> You'll find this action you'll regret
>> And hate and war will thus beget.

Of Elves so dark, beware, be warned,
  The little creatures quaintly horned:
Who build their nests beneath the fosse:
  A crenellated Ferrikross! [9]
Two legs not four, of heads, but one.
  Eyes: two not three and when all's done,
They're not as us, but copy HobB - so,
  Keep safe away and follow GoD.

'That's exactly what they're like, Dark Elves, and they're turning up all over Sammowa. And they're kissing every Trisep they come across; kissing them on the hand. They're so friendly. They're going into their homes and all drinking lactinfuse together. We have warned Sammowan Triseps on local e-commenters but the Dark Elves are just so friendly and generous that all warnings are being ignored.'

'Generous? Has there been any Contaigen?' asked Sammowapolit7 through the autotranslator.

'Contaigen? Do you mean itching? No, nothing; nothing at all. There's been no sign of it.'

'What did you mean by generous?'

'They're giving everyone beautiful Jewellery, all made of solid gelt. And their holes seem to appear anywhere, not just in the squelches as they are supposed to.

'What else is happening?'

'Nothing. Cate'aeddy is on her way, so all Eqinox will soon know. Oh, and I've asked Profmed to come. He will be here soon.'

'The Contaigen is very painful and unpleasant.' commented Smelt, 'but Profmed has now programmed his analysing sequences and new cure into all automeds, so there should not be any problem, but all Triseps who touch your Dark Elves must be checked by the automed as soon as possible.'

'Profmed said that already and we've bleated it, but they're ignoring it.'

Polit46's personal callall berped with the emergency tone.

'I heard that, I won't interrupt, good-bye.' said Sammowaprecedent.

'Good-bye, Prez.' responded Sammowapolit7.

Polit46 answered his callall. Even though he was Precedent of the Eqinox Government, he had not met all the precedents of hundreds of local governments of the smaller countries.

---

[9] *A Ferrikross, (Iron Cross), more correctly known as a Quadric Gammagram is remarkably similar to a the medal given by a bunch of marauding Riffs called the Third Reich. Remember that names of lucky charms, like spiritual entities, are always written with a capital letter at each end to keep out evil spirits from the centre of the name of the charm. Otherwise, the name of the lucky charm will have a seriously negative effect on the writer.*

A strange little Trisep wearing olde-fashioned glasses appeared. This was a very unusual sight since automeds have been able to cure all eye problems for hundreds of cycles. Only the most eccentric wear glasses, mostly for effect, except Mycroft, of course, who still wears a monocle.

The callall's infobox told him that his interlocutor was Makkaan, Precedent of that verdant corridor of land called the Green Aisle.

'Hello, Makkaan,'

'Hello. You should know what's happening here. Little green Gobblings with pointed ears, just like the tales of the Lepperdcorns. Lots of them everywhere. Everyone loves them. They're laughing like lepperds and telling their corny jokes; really living up to their name, so they are.' he ran out of breath and stopped. But only for a breath or two, 'I've just had Lynkern, Precedent of the Amorics on the callall and he said that he was enjoying being kissed by Faeries. The whole of Eqinox has gone mad, so it has.'

'Are they kissing you? Not the Faeries, the Lepperdcorns?' asked Maecenas from the background.

'To be sure. Now, how did you know a thing like that, I wonder? They come out of their little holes in the ground. Triseps see them and stop. They stop on yellow lines where they shouldn't park at all. *And* they stop on double yellow lines where they shouldn't park at all at all, just to talk to the little bipeds, the Lepperdcorns. I thought you might be interested, that's all.'

'Well, Makkaan, have they ... ' began Polit46.

'Don't call me that. Call me Dick.'

'Dick?'

'Yes, Dick, or Big Dick, if you prefer.'

'Big Dick?'

'When I was tiny, I dismantled things - anything - with a giant spanner called a Big Dick, so that's what they called me. I wanted to be called Spanner, but they wouldn't let me. Told me, so they did, that Spanner was another word for tool, which was a rude four letter word, so it was. I never knew what a tool was; they never told me. Said I was too young.'

'What's wrong with calling you Makkaan?'

'Most Triseps on the Green Aisle can't because of the high viscosity of their brains, but because I can, they called me Makkaan. My mother couldn't spell. Triseps from the Aisle who can't don't like those of us who can. Well, they think I am boasting by my name and punch me on the nose, so call me Big Dick instead.'

'OK Dick, now have the Triseps been warned about the danger of touching the Lepperdcorns?'

'Danger? There's no danger, so there isn't. They're very helpful and friendly little critters.'

M shook his front head in frustration at everybody else.

'And what would you know, even the nüns of the Triseptokatholicus Order, the black and white ones who always said that Lepperdcorns are from the evil HobB and not of GoD are talking to them and laughing at their corny jokes. I'm still laughing at the one that the Lepperdcorn told me about the Green Aisle Trisep, the shovel and the rubber boot! And have you heard the one about ... '

Lynkern

'Listen!' interrupted Maecenas, forcefully, 'we need to know whether any Triseps of the Green Aisle are listening to warnings at all.'

'Warnings? Warnings! We don't need warning at all. Not at all at all. Now we've met them, we *know* that we don't need to be warned. All the folk tales have turned out to be true. They're so friendly, so they are, too.'

'You said they kissed you and your nationals?'

'Kissed? How else would you expect a good Lepperdcorn to greet you?'

'Do they kiss everyone?'

'Yes, even the Triseptokatholicus nüns. They like being kissed most of all, so they repeatedly ask for more. A bit sex-starved, if you ask me.

Do you know, they don't even allow Sharen inside the walls of their tonsurages.'

'¿Tonsurages' asked Sammowapolit7, who had little experience of the customs of either Triseptokatholicus nüns or the Green Aisle. Actually, that isn't true. The truth is that he had never even heard of it.

'A tonsurage is a home for the nüns;' replied Big Dick, 'so called because it has trees round the edge and a skating rink in the middle for their religious observances.'

'What a quaint and obscure custom' said M, translating Sammowapolit7's retort.

'Listen carefully,' began Maecenas, 'it is vital that every Trisep visits an automed immediately. At least, every Trisep who has been in contact with a Lepperdcorn. If they do not, they will almost certainly die.'

'But the Lepperdcorns are not like Gobblings. Lepperdcorns are good, very good. They wouldn't hurt Triseps of the Green Aisle. Never in forty-seven million cycles, they wouldn't, to be sure.'

'Thank you for your assay of the situation. We will discuss and advise later. Good-bye.' said Maecenas who was a bit fed up with the conversation.

No sooner had Polit46 terminated the callall than it berped again. Kernal, still on Scotaisle was calling on an emergency code, using over-cipher.

'We're being overrun by Sprites.' said Kernal.

'Sprites?' Responded Polit46.

'Do you mean Holy Sprites?' asked Smelta, who still had her research in mind.

'Holy Sprites?' asked Kernal. The Necropol Club clump all looked at Smelta with both heads, waiting for an explanation.

'Yes. In the folio from Planet Three, there were three images of GoD, like the three thirds of a hole, inside, outside and hollow. They were an old Gobbling sitting on a cloud, a young, bearded Gobbling tied to a golejibbit and a bottle of brown fluid called Wholly Spirit, which I am sure means Holy Sprite. Actually, their multi-folio bears a remarkable resemblance to *The Folius.*

'It might be,' replied Kernal, 'but they're not bottles, they're like Gobblings, but not Gobblings. They are all wearing critter skins and are running round making little spherical houses out of the ice. They're very friendly. They aren't interfering with us or our work at all. They just keep offering their wives to keep us warm for the night. Nothing to worry about at all.'

'Have they kissed you?' asked Polit46.

'Kissed? Why? Well, yes, of course. How did you know? They're just like that, they love kissing. They're very friendly, you know.'

'Get rid of them.' ordered Polit46.

Sprite

'We've tried, but we can't. Their holes just appear like they did at the Conventionium. Such ingressions keep moving, so we can't catch them. I suppose we could shoot them, though, but the pretty little creatures are too much fun - and too sexy. They're not armed and it seems unfair to shoot them with our weapons.'

'But they *are* armed.' said Maecenas.

'No, they're not, we've checked very carefully.'

'You must get rid of them and treat all those who have been kissed.'

'The automeds have been taken out of stores and Vittler is sending them down to us after complaining that they insisted on keeping him alive. The first automed should arrive at any moment.'

Kernal explained that the hoverfloat autobridges needed to be rebuilt from scratch, and that Nanotech329 was doing it.

'Tell the Gobblings that ... ' began Mycroft.

'They aren't Gobblings,' interrupted Kernal, 'they are, well, I don't know what they are but they call themselves Esquimeaux.'

'Just a sub-tribe of the Sprites tribe of Gobblings.' said Mycroft, 'Now tell the Esquimeaux sub-tribe that they are to keep off Scotaisle or they will be shot on sight.'

'Sir,' replied Kernal, 'You know that all Defenss carry a micro-neutron gun pin attached to the uniform and use a psycho-trigger hairclip. However, we are not allowed to use them under the Helvetica War Crimes Treaty.'

'Yes you are.' replied M.

'No. I have learned the Treaty, it says, *Any Defenss or any other personnel who kill or injure with intent to kill any other where the injured party is unarmed and can be captured and there is no immediate danger to the former shall be guilty of a Type One War Crime.* So we cannot use our weapons against the Esquimeaux.'

'Yes you can.' said M. 'As Maecenas said, they *are* armed. Their weapons are their kisses. Whenever they kiss, they pass the Contaigen to you. That is their weapon which is as good as any gun or lethal chemical.'

'Well, it sounds good, but if you know the Treaty, you must also know that the Treaty says, *Punishment for the perpetrator of a Type One War Crime is to be kept alive in permanent excruciating pain for one whole lifetime on each count to a maximum of one thousand lifetimes. On completion of the sentence, pain shall be increased very slowly until the prisoner dies in screaming agony.* Can I have confirmed and witnessed assurances from Eqinox Government that I will not be accused later of War Crimes? There could be thousands of counts. I can't risk that.'

'You have that assurance.' replied M.

'No, I must have it from the planet's government.'

Polit46 looked at M, who nodded confirmation. 'I will give you such an undertaking.' he said.

'I don't want to be a pedant,' retorted Kernal, 'but you know what happened to the infamous Herrhess: he said he was acting under orders but he was still convicted and was kept alive in excruciating pain for six hundred and twenty lifetimes. I do **not** want the same to happen to me. I need a pulpleaf with this order confirmed and appended with a non-prosecution statement.'

'You don't need more than my word but ... ' began Polit46.

'You will get it immediately.' interrupted M.

Polit46 looked at M with a degree of uncertainty and annoyance that his authority was being usurped. 'Wait.' said Polit46 and set the callall to shush.

'You can't say that over my head, Mycroft.'

'It's your choice. This is the Gobblings' way of fighting a war. They have declared it by their actions. We have to respond with reasonable force. We have the right to declare a nogozone around any Defenss installation. That is what Kernal will be doing. When he reaches Ozzilland, we will all know what the Gobblings are really up to. Until then, we are at war.'

'Yes, but … ' began Polit46 and was interrupted.

'As I am Chief Security Adviser to the Eqinox Government, it will do as I recommend. It always does because the precision of my logic is unfaultable. I recommend this action now. You can convene the Government or you can take the decision yourself: you have the power. Not to do so will waste time and render us liable to earlier attack.'

Another callall berped. Maecenas answered it.

Polit46 hated to be overruled, it seemed, and this, effectively, was what was happening. He dropped his eyes to the floor and eventually nodded in agreement, knowing that he was cornered by the logic of M's argument.

M unset the shush on Polit46's callall and gestured to him to continue.

Polit46 hesitated and looked back and forth between his colleagues before continuing, 'You will have your confirmation as soon as it can be set up. Meanwhile, you must declare a defensive nogozone of at least 4747 lengths around your Scotaisle installation.'

'But that means total annihilation of everything in the area. We will have to destroy any Gobblings or Esquimeaux, even if they are friendly. Surely we can't do that.'

'No choice, Kernal. We have already had reports of Gobbling invasion in Sammowa and the Green Aisle as well as from you. It looks like Maecenas is taking another now from Yishrel. So this is your order. Tell the Esquimeaux to go. After that, shoot on sight. Good-bye.'

Polit46 terminated the callall. M had arranged for the pulpleaf to be prepared immediately. The Necropol Club was well equipped with such olde-fashioned facilities, for its members preferred it that way.

Polit46 joined the conversation between Maecenas and Yishrelprecedent.

' … kiss, kiss, kiss, all the time kissing hands and slobbering. Of course, we're sorting them out. We saw what happened to Smelt.' he said with his own breed of accent, 'We have set up nogozones throughout Yishrel, but we haven't started killing yet. We don't believe in killing, even the sprightly fun-loving, clown-coloured, Gobbling-like Kobolds, unless we have to, hence this callall. What do you suggest?'

'May I?' offered M and Polit46 gestured for him to continue.

'Hello Yippy, I see you are well. You are doing the right thing. The invasion is Eqinox-wide. I am recommending to set up nogozones everywhere and to shoot on sight. Clearly, their charm and kisses are their weapons, so they are not unarmed, and you will not be contravening the Helvetica War Crimes Treaty. Actually, that treaty was set up between Triseps without reference to Kobolds, so it shouldn't apply in any case.'

'Thank you for your advice. Our Defenss is equipped, efficient and effective. You know our history. We will defend to the last individual's deceasement. The Kobolds, the Underplanet Gobblings of this area, are too friendly and my people want to befriend them, but we know from our history that we must not mix. Did you see the quadric gammagram? We have foul experience of it and loathe it.'

'I saw it.' replied M. 'I know what it must mean to you and your kind. Keep the Kobolds down. They have declared war by attacking us. Good luck.'

Old Troll

As soon as he terminated the callall, another emergency callall came in for Polit46 from Walled Faience, the great country Sunriseward of Squeith where the yellow race lived (they were actually bright pink, just *called* the yellow race); one third of all Triseps on Eqinox. The clump all looked at each other with both heads. Walled Faience was known for being independent of the Eqinox Government; so exclusive were they that a great wall surrounded the entire country.

M raised his eyebrows and said before Polit46 answered, 'If Walled Faienceprecedent is making an emergency callall to you, there must be something pretty drastic happening.

'We are being overrun by Trolls, all over the country … ' he began and told the same story.

And another call, speaking in Pijin, 'Dis am de Pressid Idi Dada, Ah Meen am wi dat bobble hat on an wi dem Urchins in Zimgululland an ahl we am got wi dem kis-kis lots an lots for dey luv us an ah dun giv dem medals, no sur, dem am got de voodoo off dem antsisters an it dey do giv dem bubble-bubble on me han of kis-kis.'

The autotranslator jumped up and then retired again, not sure whether this needed translating or not. Even though the gathered clump all exchanged puzzled glances, nobody said the prompting query, *Eh?* so it remained silent.

And another callall came in from Lynkern, Precedent of the Amorics, 'Say, we've got lots of Faeries in the Amorics. They're even more amorous than we are. Some of us in Congress here are worried about us getting the lethal Contaigen from these Faeries. What about aids? Are there any aids you can suggest to stop us getting the Contaigen? Has Profmed looked at aids yet?'

And so details of a love-invasion continued to be received from all over Eqinox.

Chapter 8   Let Battle Commence

'Well, that accounts for the seven tribes.' said Mycroft privately to Maecenas after the others had retired for the night. Smelt had stayed over in the Necropol because he wanted to go to sleep and Smelta wanted to practise replication techniques with Grounsell.

Maecenas had written out the names and locations of the seven tribes as they had shown themselves:

The Seven Tribes of Gobblings:

	Tribe	*Location*
0	Hobbimps	Squeith
1	Dark Elves	Sammowa & Ozzilland
2	Faeries	Amorics
3	Kobolds	Yishrel
4	Lepperdcorns	Green Aisle
5	Sprites or Esquimeaux	Scotaisle & Antipole
6	Trolls	Walled Faience
7	Urchins	Zimgululland

'You know,' commented Maecenas in passing, 'it's funny how some add up such lists to be more than seven, actually counting zero as a positive integer: a number; but if it is zero, then it is nothing. If it is nothing, then it doesn't count and thus seven plus zero remains seven.'

'I know,' laughed M heartily blowing a netherwear smoke-ring full of Sigmata: Σ, like those which arithmates sometimes discover emblazoned on their hands, feet and foreheads, 'strange how some otherwise intelligent Triseps can't grasp the most simple of arithmetical concepts.'

'They don't even realise that you can have as many zero-numbered items in a list as you like, and it still only adds up to seven. Aren't they odd?'

Maecenas chuckled and then - for some strange reason - couldn't stop laughing at this reminder of the difficulties of the less-bright and nearly fell off his armcowch in a fit of mirth.

'Perhaps they should integrate more!' added M, multiplying the negative division of his unequalled statement, 'but I wouldn't denigrate the unfortunate arithmates' state.'

Maecenas fell off, so that dying with laughter nearly killed him.

* * * * *

There was a party going on in an olde-fashioned warehouse just outside the old Speed-Route Ring, an olde-fashioned road circumscribing the Squeithian capital, Selondre. Actually, it wasn't a party it was more of a raving orgy.

Everybody was there; well, almost everybody. Except those staying at the Necropol Club and a few other old fogies.

What better excuse for a party than imminent war, seemed to be the consensus of opinion. Most were dancing to the most up-to-date autoerotic nanogroove.

The e-commenter said that Cate'aeddy had changed destination and landed in the giant walled country of Faience, where had appeared Trolls with their black pointed faces, long dangling arms, long dark hair and a lolling gait that reminded more of primitiveness than civilisation. She was appearing in a giant holoquadrant in one corner of the old warehouse, although what she was saying was no longer news. In any case, she could hardly be heard above the flickering boom-clang of the autoerotic nanogroove.

Most of the Triseps kept one of their eyes trained on Cate'aeddy's holoquadrant checking for further news; another on their drinks in case anybody pinched them: a common problem as most were liberally sprinkled with intoxicants of varying legality, strength and availability.

Smelta had contrived never to admit to Smelt that she was a secret party fiend. She wouldn't have admitted it to Grounsell either had it not been for a pirate e-commenter holoquadrant giving details of the illegal raving orgy.

She didn't need to worry about the lorr as the illegal raving orgies, where and when they occurred, were public knowledge within a very few breaths of the location being decided upon by the less than honest rave hosts. She did, however, need to worry about her partners' views: they would, outwardly, have scorned her participation.

At times of trouble in particular, virtually everyone joined in. Policing officials right up to Lorranordå at the top all enjoyed participating, so everyone was happy and the illegal raving orgies became commonplace.

All were happy, that is, except the spare Triseps who were inevitably conceived at these events. These, for a complex reason connected with Natural Genetics were always girls. The first child of a Trisep male was always a son; the second was sometimes a son. Except for rare accidental deviations, or to replace an infertile male, all subsequent offspring were daughters.

There was not a case in recorded history of a Trisep having more than a single offspring at a time, although it did happen in some other critters.

So the reason why each herd had so many wives was simple: there was too much extra-nuptial replication practice.

But some of it wasn't practice. Some of it was for real.

* * * * *

The next morning, slimmer Triseps had a hangover. Fatter Triseps still had an overhang. They all had headaches except those who stayed at the Necropol Club.

'Seems like Chequemate, mate.' Ozzipolit7 said as an opening remark to the reconvened meeting in the Necropol Club foyer. 'I've been watching Cate'aeddy on the e-commenter. She's gone to Walled Faience; I didn't think the yellow people would let her in, but she's there and Precedent Chi Nar Mao is talking to her.'

'Equinox gone has of mad the whole.' Sammowapolit7 remarked.

The whole of Eqinox has gone mad. The autotranslator responded

'The whole of Eqinox has been invaded.' Smelt retorted.

'Ah, but not quite,' said Maecenas, 'have you noticed that Squeith hasn't been invaded by the Gobblings? Selondre should be overrun by now.'

'Not so;' said M, 'the Hobbimps under Squeith are the most intelligent of the Gobbling tribes of the Underplanet and are controlling the others. They already have Bodgitt and they know that we know of their devious kissing tactics, so they wouldn't work here. They also know that we know that they have been monitoring our e-commenters, including ENN.' he puffed some weaponry from the netherwear smouldering in his pipe.

'Deduce therefore my friends,' he continued, 'that they would expect us to be prepared. An invasion by them, they rightly think, would be anticipated and repelled with some force and certain precision. They wish to avoid casualties. From their point of view, why should they fight us when the other tribes can fight first.'

'Surely, if they had surprised Squeith, they would have had the advantage, particularly as Defenss are out of the country at the moment.' argued Polit46.

'Again, not true.' said M, 'This way, the Hobbimps win either way. You see, if the other tribes win in the rest of Eqinox, the Hobbimps will order them to overrun Squeith too, so they win without casualties.'

'But what if they lose?'

'Ah, if the Gobblings lose the rest of Eqinox, the Hobbimps could claim that they were not involved in the fighting and so have a chance of winning the peace and gaining some surface land that way; if not land, certainly credibility. So by showing a pretence of integrity, their overall credibility remains intact. Additionally, if the other Underplanet tribes are effectively annihilated, the Hobbimps will be able to colonise much of the space left clear under the rest of Eqinox.'

'So are you saying that the Hobbimps can't lose, whether the Gobblings win or lose the war?' Maecenas suggested.

'We're not at war,' said Polit46, 'or are we now?'

'Possibly and possibly not;' said M, 'and so the solution is obvious.'

The whole clump nodded in agreement, but not all understood. Only Ozzipolit7 admitted confusion, 'I don't understand the problem, so how can you have worked out the solution?'

'The puzzle is,' sighed M in frustration and waited for them all to catch up mentally, 'is that Eqinox is being invaded by seven of the seven tribes of Gobblings of the Underplanet.'

'What do you mean, seven of the seven? You using that magic maths again, mate?' suggested Ozzipolit7.

'Not quite magic, just honest.' replied M, 'the zeroth, Hobbimp tribe do not count on this invasion occasion.'

'We don't know it's an invasion, mate. They just want to be friendly.' continued Ozzipolit7.

'About a one percent chance of that, I think.' said M,

'So tell us the solution, mate.'

'That would not be prudent; not yet, anyway. If you have worked it out for yourself, remain silent.'

The clump looked at M, seriously puzzled.

'Why?' asked Ozzipolit7.

'Because walls have ears. And so do floors, especially if there is a possibility of Hobbimps listening through them. They could have linked into our computing and callall network, too, so communication by that method, or even by the autodiary, is not necessarily safe.'

Nobody dared speak. Glances were rapidly exchanged between front and back heads. Mouths opened several times to speak, but closed again after the floor threatened, not to mention the walls.

M signalled Steward and mimed an olde-fashioned writing pad of pulpleaves and a quill. Whereas the others had been taught about handwriting only as a matter of historical interest, Mycroft was fluent.

* * * * *

Cate'aeddy appeared on a holoquadrant. She was trying to report a very difficult battle.

The Trolls of Walled Faience were appearing from holes in the ground, running from one Trisep to another in Tournäment Square behind her and trying to kiss everyone.

'Trolls are pretty little creatures,' the infobox said 'if you like that sort of thing, with levva-like, pointed black faces. Their bodies are covered in long black hair. Sometimes they almost walk on their two long and dangling arms, which they also use to swing from branch to branch in trees. You also notice their protruding red nether regions. They have a particular penchant for bananas and are easily captured if offered one.'

'None of the trolls have tried to kiss me yet,' said Cate'aeddy. 'although whether that is because I am not yellow or because I'm ugly, I don't know.' As she was transmitting to the world, she was unable to get a response to her claim of ugliness, but had she had one, it would have been a contradiction, for all thought she was delicious. She only paused for a breath, 'They are quite pretty in their own way and very friendly. Too friendly, in fact. The precedent, Chi Nar Mao, whose name means *Rod of Iron* has ordered his people to stop the kisses and ignore or capture.' she looked round at the battle raging in the square behind her. 'To the untrained eye, this is not a battle, but a tug of love between the unmatched marriage partners of hundreds of pairs of disparate creatures. But far more is going on behind the scenes. Look at this, for instance.'

She opened a third holoquadrant showing Trisep thaumas flying their besom brooms, a sight to behold. One of them was already a fully qualified WitcH and she was just depositing her septics into a storage tank.

'I have never seen thaumas or WitcheS before, because they only appear in public in times of the deepest distress and emergency. I always imagined they would fly olde-fashioned besoms. I was wrong. These are not ordinary besoms, but triple besoms arranged, surprisingly, in a sort of seven-sided triangle, and they seem to be armed and firing something.' said Cate'aeddy. Suddenly she peered more closely and with a surprising lack of embarrassment, 'There seems to be one WitcH depositing her septics into a septic tank. For the uninitiated, septics are seven-sided, cube-shaped droppings. Well, in this job, you see something new every day!'

The Summit clump at the Necropol Club were watching. 'Faience does not have a good local Defenss force,' commented M, 'so their WitcheS and thaumas will make a lot of difference there. Unlike the Faerie Gobblings under the Amorics, Trolls in Walled Faience cannot fly.'

Cate'aeddy ducked on the e-commenter holoquadrant as a twig flew past her ear. So did the Necropol Summit clump. 'Never got used to them holograms,' said Ozzipolit7, 'get me every time, they do. Hey, M, can you tell Steward I think I need a drop more four-ecks.'

On the holoquadrant showing WitcheS, the triple besoms were everywhere and firing at the Trolls. 'I can see now,' said Cate'aeddy in the casual way that she always reported wars carrying on around her, 'the ordinary thaumas are wearing white pointed hats with bobbles on, but the WitcheS are the ones wearing black pointed hats with tassels. I wonder if it's the hats that give them their power? They're firing twigs from their besoms at the Trolls and the Trolls are returning their fire by throwing stones and trying to knock their hats off. But no, the triple-besoms are returning fire automatically, it seems, and flying too high for the stones. Just before each twig is fired from the besom, the WitcH's hat's tassel stands up on end three times and points at her target.'

She paused her commentary as she was surrounded by a ring of Trolls all holding hands and dancing round her. 'As you can see, the Trolls are all friendly, very friendly indeed. A bit too friendly, really. Perhaps one of you trolls can tell me ...'

A couple of thaumas and a WitcH swooped down towards Cate'aeddy and fired twigs at the Trolls, killing two of them instantly and sending the others scuttling.

'Well, you saw that attack,' said Cate'aeddy, 'and as I look down at the bodies of the dead Trolls, I can't help feeling a mixed sense of, of, er, oh!'

A new, wider angled holoquadrant showed a view of the Trolls lying at her hooves.

'Well, as you can see, they were only shot a few breaths ago but now they seem to be decomposing already. No, not decomposing, more sinking. Yes, they're sinking into the ground. The ground seems to be swallowing them. One is lying on the surface soil and one, as you can see, is on stone, but they both just seem to be, sort of, well, just melting into the ground. I've never seen anything like this in my life. Where are they going?'

She looked around as though searching for their remains, 'They have almost gone now, in only about ten short breaths. In all my days of reporting, I have never witnessed anything like this necro-vaporation. I have studied all the histories of creatures on Eqinox and there is no record of anything like this. This is new to our knowledge, and remember you saw it first here on ENN.'

Cate'aeddy watched the necro-vaporation of half a dozen black lolling trolls before speaking again.

* * * * *

'What *is* the solution?' Smelt asked Mycroft.

M opened his mouth to reply but was interrupted by a berp from Smelt's callall.

Smelt answered the confidential shushcallall on his personal unit. The others were excluded by the anti-sound. 'I need to talk to you.' said Grounsella.

'What, *now?*'

'Yes, now. Now, now, now! *Right now.*'

'Yes, yes, yes! I've got the message. But I'm in the middle of an important war meeting. What is it?'

'A problem. A big problem. It's confidential.'

'You're on shush, tell me now.'

'No, it's got to be face to face.'

'OK, but … '

Polit46's callall berped an emergency code. Kernal, on Scotaisle was calling using over-cipher.

'I'll callall you as soon as I'm free. I must rejoin the meeting now, there's an emergency callall coming in.

'Make it soon. Very soon.'

Polit46 answered the Kernal.

'Sprites everywhere. We're still building the bridge. Shoot sprites and they won't die. They just seem to walk through the fire of the micro-neutron guns. We need reinforcements. We need Trisepitarian help for our injuries. We need the Yellow Cross Organisation of Helvetica to bring in more bandages and nurses. It's not just the Esquimeaux any more, there are other Sprites without the animal skins and who don't build little spherical ice houses. We can't stop them kissing and now most of the Sqoddies have contracted the Contaigen too, we think.'

'At least it's curable now,' said Polit46.

'The automeds don't recognise it, it must be different.'

'Different? Have you talked to Profmed yet?' asked M.

'He said that it can't be different. He said that the automeds must be malfunctioning. He said that he has updated all automeds to include the Contaigen and automatically report to him any previously undiagnosed disease.'

'When were the automeds last tested?'

'Vittler took them from stores and tested them on himself. He complained that they wouldn't help him commit decession and wanted to give him a Phroydtest.'

'Obviously they weren't updated while they were in stores and switched off. Vittler should have done that.'

'OK, you've solved one problem. Now, how can we stop the Sprites?' asked Kernal.

'Have you tried auto-lasers?' suggested Mycroft.

'They're olde-fashioned. We haven't used them for generations. We wouldn't even know how to operate them.'

'You must get them out of stores and use them for the moment. You must maintain your nogozone. I've got some other ideas you will have later.'

M terminated the callall and said to Polit46, 'I want all the thaumas and WitcheS in Squeith to assemble at the Conventionium as soon as possible.'

* * * * *

'How many auto-lasers can you supply?' Kernal asked Vittler.

'You don't want me, do you. You're not interested in me, are you. I suppose I can look for you if you insist. How many do you want?'

'All you've got. And have you got any holo-video-manuals for training?'

'Been using one myself. Trying to modify one.'

'Why?'

''Cos they're designed not to shoot the operator.'

'You sound depressed again.'

'So would you be if nobody wanted you. You've got a useful job to do. Mine could be done by machines. I'm only used to make something for me to do. I would jump off the top of the store-tower here, but it's surrounded by spunj-squelches, so I can't even break an arm. Even Vittlera said she doesn't want me to go home because she says I depress her. Actually it is the other way round, now that she's become a mother-in-lorr herself. And another thing … '

'That's enough! Can you provide training or not?'

'I can train you if I have to.'

'No, I mean, can you provide me with holo-video manuals for training?'

'If I have to. That proves it, you see, nobody wants me, only my vittles.' replied Vittler.

'Go away. Go, go, go! Go away! Get lost! Leave me alone. Clear off.' interrupted Kernal.

'I've got the message. Even you hate me, Kernal!' Vittler terminated the callall.

'Not you, you twit, I was talking to the Esquimeaux. Hello? Hello? Damn. He's gone.'

* * * * *

Cate'aeddy arrived at The Septagon, the seven-sided seat of local government at Launder, capital city of the Amorics, and where you get the washing done. 'Mr. Precedent Lynkern, Sir, I can't see any problems here at present, but I understand you've spoken to Eqinox Precedent, Polit46 about some problems with Faeries in your country.'

Young Troll

'Yes, Cate'aeddy, Sir, we wants aids.'

'Aids?'

'Yes, Sirree, we wants aids to rid ourselves of them Faeries. This country was a good and wonderful place to live until the Faeries came along and what we want now are some practical aids from somewhere to get rid of them.'

'What sort of aids?'

'Anything. Micro-neutron guns don't work, so new types of guns. Most Triseps don't believe the propaganda, so better training for

Triseps that really works; barriers that will keep out the Faeries.' Lynkern set his front head into his three hands. 'Our Defenss have run out of ideas. We've given aid to other countries when they were poor and needed it. In fact, we've given aids to everybody else and now we need some aids for ourselves to get rid of the Faeries. We've had everything here, Granny Abuse, Fobofobia, Second-Head-Collapse-Syndrome, Mother-in-lorr Naggits, Husband beating, Feminism and now we've got Faerie Contaigen!

'Did you see the ENN e-commenter report from Faience?' suggested Cate'aeddy.

'Of course, of course.' he looked up and raised his front eyes GodwarD. 'And I got my mother-in-lorr to organise thaumas and WitcheS from all over the country, ready to attack.' He shrugged and dropped his head again.

'And what happened?'

'Nothing happened. The Faeries didn't like being shot at with twigs from the besoms. They can fly, you know. That's the main difference between our Faeries and the Trolls in Walled Faience. All they did was fly up, avoid the twigs and start attacking with their kisses again.'

'What do you propose to do next?'

'We have a plan. Call it a secret battle plan if you will, but we are still open to any advice from any quarter to overcome these bright, merry, jolly, gay and happy Faeries.' The Precedent rocked back onto the back two legs of his cowch.

A pretty white creature like a Gobbling but with a pair of double white wings and a long white dress landed at the open window, chirped twice like a bird and dived at Precedent Lynkern.

The Precedent lost his balance and fell back off his cowch and flailed around on his back with his hooves in the air and screamed a long and bloodcurdling, 'Aaaagh!'

Cate'aeddy was standing opposite his desk and ran round it to pick him up. The Faerie attacked from the other side and kissed him all over and managed a few kisses on Cate'aeddy's hands.

The door to the Precedent's office flew open and a pair of Secret Service security Triseps ran in. It was obvious what was happening, a woman and a Faerie were attacking Precedent Lynkern.

The first to enter looked at Cate'aeddy and the Faerie and mentally shot them, thus triggering the psycho-trigger hairclip above his ears. The micro-neutron gun pinned to his uniform fired a lethal round straight at the Faerie and a second at Cate'aeddy. The Faerie flew up out of the way, cackled a bewitching laugh, turned round three times and flew out of the window.

Cate'aeddy was hit in the back and rolled forward over the Precedent, landing on her back behind him, legs and hooves in the air. She curdled a yell.

They picked up Lynkern and helped him back to his cowch.

'I sure thought I was done for,' said Lynkern, 'and I sure don't want Deputy Effdeearr to take over as Precedent of the Amorics.'

A dozen or more other female aides appeared at the door, and a couple ran across and dropped to their knees to pick up Cate'aeddy. They had seen the attack on e-commenters. Being American Precedential aides, they were all quite used to being on their knees in the office of the Precedent.

They helped her to stagger to a cowch, 'G-g-g-good j-j-job I was wearing my-my-my-my-my er-er-er anti-f-f-flack sh-sh-shield,' she stuttered.

Cate'aeddy's image was still being bleated through her personal autofollowing holocam to the whole of Eqinox's e-commenters.

* * * * *

The meeting in the Necropol Club foyer was reconvened and other ambassadors invited, including Amoricspolit7, Yishrelpolit7, Faiencepolit7 and Zimgulupolit7.

Maecenas chaired the meeting and immediately introduced and handed over to Mycroft.

'I am delighted that at long last, all Eqinox will listen to logic and …
'

Smelt's callall berped. He set it to shush. He was right. 'Hello, Grounsella, I *will* get back to you soon, but this meeting's important; it is vital to international security.'

'So is this. We *must* meet. I've got to talk to you. I've got to tell you.'

'You're pregnant, aren't you?' Smelt looked around, embarrassed, even though he knew that the anti-sound stopped them from hearing either his words or hers. All eyes were on him for interrupting the meeting with an obviously personal callall.

'Yes. You know it's not done for a herd leader to get pregnant. Sorry. It must have happened at the very moment when Ozzilland disappeared. I thought the earth seemed to move. What happened?'

'I must have forgotten to take the morning-after-pill-for-men.' Said Smelt, sounding apologetic and wishing himself more competent.

'Wonderful! And now look how that's left me. It's all right for you men, you don't have all the problems or the worry of it all.'

'Don't you believe it, we most certainly do.' Smelt replied.

He looked guiltily at Smelta who had been watching him with some degree of suspicion. She knew who he was speaking to and he wondered if she guessed why. Females were better at the intuition bit than males. No, he decided, she couldn't possibly guess, but he did need to *look* a bit more innocent.

'Does Grounsell know?'

'Not yet, I had to tell you first.'

'So what happens next?'

'Grounselldort, presumably.' she corrected herself, 'No, Smeltdort, sorry.'

'Most likely, but what must I do now? This is my first time outside my own herd.'

'Do? What do you mean, do? It's too late now. Abortion's been banned for centuries. You should have seen automed the next day and taken the male-morning-after pill. That would have been the most effective, then I would not have become pregnant.'

'We were busy. So much was happening.'

'That's a fact it was.' responded Grounsella.

Maecenas summoned Smelt rather forcefully. 'This is an *important* meeting.'

'I'll have to meet you later, Maecenas is calling the meeting to order, and there's much to discuss.'

Grounsella gave him a filthy look, 'You males, you're all the same. You never care about the *really* important things, do you?' She terminated the callall.

Smelt looked around, embarrassed. He looked at Smelta and blushed a bright shade of blood yellow. 'Sorry.' he said weakly and shrunk into his armcowch, pretending to be an invisible part of the scenery.

'They've still not attacked.' said Polit46 to the Summit, trying to break the ice.

The new delegates looked at each other, puzzled by such a comment and pretending not to notice the obvious tension between Smelt and his herd leader.

Maecenas broke the silence, 'To clarify, Polit46 means that the Hobbimps - that is, the Gobblings under Squeith - are the only one of the seven tribes not to have attacked the Triseps on the surface above them. Although we don't know why, we do have our suspicions. Perhaps Mycroft would like to speak now.'

Mycroft looked round. He was not used to addressing so many senior politicians, but he was neither deterred nor affected in the logic of his flow.

M took a long puff on the netherwear in his pipe and blew a few boolean symbol-shaped smoke puffs to ensure he started in the right place, 'I still haven't eliminated the possible reasons for the disappearance of Ozzilland, but it appears that we and the Gobblings are blaming each other. There is a less than evens chance that Gobblings were responsible, but at present at least, they are holding us liable and assuming that we made a pre-emptive strike. There is a tiny and diminishing possibility that they are right and somebody in Ozzilland managed to take some undetectable premature action but I think it more an improbability than a possibility. We probably won't know until Kernal reaches Ozzilland - or until he reaches where Ozzilland was.'

M looked at each of the assembled Summit clump in turn before continuing.

'I have a plan of action proposed, but first I suggest that we should talk to Quax on the private callall line. Let me explain.'

M explained his requirement in detail and Polit46 arranged for the connection to be made through to the foyer of the Necropol Club.

'Hello Quax,' began Polit46, 'I trust that you will not be offended by this communication.'

'That depends on your statements and requests.'

'We believe that you are honourable, as we are, and that we can discuss Eqinox -wide matters with you.'

'You can try. We know that we are honourable, but we are not so sure about you or your intentions.' replied Quax with a curious combination of hesitancy and firm purpose.

'You know that we have sent a Defenss force to Scotaisle in order to build a giant hoverfloat autobridge to Ozzilland. We believed that this was with your blessing.'

'It was in part, so long as you kept us informed. You did not, so we had to do our own researches and collect intelligence on your activities.'

'Unfortunately,' said Polit46, 'the Gobblings who appeared at Scotaisle near Antipole have been most unhelpful and interrupted our Defenss preparations for building a bridge to where Ozzilland is or was.'

'Why are you telling me this?'

'We would ask you with the greatest of honour and would be most grateful if you would call off the Sprites who are attacking us there.'

'As you are fully aware,' replied Quax, 'the Sprites are a different tribe and we have no control over them at all. Each tribe has its own leaders and I, as a Hobbimp, have no control whatsoever over the Sprites.'

'But I presume that you must surely be in contact with their leader. Is that not so?'

'Yes and no. Yes, I can contact their leader, but it will take time because a message has to be taken physically, the olde-fashioned way. But no, we neither have nor need your advanced automatic callall systems. Our societies are organised without such a need.'

'I understand. How long will it take for a message to be passed?'

'Depends.'

'Upon?'

'Movements.' replied Quax as unhelpfully as possible.

'What movements?' asked Polit46.

We could be lucky and have a message in a few hundred breaths or it could take several of your days. It depends who is moving and how well the relay is working.'

'Will you please pass a message asking them not to interfere as a matter of urgency?'

'I will pass such a message and add my recommendation.'

'What will your recommendation be?'

'That depends on what you offer or how well I trust you.'

'What would you like us to offer?'

'Just a promise that you will not attack us, the Hobbimps under Squeith.'

'At present we have no reason to attack you.' replied Polit46.

'That does not answer the question. Will you promise not to attack us?'

'We will not attack you without good reason.'

'Reasons are excuses. Will you promise not to attack us?'

'So long as we are not provoked, you have my promise that we, the country of Squeith and the Eqinox Government, will not attack the Hobbimps.'

'Thank you. Why must you be so obtuse in your answers? I will try to ensure that your operation on Scotaisle is not interrupted further.'

'Thank you.'

'Are there any other matters?'

'Not at present unless you wish to discuss the rest of the world.'

'No, we have no control. The rest of the world is of no interest to us.'

'We will talk again. We wish you well.' said Polit46.

'We also wish you well. Good-bye.' replied Quax and terminated the callall.

'Are you satisfied with that?' Polit46 asked Mycroft.

'Exactly as anticipated,' said M, 'now, perhaps, we should count to forty-seven.'

Everyone looked puzzled. Nobody admitted to it but each of the delegates silently counted to forty-seven in the ensuing inevitable silence.

Exactly on the count of forty-seven, the callall berped.

Kernal appeared.

'Good to see you, Kernal,' said Polit46, 'have you some news?'

'Yes. You should know that the Sprites are retreating. No they aren't, they have already retreated. Suddenly, they started walking backwards away from us and waving as if they were saying *good-bye.* Do you know what is happening? We saw the e-commenter with Cate'aeddy in The Septagon, and another holoquadrant is still showing attacks in Walled Faience. Why have the Sprites suddenly left us alone?'

'Well, it's because … ' Polit46 began but was interrupted by M.

'Uh, uh!' said M and waggled a reproving finger.

'Perhaps,' said Maecenas, helpfully, 'the Sprites have guessed the usefulness of your work and decided to let you continue in peace. That is our best theory.'

'Thank you,' said Kernal, 'and the hoverfloat autobridge is growing to schedule. I have nothing further to report, except the problem with the automeds was that they were not updated when in storage, as you surmised. Profmed has now updated them and my Sqoddies are recovering. Report ends.'

Polit46 terminated the callall.

'Now we sit and wait' said Mycroft, relaxing back on his cowch and blowing smoke bubbles.

* * * * *

Maecenas raised his hand for silence as everyone seemed to speak at once. 'I know that you are all being updated constantly by your respective governments. Perhaps we can start with a report from Zimgululland.'

Zimgulupolit7 watched the eyes of his audience for a few breaths and began, 'Dem Urchin in dem Zimgululland wi dat bobble hat cum kiskis in dem Trisep han an mah Pressid Idi Dada, Ah Meen he do go big WitcH daktari an go um voodoo wi dat besom for mu ka Urchin dey gogo per hap fro pon face to unnergro.'

The autotranslator got up and hesitated. It was sure that there were some present who did not understand Pijin, but eventually decided to wait for the cue password.

'What did he say?' Amoricspolit7 asked, undiplomatically.

'Eh?' said Zimgulupolit7.

The autotranslator picked up its cue, albeit from the wrong Trisep and in the wrong context, *'The Urchins in Zimgululland with the bobble hats on are coming to the surface to keep kissing Triseps. My Precedent, Idi Dada Ah Meen has found an important WitcH-doctor who does voodoo with a besom broom and who will hopefully make the Urchins go away from the face of the earth to their underground homes.'* its programming ensured that it would henceforward translate Pijin for the rest of the meeting without a prompt.

'¿Performs the voodoo who' asked Sammowapolit7, but the autotranslator didn't think the sentence worth translating.

'It dem big WitcH daktari of cos.' *'It is the senior WitcH-doctors, of course.'*

'How do they qualify?' asked Maecenas.

'Ah, dem bon wuns dem am de big dada wi dem sevn mama her an him het sevn baba mama cum.' *'Ah, they are the males born in cycles when there are seven females in a herd and also after they have fathered seven daughters.'*

'Of course!' exclaimed Maecenas, 'That make them more powerful than WitcheS, surely, as here in Squeith, where such become WizardS[10] with but a minor generational variation in the conditions.'

'Ah, dem it do dat is em so.' *'Yes.'*

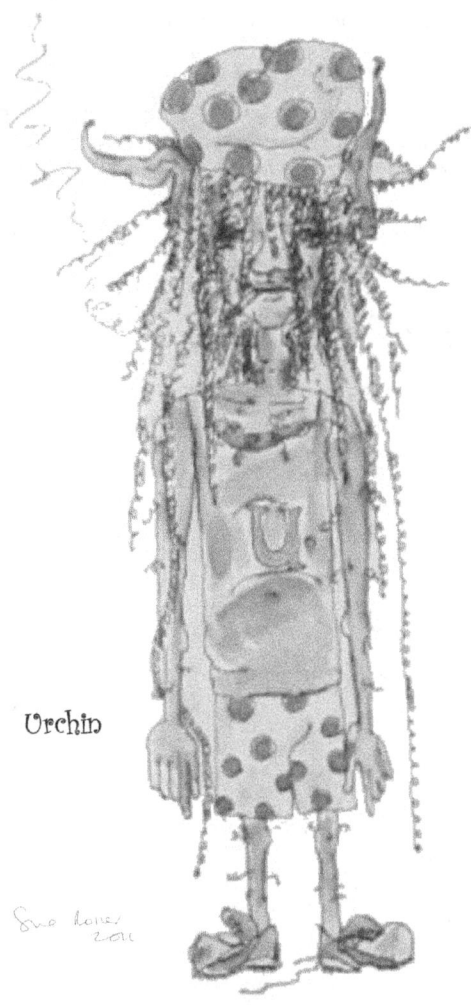

Urchin

'Is em so Amorics jus?' *'Are you having the same problem with Faeries in the Amorics as we are having with Urchins in Zimgululland?'*

---

[10]   *WizarD and WizardS are special words, like names of lucky charms and are always written with a capital letter at each end to keep out evil spirits from the centre of the name. If written otherwise, the word will have a seriously negative effect on the writer.*

'Sure am. We don't go too hot on them Faeries. That's good, very good. Thank you, Sirree, it don't help at all for me;' began Amoricspolit7, typically chewing on a revolting piece of Coker Tree Gum and swigging a can of Coker sap, 'we still got gay Faeries trying to kiss every Trisep they meets. At present time, we've got no hope of dealing with them. We are a very tolerant nation and have a history of letting ethnic groups settle. But the Faeries are a different matter. We don't want them interfering with us or our lifestyle. We are settled and staid. They are a bit too bright and gay and merry for our liking. We again ask for your help in removing Faeries from the Amorics.'

The autotranslator waited to translate because of the strange laid-back kind of drawl that wasn't really Squeithian, but nobody bothered to ask, so it got depressed with not feeling wanted and returned to its corner. *'Trouble is,'* it muttered to itself, *'is that Squeith and the Amorics are two countries separated by a common language. Everyone knows they mean different things but no-one is ever prepared to admit that they don't understand the other. Stupid Triseps.'* He felt smug, knowing that only autotranslators *really* know everything.

Smelt's personal callall berped. It was Grounsella, again, much to the increasing chagrin of Smelta.

Chapter 9   The Double Cowch

Gerry was reading some of the dirty magazines left behind by Bodgitt in the builder's hut by the Dagoba in Eden Garden, formerly known as Squelchpool.

No he wasn't. He wasn't reading them, at least. He was looking at the pictures of naked Sharens.

He was expecting Gerrya, his herd leader to arrive at any moment, so he was positioned to both see Gerrya coming and hide the dirty magazines very quickly. The doors were locked against any possible attack from Gobblings, or Hobbimps as they were in this area. Of course, there was no attack. Hobbimps were not attacking. Hobbimps were not even appearing.

Suddenly the building control computer in front of him started to bleep loudly. At 100 breaths to completion (2209 breaths in base 10) and an instruction to call the Eqinox Government for senior politicians to come and open the building. Actually, he didn't have to bother because the autodiary system told everyone to go to the grand opening anyway. At least, that was the theory.

Gerry went to find one of his little blue plaques. There it was. Now all he had to do was attach it to the building. He couldn't hammer a nail into it because it would be rejected with the self-repair system built into the nanomachines which made the Dagoba in the first place.

With no respect for Bodgitt, he stood on the side platform of his moovacar hovering at about five hites and glued his big blue plaque to the wall. It bore the legend, *Gerry Built* in large white letters. He stood back and looked at it proudly. Then he entered through the great entrance doors to inspect and admire the inside of his handiwork. Or more correctly, the handiwork of the computers with a little help from Bodgitt and some late supervision from Gerry. Actually, Gerry's help had been really rather more oversight than supervision.

But tradition must always be observed and tradition says that whoever completes a piece of work will take the credit, not those who do not bother (for whatever reason) to finish it.

Back on the ground, Gerry admired the handiwork of his well-placed plaque.

'I really must invent a nail with soldiernanos on the tip so it stays in place and doesn't get pushed out by the building repairing itself.' guttered Gerry aloud but to himself as there was nobody there to listen.

'Do soldiernanos fight?' asked a voice behind him.

Gerry jumped, physically, in utter shock, into the air at least half a hite. 'Who in HobB's name is … ' His dozing second head opened its eyes and he turned his front head to face the intruder.

So ferocious and violent was the internal reaction to the vision before him that his body threw itself against the wall behind. His jaw dropped open on sight of his first face-to-face meeting with a Hobbimp Gobbling.

The Hobbimp raised his hand in a gesture of friendship. 'Fear not, for I see that mighty dread has seized your troubled mind;' it said, 'but I bring you glad tidings of great joy, not just to you but to all Trisepkind.'

Gerry raised his eyebrows, jutted his chin and scratched his ear, 'I've heard that said somewhere before.' said Gerry, 'Reminds me of a song sung by nüns of the Triseptokatholicus Order. So what do you want from me? Why are you coming to me?'

'I want nothing from you. I come in peace. I am here to tell you that my tribe, the Hobbimps, approve of your erection.'

'My erection?' said Gerry, feeling guilty about looking at the pictures of Sharen and wondering whether his feint excitement was so obvious.

'Yes,' replied the Hobbimp, 'the erection whose creation you are shepherding and in whose shadow you now stand. When you have installed the Orijin, we would like to come on pilgrimages alongside you.'

'Why are you telling me this? This is a matter for the politicians. Your leader should be talking to my leader, Precedent Polit46.'

'In time, they will, they will. For now, I make my peace just with you, the shepherd of this Dagoba. Let me kiss your hand in friendship before I take my leave.'

'No!' Gerry tried to take a sharp step backward, forgetting that he was next to the solid wall of the Dagoba. He slithered gracefully to the ground, all consciousness drained - virtually to his extinction.

He remembered no more … for the time being, at least.

* * * * *

'What do you mean, *gone?* It's a vast structure. You must remember that it is the largest building on Eqinox. Can't just disappear. I expect he's in a turret somewhere looking at the view,' Carehedd said to Gerrya on the emergency callall link.

'No, I can see his hoofprints in the x-ray spectrum. It looks like he just sidled away from the side of the Dagoba and disappeared.'

'Is his moovacar still there?'

'Yes.'

'Have you tried his personal callall?'

'Of course I have.'

'And he's not answering?'

'No response at all.'

'We are already on our way, but I wonder if … ' he feared the worst but dared not speak for fear of upsetting Gerrya while she was alone. He decided on prudence. 'Stay in your moovacar and lock yourself in; we will arrive very soon.'

'Lock myself in? There's nobody else here.'

'Even so, stay in your moovacar and hover at not less than ten hites. We're coming now.'

* * * * *

Smelt terminated the callall from Carehedd and looked round at the clump of very senior Triseps. 'You all heard that.' he said, pouting his lips in mock depression. 'So what next?'

Nobody spoke, but all assumed the obvious for Gerry.

Mycroft blew a few smoke-rings and shook his head. 'It's not from the top. Might be a breakaway faction.'

'Listen, mate, how comes as you always knows so much about what the enemy are gonna do? Are you in some sort of league with them?' asked Ozzipolit7.

'Yeah, worries me too,' added Amoricspolit7.

'It's my job to know,' replied M, with such great an air of authority that he could be questioned no further.

The normally vocative members of the clump seemed to lose their voices and it was difficult to break the silence.

Eventually, M looked at Polit46. 'How long will you leave it before talking to Quax?'

'Should I callall now?'

'The sooner, the better. If a marauding band of out-takes *has* taken Gerry, then we need to cap it before they make their excuses to Quax.'

'What a cute expression, *out-takes*. You mean outlorrs, don't you?' suggested Amoricspolit7.

'No, I mean out-takes. Your nation should learn its own language. Outlorrs are bands of marauding Triseps who, as their name suggests, live outside the lorr. Out-takes, on the other hand, are simply a faction, possibly acting within the lorr but *taken out* of their originally defined rôle.' replied M.

Amoricspolit7 looked down at his hooves, suitably accepting his reprimand more readily than might be expected for his rank. Mycroft had that effective power of being a natural leader, even though it was a gift he rarely practised.

Polit46 initiated the callall on the private line to Quax.

'Yes.' Quax responded abruptly, clearly annoyed at being interrupted.

'We have lost a builder called Gerry at Squelchpool. He apparently just disappeared. Can you tell us anything about this?'

'Me? Why should I know if your builder falls into a squelch?'

'Because we have good reason to believe that he was taken.'

'Then look to thine own outlorrs. Do not look unto us for surface problems.'

'But Gobblings of all tribes except Hobbimps have attacked Triseps all over Eqinox.'

'But as you say, not Hobbimps.'

'You haven't openly attacked, no, but then Gerry was alone and in a place where we know that you roam.'

'If thou hast evidence, thou couldst be believable.' said Quax. 'I did not say believed, but believable. But thou hast no evidence. Neither wilt thou have because there is no evidence to be had. There is no evidence to be had because Hobbimps are honourable and I have issued no orders for any such occurrence.'

'I believe that we have an understanding which is paramount to a treaty. Would you confirm that?' said Polit46.

'I confirm that we have an understanding about Ozzilland.'

'I repeat that Squeithians will not make a pre-emptive attack. Will you make the same undertaking?' offered Polit46.

'I have confirmed previously that my people have orders not to make such a pre-emptive strike. You already have our proposal for peace.'

'Just for my peace of mind, I ask you again, Quax, do you have Gerry?'

'My people have been given no such orders.'

'Thank you, Quax.'

Polit46 terminated the callall, feeling smug.

Mycroft took a fresh puff and said, 'You can believe her if you will, but listen to every word and believe only and precisely what she says, not a syllable more, not a syllable less. Do not believe what you *think* she says, but only believe what she *actually* says, for she speaks true and with precision, but any lie would be found in omission and in your belief that she has said something different.'

'Did Quax not say what I thought she said?' asked Smelta

'Probably not. You of all with your cipher skills should know that.' M returned to his reverie.

'Are you saying,' suggested Polit46, 'that the Gobblings ... er ... I mean the Hobbimps are now holding Gerry as well as Bodgitt: both the builders?'

'I didn't say that.' replied M, deeply.

'So where is Gerry, then?'

'With the Hobbimps, most likely.'

'So they *are* holding them both!'

'Not necessarily. There are other possible explanations.'

'Like?'

'He fell into a squelch; he went away in his moovacar then sent it back again; he is sensibly hiding from his female, for example in one of the casponite towers of the Dagoba; he went off with another Trisep; he is with bridies or Sharen. Perhaps he got confused with Purkinje's after-image and went off with Bidwell's ghost or became lost and realised that he is nothing more than a product of his own instinctual fusion. Do you want me to continue the list?'

Smelt and Polit46 each scratched and then shook both their heads.

'It's all a matter of defining the thresholds of possibilities to the point of subjective equality.' M continued.

Smelt and Polit46 shook their front heads to bed down the new comments and then gave up trying to understand it.

* * * * *

Smelt and Grounsella lay across a double sleeping cowch, plaiting their arms and becoming increasingly intertwingled. 'It's been a long hard day, Grounsella; Smelta has gone to relax for the night with Grounsell, pass me a Caleptic hi-ball, will you.' He kissed her on the forehead.

'Is that all I get, your daughter number six and all?' She held his front head firmly with three hands to make sure he didn't move while she kissed him. Properly.

She wasn't fooled, though. 'What are you thinking about? What's up?'

'I'm puzzled. Why should I, an ordinary, everyday Trisep with no political or scientific achievement?'

'Why should you what?'

'Eh? Oh, yes. Why should I er ... ' he hesitated, not quite sure how to put it, 'why am I included at the highest level of international decisions. I really shouldn't be there. I'm not at that level. Why am I there. We've been making vital decisions that will affect the entire future of the planet and I am ordinary. Too ordinary to make such decisions. Far too ordinary. Why?'

Grounsella sat back on her side of the cowch and looked at him straight. 'You really are depressed, aren't you.' she unloosed his top button. 'I think you want ... something ... to cheer you up, don't you my dearest.' He suffered the pang of delight as she ran a finger down his neck to his chest.

Bang on cue, Smelt's callall berped and interrupted a promising interlude.

Kernal said, 'I need your help.'

'Mine? How on Eqinox can I help you? I am not a military expert.'

'No, but you *have* been through detoxification.'

'I don't think so - what do you mean - detoxification?'

'Now that the automeds have been reprogrammed to deal with the Contaigen, yours is one of the case histories that they detail. It said that you had an aphrodisiac side-effect reaction. Is that true?'

'You embarrass me, but yes.'

'Some of my Sqoddies are having the same reaction. They're all asking for Sharens.'

'I would expect that.'

'We're going to need some Sharens sent down to us. The Sqoddies are spending all their time watching and re-watching The Seventy Six Sexploits of Sharing Sharen.'

'It doesn't last, I assure you, but I'm sure I can persuade the government to send some of the brainless bridies of Ballam.'

'Whenever I think of Ballam, I think of the infamous bridie, Madame Sinn.' replied Kernal.

'Is she any relation to Cardinal Sinn?'

'Sister! You know what they say, if one in the family is especially good, another must be especially bad to keep the balance. I'm never convinced by that argument, myself, but it worked with them. They're both a bit of a pain in their own way!'

'Agreed!'

'Anyway, can you persuade Polit46 to send them?'

'I'll do my best, but I have no power.'

'There's one other thing,' said Kernal, 'and I may as well ask you: the Sqoddies are getting restless. Can you possibly arrange for Belcanto to provide some minstrelsy and entertain the troops?'

'Won't Sharen be enough?'

'I'm trying to dissuade them.'

'OK, I'll do my best, but she's a bit temperamental, isn't she? Wouldn't you like a load of Cher-ants instead?' suggested Smelt with a smirk, 'Are you still being attacked by Sprites?'

'Sprites? Thank Cronus, no.' replied Kernal, raising his eyes GodwarD, 'You know they've gone and no, they haven't returned, but we've been left with the Contaigen in a big way; nearly every Sqoddie has gone down with it.'

'And the bridge?'

'The hoverfloat autobridge has reached about one-third of the way to Ozzilland. From those who have not been infected with the Contaigen,

I have set up a complete string of Sqoddies so that each can see the next. At the leading edge is a platform, complete with sleeping quarters. A team is already testing the air and sea ahead.' replied Kernal.

'How are they doing that?' enquired Smelt.

'By keeping in constant touch by personal callalls. Also, a moovacar is being remote controlled, within sight, from the platform, so that there is always a test of what is happening up to about forty-seven squared lengths ahead of the leading edge of the growing hoverfloat autobridge. A simple test, but it is the one recommended by Mycroft. So far, we've discovered nothing unusual.'

'What about visual?'

'We are obviously using trinoculars to see the ocean and sky ahead, but it looks quite normal to us. There has never been an operation as simple, yet as potentially dangerous as this in the entire history of Triseps on Eqinox.'

'Glad to hear that you've no other problems. The Contaigen is bad enough without anything else.'

Smelt terminated the callall and turned back to Grounsella. 'Sorry, my love,' he began and their arms plaited themselves, his with hers and hers with his, 'now, where were we?'

'I think you were going to switch out your personal callallcode. Then we can start where we left off. We were just beginning to get seriously intertwingled.' her eyes glistened and she was alive. Glowing her warmth, she took the demonstrative lead and the adoring pair were soon utterly engrossed, each in the other, and practising replication in their own special way.

If there ever was, there could no longer be any doubt that the two halves had become somewhat more than a veritable whole.

'I don't need an aphrodisiac tonight.' replied Smelt as he moulded himself like a jelly into her crevices.

The night was long. And rewarding; most rewarding.

The post-copulate high raised Smelt's excitement as he left for the Necropol the next morning. Even the bad news that greeted him could only lower him to fractionally under total excitement.

The bad news? Well, it was agreed that he would be separated from Grounsella. He and Maecenas were to set off straight away for Scotaisle; that small corridor of land, a sort of one-ended isthmus, just Poleward of Antipole from where Defenss were growing their hoverfloat autobridge to Ozzilland.

* * * * *

'We'll route our journey over the Amorics. We can thus see the events there for ourselves.' said Maecenas.

'You must all have started the meeting very early this morning.' said the latecomer.

'No, you were late. What *were* you up to last night?' he glanced at Smelt who was busy blushing bright. 'On second thoughts, you'd better not answer that.'

He didn't. Smelt decided that this was one of those occasions when silence was the better part of valour and any attempt at improving or recovering the situation would also be to announce one's guilt all the more powerfully. He sat back, closed his eyes, ordered a geeantee and relaxed for the long journey as they crossed the coastline and began to climb over the ocean.

'Look! Look down there.' Maecenas pointed across to a coastal area below. He ordered the moovacar to stop and hover for a moment.

Below were tall, graceful cliffs rising sheer, clean and white from the sea for hundreds of hites and above were the rolling hills of Sunsetward Agwgwlland.

'Yes, it is beautiful,' admired Smelt casually, still not fully recovered from his post-copulate reverie and downing a spec of four-ecks for a change.

'No, look. There!'

Smelt followed the pointing finger and then he saw them. Giant caves at the base of the cliffs, and with a deep-water entrance. Over the entrance was a giant canopy; a sort of porch.

'Have you noticed, that from any other angle,' began Smelt, 'you wouldn't be able to see those caves? The canopy is brilliantly manufactured; it's not natural. And yet it all looks so natural. It must have been some old naval installation because those caves are big enough for the largest ships.

'That wasn't what caught my eye,' said Maecenas, 'look at the ground on the cliff top.'

The back of Smelt's cowch took the impact of his shock. The ground was covered in hundreds of mound-rings, which in themselves would have been unremarkable. From this height, however, and with the sun setting to form shadows even of these low rings, they formed the very clear image of a quadric gammagram.

'Yes,' said Maecenas bearing the look of fear, 'it's the sign of the Ferrikross.'

Smelt turned a single, puzzled eye to Maecenas.

'You know! You, Smelt as a smelter should know, of all Triseps! The ancient lucky-charm symbol of the Iron Cross, or *Ferrikross*.'

'I must read it up. I've always known the design as a quadric gammagram. If we weren't so high up, we would never have seen the pattern of it.'

'Aha! that only proves that you are a classical arithmate and not a historian of fortune.'

'True, but what does it mean?'

'Well, in ancient Greasy ... '

'No, no, no! I mean, what does it mean *there?* I mean, why is it there?'

'That, my friend, I intend we find out, but first we must call in.'

'Call in what?'

'Call in to M. Ask his advice.'

The callall was connected instantly. Maecenas turned the moovacar's holocam to the ground far below.

'It's new,' responded M, 'and a development not totally unexpected.'

'Why?' asked Maecenas.

'Why is it new? Because it wasn't there before.' said M, contemptuously.

'No, why was it expected.'

'I didn't say it was expected. I said that it was not totally unexpected.'

'OK, but on what grounds?'

'I would have thought you could have worked that out for yourself.' Mycroft leaned back on his cowch and blew a few quadric gammagram-shaped smoke symbols. He objected to explaining things to lesser intelligences. He always believed life was unfair. If he had to work things out from basic principles, why shouldn't others do the same?

Maecenas sighed deeply. 'I'll callall you back.'

'He *knows* that nobody else has his legendary powers of logical deduction, yet he seems to want us to work out answers that he has already deduced. I sometimes wonder whose side he's on.'

'He must know that we're not in danger, or I'm sure his reaction would have been different.' replied Smelt.

'True. Any other suggestions? About the Ferrikross, I mean.'

Smelt's heads turned and looked at each other, then back to Maecenas, who opened his mouth and raised his eyes GodwarD in sudden realisation. He callalled M.

'Wasn't it in the Great Western Wars, M, when the Gobblings were discovered under Eislland, they had been amassing there to join in the battles.' began Maecenas.

'What about it?' retorted M with half a smile.

'Well, the Triseps who dropped the atom-splitting molotov reported seeing a giant quadric gammagram on the ground. They aimed at its centre. It wasn't until later that it was discovered to be the symbol below which the Gobblings had their underground headquarters. Is that right?' suggested Maecenas.

'Almost.' replied M.

'And so this symbol on the cliff-tops of the Sunsetward coast of Agwgwllland suggests that Gobbling headquarters is underneath?'

'Of course. Did you notice some large caves leading out to sea?'

'Yes, we were just talking about them. How did you know they would be there?'

'Elementary, my dear fellow. The Gobblings need to use olde-fashioned ships to cross the oceans to Ozzilland, so they need a harbour near their headquarters.'

'But I thought their headquarters point was at Qontûm.'

'It is.'

'But Qontûm is under Squelchpool, near Selondre.'

'It is.'

'Then it can't be under here. Qontûm wasn't large enough to spread this far.'

'It isn't.'

'Then one of your statements is false, isn't it?'

'No, they are all true. So far, you have asked a lot of irrelevant questions. What you really want to know is what is the nature of that which you have stumbled upon and also that which you seek.'

'Er?' chorused Smelt and Maecenas.

'To the best of my received, perceived and deduced intelligence, the city of Qontûm is the Gobbling headquarters. It is located directly beneath the quadric gammagram. I always expect reports such as yours specifying its latest location, which is currently and logically on a coastline from where ships can be launched, hence the caves. Gobblings may be advanced in some ways but are not advanced in others. If you had looked at the ground from a great height when you visited Qontûm, you would have spotted a Ferrikross there too. Actually, you still will, and anywhere else where there is a probability of Qontûm being, at any one moment, located or passing beneath or both, or indeed having been. Where it is, it may not necessarily be and where it is not, it may be - with a degree of probability verging on a hyperprobability factor. The problem is one of time and space relativity of yourself versus Qontûm. Probably.' M sat back on his cowch, puffed some Qontûm maths symbols from his smouldering netherwear and stared up at the ceiling as well as one can with closed eyes.

M added in a mutter, 'I refer you to the writings of Stephen. Actually, there is a greater final solution, but you will not be ready for that until the precursors have heralded a replacement era.'

He puffed again on his netherwear and appeared to sleep.

Those meeting with him in the foyer of the Necropol Club stared at him, mouth agape, sharing the moment of speculative numbness. Not one understood him; yet.

The silence was intense to the point of pain, when Smelt had the courage to be the first to speak, 'So should we investigate or not?'

There was no response, so he tried again, 'Mycroft, do you think we should investigate?'

'Why?' replied M without opening his eyes.

'To see what's there, of course.'

'Why do you need to look when we have already deduced what is there, with the absolute certainty of the Qontûm probability?'

'He means, *don't bother;*' translated Maecenas. 'you know there are times when I wish the autotranslator would translate scientific statements and Mycroftese as well as other languages.'

The autotranslator woke up, performed the electronic ritual equivalent to a yawn and sprung to life, *'I do, but nobody ever asks me.'* it said, making both Maecenas and Smelt hit their heads on the moovacar roof with startled jumps, *'in any case, what M said was quite clear. My translation could only obfuscate and not clarify. Your perplexed brain would become further bewildered.'*

They both turned their front heads to look at the autotranslator, now being studied by all four heads. Smelt put a hand over his mouth and whispered to Maecenas, 'It's laughing at us, I'm sure it is.'

I cannot laugh. I have explained my duties and their consequences. I am not able to overcome any deficiency you may have in intelligence or lexical analysis. Unlike you, I am not deficient.'

'Shut up and sit down.' barked Maecenas.

I cannot close up as I do not open. I cannot sit down, only fly or return to my closet.'

'Then do so!'

'Look down there!' said Smelt.

Maecenas looked down. 'What's that with all those Gobblings near the middle of the Ferrikross?'

'What in HobB's name is it? It's got a long tube, like an olde-fashioned gun barrel. And it's pointing straight at us. It's time to make a sharp exit, methinks. GoD, I need a drink.'

Maecenas yelled at the moovacar's computer to move and it did, only a few breaths before the Gobblings would have fired their rounds.

'Once again,' muttered Smelt, 'saved by the bellow.'

'Eh?' asked Maecenas.

'A further occasion now it is that I have been protected by the shouting.'

'Who asked your opinion?' asked Maecenas, metaphorically.

'You did.'

'I didn't.'

'You did. You said, "Eh?". That is my cue.'

'Well just keep quiet in future.'

'I cannot, I am programmed to respond to "Eh?" and thereafter to translate all of that language in any one conversation into Squeithian.'

'Oh, shut up.'

And they all did. But only for a while.

* * * * *

'Look out!' yelled Smelt, ducking.

Maecenas ducked at the same time. The moovacar suddenly changed direction, backwards, up, down, flying around, looping the loop and defying what it saw as a sudden attack, but eventually it saw a way through and took it.

'What was *that?*' said Smelt.

'Faeries.' replied Maecenas.

'But there must have been thousands of them, and at this height too!'

'We're on a direct route between Qontûm, the Gobbling headquarters and Launder, capital city of the Amorics. They must want the Faeries for the ships so that they can fly back at the first sign of trouble. I must say, this gives me confidence that, perhaps, M was right and the Gobbling tribes are not behind the disappearance of Ozzilland.

'Talking of Faeries, I want to see how Lynkern is getting on.' said Smelt.

'Annoying how news reports never show you the end of a story, only the juicy bit at the beginning.'

On cue, Cate'aeddy appeared on the e-commenter, kempt but fraught.

'I am now fully recovered from the friendly fire from Lynkern's aides, thanks to an automed. You will be pleased to hear that Lynkern himself is also fully recovered after a period with his automed. He will be making an official statement this evening concerning the state of the Amorics and the current security crisis.' She stopped and took a sip of geeantee.

'There was a report earlier of Faeries amassing in huge numbers, and nationals here were warned to be prepared for attack. Suddenly, the huge clump of Faeries all flew into the air as instantly as they had appeared out of the ground. This clump were last seen crossing the Sunriseward coast towards Squeith, flying in formation like olde-fashioned bombers in the old non-holo films about the Great Western Wars.'

A new holoquadrant opened up and showed the Faeries flying overhead.

Smelt callalled ENN. 'Link to Cate'aeddy please, we've just flown through the Faeries.'

Cate'aeddy heard the report from her portoffice through her ear piece. 'We've just had confirmation that the Faeries were spotted flying towards Squeith. Smelt is on a callall now.'

'Yes, I confirm that we passed through the cloud of Faeries with no difficulty. The moovacar hadn't encountered anything of the kind before, so took evasive action initially, as if under attack, but then saw a clear way through and the Faeries did not attempt to attack. Had they done so, we would have been a sitting quack for them, even inside the protected moovacar.'

'Well, there you have it, straight from the Trisep's mouth. There's nothing I can add to that!' concluded Cate'aeddy in a rare moment of terminal asseveration.

* * * * *

'I'm worried about the inconsistencies.' concluded Smelt after a pregnant and most thoughtful lull.

Maecenas looked at him with one eyebrow raised on each head. 'Oh?' he mused.

'Yes, it doesn't fit. It just doesn't fit.'

'You've been dreaming about Sharen again, haven't you?'

'Sharen? Ah, Sharen! You HobB, no! Quax and Shealar.'

'Now you *have* fooled me.'

'Well, Quax said in the Conventionium that she was annoyed about being called *Shealar* by Ozzipolit7, and yet when she was talking to Polit46, earlier, she said, "We have no objection to your title of Gobblings; words mean nothing to us." so which was true?'

Maecenas shrugged, 'We all make mistakes; perhaps she was in a different mood.'

'No. in all other things, she has been precise. She is like a military leader. As precise as a computer. She does nothing that is not pre-planned. She says nothing that is not pre-planned. She operates with utter precision.'

'So what is *your* theory?'

'*My* theory?' said Smelt, pursing his lips and looking at the ceiling for inspiration, 'is twofold. First, it could be that the word means something rude in her language.'

'And more realistically, what is your second theory?'

'My second theory is that she was nervous about talking to Ozzipolit7, in view of Gobblings being removed from Ozzilland in the rookanga scare and their wish to take the country over for food production. The word being, as it were, not exactly non-derogatory wouldn't help, either. Yes, I think it was more of a nervous reaction, although even that wouldn't fit her character. It's just the best I can come up with at the moment.'

'I think,' said Maecenas, scratching his chin, 'that you're right and wrong. Right that she was nervous and that she is precise in all she says and does, but wrong in your final analysis. There's got to be a simpler and more logically obvious explanation. Do you think it matters enough to expose the problem to Mycroft's brain power?'

'I'll have to think about that; he'll probably just give us another question. Aha! We're passing over the coast. Nearly there now!'

Maecenas looked down, 'Look, There's another one!' he exclaimed, 'Look! Look!'

Smelt followed Maecenas' gaze. 'I've never seen so many Faerie-rings before, and they're all making up another giant quadric gammagram, another Ferrikross. They must be some sort of signpost or marker.'

Maecenas scratched his head, 'Time to call Mycroft again, I think.'

The thirty-breaths-to-landing warning ping sounded.

'He said it was the sign of the Gobblings' headquarters. He must, of course, have meant that there is one in each country; one for each tribe.' suggested Smelt.

'Mycroft is far more precise, even, than Quax. That is not a mistake that *he* would make. What he means he says. What he says he means. Nothing more, nothing less. What are you expecting him to say?'

'Let's find out. I'll callall him now.'

* * * * *

'Look, there's The Septagon. The Precedent sits in Side Zero. He is expecting us to visit him. It looks like there is a reception committee waiting for us on the lawn.'

'Yes,' replied Smelt, alternately sipping geeantee and lactinfuse, 'but can you see the Faeries looking down. They're hovering like angels in olde-fashioned religious pictures, just hovering.'

Enough of this for the moment; something big was happening on another side of the planet.

Chapter 10   A Lesson in Geography

'It kinks. The air is kinking. Not so much bending or warping; it's more of a kink.'

'A kink, Kernal? A kink?' responded Polit46 to the callall as though he were talking about a handbag in which a baby had been found.

'Yes, at 2209 lengths from Ozzilland, the remote controlled moovacar was flying perfectly, dead ahead, when it slipped sideways to the left while still but remained still when moved to the right.'

'Eh?' asked Polit46. Mental confusion ruled at the Necropol Club.

'At a distance from Ozzilland of two thousand, two hund ... '

'Oh, shut up.' said Polit46.

'I thought you wanted me to tell you what happened.' said Kernal.

'I do.'

'You do? Oh? Er, oh! The very air is kinking.'

'You said that.'

'There is a line. An invisible line. If I didn't know better, I would call it a Magicknot Line because of the knotting or confusion of callall signals and brains that cross it. Beyond that line, things move where they shouldn't move. I'll put you through to the senior Level Seven Sqoddie, Sqoddie747 who is on the bridge at the point of the kink.'

At the same time, Polit46 linked Smelt, Maecenas and Lynkern into the callall conversation. He would have preferred to keep the knowledge secret, but Mycroft insisted.

'What ho, old chap.' began Sqoddie747, 'School together, remember?'

'So we were, you old bugger!' replied Polit46.

'Not any more, I'm not. Left all that behind at school. Got wives and kids now.'

'Called you Jumbo, didn't we, due to your excessive girth?' said Polit46.

'Still a bit on the beer-belly side, old chap.'

'That's the way! Anyway, how are things down there? We hear the air's kinky.'

'That's a good expression, coming from you!' he retorted, 'Yes, as you can see behind me, the hoverfloat autobridge is growing still and just behind me is a line across the ocean. This side of the line, everything is still. The other side of the line, the air and the ocean are moving. As I passed through the line, I felt sick and ill, but recovered immediately on emerging. I've done it three times now and the slower I moved, the more sick I felt.' Sqoddie747 pointed the callall to the line.

'You can't see the line very clearly, because although the other side is moving, when you are there, it is this side that is moving. Each side is still, or so it seems.'

Sqoddie 747
(Jumbo)

'What shape is the line?' asked M.

'Eh?' replied Sqoddie747.

'Please define the geometric characteristics of that which has length between two points but no thickness.' said the autotranslator, *'by the way, did somebody mention the majin-owe-line?'*

'Oh, shut up! said Polit46 without turning away from facing the callall, 'in any case, you may pronounce it majin-owe-line, but it is spelled, *magic knot line*! Now get lost, will you.'

'Very well, good to talk to you again.' said Sqoddie747 and terminated the callall.

'Aaaaagh!' yelled Polit46 and hit his back head against the brick wall behind him in frustration, 'Reconnect me! Now!'

It did, but moaned.

'Right. Good. Let's start again.'

'I need to know the shape of the line.' began Mycroft.

'It goes from left to right. Roughly from Sunriseward to Sunsetward.'

'But what is its exact angle, and I need to know whether it is straight or curved. I suspect an answer, but I need you to confirm it.'

'I will have to do some tests. Is it really important?'

'Yes. Very important.'

'I am sure Ozzilland will still be there beyond this wall, I expect.'

'Do you have any direct evidence for that?'

'Yes. Both callall signals and standard remote controls for moovacars have very weak signals through the wall. They are at full strength on this side, and on the other side, but attenuate dramatically when passing through the wall.'

'Good. You've done your research well. Is there anything else you can tell us?'

'No, not yet. I will call an armoured surveying vehicle and tell you the answer to your question.'

'I have one further test for you to perform,' added Mycroft, 'Please go across the line and make an internal callall to a Trisep in Ozzilland and see what happens. If your response is positive, then all is well. However, if, as I suspect, you get no response, it does not necessarily mean that all is lost. In simple terms, Ozzilland may not be lost; it may just be hiding.'

* * * * *

Lynkern wanted to go public immediately, as is the custom in the Amorics. Polit46, as Planet Precedent of Eqinox took the exceedingly rare decision to overrule him. The stated reason was that it was too sensitive, Defenss-wise, to go public. 'It is possible that we have some enemies, including the Gobblings who monitor our e-commenters. No, Lynkern, now is not the time. I will make an announcement when the time is ripe.'

The real reason, of course, was that Polit46 was a good politician and wanted to have the kudos of announcing the find for himself; when he had understood what had been found, that is.

'So what *is* your theory?' asked Polit46.

'I do not have a theory;' replied Mycroft, 'I never have theories for anything. I calculated many possibilities and determined probability factors for each. There were once nine possible solutions to the disappearance of Ozzilland. Now there are only two; one is probable and the other is an unlikely scenario. We should know soon. That reminds me, where *is* Grounsell?'

* * * * *

Smelta and Grounsell had overslept. Again. Overslept, if that is the right word for practising their replication techniques on a sleeping cowch.

'No sleep again,' Grounsell said in a rare break between prolonged kisses, 'I can't keep this up every night. I *must* have some sleep *sometimes!'*

'But my love, you're good at keeping it up all night!' She arrested his move away and ensured that they remained wholly intertwingled.

Grounsell, for his part, was too tired to resist and let himself be pulled back to his proper place on the sleeping cowch.

He confessed only to himself that he wanted to get back to the meeting and discover the latest news. He would not have dared admit even a hint of a wandering mind. Smelta was most demanding.

The ground rumbled.

The earth shook.

'The earth moved.' said Grounsell.

'I know. Wonderful, wasn't it.'

'No, I mean the earth. It moved.'

Smelta tightened her intertwingling grip. 'I know, I know! You don't need to tell me. I know! The earth shook. It definitely moved.'

The earth shook again.

'GoD, it's an eqiquake!' Grounsell leapt off the sleeping cowch and Smelta, leaving her in a delighted reverie for a few breaths longer.

'The whole room is shaking,' she replied, holding on to him for balance.

'But we're not in an eqiquake zone.' he protested, 'Are we?'

'No. No, we're not.' Her more logical mind was suddenly beginning to work overtime, if that's possible when you haven't worked your hours in the first place.

He held on to the sleeping cowch.

She held on to him and to the sleeping cowch. Half her mind was still hoping that the quake was really a result of her recent coitalising. Sadly, she feared that it was not.

Neither did Grounsell really want to believe that the earth could shake in any other way at that moment than that which he desired most.

Grounsell's personal callall berped.

'What are you doing? Are you all right?' asked Grounsella without really looking. Then she saw him, somewhat compromised by his disrobed state, 'I seem to have caught you with your trousers down.' she said, with more than a hint of jealousy.

'Sorry, I thought you knew where I was.'

'I guessed. It's not very fair for you to be there when Smelt is away and I am left alone, is it? My only remaining option was to call for Sharen, and you know I don't like *that* idea.'

'Sorry.'

'So you ought to be.'

'Just before you callalled me just now, did the earth move for you?' asked Grounsell.

'As you weren't here, no.' Grounsella retorted with more of a sneer than a laugh.

'What have I got to do with it? Did the *earth* shake? I mean, did you have an eqiquake? I mean, was it just local to here or did you get it too?'

'Of course I did, why do you think I callalled you?'

'Was it bad?'

'Not really,' she replied.

'Any damage?'

'Only superficial. You?'

'Only to my brain. It came at the wrong time.'

'Serves you right. You never made an eqiquake for me.'

* * * * *

'What in HobB's name was that?' said Ozzipolit7.

'an Eqiquake it was.' said Sammowapolit7, calmly, *'It was an eqiquake'* Said the autotranslator with a shaky voice.

'A come from I quake remember that them; to used we're zone. About - all and are breaking buildings built flashes Great I Nothing nuclear quakes since the to up Wars Western without withstand worry would.'

'We're used to them; remember that I come from a quake zone. Nothing I would worry about - all buildings since the Great Western Wars are built to withstand quakes and nuclear flashes without breaking up.' The autotranslator's voice was increasingly shaky.

As soon as it had finished the sentence, the autotranslator flew to the door and disappeared into the distance before Sammowapolit7 had a chance to speak again.

Sammowapolit7 opened his mouth to speak but realised that there was no point and gave up.

'This building,' began Mycroft, puffing a shivering creak from the netherwear in his pipe, 'was built two hundred cycles before the start of the Great Western Wars.'

'Does that mean that it's not eqiquake-proof then?' asked Ozzipolit7.

'Not officially.' replied M and smiled.

'Is it or not?' asked Ozzipolit7 with unaccustomed precision, concern and alacrity.

'Almost. It is built with an olde-fashioned wooden frame held together with soft wood pegs. In an eqiquake it would flex and bend. Some plaster from the ceiling may fall on you, but that is all. Just don't sit under the giant crystal chandelier, that's all. I never do.' He sat back. His netherwear puffed a picture of a chandelier rapidly descending as a downward flying missile. Ozzipolit7 moved rather rapidly from beneath the offending and potentially lethal projectile.

'How do you *do* that?' asked Polit46, looking at Mycroft's netherwear smoke patterns.

'I just moved.' replied Ozzipolit7.

'No, Mycroft. How *do* you do that?'

'Which?' asked Mycroft.

'Eh?' asked Polit46, realised what he had said and looked round rapidly for the autotranslator to tell it to shut up. But it wasn't there. 'I mean, which what?'

'Well,' responded M with a word uncommon to his vocabulary, 'which question are you asking? was it: *how do I* **do** *that? or how* **do** *I do that?* ?'

'What's the difference?' asked Polit46.

'I don't know,' replied M, 'you asked the questions. I would have thought you would have known the answer to the question of what questions you were asking. Try asking again and I will reply.'

'Well, I mean, *'how* do you do that?' said Polit46.

'That's a different question again.' said M with a sigh, 'How do I do *what?'*

'What? Er ... I er I, I, I er can't remember now.' stuttered Polit46.

Mycroft rested back and closed his eyes again. His levva armcowch was about as far from being under the chandelier as it was possible to be.

The earth shook again.

The assembled clump all looked at each other, which with six eyes each they could all do, all at the same time. All, that is, except M, who appeared to be asleep with his eyes closed and the netherwear in his pipe gently puffing holographic images of flying crystal chandeliers.

'Mycroft, were you expecting this eqiquake?' asked Polit46, carefully.

Mycroft opened one eye and pointed it at Polit46. 'I never *expect* anything, but anticipate everything. Everything that ever occurs always does occur as a direct result of two things: first, a previously existent set of conditions, every characteristic of which may or may not be apparent to all observers; and second, influences upon that set of conditions which, as the conditions themselves, may or may not be apparent to any observer.'

'You, Mycroft seem to the only one of us who is not panicking, so what is your analysis of this eqiquake?'

'We are not in an eqiquake zone. Selondre is not on a geofault. It is most unlikely to the extent of being more of an improbability than a probability. We are therefore restricted to looking for a far more local reason for the ground movement. While there are at least ten possibilities, we do have external evidence from elsewhere.'

Everyone turned their front heads and stared at him. 'What evidence?' seemed to be the general mutter through the room.

'Just look at the weather holoquadrant on the e-commenter.' replied M.

Nobody else had thought of that. Sure enough, it showed reports of eqiquake activity all over Squeith, including in the capital city of Selondre.

'Wow, it's everywhere!' said Polit46.

'No it isn't, there is a distinct pattern, as I expected.' corrected M and ordered the e-commenter to expand the weather holoquadrant picture to take up the space normally occupied by eight holoquadrants.

'It's a, it's a … in HobB's name it's a quadric gammagram!' exclaimed Polit46.

'Yes, indeed, it is the shape of the Ferrikross.' said M.

'Can you elucidate?' asked Polit46.

'I doubt if you are fully aware of the evil magic which can be done in HobB's name by using the shape of the quadric gammagram or Ferrikross.' replied M, 'It is a power which may not be overcome by any normal means. Have you noticed how it touches the Poleward edge of Squeith at the top; the Antipoleward edge at the bottom; the Sunsetward edge on the left and Sunriseward on the right?'

Everyone nodded.

'That could be a warning,' said Mycroft. 'remember Eislland?'

Sammowapolit7 had a particular interest in Eislland, '¿Why' he asked. One word in Sammowanese, of course didn't need translating, so that was all right.

'Because when Sammowa dropped the atom-splitting molotov on Eislland, nobody believed that they really had the technology. And second, the Triseps who dropped it said that they fired it into the centre of a giant Ferrikross. There were doubts for many cycles afterwards about the truth of it all. There were many who suggested that there was an underground battle at the same time and that the real purpose of the atom-splitting molotov was that Sprites or Pole-Esquimeaux were attacking the multi-raced Gobbling condominimum under Eislland. Helping Sammowa to attack Eislland was a cover up, helped by the

Triseptokatholicus Order who disapproved of condoms, minimum or otherwise.'

'¿Evidence for is that there What' asked Sammowapolit7, who could always understand but never speak correct Squeithian.

'You mean, *what evidence is there for that?*' said M, who had to translate in the absence of the autotranslator, 'Well, there must have been a cover-up. There were doubts that the entrance or *gate* to Eislland had been abruptly and corruptly moved by magic. There was a huge investigation called Eisllandgate. To add circumstantial evidence to the theory, everybody involved has conveniently died since then.'

Only Smelta laughed.

'I didn't see you come in.' said Polit46.

'Sorry, I've only just got here. I overslept again. I came straight away.'

'No you didn't,' laughed M, in a rare bout of obtuse adult humour.

'I *did* come straight away.' said Smelta, protesting a little too much and suddenly realising that her statement had two meanings.

'No, I meant that you didn't oversleep. You cannot oversleep if you do not sleep. Your bags show that you did not sleep, and here is the reason.' M looked towards the front door and everybody else's gaze followed.

Grounsell was standing in the door, rapidly blushing a bright shade of blood yellow. 'Sorry I'm late,' he blurted, 'I sort of overslept.'

'Only sort of?' smiled M, 'that's a euphemism if ever there was one!'

'Don't you think we ought to worry about the eqiquakes?' suggested Ozzipolit7.

'I am not worried. I was trying to lighten everyone else's mood and stop them worrying.' said M.

'But why aren't you worried?' asked Ozzipolit7.

'Because there is plenty of time. There will be no more eqiquakes. The pattern has now been made as you can see from the weather holomap. We should talk to Quax and demand an explanation.'

'You mean that *I* should talk to Quax.' corrected Polit46.

'Yes and find out what they are really planning.'

* * * * *

'Not available?' Polit46 enquired to the voice-only callall, 'When *will* she be available?'

'I am unable to answer that question.'

'Do you mean that you do not know or that you are not permitted to answer?'

'I mean that it is not possible for me to answer the question.'

Polit46 looked at Mycroft and frowned at being given yet another non-answer.

'When do you suggest that I should callall her again?'

'I do not make a recommendation.'

'Will you please ask Quax to callall me as soon as possible?'

'I am unable to do that.'

'Well, what can you do?'

'What would you like me to do?'

'Tell me when I can talk to Quax.'

'Try again next year.'

'She must *surely* be available before that!'

'I am not advised of whether that will be the case.'

'Does she have a deputy?'

'Yes.'

'May I speak to that deputy please.'

'That will not be possible.'

'Why not?'

'Because he's not here.'

'Can you pass a message?'

'I will listen to your message.'

'Please state our urgent need to discuss certain matters of mutual interest with Quax or her deputy. Please remind Quax that we have a written agreement. Please say that we have intelligence on matters concerning Ozzilland. It may not be lost, it may only be hiding. This will be explained in full to Quax or her deputy. Is that clear?' Polit46 paused for a response, but answer came there none.

'Is there anybody there?'

'Yes. Are you to add to your message?'

'Yes. In addition, please inform Quax that we have early intelligence of their battle plans.'

Mycroft raised one eyebrow and looked at Polit46. Frankly, he was surprised that Polit46 had really understood what he had been saying. More surprising still was Polit46's ability not to tell too much. At last, somebody had got something right. 'Oh well!' he muttered, shrugged and closed his eyes again.

Polit46 terminated the callall. He was left rather confused as to whether he had actually left a message and whether he had said what he thought he had said. Or not, as the case may be.

He was worried. Ozzipolit7 was worried and seriously considered flying home immediately, until he remembered that there probably wasn't an Ozzilland to go back to. Anywhere but here, he thought.

Sammowapolit7 was in the same dilemma, '¿and do go home I leave should think you'

M didn't bother to translate, just replied in Sammowanese, 'Danger is not yet. Go not now you.'

* * * * *

The callall berped. It was set to over-cipher.

'I've got your answer.' said Sqoddie747.

'Yes.' responded Mycroft.

'The line must be straight but it appears curved.'

'How?'

'From either side, the line is concave; quite definitely: we've checked and re-checked it. It appears to be curving with a radius which is exactly the same as the diameter of the planet. And what is baffling is that it is the same when measured from the other side.'

'That is as expected.' responded M without opening his rear eyes. 'And are the water and air the other side of the line still moving?'

'Yes. We've taken some very careful measurements and it is increasing.'

'You mean it's going faster?' M looked firmly into the callall with some degree of surprise and obvious concern.

'No. It's going slower. The rate of deceleration is increasing, I mean. I calculate that at the current rate, it will stop completely in less than eight days.'

'Ah! you mean it is slowing down faster! About six and a half days, actually, I think, from the data you sent me previously. Well done. Good work.'

'How did you know that? We calculated six and a half days but said eight to allow for all the error factors. By the way, what did you mean that the shape of the line was as expected, concave from both sides? Is it some sort of illusion?'

'Almost, but actually, no. It is because of Eqinox being a vexal septiquadecahedron and not a sphere,' replied M, 'Normal spherical geometry doesn't quite work. You should use Convinciing Geometry. Remember that the radius of the surface on which you are standing at any point in the planet is the same as the diameter of the planet as a whole. And there is another Qontûm factor that is built into Convinciing Geometry, but that is too complex to explain here.'

Sqoddie747 nodded, but felt pangs of doubt about the explanation. He had never quite got to grips with spherical geometry, let alone that of a vexal septiquadecahedron!

'You'd better forward to me the precise location and characteristics of your findings. I will then check them against the various options.' M instructed.

'Yes, Sir.'

* * * * *

The private line callall to the Gobblings berped.

'You wish to discuss The Agreement with me?' Quax said to Polit46.

'Yes.'

'Then discuss.'

'Tenet Five of The Agreement states that Triseps and Gobblings should remain warless for all time.'

'That is subject to Triseps keeping to the contract of The Agreement in every word.'

'We did.'

'You did what?'

'We did keep to The Agreement.'

'You bleated throughout the planet details of our visitation pipe at Squelchpool. This was contrary to the Second and Third Tenets which were that: Triseps would not admit the Gobblings' existence or the existence of The Agreement publicly; and that publicity about any contact should be suppressed or dismissed as ridiculous. You have broken these Tenets. We are still considering whether you have broken either Tenet Five, that you should not war, or Tenet Six that Triseps would warn us of an impending disaster.'

The statement was clear but nevertheless beyond the experience of Polit46.

'Does that mean that you are abandoning The Agreement?'

'We have not, but you have.' said Quax.

'It is my firm belief that we have not.' replied Polit46.

'Then why did you publicise the finding of our city of Qontûm.'

'Perhaps you can tell us why you left the hole open when you are usually so meticulous in closing and sealing them.'

'We were exchanging our air. We do it twice every cycle. We always choose a position where no Trisep has walked near for at least five cycles. It is agreed in clause twenty-nine of The Agreement.'

Polit46 looked at M, who nodded confirmation. 'Why didn't you place a safety grill over the top?'

'Because it is not in The Agreement.'

'Will you return Bodgitt to us and his herd?'

'That depends on you proving to be honourable.'

'Do you mean me or us?'

'Had I meant *thou,* I would have said so. I said and meant you. Plural. All. Your race. Triseps. Any part clump and every one. Is that clear?'

'Eminently, Quax, thank you.'

'What else dost thou wish to say to me or us?

'Well, er, nothing, really … '

'Ahem!' interrupted Mycroft. Polit46 turned his front head to follow his rear gaze to M. 'May I speak?'

'Of course. Quax, I would like to introduce Mycroft, a counsellor of great wisdom, who has some news which I hope will encourage you and yours to show that we are honourable.'

'I will listen. Go ahead.'

'Hello.' said Mycroft, 'We have received some intelligence from the Ozzilland area. Tell me, are you familiar with Convinciing Geometry?'

'I have a little knowledge. Would you like to speak to our profgeol?'

'Perhaps your Profgeol can join in with our conversation?'

'He is already listening.'

'Very well. We have so far discovered the most Antipoleward of the seven geoplatelets making up Ozzilland has moved. It seems to have moved, or perhaps rotated, Temporra-wise.'

'How did you move it? I was not aware that even you had the technology to do that.' replied Quax.

A new voice joined in. 'Hello. I am, in thy language, Profgeol. Now, did you permit anti-friction making nanomachines to escape between the geoplatelets, thus enabling such a movement?'

'I don't know the answer to that, but I think it most unlikely, particularly as the rotation has so far only been confirmed in the ocean and the air above it.' replied M.

'If Triseps claim not to have caused that effect, my presumption is that thou art blaming us.'

'I attach no blame either to Hobbimps or to any other of the Gobbling tribes.'

'Then you must be speaking false, for as the rotation was not caused by any mechanism of ours, it must have been caused through action of the Triseps from the surface.' said the Hobbimp Profgeol.

'We Triseps have not developed a class of nanomachines that would create a lubricated layer between geoplatelets to enable such a movement.'

'Are you suggesting,' said the Gobbling Profgeol, 'that the geoplatelets moved of their own accord?'

'I see no alternative. Have you any more advanced ideas?'

'No.'

'We have never studied the sub-planet structure as you have. What is the shape of the geoplatelet structure beneath the surface?'

There were a few embarrassing breaths of thoughtful silence before the Gobbling Profgeol replied, 'All geoplatelets are like a sphere cut in half with a knife. So the surface you know is the flat part with a simple hemispheric vexal beneath each geoplatelet, leaving an *Ovum box* shape of magma below. There is constant movement, but it is always very slight; never more than one tenth of a hite per cycle. That is why the magmablasts forming mountains such as Alp-Etnavolc and the eqiquake zones are all on the joints between geoplatelets.'

'I knew about the small movements and density fluctuations due to the gravitational, magnetic and heat effects of the seven-yearly cycle visit of the second sun,' replied M, 'but I was unaware that the movement could ever be enough to move an entire geoplatelet with any rapidity, let alone the seven needed to move Ozzilland.'

'We still do not believe that such massive geoplatelet movement would take place without some intelligent assistance. Clearly you must be held responsible for the continent's disappearance until we have evidence to the contrary.'

'But surely *you* must understand that we could not have had anything to do with it any more than I now believe that you could have. Don't you?'

'I see no alternative to my own view and disagree with thine own.'

M thought for a few breaths, considering the best next statement to be made in judgement of the evidence. Mycroft's train of thought was interrupted by Polit46.

'There is no point in unnecessary mutual carnage.' said Polit46.

Mycroft looked at Polit46, not quite sure what he was getting at but before either of them could expand on their thoughts, Quax retorted with power, 'Is that a threat?'

'A threat?' puzzled Polit46.

'Yes, are you suggesting that you will attack us? You mentioned unnecessary carnage. We have never forgotten what you did to us beneath Eislland.' said Quax.

'That *was* a long time ago, *and* there is not inconsiderable evidence that Gobblings themselves were instrumental in assisting Sammowa mount the attack on the condominimum.' said M with considerable emphasis.

'Our History Records show an entirely different picture of the events from your own. Remember that you are not providing propaganda for Triseps now, but are involved in serious negotiations at planetary level.'

'I had not forgotten that. We do not use propaganda. Triseps have no need of it.'

'But you tell stories that are not true, sometimes, for the good of the nations?'

'Naturally.'

'Then that is propaganda!' replied Quax.

'No, it most certainly is not,' responded M, 'we sometimes provide partly true or untrue information to avoid confusion or to avoid upsetting the sensitivities of others.'

'Clearly, our definitions vary, as do our definitions of war and peace.' said Quax.

'Not significantly.' replied M, 'Our aim is to be peaceful with you, at least until we have both had a chance to prove the culprit of the Ozzilland crisis. Unless unavoidable, we would prefer to avoid war until there is a ... '

Quax interrupted, 'The expression, *avoid war until* is the same as saying *postpone war*. Either expression implies that war is inevitable but that you wish for a delay in order to arrange adequate armaments. There are precedents aplenty for countries negotiating treaties to give them more time to re-arm prior to declaring war. I remind you that your Precedent, Polit46 has negotiated a treaty with us. You will recall that he stood before the Eqinox's leading Triseps in the Conventionium, held up a pulpleaf and said, *Peace in our time.'*

'I did not say that to give us time to re-arm,' insisted Polit46, 'but to be sure that we all pooled our resources to discover the mysterious cause of the missing Ozzilland and work together to solve it. We are not re-arming. My purpose in contacting you is that there are signs that you, the Gobblings are preparing for war while we are peacefully attempting to investigate the Ozzilland problem. To that end, we appreciate your assistance in stopping the attacks on Scotaisle.'

'What concerns us,' added Mycroft, 'is that we have spotted your quadric gammagrams all over the planet, and these appear similar to the one on Eislland used as a target for the atom-splitting molotov. We ask you to make a statement that you are not planning an attack.'

'Then ask.'

'I so ask.'

'Dost thou wish me to make the statement specified as required or to tell the truth?' asked Quax.

'I prefer you to tell the truth.' replied M.

'We always plan to respond to any emergency, including war declared by Triseps.'

'Will you guarantee not to strike pre-emptively?'

'Subject to being wholly satisfied that you are not re-arming, I am prepared to offer that guarantee.'

'I confirm our similar intentions also.' replied M.

'I confirm that.' added Polit46.

'Then there is no problem.' said Quax.

'I fear there is,' retorted M, 'and our fear is that we still do not have a reason for the Ferrikross or quadric gammagram appearing so frequently across the planet.'

'Thou needs have no fear of the symbols.' replied Quax.

'We have no fear of the symbols themselves, but of your purpose for them. Are they targets?'

'No. Why do you ask? You already know that each corresponds to a local military headquarters. You already know that we are using our military power to investigate the Ozzilland problem. You know as much of us as we know of you.'

Polit46's callall berped on emergency and over-cipher with a report from Kernal.

'Thank you,' said Polit46, 'please excuse me to take an emergency callall with a report from Ozzilland. I am sure you understand.'

'I understand that, but I do not understand your fear. Good-bye.'

* * * * *

'We have discovered land.' said Kernal, but it is not quite where it should be.'

'I expected it to have moved.' said Mycroft, 'Please describe the movement precisely.'

'Ozzilland is upside-down.'

'Of course it's upside-down,' said Ozzipolit7, 'it always has been.'

Polit46 was baffled. All the others each scanned from one to another in querying debate.

Mycroft just nodded.

'No, it has turned upside-down. According to Sqoddie747, the land discovered seems to be the top or Poleward side of Ozzilland, and not the Antipoleward side, which we would expect. It appears that the land may have rotated too because we found an inland signpost on the coast.'

'How far inland, mate?' asked Ozzipolit7.

'The signpost says, *Welcome to Allysp Rings.'*

'But that's right in the centre of Ozzilland, where the great expeditor Allysp discovered a Ferrikross of Faerie-rings and endlessly chased-up other Triseps for their theories.'

'And Triseps? Signs of life? Have you found any signs of Triseps, either alive or dead?' asked Mycroft.

'But it's not on the coast.' said Ozzipolit7, still puzzled.

'It appears that it is now,' said Polit46, 'wherever it was before.'

'Not yet.' Replied Kernal to Mycroft's question. 'But remember that all communication is transmitted from the Ozzilland end of the hoverfloat autobridge to the edge of the geoplatelet where the movement is still occurring. We then walk across what we have termed the Great Divide with the message and then re-transmit to Scotaisle.'

'Thank you.' said M, 'all of that is exactly as expected, so far, but please advise as soon as you have news of life in Ozzilland.'

'Er, I think you should know,' began Kernal, hesitantly, ' that there is, er, a er, well, another matter.'

'Then spit it out.' said Polit46.

'Ozzilland is tilted.' said Kernal.

'Tilted?' replied M, 'you have already said it is upside down.'

'Yes,' replied Kernal, 'can you imagine an Ovum in an Ovum cup, knifed in half and then tilted so that half is raised up and the other half is sunken, leaving the surface angled?'

'I'm not sure.' said Polit46.

'I can.' replied M.

'Well,' continued Kernal, 'that is how Ozzilland currently appears. We have not explored inland or round the coast yet.'

A pregnant silence followed while Smelta and Sammowapolit7 put their hands on Ozzipolit7's shoulder in moral support.

'I presume that the ocean has ingressed on the subsided part of the land?' asked Polit46.

'That's the funny part of it, There is a rim where the edge of the land used to be and it appears as though the land is a hemisphere that has twisted within its shell.' Kernal paused, 'Ah, oh, and the surface that used to be below ground is perfectly smooth. It reminds me of the unprecedented smoothness of the lining around the pipe from Squelchpool to Qontûm.'

'Then the first part of the answer to our puzzle must be that Gobbling activities of the Dark Elves has transgressed the natural boundary of geoplatelet formation enabling rapid re-alignment to compensate according to local magnetic deviations.' said M.

'But will the Ozzillanders be harmed?' asked Ozzipolit7.

'I doubt it. They should have survived because the initial acceleration would have been slow. And it has slowed again. The geoplatelets have virtually stopped moving now.'

Ozzipolit7 nodded, jutted his chin and smiled in thanks.

'Good luck nation to your.' said Sammowapolit7.

'It am luk do me mak it gud.' said Zimgulupolit7.

'Muzzeltoff' said Yishrelpolit7.

'The yellow ribbons of my country are set for you.' said Amoricspolit7.

'Good on you mates,' replied Ozzipolit7 on behalf of his countrymen.

'You will all need to re-learn your geography;' said Mycroft and puffed an upside-down smoke map of Ozzilland from his netherwear before adding with a wry smile, 'as Ozzilland is now upside-down *and* upside-down and is currently turning its hemispheres to become upside-down on a third plane, we will have to teach all geography students that Ozzi = upside-down cubed.'

'Shouldn't that be upside-down sphered, or even hemisphered?' suggested Smelta in a poorly received attempt to add humour to M's combination of perfect wit and apparent obfuscation.

Chapter 11   A Town Like Allysp

'Where are they all?' Sqoddie747 asked an aide.

'They've got to be here somewhere, Jumbo, it's still only at fifteen degrees.' replied the more junior Sqoddie638.

Sqoddie747 opened another front door to yet another house. Again, there were the signs of an evening meal, olde-fashioned crockery and cutlery all dropped into a sink ready to be washed up, as they did in the old pre-holographic and pre-nanotechnology films.

'This is archaic,' said Sqoddie747. 'you'd think they would have nanomachines like the rest of Eqinox.'

'Mm. A bit odd, these Ozzillanders, if you ask me.' replied Sqoddie638.

'What puzzles me more than anything is that if they all left in a hurry, there would have been signs. If they were forced to leave quickly, they would have taken things with them and their hurry would have caused them to drop various items, like toys. If, however, they left without being forced, they would have taken more clothing, jewellery and other items along.'

Sqoddie638 nodded in agreement, 'It's like a ghost town: there are signs of Triseps but there are no Triseps; there are signs of moovacars, but there are no moovacars; there are signs of recent movement, but there is no movement. Do you think they were all abducted? Gobblings, perhaps?'

'Dark Elves, here, to be precise. But no, they were not abducted or the mess in their homes would have indicated the sudden exodus. Anything being held would have been dropped; nothing *has* been dropped.' Sqoddie747 raised his front eyes GodwarD, stroked his imaginary beard, scratched his left ear and continued shaking his head in utter bafflement.

'So let's get this right,' said Sqoddie638, 'they didn't leave gradually at their own pace, they weren't forced to leave suddenly and they weren't abducted. That only leaves a sudden disappearance, as forecast by the religiots who read us the Folio of Revealment from The Folius, *For next in my vision, GoD took up His own into His Kingdom and they knew not the Temporra nor the breath when they would be taken unto*

Him, but He had most surely taken them to Himself when they were least prepared. Do you remember that appalling rhyme we learned at school as a mnemonic to this passage:

> For next in my vision did GoD
> Come forth and engage with His rod;
> By night did He take them, and day;
> And forced HobB to keep well away.
> The breath and Temporra they knew not,
> Nor place nor the fate of their lot.
>
> GoD took His own from poor slavedom,
> Brought each, his own, to His Kingdom.
> To each, of His own He afforded
> With Heaven-sent goodies rewarded
> To Heaven, their souls, they were driven
> GoD's from HobB's, then, ever were riven.'

'Yes,' replied Sqoddie747, 'it really was a dreadful rhyme, but it did help remember the passage.'

The two eyed each other for many breaths, watching for a sign of deference to the GoD they both doubted, somehow wanting to believe in a supernatural omnipotent being, yet not quite knowing the runes to conjure this dubious reality. Suddenly the pair were experiencing that unnerving awareness of the potential presence of that which is beyond understanding.

'Do you believe in a GoD?' asked Sqoddie747.

Sqoddie638 raised his eyebrows and laughed. He raised a finger in mock censure of a question contrary to the Freedoms for Religious Equality Amendment Kreed, F.R.E.A.K. 'A senior officer is not supposed to ask that question, but no, I don't.' he said.

'No, neither do I, so let's stop being emotional and start thinking logically.'

'OK, then the obvious logical response is to ask why Triseps should only disappear from Ozzilland. Why not from the whole of Eqinox.'

'Correction, old chap' responded Sqoddie747, 'we only have evidence so far that Triseps have disappeared from this one town which is at the edge of a geoplatelet and set like a gyre, gimballing in its socket, or wabe, if you prefer. But I agree. If the disappearance were down to GoD, the effect would be planet-wide, whereas it is not, so it *is* not, is it not?'

'Yes. Do you think the gimbal effect caused the geoplatelet to tip further than at present, thus tipping the natives to the edge?' Sqoddie638 looked around for evidence, but couldn't actually see any; but then, he wasn't as bright as Sqoddie747.

'No. The evidence disproves it. Were that the case, then ornaments and other items would have slithered and lodged away from their set places.'

'Do you have another theory?'

Sqoddie747 glanced back at the houses he had visited and thought carefully, 'The evidence suggests that they all left as though they were going out for the evening. Did you notice that in some of the houses, meals were left cooking on an automatic timer. Well and truly cold now, of course, but that was how they were left, and with no interference since. Others left meals cooking on a stove with a genuine log-burning fire.'

'So do you think they were lured somewhere?'

'Yes, I do, but I am worried by what could lure an entire town away without frightening the inhabitants. I think we should go up in the moovacar and look for Faerie-rings as Kernal instructed.' replied Sqoddie747.

* * * * *

Having arrived from the Amorics, Smelt and Maecenas immediately sought out Kernal and the three were chatting.

'Mycroft has been keeping us up to date in the moovacar.' began Maecenas, 'We saw a number of quadric gammagrams over every country we crossed. It's as though the Gobblings are trying to put their mark on the surface for some reason. They certainly weren't there last time I travelled across the Amorics.'

Kernal nodded and excused himself to take a callall from the Magicknot Line.

Sqoddie747 had reported via a link on the other side. Reception was still too difficult for the callalls to work across the Magicknot Line, the boundary.

The report said, *'Sqoddie747 reporting. We have flown high enough to see the whole of Ozzilland and confirm that it appears to be almost upside-down. If it continues its current deceleration, then when it stops its movement it will be exactly upside-down. As expected, we were unable to see any movement or life from there.'*

Kernal looked at Smelt and Maecenas, expecting a reaction, but detected only the raised eyebrows of impatience.

The report continued, *'What we were not expecting to see was the state of the surface. All of the geoplatelets are quite clearly defined like cup rims while the geoplatelets themselves appear as though they are hemispheres which have just been dropped into the hollows at random. The rivers, such as there are, are still following their original courses, often uphill and then falling over the edge of the geoplatelet into the correct place on the next one. There are two rotations. The whole of*

Ozzilland has rotated and each geoplatelet has gimballed through a rotation of between 10 and twenty-five degrees. When standing on it, you remain at an angle exactly half way between the gimballed rotation and vertical; it's a very strange feeling. Still no signs of life. We will continue searching. End of message.'

'Well, you heard that, gentletriseps,' said Kernal, 'what have you to say?'

Smelt took a heavy intake of breath and looked squarely at Maecenas, who reciprocated in like fashion, then glanced back to return the implied query to Kernal. 'I have never heard anything quite like this before. They must continue with their explorations to seek for signs of life.' he paused to think, 'Oh, and perhaps you should forward the message to Mycroft, Polit46 and the Summit meeting at the Necropol club.'

Smelt and Kernal nodded in agreement.

'And ask them to measure the precise positions and rates of gimbal movement, if any, of the geoplatelet hemispheres, specified in terms of roll, pitch and yaw measured from Antipole towards Pole.' suggested Maecenas, as he peered in vain across the sea towards Ozzilland.

'It might also be worth asking what, in his opinion, caused the movement of the geoplatelets within their gimbals, if he has any ideas at all.'

'Top o' the morning to ye all.' said Big Dick Makkaan.

'Where in HobB's name did *you* come from?' asked Kernal.

'Well now, there's a question, to be sure. To tell you the truth, I really couldn't say. I was walking along, nattering away between these two Lepperdcorns when what do you know, suddenly I wasn't there.'

'Where weren't you?' asked Maecenas, baffled by the sudden unannounced appearance of the Precedent of the Green Aisle.

'Well, let me see now, I wasn't where I was, so I wasn't. I was there but then I was somewhere else as soon as you could put a Dalli on a head to win at the races. Fell down one of they pipes, so I did, with a Lepperdcorn either side o' me. Now who'd have thought they'd let me do that, eh? And they laughed and laughed all the way down and they sounded so much like Lepperdcorns with their laughs like Zimgululland lepperds. And their corny jokes are so bad, so they are.'

'But how did you get *here?'* asked Smelt.

'Well now there's a question, so there is. They Lepperdcorns was kissing me all the way down the pipe and I don't remember landing at all, so I don't. And do you know the last thing they said to me?' he paused for a response.

'No, tell us.' suggested Smelt with half a smile.

'Well, now, one of they Lepperdcorns said to me that I would be more use to them if I were here with you. Said something about Scotaisle. Is that where I am?'

'Er, yes, you are.' replied Kernal, somewhat perplexed.

'Now there's a thing, so there is.'

'Tell me,' said Smelt, 'how did they think you could be more use here?'

Big Dick shrugged both ends and replied, 'To be sure I'm hanged if I know. Why?.'

'Perhaps more to the point,' said Maecenas, 'why would they think you would be more use *to them* if you were here? I mean, what could *they gain* by your presence here?'

'Nothing.' shrugged Big Dick.

'Or more to the point,' added Smelt, 'What could they possibly gain by your absence from the Green Aisle?'

'If it were only me, then I would agree with you.' replied Big Dick.

'Why? Have many others disappeared?' asked Maecenas.

'I don't know. They may have done.'

'But you said … oh, never mind.' shrugged Smelt, 'I mean, do you know of any others?'

'No.'

'OK,' replied Maecenas, 'do you want to go back?'

'Yes. Well, no. I mean, what do you suggest?'

'I think you should go to the hospivoid and rest with some tests.' suggested Kernal.

'And a good black stout drink.' said Big Dick, suddenly feeling more chirpy at the thought of a large spec of a stout liquid refreshment.

'Meanwhile, we need to warn Polit46 so that the Eqinox Government may discover what strange occurrences are happening in the Green Aisle.' added Maecenas.

'There seems to be a trend here, somewhere,' said Smelt. 'there have been small attacks of Triseps all over Eqinox, but I think this abduction is new. Do you think we can learn from all this?'

'Oh, we can learn,' said Maecenas. 'we can certainly learn.'

'What can we learn?'

'Never trust Lepperdcorns!' laughed Maecenas in reply.

* * * * *

'These harbingers are just the precursor.' Smelta muttered to herself, half in a post-coital reverie, half in a drunken reverie and three-parts into a sleep-ridden dream.

'What?' asked Grounsell, not sure that he had heard correctly.

Smelta and Grounsell had taken a long lunch break together. A very long lunch break, and they were determined to enjoy every deliciously naughty moment of it, but suddenly Smelta had sharpened up and looked straight into his eyes.

'Do you think the end of the planet really is nigh?' she asked as they plaited their arms and intertwingled their bodies on the sleeping cowch.

'We have all witnessed the signs that the religiots have been predicting for so many hundreds of cycles,' replied Grounsell, 'the wars and rumours of wars, The Contaigen to be spread planet-wide, pestilences, a spreading of eqiquakes. These are all happening now.'

'Are they happening more or are we noticing them more? Look at history. Remember that the Triseptokatholicus Order was founded when there were wars and earthquakes. Then everyone said the world would end after the invention of the atom-splitting molotov. It didn't.'

'You don't think that this situation is a harbinger, then?'

'No.'

He looked at her curiously and raised his eyebrows. 'Does that mean that you don't believe in GoD either?'

She nodded her front head. 'Yes.'

'Yes you do or yes you don't?'

'I suppose I'm a bit of an agnostic. But you must admit that they do have a point.'

Grounsell kissed her and secretly wanted to return to their more succulent activities, 'There's a great deal more under the surface than any of us are aware; a great deal more hidden power and magic lurking than any of us have ever considered.'

She frowned slightly, 'Exactly what are you saying?'

'Nothing really, just that you could be right about these harbingers being just a precursor to absolute change in life structure on this planet as we know it.'

'So what do you know that I don't?'

'Little, I doubt. It is all stated or implied in the history archives if you care to look hard enough and read between the furrows.'

'Just *tell* me. You're making me more frustrated to know what I am missing with every word. What *do* you know that I don't?'

'Well, simple miracles and healing magic can be performed by thaumas. And every forty-seventh thauma becomes a WitcH. Much of what they used to do is now taken care of by machines like automeds.'

Smelta sighed, and screwed her lips in simulated boredom, 'I *know* all that.'

'Then there are the WizardS.' said Grounsell.

'Nah. They're just folklore!'

'Ah! They may be folklore, but they are nonetheless real for all that.'

'I've never really been convinced,' she said thoughtfully. 'I've never met one.'

'That's because there haven't been any for over a hundred and twenty cycles. The truth of who will become a WizarD and why and when is a well-kept government secret. The fact is that we now have a rare generation when many ordinary Triseps could become WizardS and it is theoretically possible that one or two could become GrandwizardS.'

Smelta felt a jam-chiver creeping along her spine, bouncing back and forth from head to head in waves. 'You're being serious, aren't you? In *my* lifetime? You mean, *real* WizardS? And *real* GrandwizardS?' She continued to look at him with open mouth and drooped chin.

Grounsell nodded carefully, not fully sure whether he dared expand and tell her all he knew about the heights and depths of magical powers. Not, as he was well aware, that he was in a position to know more than even a few percent of the truth. Perhaps it would be acceptable, he thought, to tell her the main points, 'I confess that I know little myself, but we are at the beginning of an era where everything will change. WizardS and WizardrY will become commonplace and so will voodoo. Powers beyond anything ever previously experienced are about to be unleashed. Thence onward will the very time and space in which we have for so long been thriving be threatened. Challenges of nature will strike from HobbS to GodS and back again.' He watched her for a reaction.

'Phew!' said Smelta, raised her eyebrows and stared, without noticing, right through the ornate carved headstead of the sleeping cowch.

Grounsell was in the swing now and continued, 'Triseps will come and Triseps will go. Even WizardS will pass in time, but while they may intermittently be killed, and while such predeceasing prepares them to perform their own spectacular conclusion to the preparatory acts of permanent deceasement, they will meanwhile perform magic that transgresses every known lorr of nature.'

'Like what?'

'You mean, you want me to give an example of my generalisation so that you understand?'

'Yes,' said Smelta, seriously, 'I need you to explain.'

'Oh dear, well, er, nobody knows. it is so long since it happened that even the History Records have been corrupted.' replied Maecenas.

'By the magic?'

'Yes, most probably the records of the magic were corrupted by the magic itself as its dying act.'

Smelta drew in her breath and lips, raised her eyebrows and rapidly declined into a not unreasonable cold sweat by the image of uncontrollable WizardS corrupting all in their paths by what sounded like equally uncontrollable magic. 'Sounds more awful than a worst nightmare.'

'It could be degenerative or it could equally be regenerative. We will just have to wait and see, but there's no point worrying about it, is there?'

'Why not? I like worrying. I have a predilection for the horror of potential disaster.'

'Oh, it may not be disastrous. Not totally, at any rate. Nobody knows, really.' He leaned forward and kissed her gently on the forehead, but she was well and truly engrossed in the depths of a new wave of thought. He pulled back and looked at her, wishing that he had never bothered with this conversation which was sadly keeping her from joining in with mutual extra-nuptial replication practice.

* * * * *

Smelt and Maecenas crossed the Magicknot Line surrounding the Poleward side of Ozzilland and immediately felt different.

'I feel different.' Smelt said.

'So do I.' replied Maecenas.

'I don't know why; it's a bit like those nerves you get just before exams. Not fear, exactly, but not elation either and it's not like being ill.'

'I know. I feel the same. You can't really explain it, can you.'

'Only as elated queasiness.'

Smelt looked at him askance and almost smiled, 'That was double-Zimgulu if ever I heard it.'

The pair flew on towards Ozzilland retaining the curious double quizzic of nervously exhausted elation as encouragement for their next stage. They were to continue to the end of the hoverfloat autobridge, following it closely lest they get lost as the country moved from its projected course.

Their last words from Mycroft before they crossed the Magicknot Line were to be careful and to expect nothing but the unexpected and he had added, 'Remember that you are entering unknown territory, physically, metaphysically and possibly even in terms of Qontûm probability leaps.'

'But it doesn't happen at this size and level, Qontûm-wise, I mean, does it?' Maecenas had asked.

'That is a possibility that must always be considered.' M had replied, adding finally, 'so that what is, may only apparently be and what is apparently not may, in practice, be the contrary of its own apparency.'

Maecenas and Smelt had expended considerable conversation immediately before and after crossing the Magicknot Line wondering whether they understood this and deciding eventually that they thought they did; at least, each apparently thought that the other probably did, which both apparently felt was acceptable, private views notwithstanding.

Ozzilland was now in sight. Or at least, before them was a gigantic landmass tilted at about seventeen degrees and appearing to disappear into the sea in front of them.

'Look!' said Maecenas, 'See before you. The nearer we come, the more we can see that the land is next to the sea. And the land which is next to the sea is below the sea and the sea covers it not.'

Smelt looked at Maecenas and responded to his curious style, 'You are beginning to sound like a religiot reading The Folius.' he remarked.

'I was reading some of a GodspelL from the New Promisings of The Folius last night and then some of the last folio, the Book of Revealment.'

'That explains it. Magic on the one hand and GoD on the other; the two don't mix. There's definitely something strange going on in your brain.' Smelt remarked with his dry, wry smile and fully aware of GoD's injunction: *'There shall not be found among you any that useth divination or an observer of Temporras, or an enchanter, or a WitcH, or a consulter with familiar spirits, or a WizarD or a necromancer.'*

'Ah!' spotted Maecenas, 'the eighteenth chapter of the folio of Deteriorations, if I recall correctly.'

'I fear you do.' Smelt confirmed.

'But have you ever noticed that prescienters are sometimes right? I mean, just look at that amazing sight laid out before us. Was it not predicted that countries would be overturned in the End Times, and that is just what is happening before our eyes.' said Maecenas.

'Sometimes. Occasionally. Less than statistically predictable, but yes, they are sometimes right. So what?'

'Could there be something in the prediction that whole countries will be overturned?'

'Overturned can mean many things. *End Times* can mean many things, such as the last days of individual Triseps. Even *countries* can mean many things.' Smelt replied, 'And for the most part, national borders are arbitrary and certainly not divinely defined.'

'But you can't get more literally accurate than this one, surely?' checked Maecenas.

'Perhaps. Just look at it. It's like a gigantic twist. The land just drops below the sea. How does it do that? I can't see an edge. The water just stops. And to the left. Look to the left. The cliffs have risen with perfect smoothness straight out of the water and into the air and look, they rise and fall into the distance as far as we can see.'

'No. Look to the right.' Maecenas pointed. 'In the far distance. There is a sheer wall at the end of the land. It must be hundreds of thousands of lengths away. And look, see how it rises into the air, high in the sky, like the highest of alps.'

'It's so far away, I didn't see it, but yes! Yes, it's higher than Alp-Etnavolc. Higher, even, than Alp-Ever-rest.'

'And it appears even higher coming out of the lowered ground betwixt here and there. The whole land is like a ball cut in half and put down at an angle. I can't believe what I'm seeing.'

'You'd better. There's the team.'

Ahead of them, the leading exploratory team of Defenss personnel were waving a greeting from the cliff-top just to the left of the point where the ground rose above the sea.

'This must be the centre of the geoplatelet twist that Mycroft and Kernal talked about.' Maecenas said, still taking in the magnificently fearful sight with all his eyes.

The reality of the twisting of the whole of Ozzilland was hitting Smelt with a vengeance. When he first saw it, he had been awe-struck. Now, only a few hundred breaths later, the full impact was becoming utterly apparent. Smelt was struck dumb and staring agape. He hadn't heard Maecenas and was now slowly shaking his head. Ozzilland wasn't like this last time he visited. It was flat and, er, well, just flat and boring. Relatively, at least.

Smelt and Maecenas were still looking around with their minds blown open by the facts and implications of the twisted scenery around them.

As they landed beside the saluting Sqoddies on the land-ward side of the land-sea boundary, the inside edge of the sea became visible. Maecenas pointed to it but Smelt was already looking. It's smooth, perfectly smooth, like the cliffs on the other side.' He shook his head, 'The sea is just holding itself up. Look, you can see right through the water. What's holding it there? Can you see?'

Smelt was also staring, still agape, at the sea, from the sunken land-ward side, 'It must be some sort of window, I suppose. For something like that, you would expect a traditional concrete dam. I wouldn't expect a glass window tens of thousands of lengths long - and look, it hasn't even got any seams in it. It can only have been built with nanotechnology. It couldn't have been done otherwise.'

Having momentarily forgotten their mission, both suddenly, both were aware of the Sqoddies arriving at the window, including the over-sized senior Level Seven Sqoddie747.

When Smelt and Maecenas finally acknowledged the Sqoddies by a nod, Sqoddie747 offered his hands to greet them. 'Good afternoon, gentletriseps, Maecenas and Smelt, I presume.'

'Good afternoon.' replied Maecenas and Smelt together. How pleasant, thought Smelt to meet such a polite welcome in these curiously less than civilised circumstances.

'Have you seen any life?' asked Maecenas.

'No,' replied Sqoddie747, 'no life except felines, canines, dingoes and a few rookangas.'

'No Triseps?' asked Smelt.

'No, none.'

'None at all?' asked Maecenas.

'None, but neither can we work out why not.'

'Perhaps you can follow us and look at the houses, then you'll see what we saw and understand why we can't guess where all the Triseps have gone. But one way or another, gone they have. The best guess we can make at the moment is that they have gone that way.' Sqoddie747 pointed out to sea, to the line of hoverfloat autobridges stretching as far as the eye could see to the horizon. 'That theory is based on the tyre tracks of vintage non-flying moovacars as they left the dirt drives of the houses.'

Smelt and Maecenas both glanced out to sea and immediately back to Sqoddie747 in case they had not seen correctly. They had. They both looked back out to sea for a few breaths longer, but saw nothing new.

'They couldn't have gone that way with non-flying moovacars.' said Smelt, still staring out to sea.

'The road stops at the cliff-edge and anything that continued on it would end up in the sea without any doubt.'

Smelt drew in breath, raised his eyebrows and scratched his imaginary beard.

Maecenas frowned and closed his eyes to help him think. 'When did they leave?' he asked, still with a frown.

'We don't know, but to look at the staleness of food I would say it was the first day, when we all thought that Ozzilland had disappeared.' replied Sqoddie747.

'But it hadn't.' replied Smelt, 'and now we have the probable answer. Only the Triseps disappeared. That would explain the sudden disappearance of all communications.'

'Only partly.' corrected Sqoddie747.

'How so?' asked Maecenas.

'Because many communications would have continued automatically, so only manually controlled communications would have been disrupted. Automatic bleaters would continue until changes were programmed by Triseps. As each bleater has its own private power source, something pretty drastic must have occurred to stop them all at precisely the same time. It can't be accounted for by anything we see here because all the movement occurred gradually and all automatic equipment we have discovered has never stopped. If this is an example of the whole of Ozzilland, then the bleaters would have continued bleating, and we would have continued to pick up their signals. No, something more dramatic occurred in Ozzilland at the start of the movement, and we haven't worked out what it was yet.'

'Sudden Contaigen?' suggested Smelt, 'A Contaigen could kill or cause serious incapacity, couldn't it?'

'In which case there would have been bodies.' said Sqoddie747. 'No, I don't think that was what happened. Come, I will show you the evidence we have discovered; oh, and I'll show the Faerie-rings while we're there.'

* * * * *

'Here, have my can of Coker sap, I'm settling for the night.' Smelt passed the can to Maecenas before falling onto the moovacar's sleeping

197

cowch. Almost immediately his brain switched to sleep and dream mode.

Smelt snored, but only about seven times.

Maecenas watched Smelt with certain concentration, surprised at his precipitate entrancement; suddenly, he began to recite a trirhythmic-septaline, a poetic style only usually practised by the upper class Triseps of Ånjap on the Nipoff Archipelago,

The rings of Allysp found around the ground -
Caught Triseps unaware from care just there;
So where the holes had been once seen, so green
We Triseps here were brought: they sought; all caught.

Late search could find no trace of race - or place a face,
Nor any praying soul obeying, straying, playing.
Ozzis now away are tossed, riposte lost, what cost!

Maecenas recognised the poem immediately for what it was, and opened his mouth to speak and interrupt the narcolexic attack, 'I could never ... ' when the sleeping Smelt began another,

'So proud she sat, her bones on throne of stone;
Undaunted yet, her heart was ... Eh? er what? did somebody
speak?'

'Sorry to wake you, but I never could make much sense of those Nipoffese trirhythmic-septalines. The words never seem to make much sense and the scan is only interpretable if you attended a Nipoffese university. What brought that on anyway? The day's events, I suppose. But never mind, we'll go further inland all day tomorrow.'

Smelt stretched and opened his eyes properly, 'Eh? What? What did you say? Is it morning already? It's still dark outside, Eh?'

The autotranslator ignored the double prompt.

'I said ... oh, never mind. Don't stop. Tell me the rest of your poem.'

'What poem?'

'Your trirhythmic-septaline, the one that began, *So proud she sat.* '

Smelt looked at him as though he was out of his bassinette. 'What on Eqinox are you talking about?'

'Your poetry.'

'What? I'm Smelt, not Wordsmyth. I've never seen the point in poetry, really. Never uttered a word of my own poetry; I've written none. Precious little of other people's, to be truthful.'

'Do you not remember reciting poetry in your sleep?'

'No, I don't remember. Tell you what, make a recording of it for me next time. Any of that can of Coker sap left?'

'Don't they have magical powers?' asked Maecenas.

'Who? What, Coker sap?' asked Smelt, quizzically.

'The poems, the trirhythmic-septalines?'

'So it is said by them of old, but believe it if you will.' said Smelt, still slightly sceptical of his own powers as a poet.

'And every single word has a deep and hidden meaning as well as the superficial meaning.'

'Even though it appears to be nonsense at first glance.'

Maecenas laughed. 'They may appear to be nonsense, but they are all deadly serious. It is said that every one portends an event of planet-wide significance, but I could not interpret your prophecy, if that is what it was. Perhaps we can interpret it together tomorrow when we're rather more awake.'

In less than forty-seven breaths, Smelt was asleep again and muttering, but this time it had the effect of turning Maecenas ever more white as he listened to Smelt for this time the significance was less obscure,

> *Now is the time the force proports its course,*
> *For each new pack, full grown, must hack its track*
> *And weave from gate to wait 'neath geoplate;*
> *The future's known: yet never shown full blown.*

> *Within the crust now look and hook what crooks have took.*
> *Beneath the sand do stand the band from Ozzilland,*
> *Where lies betrayal; a tale to hail from past the pale.*

Maecenas was worried; he was very worried indeed. He played back the recording and replayed it and replayed it again. He told the computer to put the words in a holoquadrant and he stared at them, having only partial success in interpretative guesses. There was no doubt in his mind that here was a great deal to interpret.

He double checked that it was genuine. Yes, there were seven lines (although he had correctly heard that only WizardS could produce line zero as well, making a *full* seven lines); there were four lines with three rhymes and three lines with four rhymes; it seemed to portray events which would need interpretation. So yes, it seemed genuine enough.

Maecenas kicked himself for interrupting the second trirhythmic-septaline poem, having some sort of secret unclassifiable inkling that it could have been of serious significance.

His mind churned the consequences of the words before him and he decided to give Mycroft a callall. Nobody else, he was sure, could interpret such a text. At the same time, he feared waking Smelt in case there would be more such gems of wisdom so divined.

He told the callall to connect him to M. It complained that it could not make a link. This had never happened before.

Then he remembered that he was in the moovacar hovering, for security reasons, above Allysp Rings of central Ozzilland, now located on the Antipoleward edge.

He put in a callall to the Sqoddie on the geoplatelet boundary, now better known as the Magicknot Line and asked for the trirhythmic-septaline poems to be sent to Mycroft in the Necropol Club in Selondre for interpretation.

Now it was time for Maecenas himself to drop onto the sleeping cowch, but sleep was not an easy option. Too many events of the day were still singeing the edges of his brain cells.

* * * * *

Back in Selondre, all had retired at the Necropol Club except Steward, who took the callall from Kernal and passed the fourth-hand messages on to Mycroft taking a rare nap in his private suite.

He read the first of the poems in the holofolio. It was of little consequence, relatively speaking, to him at least. He read the second and sat up with a start and suddenly realised what he had missed in the first, 'Only seven lines. I would expect seven.'

'Sir?' puzzled Steward.

'I said, only seven lines. I would expect there to have been a full seven by now.'

'Begging your pardon, Sir?' responded Steward.

'Line zero. Ah! Perhaps it hasn't happened yet. He must be on number six.'

'I'm sorry, Sir? Number Six? Olde-fashioned cancer sticks?' suggested Steward, who was quite used to Mycroft's curious monologues about things that nobody else understood. He nevertheless understood his own position. He was useful for Mycroft to talk to, a brain, albeit of lesser ability, to bounce ideas off; to respond with the common Trisep's firmly held but unresearched and only partly informed opinion.

'No! Daughters, Steward, daughters.'

Steward raised his eyebrows and twisted his front head to a questioning angle. He was even more baffled than before. cancer sticks he understood. Pipes filled with netherwear blowing obscure mathematical symbols as smoke-rings, that he understood. But daughters. Daughters? Daughters! What would Mycroft of all fellows know about daughters? Now, *that* was a puzzle.

'Would you arrange to reconvene now, please.'

'Do you mean the Summit, Sir?'

'Yes, please.' said M, shutting his eyes as if to doze.

'*Now* Sir?'

'Yes please.'

'With the greatest of respect, Sir, it is the middle of the night and everyone from the Summit will be asleep.'

'Then we must wake them. We must reconvene with the greatest of urgency. This message has provided me with the missing links.'

'The missing links, Sir. Yes Sir, I will arrange it straight away.' He began to walk away to carry out his orders, 'the missing links.' repeated Steward to himself, always hoping but not now or ever expecting to learn much more at this stage, and he was right, he would be told no more for the time being, but he knew that something of a grand order was afoot, or awry perhaps. It was always rather difficult to tell with Mycroft's expressionless visage.

* * * * *

'Aaagh.' said Grounsell in pretence of a scream. Smelta woke up and looked at him, wondering what he was complaining about.

'It's the damned callall. Probably a wrong number.' He turned to the callall, answered it and rapidly regained full consciousness on seeing Mycroft's reference but not noticing the face. 'GoD,' he said, 'it *must* be important if you are waking me now. What's happened?'

'It isn't Mycroft.' said Steward, whose face now appeared. 'I am using Mycroft's callall for security reasons. I have been asked to reconvene the Summit.'

'But it's the middle of the ... '

'Yes, I know it's the middle of the night.' interrupted Steward, 'but there's been a development. All I know is that there has been an emergency communication from Ozzilland and you are respectfully asked to reconvene. Please. Urgently.' he paused and added, 'He means now.'

'I'll be there.'

Grounsell terminated the callall and turned his front head to Smelta. She was fully awake now and equally puzzled, particularly knowing that Smelt was there with Maecenas.

'You should tell Grounsella. She will want to know what is happening to Smelt.'

Grounsell raised his eyebrows in surprise and frowned with jealousy, not wanting to tell her.

'If I were carrying *your* daughter, I would want to know if you were in trouble, whatever the circumstances.' said Smelta.

'We don't know if he's in trouble. Yet.'

'But he must be. The message was from Ozzilland. Smelt is in Ozzilland. Mycroft would not have callalled us in the middle of the night unless it was life and deceasement.' said Smelta, wearing a most worried frown.

'We'll see, but if it were that bad, I am sure you would have heard directly. He probably just wants approval of his actions for the next stage of his plans. Remember what an eccentric he is.'

'You're right, perhaps. Perhaps he doesn't know what night is!' she grinned.

'That's better.' he laughed, 'I was getting worried about you.'

She pulled him towards him, 'Trouble is,' she said as she kissed him, 'trouble is that I was about to wake up with better plans for tonight. I think we are, er,' she kissed him again, 'er, we're a bit behind with practising our replication techniques!'

'Not now, darling, we'll have to practise our marital arts later.'

* * * * *

'They're ready.' Nanotech329 reported to Kernal.

'Eh?'' asked Kernal, who was deeply engrossed in a virtual holomap made from reports of where Ozzilland had moved to.

'*Er,*' began the autotranslator, not sure how to translate two simple words of a language into itself.

'Shut up.' said Kernal without turning his head away from Nanotech329.

'Sorry. I thought you would like to know.' said Nanotech329, still unused to Defenss protocol and the Kernal's manner.

'Not you, I was telling the autotranslator to shut up before it reached full speed.' He looked up at Nanotech329 for the first time.

'Ah, you mean the armoured moovacars? They're ready?'

'Yes.'

'All of them? You only did it in your spare time.'

'I know. Yes, they're ready.'

Kernal ordered his troops to be ready to go into Ozzilland. He had prepared a whole septallion of one level seven officer and seven level five officers, each with seven level three Sqoddies, each in turn commanding forty-seven ordinary Sqoddies. They would all go to Ozzilland. Each would take one of the armoured moovacars and explore a different area.

All Kernal needed now was the go-ahead from the Convention, although he was wondering where the real power lay now that the Summit seemed to have taken over power, and Mycroft from the Summit.

'Have I permission to go?' asked Nanotech329.

'Yes, off you go.' retorted Kernal, undefenss-like.

'No, I mean to Ozzilland?'

'Ah. Later, perhaps, when it has stopped moving, but for now, it is safer here and I would rather you stayed. We may need you.'

'Many others can do my job quite as well.'

'But you know our position. A new Nanotech Trisep would need to be trained. No, I can't permit you to go to Ozzilland.'

Kernal dismissed Nanotech329 and made a callall to the Necropol Club, forgetting the time difference between Scotaisle and the Squeithian capital of Selondre.

Mycroft was, of course, awake. The Summit was reconvening. Kernal had forwarded a couple of rather silly poems because he had been asked to as a matter of urgency. For the life of him, he could not see what significance they had or why they were so urgent. But Maecenas had and he outranked Kernal, so his orders had to be obeyed. But why send a couple of singularly childish poems on over-cipher? Now that really was a puzzle.

Never mind, he shrugged, and called his herd leader to join him in a dance to the latest autoerotic nanogroove.

* * * * *

'Steward here has known me a long time and is a sort of confidante.' began Mycroft, 'He will be joining us and if there is anything you don't understand, he should be able to translate it into everyday language. I'm not such a fool that I don't realise how I am stuck here in my casponite tower away from any reality of the real world.'

Mycroft spent the rest of the night explaining the significance of the two trirhythmic-septaline poems to the assembly including all the peripheral details.

'Shouldn't we tell the Convention and then prepare the world?' suggested Amoricspolit7.

'The world is not ready yet, we must first straighten the Ozzilland position and announce that.'

'Wiz dat ism how-how do Zimgululland is voodoo dat nuf im dism off?' asked Zimgulupolit7.

'Will the new situation affect my country, Zimgululland, and will voodoo help us to make a difference?'

'Good job the autotranslator came back.' laughed Grounsell quietly to Smelta.

'I thought it was clear.' replied M, 'nothing has happened or is likely to happen that will make too much difference to Zimgululland, except for the increased powers of thaumas, WitcheS, WizardS and GrandwizardS.'

'Adjacent affect are because but closer. dramatically immediately in much Ozzilland problems quite surely the us we we're will?' said Sammowapolit7, adding, '¿About and eqiqakes climate, even tides what'

'But we are much closer; surely the problems in Ozzilland will affect us quite dramatically, because we're immediately adjacent? What about climate, tides, and even eqiquakes?'

'My answer is the same as for Zimgululland. Neither will you suffer excessively from unexpected climatic, tidal or geoplatelet activity.'

'¿Excessively' asked Sammowapolit7.

'No more than can be expected in the circumstances already defined,' replied M, 'but you must remember never to forget the potential of the Gobblings!'

'And the Faeries?' suggested Amoricspolit7.

'The Faeries will always have a jolly gay time, old chap, whatever else happens.' replied M.

* * * * *

Mycroft asked Polit46 to remain for lunch.

'I'm going to callall Quax.' he announced when they were finally alone.

'Don't you think I should do that as a matter of protocol?' replied Polit46.

'Yes and no.' M looked firmly at Polit46, 'Yes because you have always been the primary contact and no because I have to go myself. I and I alone can speak Gobbling. More to the point, I can speak Elfin B, the language of the Dark Elves of Sammowa and Ozzilland.'

Polit46 stared at him and stopped chewing halfway through an open-mouthed chew, displaying his half-digested critter rump. 'I see.' he eventually spluttered out, having forgotten that he was eating.

'Oh, and I can also speak Esquimeaux and that may be useful in Scotaisle and Antipole, should we need to go that far. As I implied earlier, we are unlikely to need to go outside the seven geoplatelets of Ozzilland; there being a theoretical $46.776+0.001$ in forty-seven chance that the Qontûm solution will be wholly contained within that area.'

Polit46 nodded approval and agreement. 'A high chance, yes. So there is a small chance of - well, of what?'

'That the phenomenon may have spread beyond Ozzilland, but I have no evidence whatsoever to support the reality of that theory, thus the probability factor diminishes with every breath that passes.'

'I am still worried about the Qontûm solution. I never did understand science subjects. I only just understand basic relativity and we are supposed to understand that in the first year of education.'

'I suggest,' suggested Mycroft, 'that you read the famously hawked folio, *Qontûm State Has Moved Here, Probably* by Stephen.'

'There's got to be a simpler solution.'

'There is: forty-two, but that's another story.'

'And in base thirteen, so I hear' said Polit46 with an *I'm-not-sure-what-I'm-talking-about* kind of smile. The returned look from Mycroft instantly warned him that trying to outdo him could end up as a multi-dimensional metaphysical brawl. He thought for a moment and then pondered what a metaphysical brawl would look like, and whether metaphysics had multiple dimensions. Then he determined to look up the *metaphysics* word next time he had an opportunity.

Logic told Polit46 that he must inevitably go against his political training and instinct and shut up as the better part of valour. 'I'd better follow my own logic, then.' he said with that condescending equivocation practised only by defeated politicians.

Mycroft raised one eyebrow at Polit46, not having been privy to his innermost thoughts.

Chapter 12   This Land is Your Land . . .

The Summit clump returned to the Conventionium at Polit46's behest and reported the agreed statement on the known facts of Ozzilland. Meanwhile, the Convention had not so much been unconvened as allowed to degenerate into a public debate with virtually no knowledge of the real events.

Cate'aeddy repeated the statement through the public e-commenter network and immediately departed to Scotaisle to witness the final preparations for the invasion by Squeithian Defenss force Sqoddies.

Meanwhile, Mycroft spoke to Quax in Gobbling on the private callall, borrowed a moovacar (he being in the unprecedented (and unique on the planet) position of not having one of his own) and collected Quax from a secret location somewhere near Squelchpool.

Unknown to the rest of the planet, including Polit46 and the Eqinox government, Mycroft had been negotiating with the Gobblings in the utmost secrecy for many years. There was no reason now for this secret to be broadcast, even though amongst Triseps generally, the definition of a secret is something told to only one other Trisep at a time, expecting it to be treated with like respect when forwarded.

Mycroft experienced no difficulty in explaining the significance of the trirhythmic-septalines to Quax, who knew him as the only truly trustworthy Gobbling, despite all she may have said for public consumption. Indeed, Mycroft, too, had said a great deal for public and even Summit consumption that could be considered to be doubtful by comparison with reality.

It only needed the two of them to effect Mycroft's plan for Ozzilland.

Mycroft made an adjustment to the callall. 'I'm adjusting the dingdong to cut you out.'

'Adjusting the what?' asked Quax who had never heard the term before.

'The dingdong. Some of us older Triseps still call a callall a dingdong after Alexigram Dingdong who invented the first primitive communicator, that worked with electricity moving along wires. I'll refer to dingdongs as callalls in future.

He finished setting the callall so that Quax could not be seen by his interlocutors and immediately callalled Kernal. 'Have you yet received instructions from Polit46 and the Eqinox Government?'

'Yes. I have been commanded to follow your instructions to the letter.'

'Good. Your septallion of troops must be stationed evenly in every town of Ozzilland in direct proportion to the number of residents from that area. Do not, I repeat, do not place any in Allysp Rings; that town is to remain empty. Remember that not only has the country rotated to be upside down, but that each of the seven geoplatelets has rotated. But there is some good news.'

Kernal was already beginning to lose track of Mycroft, technically - or rather, geographically, 'What's the good news? You surely cannot add anything as you haven't been there yet.'

'Perhaps not, but I have logic.'

'The seven finely balanced hemispherical geoplatelets of Ozzilland, which are not actually hemispheres but only appear to be, have moved on their gimbals due to the combined movement of the planet and the new movement of the continent of Ozzilland as a subset of geoplatelets. Straightforward. It works with simple centrifugal forces, rather like a governing set of heavy balls in an old pressure-vapour engine. The angles, relative speeds, characteristics of acceleration and deceleration and general descriptions you have forwarded to me wholly concur with my own calculations. There is no doubt about my conclusions.'

'I can't envisage the outcome of that statement.' said Kernal, trying to sound as though he understood it - a bit at least.

Mycroft secretly despaired for the future of intelligent life on Eqinox, 'Listen carefully, this is important. By the time I reach Scotaisle, the septallion must have completely left. I will follow them and I require purple air space throughout. To remind you, that means that there must be no other moovacar or other object within 4747 lengths of my own location.'

Kernal had already detected that he was not receiving the normally complete holopicture of the whole of the inside of the moovacar. Initially, he had put this down to Mycroft's eccentric and paranoiac penchant for privacy. Now he wasn't so sure. What had he got in there?

'In HobB's name, what are you carrying? Have you got an atom-splitting molotov on board?'

'I confirm that I do not have an atom-splitting molotov, but I do have a top-secret classified cargo.'

The out-of-sight Quax raised one eyebrow and laughed silently at being described as a cargo.

'You will have your purple air space. As soon as you come within range I will provide an escort.'

'Outside the specified distance for my purple air space please.'

'Of course, Mycroft. They will come no closer.' replied Kernal, 'Can you give me further details of your mission?'

'The destination is Ozzilland via Scotaisle. I shall be following the line of the hoverfloat autobridge. You have no need of further information at this stage. Remember to clear Allysp Rings of all live activity and all autofollowing holocams.'

'Yes, Sir.' replied Kernal with appropriate deference.

Mycroft terminated the callall and turned to Quax. 'That should clear the route for us. Do you know, there was a short period when I was seriously worried about your intentions. Of course, as the Hobbimps are the most intelligent of the Gobblings, you would have been the *nerve centre.'*

'Naturally,' replied Quax, 'so your best solution would have been an underground detonation of an atom-splitting molotov beneath Squeith, particularly based on the hub city of Qontûm.'

'If we could find it at any one time, yes, we would have needed to destroy the nerve centre itself, even if it led to our own destruction.' replied Mycroft with only half a smile, 'Of course, we would need to take into account the probability factor of the movement of Qontûm and its location at any one time may or may not be where it actually is.'

'According to the Qontûm of its energy, external force and the elginfunction of uncertainty; remember also the pizzazz factor of attractiveness of moving or otherwise at any one time according to external factors.' responded Quax, showing off a bit.

'We have questioned many Triseps,' said Quax, 'and I have conversed with you before, but I am convinced that you are the only one of your race who really understands what is happening down there.'

'Except Stephen, of course!' replied Mycroft, and took a sip of his genuine hand brewed geeantee which he stocked up with before leaving the Necropol Club, 'Actually, quite a lot of Triseps understand the advanced stuff but few understand it all, and they don't tend to be hikers who fall down your holes.'

'Perhaps ... ' grinned Quax, 'perhaps Triseps aren't as thick as we define them to be.'

'I could say the same of Gobblings and Hobbimps in particular. The impression from the surface is a very primitive one. Nobody would guess that what we saw was only a minor trading town cross-roads within a whole Underplanet of activity and technology.'

'Hive.' said Quax.

'Hive?'

'Yes, most Triseps would call it a hive of activity. I am not sure whether that is just terminology or slightly insulting.' She moved a piece of the Financial Monopoly game between them. 'Your move, I think.'

'I haven't decided yet,' said Mycroft, 'whether it would be of greater etiquette to let you win or to declare an early chequemate.'

Quax was on a par, if not actually ahead of him, 'Do you mean in this game or in real life?' she asked.

'Does this game not reflect reality, not just to some extent but to a very high degree?' suggested Mycroft, 'Are not the wars of old simply replaced by the highest levels of sport? Is not a bail battering test match for custody of an urn of ashes our equivalent of a battle for custody of a third country? Is not international Financial Monopoly the equivalent of a trading war where the rents go to the winner? Isn't chequemate the equivalent of financial domination in the real Eqinox ? Isn't lobbing an odd-shaped ball over a golejibbit exactly the equivalent of lobbing a cannon-shell at the enemy's camp?'

Quax nodded in agreement.

'By the way,' said M, 'Maximum of twenty three moves to certain chequemate unless I am mistaken.'

'You win this time, but next time you will lose.' said Quax, 'By the way, can we challenge you to a game of bail battering one day? We play it ourselves, with the same size equipment as you and we have certain advantages of speed, while you have the advantage of an extra hand and the stability of four legs. I think we would be evenly matched.'

'And the golejibbit game?' suggested M.

'Now that's a different matter entirely,' said Quax backing down, 'but we could have an inter-being intelligence contest. You already have Mensa, the Mental Exercises and Neural Stimulation Association and we have a similar body; Gobblings who claim to be intelligent meet to play tyddly-wynks and drink too much. The ultimate in non-volatile war must surely be pure mental activity, battling wit against wit.'

'As we are doing with this game?' suggested M.

'Indeed so!'

'It's a good job for us that Gobblings can only read the minds of other Gobblings and not of Triseps. By the way, I never did know the secret of that. What is the mechanism for it?'

'Ha!' replied Quax, 'simply that Hobbimp neural activity is displayed as visible rapidly changing micro-pimple skin variations on the forehead. Once you have been trained to decipher the code, it is just like reading a holofolio.'

'Perhaps if Triseps didn't have hair,' said M, 'we may have similar capabilities. As it is, only the automed's Phroydtest is able to analyse neuronal activity, but it has never been able to analyse *every* thought.'

'That's exactly the problem,' said Quax moving another piece, 'or at least, it used to be. We have to learn at an early age to use a different part of our brain for secret thoughts from that part used for public thoughts. It can be quite useful if you are a politician and want to make a public statement at variance from private thoughts. Remember that we see each other in a different spectrum than you do by using surface light from the sun, and that makes a difference too.'

'You still can't win.' said Mycroft, moving his own piece.

'Then I concede, but only in the game.' she laughed, 'I am still puzzled.'

Mycroft looked at the game board. He knew his king was safe. 'About what?'

'About why you didn't start a war against us by a pre-emptive strike. Your weapons were ready. We would have been caught unawares and could not have reciprocated in time. Not in the early stages at least.'

'We didn't start a war because the politicians, as you know, called a Convention which prevaricated far too long. Eventually, they asked my advice. I would never start a war if it meant that the Necropol Club would be damaged. After all, I've got to live somewhere!' he smiled and she wasn't quite sure whether he was factualising or cracking a joke.

'Couldn't you have moved or replicated the Necropol Club?'

'Only if really necessary, yes. We could have cloned it, but somehow that would never be quite the same. It isn't just the place, it is the certain knowledge of so many generations of history. Even if we cloned every last precious dust particle, it would never be quite the same, somehow.'

Quax nodded in understanding.

He moved a piece. 'Chequemate! I get all your money.'

'I thought I had already conceded;' laughed Quax, 'we must have that bail battering match quite soon. I am determined to beat you at *something!*'

Mycroft laughed. 'Let's eat. Then I'll teach you how to play some printed card gambling games like Firebrand.'

'Sounds lethal,' she said.

'Triseps have been known, in certain societies, to kill over losing a mere game of cards. Gangsters, crooks and international playboys used to play it for money, when money was of value before the invention of nanotechnology. When greed became more valuable than life, they used to kill for the winnings of another, or because one claimed that another cheated.'

A warning ping sounded. Another moovacar, a Defenss moovacar had entered inside the purple air space, but only just, by half a length. It was flying exactly on the limit and had now turned to escort them for the last few thousand breaths towards Scotaisle.

Quax saw the escort and ducked.

'You need not worry,' said M, who was only slightly more used to the technology of moovacars than Quax, 'you can see out but they can't see in at that distance, even in the x-ray spectrum. You are quite safe from being seen. Are you mentally prepared for our excursion when we finally reach Ozzilland?'

'I think so;' replied Quax, 'it shouldn't prove very difficult if your theory is correct.'

'All other theories have now proved to be impossible and so what is left, although wholly improbable when viewed from a historical perspective is now the only possible answer.' reminded Mycroft. 'You know, I have a brother who is a detective and he needs to be reminded of that fact from time to time, particularly if he thinks the case too simple for his advanced brain and tries to solve it while snorting substances of dubious legality.'

'I confess that a little part of me still needs some convincing.' she agreed.

'Divide et impera. Remember, divide a problem into its component parts in order to understand and overcome it. No problem, however large or small, can be tackled unless it can be understood. Logic tells us that we can only wholly understand the characteristics of one component at a time.'

'That is indeed, and as you know, the way we organise our society.' replied Quax, 'We are divided into tribes and our tribes are divided into sub-tribes. Each sub-tribe has towns and towns have families, so you see, we work the same way. We also divide and thus conquer and control the Gobbling population, as you know.'

'I know.' said M, taking the new pack of cards from the provisions hatch.

* * * * *

Cate'aeddy reported the build-up of troops and the despatch of a Septallion from Scotaisle to Ozzilland. She stood in front of her personal autofollowing holocam in full battle dress.

With just the standard anonymous camouflage-coloured tent as background, Cate'aeddy told the story as she saw it. A few Sqoddies were filmed entering their armoured moovacars, but as in all Defenss operations, she was kept in the dark about what was really happening and she could only report superficially.

Truth was that she had a sort of internal auto-pilot, which sometimes regurgitated the facts fed to her.

There's nothing else worth saying on that subject, really.

* * * * *

Smelt and Maecenas stared at Sqoddie747, 'Cleared? What do you mean, cleared? why does Allysp Rings have to be cleared?'

'Orders, Sir.'

'From whom?'

'From Kernal, Sir.'

'Why?'

Kernal

'He's ordered a full invasion of Ozzilland. A full septallion will be arriving here and spreading out to every city, town, village and hamlet. Troops are to be located in each place in direct proportion to the population.'

'Then we can watch what happens from here in Allysp Rings.' argued Maecenas.

'No, Sir, I'm afraid Allysp Rings must be completely cleared. Nobody must remain, nobody at all.'

'Why not?'

'Orders, Sir.'

'You've said that once; but why has the order been given?'

'I only know that the reason is secret.'

'Will you please tell Kernal that I, Maecenas the Eqinox Government's Chief Scientist and Scientific Historian order him to tell me the reason for this action.'

'Yes, Sir.'

Sqoddie747 immediately callalled the Magicknot Line and ordered the instruction from Maecenas to be forwarded to Kernal. The olde-fashioned wire-less link across the Magicknot Line was becoming better at each attempt, since the movement of the plates inside the line had now slowed almost, but not quite, to a standstill. Nevertheless, direct contact from Ozzilland to Scotaisle remained impossible.

The answer came back very quickly from Kernal, 'I am unable to grant your request for further information on the order to clear Allysp Rings as the order was from a more senior source. I will, however, ask permission from that source forthwith to provide more data.'

'I am worried, Smelt, very worried. What higher authority is there, except the Eqinox Government itself, and they wouldn't make a secret order like that unless, unless, er, well, unless something very dramatic indeed has happened.'

'What sort of event?' asked Smelt.

'Like the Hobbimp Gobblings invading Selondre.'

The two men looked at each other and at Sqoddie747, fearful of what could be transpiring elsewhere on the planet.

Sqoddie747, as a most senior officer, was permitted to know virtually all government secrets and could even start minor wars if he were foolish enough to be so minded, but an order such as this, and at an even higher level of secrecy was beyond his experience.

Another callall began from the Magicknot Line. A message from Kernal. Maecenas and Smelt could stay in Allysp Rings but Sqoddie747 and all others must move away according to the distribution plan. A visitor, apparently just called M, was imminently expected with a secret cargo.

Maecenas and Smelt greeted the news with a knowing smile. At last, the alp was coming, as it were, to Ozzilland. Just what, though, could have persuaded Mycroft to leave the Necropol Club was another question that they would have to wait to discover. But the wait would soon be over. At least that was what they supposed.

Meanwhile, the Triseps of Ozzilland remained lost.

* * * * *

'CROLL TROLL TOLL TRAGEDY' read the headline in the Miroray daily chronicle, resulting in several hundred Triseps reported to automeds with bad cases of seriously twisted tongues.

The world was waking up to another ENN report, this time from Walled Faience where the Trolls had apparently taken a particularly bad toll in a small village called Croll.

Apparently, the triple-besom driving thaumas had all gone to bed early because of a deep mist and a few had unwittingly crashed because they couldn't see where the ground was.

What happened next in Croll was not so much a fact but more depended on which version of the story you heard first, although they nearly all involved magic of one sort or another.

In the least dramatic version, the Trolls appeared in the night, kissed all the male Triseps and because of the latent magic lying around and not being disseminated by the thaumas, they turned into frogs and hopped away into the night, looking for still, fresh water.

Another version suggested that the sudden appearance of a Sharen in the village gave all the males an excuse to escape from their wives for a night after they had fallen asleep. Once ensconced with Sharen in an orgiastic autostack, they all became so over-excited that, one after the other, they died of exhaustion and they were in such a heightened sexual frenzy at the time that decomposition began immediately; however, by the time the wives arrived they had more sort of melted rather than decomposed, leaving nothing more than a little heap of worthless chemicals.

Two further versions involved whirlwinds. One suggested that there was a sudden whirlwind while all the males were attending an Anti-husband-Beating Victim's Greeting and Eating Meeting and were taken up into the sky, while the other said that they had gone on a whirlwind tour of the underground cities, taken by the Trolls in a pretence of a truce, but were kept there and probably eaten as aphrodisiacs.

The fifth, and perhaps most credible version was that the grounded thaumas, the feminist mothers-in-lorr, saw the light and decided to banish all men from the village, so cast simple banishment spells which (would only work for WitcheS, unless forty-seven thaumas could actually agree to act in unison). The men were so upset that when they met together on a green hill without the city walls (as they called the wooden paling fence round the village), er, where were we, oh yes, the men were so upset that when they met, they spontaneously ignited. This last theory is given added credibility by the pile of ashes left on the hillock outside the village.

The sixth theory is similar, suggesting that the males were trying to curry favour with GoD by making an olde-fashioned Middle-Eons style sacrifice of pre-copulate daughters. The fire is said to have spread to the males, who exploded because of the excess oxygen in their bodies after hyperventilating at the exciting thought of certain illegal activities about to be undertaken for their own pleasures. This theory is only given credibility by one pre-copulate daughter who became as madly mentally unstable as her mother and refused to do anything all day except play the virginals.

All are agreed on one point only.

They are agreed that only that the males of the village disappeared during the night, every single one of them, and the next morning when a visiting Troll was captured, he denied all knowledge of the incident and offered to help solve the mystery.

By the time EBC's Eqinox Nebulus News holocam team arrived, it was all over and there was nothing left to report. A storm had washed the ashes into the ground, so it might have just been an ordinary bonfire, but who could tell? Yes, there were a lot of frogs, like there were after every storm. Yes, there were little piles of worthless chemicals. Yes, nobody trusted the word of a shifty-eyed Troll. Yes, there was a pre-copulate daughter who may or may not have previously been sane. But, no! Nobody could work out the truth of this strange event.

The repercussions reverberated around Eqinox, fuelled and exaggerated as ever by the journalists rather than by any genuine public opinion. But then, the entire universe knows that the journalists' *a storm has broken out about ...* really means that they have just discovered something to write about that the rest of us already knew, but didn't really care about. Matters like the wearing of critter furs or the hunting of anything four-legged.

But something happened and everyone will find out what in due course. Probably.

* * * *

Mycroft landed and alighted from the moovacar far enough away from Maecenas and Smelt for them not to be able to see inside.

He sidled across to them. 'Well, it certainly is good to see you.' said Maecenas from the heart, 'what is so important that you, of all hermitic Triseps, needed to come all the way to Ozzilland?'

'I needed to come myself.'

'What can you learn that we could not have told you? I know you hate travelling. I have already confirmed the facts; I am sure you will confirm them too.' said Maecenas.

'My purpose in being here is to unlock the divination key provided by the GodS through the prophetic trirhythmic-septalines.'

Smelt and Maecenas looked at each other with their front heads and back to Mycroft, 'I thought you didn't believe in GodS and HobbS or anything spiritual, good or evil. Do you?' asked Maecenas.

'Yes.' said Mycroft firmly, 'And no!' He looked from one to the other, 'The facts are contradictory. There is no direct evidence of GodS or HobbS and never has been. All evidence is second-hand through Prophets and Touchers, those who claim to have been touched by GoD. An indeterminate proportion of the claims of such Triseps become reality and perception bias thus validates the principle.'

215

'I still don't understand;' said Smelt, scratching an ear, 'does this mean that you are expecting the GodS to help you solve the Ozzilland problem through prophecy or something similar?'

'No.' Mycroft replied, unhelpfully, 'Of course not. Tell me Smelt, have you experienced any further dreams?'

'I don't think so.' Smelt looked at Maecenas.

'No, he hasn't; at least, none articulated.' said Maecenas.

'Good, then the answer is probably locked into the first two;' said M, 'if not, we should await the next. If you read them carefully, then you will see that we have been given the answers. It is not for me to judge whether your dreaming poems came from a GoD, or from the GodS, or from HobB, or from you own sub-conscious or your sub-conscientious, or from some other source. The fact is clear that they confirm one of my possible solutions. You should be reassured that I have not relied solely on your poems, but have independently confirmed my hypothesis; my hypothesis being hypothesis no longer but definitive.'

Smelt was only a little wiser, and despite his vastly greater scientific and historical knowledge and qualifications, so was Maecenas.

'To be wholly honest,' began Smelt, 'although my hobby is decryption, I haven't taken the opportunity to look at the poems because there have been far more interesting matters here to study.'

'But you should have done!' replied Mycroft, always amazed at the incompetences of lesser intelligences, 'What more interesting matters are there than the ultimate solution?'

'I hardly see how a poem dreamed could be the ultimate solution!' replied Smelt.

'Remember that you are currently replicating your sixth daughter, so the magical powers are beginning to build up within you. Only one more in your case and, as you know, the world will be an entirely different pearl-shell for you.'

'I have always tried to avoid that possibility. Number six was an accident.'

'And number seven is not a possibility, it is an inevitability. It is wholly inevitable that you will produce the seventh and become what you must become. That is also clear from your second incomplete poem.'

Smelt hung his heads, but half looked up and nodded in reluctant acceptance of the inevitable, 'Oh.' was all he could muster from his shivering lips.

'And the third trirhythmic-septaline poem,' began Mycroft with uncharacteristic enthusiasm, 'defines the current location and condition of the Ozzillanders. That is why I have brought Quax.'

'Quax!' exclaimed Maecenas and Smelt with one accord, 'Why?'

All three stood agape, each staring at the other two with one eye on each. Mycroft puzzled over how the other two were unaware why Quax accompanied him; Smelt was Gobbling-smacked (to mint a phrase) that he should be the one to portend; Maecenas quite frankly did not understand the situation at all and really could not work out what was going on.

Mycroft took out his pipe and re-lit his netherwear. He puffed a few smoke symbols which appeared to be advanced Convinciing Geometry, not surprising in the circumstances.

Smelt looked at the symbols, 'So what happens next?' he asked, eventually breaking the silence.

'Clearly the Ozzillanders are alive and below us in the hemispheres, along with the local tribe of Gobblings, the rest of the Dark Elves, who are also trapped and probably waiting for the movement to stop before showing themselves. I have brought Quax along to divine the precise current location and movement, if any, of the Poleward Qontûm which was and should currently be beneath central Ozzilland near Allysp Rings. When she has located them, she will motorphroyd a hole to them. Once the Dark Elves' situation and Triseps' condition has been established, we can recover to a more normal lifestyle; relatively speaking, that is, except that life will never be the same again now that magic is rearing its dubiously attractive little head once more.' M sidled across towards the moovacar, stopped and turned his front head, 'Oh, by the way, it is your *future*, Smelt, and not your *past* that has guaranteed your senior position in the recent governmental Summit.' He turned to continue to fetch Quax from her hiding place.

'How did you *know?*' asked Smelt, but M had already switched off and was sidling back to his moovacar.

On the return, he was speaking to Quax in a language the like of which neither Smelt nor Maecenas had ever heard. The only way to describe it in comparison to Squeithian was that it was about as similar as a magma rock from Alp-Etnavolc was to the legendary Phroydian philosopho-psychological interpretation of the Antilogic Paradox of Cantor.

Smelt and Maecenas listened to the conversation in awe and wonder, while still building more awe and further thunderous wonder from M's previous speech to them.

Smelt looked at Quax, put out his third hand and then withdrew it suspiciously, wondering whether it was safe to greet her by any physical contact.

Mycroft read his mind, 'Don't worry, Smelt, Quax is quite harmless now. It is only the wet kisses that are dangerous, and then only after a Gobbling has recently eaten leaves the venomous, self-defending vipertree. Unfortunately, even though they are deadly poisonous to us, they are a delicacy to all tribes of Gobblings and they consume massive amounts on every surface visit. You may be assured that a normal handshake is quite in order.'

Maecenas offered his third hand and it was warmly taken and shaken by Quax.

Smelt, still retaining a natural degree of doubt, followed suit. Some suffering can never be forgotten.

'You may be assured,' said Quax with what Smelt felt was a dubious adequacy of economy with the reality, 'that you will have no after effects from our meeting this time. Mycroft has persuaded me that we Gobblings have nothing to fear from Triseps.'

That depends whether I get *my* way, thought Smelt but didn't dare make his thoughts public. He was quite sure, however, that Quax knew exactly what he was thinking, and what's more, she probably knew why.

'There is plenty of time before we should begin,' said M, 'so why don't we settle down to a good meal?'

'And social conversation?' added Quax with what the others realised must be a smile, aware that she was not just talking to the relatively dour M.

'But first,' said Quax with an unexpected degree of seriousness, 'I hope you will all remember that this land is not your land and this land is not my land; while this land is your land and this land is my land, your land and my land are made for you and me so must be cut evenly if there survive hereunder no other valid claimants, despite Mycroft's specifically calculated assurances to the contrary.' She looked at the silently gathered and expressionless clump and continued, 'Now, about that social conversation with a good meal?'

'Good idea!' enjoined Maecenas gaily, yet still looking at Quax with some doubt and mentally replaying her words to extricate their precise meaning from their equally intricate perplexion. He remembered that Quax always spoke with precision, so he wanted the meaning to be clear in his mind.

'I have brought some real food from the Necropol Club.' said M, unperturbed, and proceeded, unmoved by the speech, to his moovacar to make the preparations for the first class, six-course, formal dinner that his accustomed lifestyle evidently required.

* * * * *

Smelta and Grounsell, back in Selondre were finishing their specs of wine while quietly listening to the end of the story and the last movement of a chunk of music that all came together with a combined Delius Myth recipe.

'There's not much else to do, really,' said Smelta to Grounsell back in Selondre, and smiling one of those ultric-charming smiles that said it all, 'so shall we er,' she stroked his front and rear foreheads with her own as encouragement, 'er, retire?'

Grounsell needed little encouragement for such activity, having been in a semi-permanent state of arousal for the past few weeks.

As they plaited their arms and intertwingled their increasingly excited bodies on the double sleeping cowch, the callall berped.

A reluctant separation, leaving but a kiss behind. It was a wrong number. 'Why do wrong numbers *always* happen just as things are getting interesting?' Smelta moaned, 'I was sure that was Smelt's berp. So much for hoping for more news from him.' She looked lovingly into Grounsell's tender yellow eyes, and said less mystically than she intended, 'not, of course, that I would prefer the interrupter to the interrupted.'

* * * * *

Earlier, Smelt had sent a message via the Magicknot Line and Kernal to Smelta that he was well, which didn't really tell her anything, and that Maecenas was well, which told her even less and that their work was progressing satisfactorily which was so vague he could just as well have been a politician - or worse still, Profmed. However, he failed to mention the arrival of M and Quax or their plans for the morrow, whatever they may be, probably because at this stage M's plans remained about as clear to him as a quag in a squelch.

Maecenas was rather more philosophical about the whole thing, having seen Mycroft's modus operandi before. He knew that whatever happened, Mycroft had it all worked out, probably. But as a scientist, he was still baffled as to why communications were cut so suddenly at the time of the original apparent disappearance of Ozzilland. He still would have expected most of the automatic bleatings to continue and for an emergency message to have escaped, at least.

Maecenas thus feared the worst for the Ozzillanders' lives and in one sense he was as right as Smelt in his hypothesis, but all would, with all probability, be revealed in the morning. 'Good-night' he said and told the light to extinguish, which it obligingly did, at the same pace as Smelt fell to sleep.

* * * * *

Forty-seven breaths later, he spoke a speech which, this time, Maecenas felt heartily honoured to hear,

> *That MystyK lost from woe, long 'go, you know,*
> *When WizardS last whizzed past the planet vast -*
> *Did in hide abide, obdurate to chide*
> *The many calling back who lacked the crack.*

And now Temporra's right to sight the light at night
Then MystyK will escape great fate of geoplate
Again to fly; allay betrayal and hail the grail!

Maecenas watched and listened with detailed care to every least jot of the latest trirhythmic-septaline, with mouth agape and in horror-filled wonderment while a silent query begged itself to be asked: *to wake or not to wake?* that was the question.

This latest prophecy was clearer to him than the previous and he could see the magic forces appearing in the netherlight of x-ray.

The power of the 'M' word was clear to see, for as Smelt spoke, so the unseen yet clearly visible magical light of the sound betrayed the power of a force unknown before, even in the vast scientific and mathematical knowledge Maecenas boasted.

Here was news. Here was power. Here was a poem so powerful that every word soared to the hites of his brain and bored its lexis to the very depth of his core.

Maecenas was born great, but here before him was a Trisep who was at this precise moment having greatness thrust upon him, and he, Maecenas, knew it and felt honoured to be the only witness to it.

He could recall every precision-set word, syllable and nuance without a dare of need to replay.

The natural fear of such a circumstance, however, could not so easily be suppressed and Maecenas was beginning to feel that his hearing the rhyme was for a purpose and that purpose in the immediate was to forward it and its circumstance to those in greater authority. Without further thought, he automatically made the necessary callall to Mycroft and then realised that he was on the other side of the Magicknot Line where the callall would not work.

Mycroft was not asleep, he was snoozing in his armcowch which he had brought with him in the moovacar from the Necropol Club. He was not prepared to sit on anything but the best buttoned armcowch made with the finest Wopian critter levva, grown, dried and cured exclusively in Wopia.

He was thinking about his armcowch itself at that moment, actually, and his mind had wandered onto the history of Wopia, the boot-shaped country where the art of making the finest levva had naturally been developed to make the best boots. He was actually wondering whether there was any truth in the suggestion that Wopians got the idea of boots from the shape of their country, or the other way round. Of course, it was all so long ago that the History Records, if indeed there ever were any, were well and truly obliterated; *just a vicious rumour* he concluded, eventually.

The smoke-rings from the smouldering netherwear in his pipe curled GodwardS while his brain was ever active, despite the rude interruptions of his own snoring.

It was just then that the callall caught him unaware. He had forgotten but now recalled that local callalls don't need a central bleating station. The callall must therefore, he deduced, be from the Magicknot Line, which he did not expect or from the Defenss forces now spreading across Ozzilland or from Maecenas and Smelt, the latter of whom would be unlikely to callall him while in the company of a superior government official (however theoretical this relationship might be). He prided himself that he deduced correctly that his potential interlocutor was Maecenas, a quality of deduction he never failed to achieve within half a breath of the deemed need so to do. In whole truth, he was half expecting the news he was about to receive.

'Nothing since then, I presume?' M asked Maecenas when he had carefully listened to the words.

'Only snoring.' replied Maecenas, 'no other narcolexic fit. Why?'

'Because the time is not yet ripe and because he needs one more daughter before he qualifies. Even then he will have to pass the tests.' replied M.

'What for?' asked Maecenas.

'What for? In order to qualify, of course.'

'No! What will he be qualifying for?'

'Now that is something,' replied M, 'that I think you already know, but I am not at liberty to discuss either here or anywhere, now or at any other time. Your own knowledge must also come, for the moment, from gleaned hints both from your own experience and education and especially from the latest knowledge imparted only to you, but now also to me second-hand: the pure magic of the trirhythmic-septalines, to the creation of which you have been most fortunate to be the sole witness.'

'So what should I do now? What can I do? Should I wake him? Should I tell him? Should I keep it quiet? Shall I tell him in the morning? What? Heh?'

'For the moment, I recommend that you tell him in the morning and then forget it. As for us, Quax is sleeping and I have some thinking to do before our expedition in the morning. Good-night.'

The difficulty was for Maecenas, it wasn't so simple as having a good night. It is impossible to be witness to the beginning of a new era without the greatest of emotions coming to the fore and forming their own separate quadrant of ideas; impossible to witness a birth without remembering the deceasement that caused it; impossible to witness a victory without considering the pain of the battle that preceded it.

It was at this point, in fact, that Maecenas remembered the Ovum of the planet, the Orijin and ex ovo omnia which seemed to be the auspicator of this entire episode. There really was little point in asking Mycroft, because even if he knew, he probably wouldn't tell him. There were times when Maecenas wondered whether M really was Eqinox's greatest intelligence, or whether he only appeared to be, egged-on by some sort of undiagnosed ultric-super-ego. Whatever his conclusion, there was little doubt that it would have been wrong.

Mycroft, meanwhile really was considering all matters intellectual, particularly concerning the future of Smelt, before retiring, eventually, for the night.

Maecenas could not sleep. What precisely was the connection, he pondered, then wondered, then mulled over and finally seriously considered, between the revelations of Smelt in his narcolexic fits, the Orijin back in Selondre and the strange events in Ozzilland resulting in this unprecedented outing for the head of Eqinox intelligence gathering?

Mycroft initiated a callall to the Magicknot Line. 'Please give Kernal the following message. He must contact the Yellow Cross Organisation of Helvetica and arrange immediate delivery of food parcels, food-making nanowaves and forty-seven Multicares with automeds and hospivoids. If he asks the reason, please advise him, truthfully, that this is merely a precautionary measure.'

* * * * *

The morn dawned bright with the sun rising over the horizon, but not quite where Maecenas and Smelt would have expected it to rise, having seen it set the previous evening, but that is bound to happen when the country is still moving relative to the planet around it.

'Good morning.' said Maecenas, looking at Smelt with a curiously questioning expression.

'Good morning,' replied Smelt, 'what's the problem? You are looking at me as though you've seen a ghost. Have you?'

'Not of the present,' replied Maecenas, 'no.'

'Not of the present?' Smelt echoed, looking puzzled, 'I don't understand.'

'What do you know about WizardS?' asked Maecenas changing the subject pointedly.

'I think I'm intelligent, but there's a limit to my psychic powers.' laughed Smelt, 'Exactly what are you talking about?'

'I'm talking about becoming a WizarD, the creation and control of a powerful force for good or evil but rarely neutral.' said Maecenas.

'Yes, yes, yes! I know all about that, but why are you asking the question? Are *you* becoming a WizarD? Have you had some news in the night? I can see from your eyes that you haven't slept.'

Maecenas took a brief glance with his front head and looked away and down at the floor in an involuntary admission of guilt; his second head closed its eyes and pretended to be asleep.

'Well?' insisted Smelt.

Maecenas was clearly cornered and had to tell the truth, but with the greatest reluctance to go against M's advice. Nevertheless there was little choice. 'Narcolexic attacks.' he said eventually.

'What about them? Have I committed another?'

'Committed?' laughed Maecenas, 'you make it sound as though you are breaking a lorr.'

'It's not a laughing matter,' said Smelt, looking worried, 'I know that something is happening to me and it frightens me, even though I know that whatever it is, is wholly inevitable. According to folklore, I am one and a bit daughters short of becoming a WizarD and I am experiencing the psychological trauma and inter-brain contradictions I would expect in such a curious circumstance.' He looked straight at Maecenas, 'Are you truthfully telling me that I had another attack during the night?'

'I wouldn't lie to you; yes, you did, but only one. You recited another trirhythmic-septaline with a clear message. I'll play it back to you. I did speak to M, but he advised that I should not tell you yet.'

Maecenas played back the recording while Smelt listened with deep intent and at the same time, read back his words of the previous night from a holofolio shown in a spare holoquadrant

At the end, he was even more confused and could speak no words nor even mouth a silent utterance.

'We all know the legends of the history of WizardS, but few of us ever believed them.' said Maecenas at last, 'But I never thought it would happen, not in real life, and certainly not in my lifetime.'

'It's a strange feeling, I can tell you, and I still don't believe it myself.' Smelt said eventually, shaking his head in confusion and wholly disconnected with himself in his perception of the present and future.

Chapter 13   This Land is My Land

A forked lightning flash of netherlight streaked across the sky, determined to make its presence felt. Netherlight, like the whole spectrum in x-ray, was invisible to Quax and the other Gobblings.

'There goes the secondary precursor.' said Mycroft, alone among the clump in being unperturbed.

Even Quax who could not actually see the netherlight was nevertheless able to perceive the gap in the sky, otherwise full of the remaining spectrum, where the netherlight passed.

'I understand that in the Middle-Eons there were … ' began Maecenas, but was stopped by a series of rolling, creaking, demented sound bolts thundering across the sky.

'GoD, what was that?' screeched Maecenas, not having time to duck.

'Just thunder.' replied Mycroft, casually puffing images of vexal hemispheric septahedrons, 'You see, it must all take place today, on the hepts of this month of Heptember. The greatest magic will be done on the hepts of the seventh month, the seventh day before the ides when the ideas flow forth.'

Quax listened intently, determined to learn more by listening than she would lose by admitting her ignorance on the matter.

'But surely, this occurrence of the rotation of Ozzilland is a physical phenomenon?' asked Smelt, 'and not any sort of magic?'

'You might think that,' replied M, 'but I couldn't possibly comment.'

'Does that mean that it is?' insisted Smelt.

'There are matters on which I have received or gleaned intelligence but on which it is not possible for me to remark either because of confidentiality or because making statements of affect could in itself modify the direction of their power, including, possibly, the abandonment of a good power in favour of an evil one.' For the moment, therefore, I must remain silent in reply. However, we must all wait until the seventh hour and then all will be revealed.'

* * * * *

The callall berped. It was a message from the Magicknot Line for Smelt, from Grounsella, confirming the successful arrival of his daughter, Smeltdort6. He sent back an appropriately congratulatory message, as warm as possible in the circumstances of his enforced absence and being currently ex-communicated by normal means.

'I have never before heard of a dort arriving so early.' remarked Smelt when he had recovered slightly.

'Yes, it is unusual, but not so rare in the current circumstances of your imminent conversion. I must confess openly that I anticipated a seventh by now, but I must have been wrong.' admitted M.

'Surely,' replied Smelt, 'my conversion is not *that* imminent. Even with my limited understanding, I know that I haven't fulfilled all the conditions. I am still coming to terms with the idea, so neither will I unless I can be 'converted', to use your word, without any change.'

'Conversion is change by its circular definition. What you seek is impossible.' replied M, 'for what is to be must be, regardless of your personal preference. You are not in a position, fortunately or otherwise, to control this circumstance.'

'Que serah, serah!' smiled Maecenas, quoting an old autoerotic nanogroove with a nonchalant shrug and feeling that this conversation was all rather esoteric and irrationally ethereal.

'But I can surely control my own actions. Can't I?' suggested Smelt.

'Not when your actions are controlled by WizarD potentiality.' replied M with a forceful look that also told him the conversation must be over for the time being.

'But ... er, but ... ' protested Smelt before submitting to the more powerful words of the look in Mycroft's eye.

Smelt still felt that he would surely have ultimate determination over his future and was in no doubt about his own power to control his actions and environment. He was determined not to be blackmailed into behaving such as to become what he wished not to be. He had no intention of catastrophising his position, for that is what he felt the conversion would inevitably force.

* * * * *

Maecenas was beginning the countdown to the seventh hour of this day, the hepts, the seventh before the ides of Heptember. Only a few hundred breaths now and Mycroft was not wholly sure what to expect.

Quax had followed Mycroft's requested instruction to the letter and hollowed out a pair of double-spherical caves below the surface by her motorphroyd capability. The two moovacars were ready to be carefully placed, one in each of the spherical hollows and it only remained for the clump of four to enter them and fly down the holes.

The countdown continued. At 343 breaths before the seventh hour, the whole sky lit up in netherlight and the ground dented from the thunder reigning down as solid as a Saharan rock storm in the hurricane season.

As the ground before them seemed to ruffle with the waves of sound-created indentations, Mycroft led the clump to the moovacars. 'This is just the beginning of the storm.' he said, 'now is the time to hide from the surface, although we will not remain untouched even beneath.' He turned to Quax, 'How long will it take you to seal the link to the surface?'

'Exactly seven breaths.' replied Quax.

'In that case, you should begin to seal at eight breaths before. I think we should see as much of the precursor as is safe for the History Records, but we must be sealed before the hour. If the septallion of Sqoddies have obeyed my orders, they will be dug in and safe within their armoured personnel moovacars.'

The two moovacars were adjacent and attached by the linkdoor set up between them, a bit like a corridor train, really.

'Fourteen.' said Maecenas.

The sky suddenly darkened and remained black for three breaths as Smelt's callall berped. Smelt raised his eyebrows in amazement and answered.

'Ten.' said Maecenas.

'Hello?' said Smelt.

'Magicknot Line here.'

'Eight.' said Maecenas.

'We have a confidential message for you from Grounsella. You will be delighted to know that, unexpectedly, you have … ' The signal died and there remained neither picture nor sound but just a white snow and white noise.

'Seven.' said Maecenas.

The sky disappeared above them as Quax sealed the double sphere in which their moovacars had been incarcerated for the duration.

'We must separate the linkdoor and permit free movement,' said M, doing it, 'good-bye for now, Smelt and Maecenas.'

Smelt was left agape and confused about the callall from the Magicknot Line. What could be such urgent good news and for his attention alone from Grounsella? Certainly, he had already heard the news about Smeltdort6. There was no doubt, he decided with utter certainty, that this was to have been just a second copy of the message that came through earlier.

'Three;' said Maecenas, 'what happens next?'

Smelt shrugged, fearing the worst of a nightmare ahead. The four looked up as the stripe incorporated by Quax into the lining of the double sphere moved. The moovacar itself remained upright; at least, it would be more correct to say that gravity remained in the downward direction because it was impossible to determine which way was up, but the hovering vehicle remained stable. The small gap between the two moovacars was itself rotating and each duo could see the other pair and their moovacar through the gap at the tangential conjunction of the overlapping spheres.

'We're not moving.' said Smelt stating the apparently obvious.

The locational guidance systems showed that the moovacars were accelerating and decelerating rapidly and yet the feeling of the occupants was of total stability.

'Oh, GoD, far from it,' replied Maecenas, pointing to the instrument holoquadrant, 'if the geoplatelet that we're sitting just under is rocking and rolling within the hemispherical gimbal, we could end up deep in the bowels of the earth. Do you think Mycroft's suggestion that Ozzilland could become upside-down cubed could be realistic?'

'You're the scientist.' replied Smelt, 'I must rely on your judgement.'

'Whatever my judgement of the apparent position, it will make no difference to the reality of our situation, so there is no point in either of us worrying. If we worry, the position will be unchanged so that all worry is pointless.'

'True, but I remain concerned.' Smelt added. They stopped. 'We've stopped!' he exclaimed unnecessarily.

Smelt and Maecenas looked about them. The orientation was about fifteen degrees from their starting position and Mycroft's moovacar was identically located and oriented, relatively.

Mycroft callalled Smelt and Maecenas. 'It worked. We're safe. All well there?'

'Yes, thank you.' replied Smelt and added, 'By the power of the light of the Great Archangel, I wish we could all see what is happening outside on the surface.'

He was just about to wonder why on Eqinox he should say such a thing when, at that very instant the double sphere in which they were both encapsulated seemed to explode and the moovacars rose at full speed towards the sky, still full of aurora demonstrating its ability to appear, and in all colours of both the visible and x-ray spectra. At the same time Quax watched a display of multiple coloured lights in her own visible spectra.

For some indefinable reason, best known only to magic itself, the aurora was fearsome and powerful, yet beautiful and wholly unthreatening like the clear, fresh atmosphere of a receding storm. And as it moved, revealing its beautiful power, it imperceivably changed from an unnoticed opacity to an unprecedented clarity revealing the freshest of countryside colours in the landscape below. Where there had been desert, there now was grassland and trees. Where there had been a shanty town, Allysp Rings, there now was a recognisably identical yet somehow upgraded variant. Where there had been dirt tracks, there were now clean, fresh grassed walkways with the most inviting armcowch-shaped tussocks. Where there had been barren fields with sparsely spaced fruit trees, there were now thick orchards dripping with multi-coloured fruits of all varieties. Where cottages and sheds had been tumble-down, they were not repaired but replaced, yet not replaced, for the new was wholly the same and yet wholly restored and refreshed as new.

Grounsella

'Look at the horizon,' said Smelt and the others involuntarily followed his command, 'the landscape is flat as far as the eye can see. At least, until the mountains. I mean, it's not at an angle.'

'Of course,' responded Mycroft, 'didn't you notice that when we stopped moving, Quax's cavern was fifteen degrees at variance from its original orientation? Ozzilland is obviously now as flat as it ever was and the gyres of the geoplatelets have resettled in their gimbals at their original orientation, but only in roll and pitch - not in yaw, which is now antipolular.'

Maecenas rejoined the cars with the linkdoor so that Mycroft and Quax could join Maecenas and Smelt.

They watched as the aurora receded and faded into the invisible apparency of a technical shadow.

As one, as if noticing a suddenly manifested apparition, the others looked at Smelt, who responded with an equal start. 'What's the matter?' he asked.

'Do you not know?' responded Mycroft.

'No. Know? No, know what?' replied Smelt reluctantly and hesitantly.

'The change is right now taking place.'

Smelt began to panic, 'What change? Why are you all looking at me? How am I different?' He looked himself up and down and turned his heads to look at each other. 'I can't see any difference!' he protested.

'There isn't any, but you are definitely different.' said Mycroft, 'Look at the town below. The same has happened to you. You are not changed and yet you are new and refreshed. At the same time, you look no different while you somehow have an appearance inverted from the used to the unused; restored from the unclean to the kosher.'

Smelt looked at himself again, 'I can't see it.' he retorted, 'In any case, according to your criteria, the change still requires a further daughter for me to become a WizarD.'

'Then you must have one.'

'No, it is not possible. not at all possible. Oh no. No way.'

'What was your callall message from the Magicknot Line?' suggested Maecenas, initiating a callall to the line.

'We're at the line, on the outside of it.' said the Sqoddie as an opening remark, 'it doesn't seem to be there any more.'

'Do you mean the line?' suggested Mycroft.

'Of course. The kink has gone and I am talking to you direct from just outside it.'

'That is to be expected.' said M calmly, 'now would you repeat the message that was prepared for Smelt just before the seventh hour today.'

'No.' replied the Sqoddie, 'it was a personal message and I have no authority to pass it to any other.'

M widened the callall view for Sqoddie and indicated to Smelt to speak. 'It is o.k., please go ahead.' said Smelt, not sure if he really wanted to hear it.

'Very well,' replied the Sqoddie, 'it read, "We have a confidential message for you from Grounsella. You will be delighted to know that, unexpectedly, you have twin daughters, Smeltdort6 and Smeltdort7." End of message.'

'That is simply not possible. Twins just don't happen - ever!' said Smelt and left his mouth agape for a few breaths too long before recovering his composure, 'No Trisep has had twins for hundreds of years, and in any case, the automed would have spotted and stopped it.' He hesitated, then remembered his position, 'Please pass back the message that I require confirmation of the statement from Grounsella.' He terminated the callall.

'You will find that it is correct.' said M, smiling broadly, 'You have already performed a magic feat.'

'No, I haven't!' contradicted Smelt, 'That's just ridiculous, all I have done is sit here talking to you and on the callall. That's perfectly normal.'

'How do you think we escaped the entombment from the underground cavern without Quax's help?' suggested M.

'It just happened.' replied Smelt, jutting his chin and then turning his head away suddenly and looking at the floor to try to recall the precise sequence of events.

'No,' said Maecenas, 'look.' He replayed the computer's memory of the event, showing Smelt saying that he wished that he could see what was happening on the surface and the surrounding sphere instantly exploding into the daylight above, yet without leaving a scar on the landscape nor, indeed, any evidence whatever of their period of interment in the subterranean lodging.

Smelt swallowed. He swallowed very hard indeed. 'Oh.' was the only mutter he could eventually utter. He paled visibly from yellow to red as the bright blood drained from his front face and he nearly fainted with shock. Inside, his entire brain power was dedicated to the task of understanding this new position and he repeatedly shook his head and muttered, 'I don't believe it, I just don't believe it.'

'You will just have to believe it, for the fact of the event is the situation as it is.' said Mycroft.

Smelt shook his head again and hid it, resting it on his hands, 'Oh, GoD, help me!' he said.

Immediately, as if in response, a large shrub, if not almost a tree appeared in front of them. It was surrounded by a torrential river and the whole image was in mid-air some hites from the ground.

As soon as it appeared, the shrub burst into a roaring flame and spoke, 'You called?'

Smelt looked round but could not work out where the voice was actually coming from. From within the sound-proofed moovacar he would not ordinarily have expected to hear a voice from outside. He looked at Maecenas in fear, 'Can you hear the voice? Where's it coming from? Can you actually hear it?'

'Yes, in here somewhere ... but yes, I can actually hear it ... but no, not from outside.' replied Maecenas, nervously baffled. Both his heads looked over their shoulders as if checking for ghosts.

Neither Smelt nor the others, including Mycroft, expected such an incarnation and suddenly realised the apparent truth of his new interlocutor.

'Oh GoD! You exist?' exclaimed Smelt.

'That is not for me to determine.' said the burning shrub, 'If you call upon me then I must exist, or I must, at least, exist in your mind. If I exist in your mind, I must duly respond, whether I exist in any other plane or mind or not. To answer your question in whole truth, I must say that if you do not believe in my existence, then it is due to lack of evidence and thus I cannot exist for you; therefore on this occasion I only exist for as long as you define and confirm my existence.'

This brief soliloquy left Smelt dumb with confusion and he could only stare from each one of the others to the next, aware that the next move must be his but unsure of what it should be.

'You clearly have a great deal to consider and much to learn' said M with a good degree of common sense. 'Quax and I knew that this was to come and that it would most likely come today. Now we have work to do so I will leave you in the capable hands of Maecenas, who will undoubtedly assist you almost as well as I could myself. You would do well to speak to the shrub, for therein is an incarnation of your perception of GoD, from which, or whom if you prefer, you can learn a great deal.'

'Are you suggesting that I am only speaking to my perception of GoD and not to a, or rather, *the* real GoD?' asked Smelt.

'As I said, you are speaking to the incarnation of your perception of GoD. That means that if you saw GoD as a man tied to the cross of a golejibbit, then that is what you would be conversing with right now.'

'Yes, but is this the *real* GoD in the flaming floribunda, or is he just conjured from my imagination; for example, is the river surrounding just a representation of Omeg, the Sacred River? If this is the real GoD, must I now cease from worshipping Omeg, the Sacred River? Does the combusting columbine really represent the fiery descent of the Orijin, or is it just an extraordinary exploding exfoliate?'

'Both, or all or none,' replied Mycroft with a rare smile, 'according to your whim and that of none other, in that, as The Incarnation said, what exists can only exist as that which you have defined and accepted in your mind as existing. Reality for you is reality per se, for you can see no other reality. Likewise for me and for all others reality is only what is perceived to be reality. What I see before me now is your interpretation of GoD. I am sure that if GoD exists, which is not for me to judge in your place, then he will exist in the form in which you perceive him, for you at least. Of course, you conjured him up by saying, "Oh, GoD, help me!" which proclaims a reality of existence in your mind, so here he is.'

Smelt was even more puzzled. Philosophy was not his strongest of topics at the best of times, and now was certainly not one of the best of times.

Burning Shrub

RRRAR!

'Are you suggesting that I conjured him up? That I, as it were, brought him into existence by a trick of WizardrY? That I created him for myself from my own imagination? That if I had not created him in the image I expected him to portray, then he would not exist in that image? That, even more specifically, if I had not created him, he would not actually exist at all?' Smelt looked from M to Quax to Maecenas for an answer, but could not read their blank faces, for their own knowledge on the subject was rapidly becoming less than his own, 'So, if I were to imagine a whole series of GodS of various types with many different incarnation characteristics, they would appear in those forms and I would be able to converse with them in the way I would have expected? Is it like talking to a being in a dream? Are you suggesting that if GoD exists at all, he only exists as and when we want him to exist? And if so, would it be true that he will only give me the answers

I want and expect, even though I do not consciously know what to expect?'

'There is a positive Qontûm probability tending towards the affirmative, as in all WizardrY.' said Quax.

Smelt did not expect this direct contribution from what he saw as an outsider and peered at Quax in surprise, 'Do you have WizardS in the Underplanet?' retorted Smelt.

'Maybe and maybe not.' replied Quax uncharacteristically, being unsure as to the definition.

'Not in the same form.' replied M, helpfully.

'Then in what form?' asked Smelt.

'We will have to explain on another occasion.' said M, clearly eager to leave, 'Meanwhile, be careful what you say, for your wishes will generally be fulfilled, subject to certain criteria.'

M paused for effect, 'Simple spells you can do with ease, the more complex are harder while the impossible remain quite difficult; for you at this stage, however, there is nothing more improbable than the mere difficulty of the impossible.'

Mycroft waved and returned with Quax to his own moovacar without further comment, leaving Smelt agape and agog, yet aglow with the received engrandisement of his new-found position. He instructed the confused tangle of his thoughts to sort themselves into some semblance of logical order. Such kudos, yes! Yet he full knew that the proud egotism naturally partnering kudos must not be permitted to overrule common sense.

Maecenas turned his front head from Smelt and watched M and Quax go, 'Not as sesquipedalian as he can be if he tries,' commented Maecenas, 'but he does seem to be rather good at simple obfuscation. I fear that on this occasion, you will be making more of a drama out of a crisis than he will.'

'Yes.' said Smelt, slowly and thoughtfully, 'I certainly have a great deal to learn. None of it has sunk in yet.' He peered thoughtfully at Maecenas' eyes and then out into the void. Suddenly he noticed the burning shrub, which despite burning did neither diminish its flames with time nor perish and wither.

Somehow the visitation had drifted into his visual background but unexpectedly returned to the forefront of his mind, 'Oh!' was all he could understate at the sudden recall of his new status as a WizarD, now standing before his own vision of GoD.

Smelt looked back to the shrub and shook his head as if trying to waken from a dream, 'Er,' he stammered, 'please tell me, GoD, whether you are real or a part of my imagination.'

'I have already told you that this is not a matter for me to decide but for you.' the shrub replied.

Smelt turned to Maecenas and frowned in confusion, 'But I still don't understand whether this really is GoD or, as he himself suggests, a figment of my imagination.'

'That is not what I said.' said the burning shrub with a surprising degree of calmness for an admonition.

'No, I suppose it wasn't.' said Smelt, duly put in his place by what he felt to be a rather more damning remark than it really was.

* * * * *

'This looks to be as good a place to start as any.' said Mycroft to Quax when he stopped his manually trekked moovacar near the centre of what was now the most Antipoleward geoplatelet of the middle strip of the rotated Ozzilland.

Quax looked at the rows of parked and, like everything else, apparently freshly refurbished olde-fashioned, non-flying moovacars parked around the centre of a Ferrikross of Faerie-rings. She nodded in agreement and prepared to disembark as the vehicle landed. She stepped gingerly from the moovacar onto the solid ground beneath, not being totally sure of the strength of the surface of a regenerated continent.

She took several very careful steps before feeling certain enough of the support of the terrain to look around without checking at her feet. 'Shall I begin?' she asked, almost rhetorically and starting anyway.

M nodded in equally rhetorical agreement, an automatic but irrelevant gesture as Quax was no longer looking at him.

She looked down at the ground with a far greater intensity than she had when creating the caverns for the sojourn of the seventh hour of the seventh day of the seventh month, only hours earlier.

As she looked intently, summoning up even more powerful motorphroyd than is usually required for a Gobbling's hole, so the ground opened before her, but instead of the utterly smooth pipe seen previously at Squelchpool and in the front of the Conventionium, here was a similar but larger tube with steps on the bottom side, the right size to enable Triseps to tread without either tripping from an inappropriate step size or hitting their head on the roof of the angled tube.

While Quax was preparing the tube, so Mycroft set up the autofollowing holocam for the History Records. Nothing further need be done, except talk to it occasionally and let it record the scene otherwise without further interruption.

'Thank you.' said M when Quax had done, 'That appears to be perfect.' Quax led the way down the steps, followed by M with a flashlight borrowed from the moovacar's emergency kit.

'From our experience earlier,' said M, 'I hold out great hope, at least odds of 46 in 47.' He puffed smoke-rings of the odds from his smouldering netherwear.

The steps seemed to go on forever. 'I remember in my youth before the invention of the moovacar autostack, having to negotiate the one hundred and ninety two steps of the Angelicus Underground Transit Station because the lifts only worked one day a week,' said M during one of their resting stops at about five-hundred steps, 'but I am certainly glad not to have to do this journey every day.' They both knew that they were but a small part of their journey down, and that much work must be done when the bottom was reached. Every now and again, Quax would stop and create another length of hole before them, or send a tiny sideways bore-hole to check that they had not missed a level, even though she did not expect any caverns at such shallow depth.

Eventually, the end of the hole was in sight and spread below them for as far as could be discerned in the amber of the flashlight. They stopped for a rest while Quax thought what to do next. After some discussion, she continued the steps down into the cavern to reach the floor several hundred more steps below, the alternative being to make steps in the ceiling.

'I can't yet see or hear whether it is abandoned or occupied.' said Quax with some discomfort.

'It is occupied by something living and moving,' said M just managing to discern movement with his front x-ray eye, 'and what's more, there appear to be different sized objects, like Triseps and Gobblings.'

'Should be Dark Elves in this part of the world.' corrected Quax.

'Of course. Sorry if I have offended you; I was using a generic term.'

'No offence! Just making sure you hadn't forgotten.' laughed Quax, clearly relieved at the reassurance that her fellows were, here at least, as safe as could be expected in the circumstances.

'I'm just glad, despite the Qontûm probability of movement and location, that Ozziqontûm appears to be exactly where we would expect it to be.' commented M.

Quax smiled, perhaps a little more knowingly than she intended, but M was well aware not only of her actual level of knowledge but also of her ability to imply by such devious devices as knowing smiles a somewhat greater knowledge or insight than was necessarily the case; even though it sometimes was.

Quax reached the bottom of the steps first and the pair were immediately greeted by large numbers of Dark Elves and Triseps all trying to speak at once.

After a few breaths permitting adequate rest for regeneration and the initial excitement to be expended, M raised his hand in an aristocratically styled bid to call for silence, while Quax followed suit towards the Dark Elves. A raised voice would have had no effect, the more demanding silent writ having greatest impact on this audience.

'We have come from the surface.' said M, with his hand still raised. 'You will be pleased to know that Ozzilland has reverted to something near normal and you can return to your homes as soon as you wish. If you have been ill, there are Multicares waiting for you in every major conurbation and Sqoddies to help you and the infirm with any special needs. Meanwhile, I have to tell you that the country you left has been transformed into a rich landscape, while the entire continent has rotated on its own axis and is now, according to the maps, upside-down. The surface, however, is flat now, even though it wasn't for a while. Additionally, the seven segmented geoplatelets on which Ozzilland sits have each rotated. Thus, for example, Allysp Rings which was once in the centre of the continent is now on the Antipoleward edge; only in a metaphorical sense is the country upside-down in a third manner, as the changes appear to herald regeneration rather than deterioration.'

Several of the Triseps tried to ask questions at once and Quax was drawn off to one side answering questions by the Dark Elves in their own language. It was quickly established that the Ozzillanders had suffered no damage by being underground during the rotation and subsequent violent storms.

'What were these vicious storms?' asked one, more directly than any of the other statements had been questioned, 'And did they do any damage?'

'Light and sound, mostly, and the storm's wake left the whole countryside looking and smelling as fresh as a new-mown lawn. Every tree and flower looked and sounded and smelled completely regenerated.'

'What about our homes?' asked another.

'Untouched, and if anything refreshed.' responded M carefully, not wanting to sound as ridiculously far-fetched as the truth of the scenario would undoubtedly have done. To have said that all the properties had been refurbished by an external magical power would have rendered him liable to a lynching on the grounds of psychological incompetence and a sudden loss of his elgins.

And so began an hour of questions and answers about the surface events since the apparent disappearance of Ozzilland.

A Dark Elf made his way through the crowd and was clearly treated with some respect, if not in awe by his compatriots. He and Quax greeted with obvious delight and a mutual wet kiss. Quax introduced Sophist, Precedent of the Dark Elves for this cycle.

Mycroft greeted him in his own tongue, 'A teacher of philosophy, I presume.'

'More specific,' replied Sophist, 'I am *the* teacher of Philosophical Denial of Wisdom to all Gobblings. I have written many folios on Structured Antiwisdom.'

'Fascinating, my dear fellow;' replied M, 'we would define it as irrationality and false reasoning.'

'On the contrary, such false reasoning is never false when applied to a contradictive premise, itself at variance with the base argument.'

'I would concur wholly, only insofar as the reality of a premise has a Qontûm probability of truth concurring with the invalidity factor in direct disproportion to the uncertainty of its own inverse premise.' said M seriously and added in facetious jest with a laugh, 'unless the argument is made by a woman: women always come from different premises anyway!'

Sophist looked at Mycroft with the greatest possible admiration combined with a degree of unexpressed disturbance that nevertheless confirmed his own self-doubt, 'I thought that I was alone in understanding the subject at that depth' he said at last.

'I think not. Shall we continue with an evacuation to relieve you of the burden of your guests?' suggested M.

'Good idea. That would be appreciated.' replied Sophist, who then gave instructions to his people to ensure that no Triseps were left behind.

Meanwhile those who had gathered continued to discuss the Philosophical Denial of Wisdom and Structured Antiwisdom, even though most had a knowledge level of about minus three on a scale of zero to seven, and an even lower level of understanding.

In the ensuing discussions, it soon became apparent that, so far as Ozzillanders were concerned, the loss of Ozzilland problem had been the other way round in that, to them, it was the rest of the world that seemed to disappear in all practical terms.

However, when the individual geoplatelets began to gyre or 'swing' in their gimbals, an immediate conference had been convened between the surface peoples and the Dark Elves below.

The greatest intelligences had together determined that the surface Triseps were safer underground for however long the disturbance might last, particularly as there seemed a strong possibility of the geoplatelets turning turtle completely.

That M and Quax had appeared to rescue them was perhaps the greatest surprise of all as they had been expecting to begin expeditions to explore the rest of the planet to see if there were any pockets of life left beyond their own boundaries.

The Ozzilland branch of EBC's ENN had also sent out an autofollowing holocam to explore beyond its borders, but like the other, it had lost both control of the holocam and its returning signal; it was presumed that the device had fallen into the sea.

* * * * *

Cate'aeddy was reporting from Selondre. 'Never before in living memory has a case of twins been reported in Triseps. Grounsella, you are not just of interest, you have become an instant celebrity.'

Profmed was interviewed in his own holoquadrant and expressed the greatest surprise that the automed had not detected such an unusual variance in Grounsella's pregnancy, 'It's impossible,' he said, 'it just can't happen. The automed always spots problem pregnancies. It analyses every cell, so it can't make a mistake like that.'

'It may analyse every cell,' retorted Cate'aeddy, 'but our investigators have researched the automed's analysis. It may test the quality of every cell, but does it actually *count* the babies, or does it assume that the pregnancy cells are all from the same baby?'

'Good question. You may be right. I'll look into it. I don't think anyone had ever considered that there could be more than one baby at a time. The records show that it last happened over a hundred cycles before the Ozzilland rookanga crisis.'

'Thank you,' said Cate'aeddy, 'we look forward to seeing your results.' She turned back to face her personal autofollowing holocam and removed Profmed from the image, 'So you heard it here first, the fault for failure to diagnose clearly lies in a programming fault in automeds, the machine we *all* rely on to diagnose and cure our illnesses and keep us alive. You may well ask what other potentially lethal errors are lurking just beneath the surface of your friendly, neighbourhood automed. Is it a safe machine? Is it a machine to which you really want to trust your life and health? Are you sure you are safe with this lump of twisted metal and electronics?'

She looked round at the automed behind her. 'This is Cate'aeddy reporting for ENN with Grounsella and the new twins in Selondre.'

* * * * *

The burning shrub remained in the background while Smelt was cautiously testing his newly acquired powers, not sure what the limit was or what effect his actions would have on others. If he asked for a house, for example, could he be sure that it would not land on some poor passing Trisep and cause premature deceasement? If he requested a material transformation, would that affect other material elsewhere than where his request was directly aimed?

He needed to test the limits of his conjuring-up and transformation magics, and had a deep feeling that some tasks would require external help through spells, whatever they may be - and, indeed, however one may manage to find out how to learn them.

There was also a nagging fear that the powers with which he was currently experimenting just could, perhaps, run out part-way through a task; this fear was partially confirmed by a degree of internal weakening as each task was performed, leaving a sort of void within from where the energy had been leeched.

'It would be rather tragic,' laughed Maecenas, vocalising Smelt's problem, 'if you ran out of magical energy just as you were converting a Trisep into a frog. Can you imagine a Trisep with a frog's legs?'

Smelt looked up, surprised that his thoughts were spoken. He thought for a few breaths. 'Or vice versa.' he added in a nervous reminder of the inevitable responsibility that naturally attends the greatest privilege of power that could ever be accorded to an individual, 'But I have to find out to what extent this power is safe. I need to learn a great deal about it. This is a bit like becoming Precedent without prior experience or any preparation; like attempting brain surgery without studying first.'

Maecenas nodded in understanding.

'The very power itself has a life of its own. Somehow, you know, it seems to want to take over. I may be the one with the power, but it definitely exists independently.'

'Try asking GoD.' suggested Maecenas.

Smelt nodded in agreement of a good idea. 'Tell me GoD,' said Smelt, 'what should I do next?'

'My omniscience defines that I have knowledge of all things occurring in all times; that which was, that which is and that which is yet to come. It defines that I have knowledge of what you *will* do next but not of what you *should* do next. What you will do next is fixed in the history of the future and cannot be altered. What you *should* do next is for your conscience alone and not for me to advise.'

'So are you the GoD that you claim to be?'

'We've been through this once.' interjected Maecenas.

'You say that I am.' said the burning shrub, 'and I am what I am defined to be. I do not recall making any direct claim of my own. Ever.'

'But you … ' persisted Smelt and then thought better of it, thought hard and said, 'If I dismiss you, will you return when I call for you?'

'My reality is your reality and I am thus before you at your whim.' replied the burning shrub.'

Smelt turned to Maecenas for inspiration but when he returned his gaze to the burning shrub, it had vanished, along with the surrounding river, leaving only a colourless void and a smile suspended in mid-air like that of the runcible pussy.

* * * * *

'Yer not fit, mate?' said Dundy.

The first of the Triseps, led by Mycroft and a local crocodile hunter called Dundy, and the politician, Ozzipolit23 arrived at the top of the 2209 steps leading from Ozziqontûm to the surface. The Dark Elves had been perfect hosts and provided the most delicious of banquets as each period arrived that food became a requirement, for there are no days and nights or mornings or lunch-times or tea-times or dinner-times or even any measurement of time itself in the perpetual night of the underground caverns where the Dark Elves live. Except of course for the internal clocks of the Dark Elves; a capability shared by all Gobbling species.

Burning
Shrub

While the Triseps returned to the surface, so the Dark Elves were motorphroyd-forming new underground passages with directions given by Quax and Mycroft. The interconnecting tunnels passed across the conjunctions between the geoplatelets and on into adjacent but cut-off caverns, to report the good news of the stability of the surface and thus facilitate escape of the surface-dwellers.

'Hey,' said Dundy as Ozzipolit23 reached the top, 'you really want to escalate those steps.'

'You mean, make them go faster?' said M.

'That's the idea. Got it in one. They don't go at all right now.'

'But we would need to ask the Gobblings to do that.' Said Dundy.

'Then you'd better go down and ask.' Retorted M.

Dundy turned to the overweight and rather unfit Ozzipolit23, just emerging. 'Mycroft here wants you to go back down and tell those dark little Elfin things to speed up the staircase.'

Ozzipolit23 was completely drained of all energy and could not argue, but just turned to go back, ignoring M's denial of the statement and his pleas to return to the surface.

'Hey M, what is this place, mate?' asked Dundy.

Mycroft looked at Dundy, surprised. 'Do you genuinely not know?'

Dundy looked round and shrugged. He removed a very long knife from his socks and began to shave himself with the tip of it, 'Got to look good when the top boyos arrive, haven't we now mate?' he laughed. Well, it wasn't actually a laugh, more of a comical sneer, really and somehow achieved so that only one side of the mouth appeared to rise in a half-smile, 'By the way, got any four-ecks?'

'Hecks? Ah! If you go to my moovacar, it will manufacture some for you,' M sighed and shook his head.

'Good on yer mate!' Mycroft watched as Dundy walked across, entered, ordered a "seven-pack of four-ecks" and returned with a rather olde-fashioned looking set of metallic canisters arranged in a heptagram.

'Have another look round;' said M, 'can you see any landmark that you recognise?'

'Sure. Gold Valley Mountains. Over there. Look. Some call them the MacDonald Ranges because they're shaped like a giant beefburgher.' He pointed one way and looked the other with his front head, while his rear head stared unblinking at Mycroft for inspiration.

Mycroft followed his finger, avoiding the instinct to follow his gaze, 'You're right. They're unmistakable, but if you weren't here, then I need to know where you were when you went down into Ozziqontûm.'

'Somewhere else, mate.' replied Dundy, still looking around at the scenery.

M puffed a rotating pair of exclamation and question marks from his pipe in frustration, 'Yes, but precisely where was that somewhere else?'

'Ah, now that's another question, mate. Let me see, er, I was somewhere near Kathryn, I think. Why?'

'And where was Kathryn at the time?' Dundy looked at Mycroft as though he was one elgin short of a Parthenon, 'Where it's always been, of course, about 300 Ozzikays Antipoleward of Dirwan or 1200 Ozzikays Poleward of Allysp Rings.'

Mycroft's eyes fell to the ground as he considered the consequences of this statement, 'That means that there was a greater Qontûm movement in Ozziqontûm than I calculated. Obviously the energy in the Qontûm State has increased the probability of the uncertainty factor.

'You want to know how it happened?' offered Dundy, only slightly less aware of Mycroft's capability than he admitted.

'That might be a good idea. If not for me, then at least for the History Records.'

'All right then, mate, here goes: in the beginning, when all of Ozzilland thought that the rest of the world had disappeared, the Ozzilland Precedent met with Sophist and there was nearly a war because each accused the other of being responsible for the disappearance of the rest of the world. At least, they assumed that if they weren't responsible, they at least knew about it and were thus culpable.'

Dundy looked M firmly in they eye and continued, 'I mean, Sophist's first fear was that the Triseps had somehow managed to destroy the rest of the world and Underplanet with some sort of advanced atom-splitting molotov, but he soon accepted that as being unlikely.' He dropped his distant gaze at the mountains and turned directly towards M to make sure he was keeping up.

'O.k., then, so the Dark Elves had realised that something was amiss when the passages between the major caverns suddenly became blocked and the entire Underplanet moved, not so much in the usual surprise manner of a normal Qontûm movement, nor even like an eqiquake, but more in a physical, regular sort of way.'

'How do you know all this?' asked M.

'Easy mate, keep the old lugs open.'

'So what happened next?'

'Well, it was like this, after the discussions between the Ozzillanders and the Dark Elves in the first hours of the rotation of the continent, the sky became increasingly dark from the rapid obliteration of the sun, while at the same time becoming bright with the long-tailed aurora Ozzitailish freshly minted above the rain cloud layer.' Dundy stopped and looked more squarely at M. 'Are you sure you get what I'm saying, mate?'

'I fully understand.' replied M.

'The Dark Elves extended an invitation at the last minute to join them. Well, mate, there was just enough time for the Ozzillanders to collect some necessary provisions, like condoms and flashlights because of the problem of seeing in an environment where all around saw in a light of a different spectrum.'

Mycroft watched this man carefully and with unusual interest. Clearly, this yokel was even brighter and more knowledgeable than he had given him credit for.

'Of course you know,' added Dundy scraping out the inside of his left front ear with the wrong end of a can opener, 'none of this would have happened if it hadn't been for the conjunction of the Seven Heralds.'

'Heralds … ?' M stared, opened his mouth and left it there. Never before had he stood agape in awe of an intelligence capable of the same deductions as his own brain. Indeed, until now, he knew of no other on the entire planet of Eqinox. He closed his eyes and raised his eyebrows, 'How do you know about the Seven Heralds - the Seven Precursors?'

'Obvious mate, if you look at it, really.'

'What are the seven precursors you have deduced?'

'Where d'you want me to start?' he asked, swigging some four-ecks from a hole in the top of its canister.

'Why not at the first one you noticed?'

'Not so much a matter of noticing them, more a matter of putting the list together, really and waiting for them to happen.'

Mycroft was now beyond surprise, 'Do continue.'

'The first is that all planets in the solar system were in absolutely precise alignment with the second sun on the opposite side. That has been known to be due to occur for generations. Such an Eqinox of Eqinox where the day and night are equal and all is in line with the remainder of the solar system must provide the greatest of magnetic and gravitational stresses.'

M nodded, 'And the second?' asked Mycroft.

'The second was also predictable. It is exactly 329 cycles since the last WizarD suffered what the History Records so delicately describe as a dysfunctional cognitive response leading to a negative patient care outcome.'

'Quite, premature deceasement, in other words.' confirmed M, increasingly corroborating to himself with every breath that passed the phenomenal anomaly of this brilliant yokel Trisep.

'And thirdly, the power of the residual magic building itself up to its own crescendo, as it will do if left to its own devices. It just had to explode and it could have been anywhere, except that it could not possibly have been anywhere else.'

'I praise your insight.' commented M as a passing interjection.

'Which brings us to the Fourth Herald, the inter-pressure which accumulated between the geoplatelet hemispheres, forcing them to pop from their gimbals, then roll, pitch and yaw naturally, each to reach its own level of stability according to its physical shape and individual magnetic deviation; each separate from the next. Because of the inter-pressure build-up between the geoplatelets, the magic explosion of the Third Herald could only escape itself through the seven Ozzilland segments. Nowhere else on the vexal septiquadecahedron of Eqinox is there such a tightly interconnected set of geoplatelets with so much historic magic power as there is locked within the mortal remains of Arbor-Orijinals, the original native Tree-Triseps.'

'I concur and congratulate you.' said Mycroft, puffing a gyrating set of gimbals from his netherwear, adding, 'It is rather a shame that all the

Arbor-Orijinals ever do now is to become ever richer by showing tourists the cave-paintings of their ancestors.'

'Can't stand 'em, except that they're useful.' said Dundy unexpectedly returning to character.

Mycroft ignored this deviation and said, 'And what, in your sequence, was the fifth requirement?'

'I forgot the zeroth reason , which I should have mentioned before the first, the probability factor of Qontûm. Of course, the event probability remains stable at seven in forty-seven to the power of forty-seven, as you know, unless the energy changes.'

Dundy looked at Mycroft to make sure he really did know before continuing, 'Even though it hasn't happened for a terribly long time, the Qontûm probability factor remains constant. After reading Stephen's *Qontûm: the Probability of Uncertainty,* I just felt that this had to be the Missing Link, the zeroth precursor.'

'And I think you are probably right, as with the uncertainty of any Qontûm matter, but I would offer a degree of dispute about whether it should be the zeroth or the seventh.'

'Granted, mate.' replied Dundy.

M laughed, secretly comparing this yokel's style and recalling how Maecenas nearly fell off his cowch when discussing the seven-plus-zero-equals-seven principle and blew some Sigmata smoke-rings, 'And for the fifth?' he asked with a laugh that caused Dundy to raise one questioning eyebrow, shake his front head in pseudo-astonishment and turn his second head to look too.

'Well, mate,' began Dundy, turning his front head back to the mountains, 'there's doubt in my mind about the order of the fifth, sixth and seventh, but try this for size. For the fifth, I'd rate the numerous prophesyings, both religious and the mystic visionaries. The definition of the precursor to the end-times predicted in the Folio of Revealment is one example. This last book of the New Promisings of The Folius clearly tells us how the Number of the HobB shall be upon us and predicts numerous matters now fulfilled.'

'Ah!' said M delighted. He always loved an opportunity to show off his scriptural knowledge, 'it says, *And the Number shall be upon us and shall be upon the forehead of every one of us and shall be upon the hand of every one of us and shall be upon us between our navels. And that number shall not be written by any Trisep lest he be struck down. And the Number of the HobB is Seven Hundred and Seventy-Six plus One and that Number shall not be writ by word or by digit or spoke by any but by HobB himself.'*

He had turned and looked back at M. 'Precisely, mate.'

M raised his eyebrows again. Sometimes this fellow's words seemed not to correspond to his tribal origin or yokelistic streak. Strange, that, thought M.

'Of course, if you're not even slightly religious, you've got seers, mystic visionaries and secular prophets like the nosy old woman, Old Mother Nostril-Dame with her *Septuries,* the forty-seven folios, each of forty-seven trirhythmic-septalines. Trouble is, that although some believe that her words accurately predicted the future, I think they're wrong. It seems HobbisH strange to me, mate, that all such predictions are seen and proved in retrospect and no predictions are ever exposed and accurately explained prior to an event actually occurring.'

'You couldn't have expressed my view more precisely!' remarked M, 'You didn't pick up all of that from school!'

'No,' smiled Dundy, 'but you can learn more from between the lines of the History Records than you ever can from the lines themselves.'

M laughed again. It felt good to find another able to think and converse at his own exalted level. If only, he thought, if only he were suited to become a member of the Necropol Club.

'Then number six. According to the Autocensus, there are 823 543 Triseps now living in Ozzilland.'

'Ah, yes, seven to the power of seven, of course.'

'That's right, mate, except that I don't trust any of the other statistics that the Autocensus provides. It can't keep track of everything.'

'You smile as though you've got something to hide.' laughed M.

'Haven't we all?' retorted Dundy. He looked back at the mountains. 'And precursor number seven, of course, is the magic itself coming back into the hands of living Triseps from its secret and caged existence where for so long it has been hidden to the world, while yet growing and preparing its own offensive thrust. I suppose this naturally follows on from the second herald.'

'Thrust, yes. But offensive?' queried M with yet another raised eyebrow.

'Attacking, then, if you prefer it.' replied Dundy, 'Actually, I have seen the truth in the final of the forty fifth of the Septuries' trirhythmic-septalines, but I still don't understand the bit about *Then WizardS new, where gelt is felt from spelter's smelt!* in the last line of the prophecy. Everything else is clear.'

'Ah, simple,' responded M with his ever conquering smile, finally knowing that he was holding the upper hand all along, albeit a mere deuce of a card, 'there is a Trisep called Smelt who smelts the yellow precious metal they used to call gelt, and only today he became a WizarD by becoming father to twin daughters.'

'*Twin* daughters!' exclaimed Dundy, almost wondering if he should use double exclamation marks and a question mark to boot, 'when was the last time *that* happened?'

'Not since the last WizarD, I doubt.' replied M, using a rare form of expression he copied from his father.

Dundy nodded in understanding and M noticed that he was adjusting the style and even accent of his tongue to that of his own, 'But at least now the last piece of the jigsaw can be placed into the oven for final grinding.' said Dundy.

So much for my thoughts about his style, thought M.

'Oh, by the way, I suppose I should quote Old Mother Nostril-Dame's trirhythmic-septalines for this occasion. I always enjoyed reciting them, even though I had no inkling of their meaning until now. Funny, although not a WizarD, he included the zeroth line. I always thought it was only WizardS who could do that. It never made full sense before, but now it does. Let me recite it and allow its own power to pervade us and permeate the very air we breath, forever reminding us of the seven conditions:

> *Then may the Qontûm come to show all's done;*
> *When all align: planets, nine; suns in line,*
> *And Three Two Nine since WizarD, fine, did bind*
> *The magic built to hilt 'til all did tilt*
> *The plates, which thus must fire the spiring gyre!*
>
> *From precious Folius, so thus to us adjust.*
> *Count seven times seven, to heaven sent seven,*
> *Then WizardS new, where gelt is felt from spelter's smelt!'*

'It all fits perfectly now, mate, there's nothing left to the puzzle!' continued Dundy, confidently.

'Isn't there?' smiled M and desisted from further remark.

* * * * *

Unnoticed by the duo, a huge crowd had gathered round, waiting for them to finish such a fascinating conversation that every one of the impromptu audience remained silent. If M had noticed them, he didn't care because he was wholly engrossed in the subject. Dundy certainly noticed them, as he noticed all things, but chose to ignore them as they were not interfering and to mention them would be irrelevant. In any case, he liked to play to the crowd and here was a clump worth playing up to.

Ozzipolit23, who had been back down the steps and then ridden up again on the somewhat escalated stairs, sidled up to them with a stagger, indicating his depleted energy reserve, 'Can we get our families back to their homes?' he asked in a down-to-Eqinox sort of way, 'they're all tired, and the moovacars here don't belong to them.'

'I am afraid,' said M who considered this not to be a problem, 'that you will have to use the moovacars that are here and then sort out all the right vehicles from different towns at a later date. Basically, everyone will just have to use the nearest moovacar. I haven't counted them, so make sure you fill each one, in case there aren't quite enough here. We don't want to leave anyone behind.'

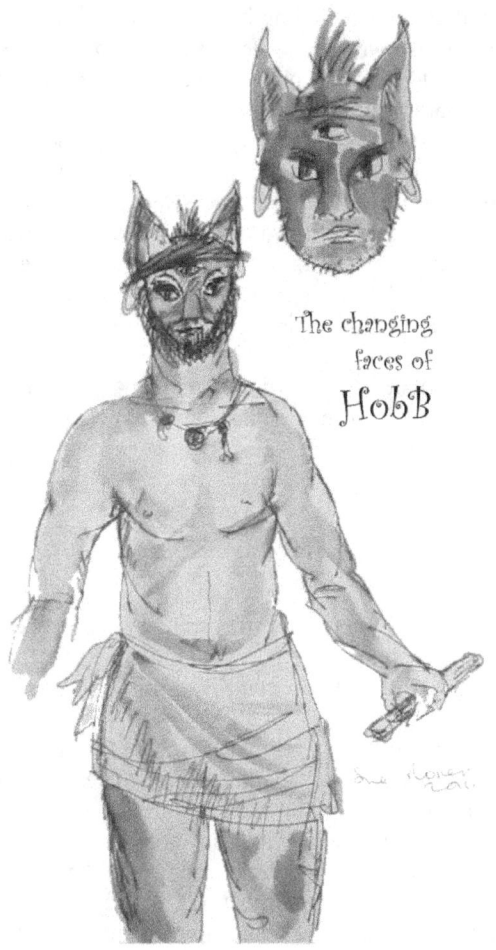

The changing faces of
HobB

Mycroft looked round in earnest, spotted the Sqoddie he was seeking and called him across, 'Will you put out a general callall message to the rest of your septallion spread across the continent and tell them to use the nearest moovacars to trek themselves home, making sure that they fill them if possible because in some areas there may be less than enough. Secondly, tell them to trek on manual. This is important. Because of the movement of the geoplatelets, the relative location, direction and actual locations will have changed. In simple terms, where they previously would have travelled Antipoleward, they must now travel Poleward and vice versa. Similarly, where they would previously have travelled Sunriseward, they must now travel Sunsetward and vice-versa. If there is any doubt, make sure that they ask one of you Sqoddies. You should all have been issued with the new maps by now. Is that clear?'

'Yes, sir.' replied the Sqoddie, noting the message with precision for forwarding, but not understanding it himself yet.

M returned to his own moovacar and he beckoned Dundy to follow. His callall to Polit46 at the Conventionium got through like in the old days, via a temporary link set up by Kernal.

'I've got the answers for you,' began Mycroft, 'and as you know by now, all Ozzillanders are safe and gradually returning to their homes. There's a minor problem in everyone swapping moovacars, but that will be overcome in the next few days. Of course, we need to sort some other matters, but that can wait until my return to the Necropol Club in Selondre.' M spotted Quax coming up from behind with his second head, 'Ah, here comes Quax ready for her lift back, I expect, so we'll be on our way to join you now.'

Polit46 was ready to receive Mycroft and Quax as an honoured guest, but he would never have guessed at the ongoing transformation still befalling Smelt.

* * * * *

'Why does Kernal command the military in peace-time,' began Smelt, 'when as soon as there is a genuine crisis, the politicians take over. I mean, Mycroft had real control of this little local problem, not Kernal.'

'Mycroft isn't a politician.' replied Maecenas, accurately.

'The principle of the principal applies nevertheless.' replied Smelt.

Maecenas nodded in slightly reluctant agreement. 'I suppose that's true, historically. They like to think they are in control, but it's still up to such as Kernal to arrange the detail and ensure the battle is won.'

Smelt was continuing to experimenting with his new-found magical powers. There was nothing he could do to help the Ozzillanders now. He could only sit and watch in fascination as the Sqoddies, effectively commanded by M had everything under their control.

Maecenas, too, was quite happy to watch what at first sight appeared to be a successful conclusion to what he was about to dub the Luke-Warm War. He sent a special callall message to Kernal to congratulate him on his good work, and also to Nanotech329 to make sure that his work would not be forgotten either.

Now that things were relatively back to normal, Maecenas tested the callall on long-distance calls and found that it worked. He had guessed that Kernal would have set up something as soon as communication was possible across the geoplatelet conjunctions.

M callalled Maecenas and Smelt, 'I think that it would be a rather nice gesture if you were both to go to Antipole, where you will find

Kernal, and thank him in person for his contribution to the planet's welfare. There is another reason why I would like you to go there, Smelt, but I won't waste our time explaining that now.'

Smelt never did quite understand M, but knew that he had his reasons for everything and often downplayed the importance of an activity while ensuring that his instructions were obeyed by his tone.

Smelt callalled Grounsella, even though he was not sure what to say. Like all absent fathers, he was upset at not being present at the time of delivery of his offspring, especially in the circumstances of Smeltdort6 and Smeltdort7 being so significant not only to him but to the future of the entire planet.

'Cate'aeddy has been here and interviewed us all because of the rarity of having twins.' Grounsella began, as an opener and to counteract Smelt's uncharacteristically embarrassed silence. She looked at him hard through the callall's holoquadrant, 'Are you all right? Are you well? You look as though you've changed, but I can't work out how. You remind me of a fellow who has just shaved off his beard; you know there is something wrong or different but you can't work out quite what. Tell me what it is.'

Smelt thought for a moment, 'Yes, I have changed, it's that, er, er, I don't quite know how to put it really.' How on Eqinox, wondered Smelt, can you tell your mistress who has made history by having borne you twins on the other side of the planet, that you went away normal and are coming back a WizarD - and all because of the twins she bore you?

'Oh, it's nothing really.' he managed to blurt out eventually, 'I'll tell you when I get back later today; you have enough matters of your own to attend to. I'll be there as soon as possible. I know I'll never get to heaven if I break your heart!'

'You certainly won't!' replied Grounsella and held up his twins for him to coo over.

'I'll tell her the moment I see her.' confirmed Smelt to Maecenas as soon as he had terminated the callall.

'You can probably magic yourself back there in an instant if you want to!' reminded Maecenas.

'I think,' said Smelt thoughtfully and with full deliberation, 'that I would rather not try any of the magic on myself until I have tried it on others.' He caught Maecenas' dubious expression, 'I mean, on things and critters, for example.'

'Ah!' said Maecenas, 'So long as you don't try it on me!'

'I won't. I've no such intention,' laughed Smelt and added jestingly and, he thought, purely for effect, 'yet!'

* * * * *

Meanwhile, Mycroft was callalling Kernal, 'Do you remember that I said you should take a bassinette and your genuine original elgins made of elgin from the Parthenon?'

'Yes,' said Kernal hesitantly, ever doubtful of M's real motives.

'Well,' said M, 'this will sound very odd to you, but it is vitally important. I want you personally to supervise it. You must go to the Antipole and precisely in the centre of the Antipole's geoplatelet, place the bassinette. Around it, I want you to make a Keltik Septagram using your original elgins from the Parthenon. You will find that there are exactly enough, however many you thought you had. I will send you the precise specifications of the star pattern, so there won't be any errors. Smelt will be joining you there shortly, so I would like you to do that immediately.'

Kernal said nothing.

Kernal could say nothing, he was awash with stunned amazement at M's latest eccentricity.

Kernal thought for several breaths and wondered whether to ask Polit46 whether M needed an automed Phroydtest for being, perhaps, less than wholly compass mendips concerning this strange Antipole activity.

Kernal decided that the activity was harmless and costless.

Kernal did as he was bid.

Kernal placed the bassinette in the middle of the Keltik Septagram, stood back and shook his head, wondering whether he had permanently lost his own elgins this time, in both senses of the expression.

Kernal was standing at the Antipole with all his elgins intact, when Smelt and Maecenas arrived.

'Good morning to you, Sirs' said Kernal as they alit.

'Good morning, Kernal' they replied in unison, staring at the strange sight of a bassinette in a Keltik Septagram of genuine elgins.

'We wanted to thank you in person for your wok.' said Maecenas, concentrating more on the vision than on his words.

'My wok?' replied Kernal wondering if the whole of Eqinox was skipping its braincells in favour of cosmic sawdust.

'Sorry,' said Maecenas, turning to Kernal and realising his error, 'I meant work.'

'Ah. Thank you.' said Kernal and slipped him a suspicious glance before looking away and noticing Smelt's strange expression.

Smelt was looking at the bassinette with an increasingly indescribably strange expression. He was silent.

Silence reigned for at least forty-seven further breaths while Smelt stared and the others stared at Smelt.

Suddenly Smelt burst, 'No longer, no more; I must do it.' and ran toward the Keltik Septagram, jumped from outside and dived headlong into the bassinette in the middle which should not have been big enough to take him.

A long-tailed aurora Ozzitailish appeared in netherlight overhead as Smelt disappeared in a puff of Sigmatic smoke rings, leaving only the brightest shadowless emptiness of light and space ever witnessed on Eqinox.

After an interminable silence, Kernal found the residual energy to ask Maecenas, 'what is the opposite of being out of your bassinette?'

As if on cue, the very air in the centre of the Keltik Septagram where the bassinette once was, curved and folded itself into a series of symbols worthy of Mycroft's netherwear smoke fountains.

Slowly but with precision and indefinable nobility, a form appeared. It was Smelt, unchanged yet wholly different. Instead of greying, he was now wholly grey; a dignified, distinguished, powerful whitish sort of grey that glowed not with reflected but with created glory.

'Please don't stare,' said Smelt, 'I'm the same old chap really; except that I am reformed. I have learnt my lesson and I will no longer practise economy or dishonesty with my nuptiality.'

'Is that all?' asked Maecenas, disappointed.

'All that I am prepared to admit at present!' smiled Smelt, 'or as Lynkern, the Amoricsprecedent would say, *There is going to be a new World Order* and it is starting today with me.'

Maecenas and Kernal stared at him, but it was a long time before either spoke.

Kernal's callall berped.

'We need you all to reconvene at the Conventionium in Selondre immediately. Good-bye.' Said M.

Kernal still didn't know what to make of M or his strange behaviour, not that he was any the wiser about Smelt. He forwarded M's instructions that this tiny but vitally relevant clump should join him forthwith at the Convention in Selondre.

* * * * *

At the Conventionium, it was as if nothing had ever happened.

Quax was arguing that because Ozzilland was now carpeted richly with vegetation following its virtual transmutation, then there was plenty for all to share, and most Triseps agreed, particularly after the Dark Elves had virtually saved the lives of the Ozzillanders by their protective custody for the duration.

Even the Ozzillanders themselves, through Ozzipolit7, had stated their desire to live happily every after in mutual harmony and co-operation with the Dark Elves. The Ozzillanders, for their part, offered the Dark Elves not only use of the land but permission to watch their soap operas covering certain neighbouring herds and their affairs, miseries and other tribulations, which the Dark Elves were not sure they really wanted until they nearly all became hooked and even timed their extra-nuptial replication practice around the daily episodes.

At one point, Quax descended into the floor of the Conventionium, only to return followed by a dubious looking character dressed in a ten-gallon hat and wearing a traditional cowboy outfit including holster and pistol.

The Trisep would have been unrecognisable in this uniform were it not for the fact that when he stood up he was clearly overweight and had a habit of sucking in his breath, shaking his head and scratching his imaginary beard. Also, despite wearing cowboy uniform, he nevertheless retained the smile-shaped gap between the midcoat and rear trousers, a vital part of the uniform for a builder.

'Why is he wearing a cowboy outfit?' Smelt asked Quax.

'Because he said that he wanted a new uniform and your people, his fellow Triseps, said he is a cowboy, even though I thought that he was a builder. By the way, is his herd-leader here somewhere? I would like to reconnect Bodgitt with his spouse.'

'Reconnect?' checked Smelt.

'Perhaps reunite would be a better word.' suggested Maecenas.

Quax nodded in acceptance, 'I bow to your better judgement of your own language.' she replied, 'Where is Bodgitta?'

'I will callall her personally and straight away,' said Smelt and wondered if this was the time to start doing some good with his newly created powers.

'Are there any other matters you need to discuss with the Convention?' asked M, looking invitingly at Quax.

'Nothing more that I need waste so much of so many Triseps' time. Not now, at least, although there are many matters we will need to discuss if we are to continue communicating at this level.'

'May I just ask you a few questions before you go, Quax?' said Smelt.

'Go ahead.'

'How did you keep Bodgitt healthy all this time, when he must have hurt himself as he fell down the hole?'

'You saw only what we wanted you to see, but we have hospitals and other methods of healing, just like you do. We're no different really, except for our shape!'

'And would you mind answering three more minor queries to straighten my mind?' asked Maecenas.

Quax nodded in agreement.

'Well, now,' began Maecenas with uncharacteristic hesitancy, 'at one point during our discussions in the Conventionium, you objected to being called Shealar, even though you had previously stated that words meant nothing to you and that you did not care about us using words.'

'I apologise for complaining, but the word sounds identical to a word in my language which means *infected brothel-inmate* and I really didn't like that term.'

'In that case, it is I who should offer apologies.' said Maecenas and rapidly dropped the subject.

'What was your second question?' asked Quax, quite willingly.

'I was just wondering when you changed from using old to modern Squeithian.'

'Simple, replied Quax, 'I listened to your educational holo-video-manuals programmed on the e-commenters.' She laughed and all those around followed suit. Except Maecenas.

'Finally, and not so unimportant, either,' said Maecenas, 'Do you know where our other builder, Gerry got to?'

'Gerry?' She looked guilty, 'Ah yes.'

Maecenas raised his eyebrows into a question mark, awaiting reply.

'I'm afraid I forgot to tell you. You were right. He was taken by one of our out-takes and they were part way through eating him when they were caught.'

'And?' said Maecenas after a long and painfully thoughtful pause.

'Ah, and we will return him to you when he is fully recovered in our hospice.'

'How long will that be?'

'When his arms have re-grown. The process is more than half completed now. You need have no further fears for him. Our out-takes have been punished. I promise his return, complete. He has one request, however. Would you please send him a visitor.'

'Certainly,' said Maecenas, 'his herd leader?'

'Yes,' replied Quax, 'if her name is Sharen.'

* * * * *

Smelta arrived from a lie-in of extra-nuptial replication practising with Grounsell. 'We've talked to Grounsella,' she began, 'and she is quite happy for us to see whether the four of us can live happily together, along with our herds and children. What do you say?'

'Are you proposing to extend it to other families?' asked Smelt.

'I doubt it, but we might, if we can all agree.' replied Smelta.

'My only concern,' added Grounsella who always liked to get in her two Dalli's worth, 'is that all of this might fail. After all, it's a bit like marrying on the ricochet, isn't it? But otherwise I'm agreed.' She felt happier now that she had been able to contribute negatively to the discussion, even though her concern was overruled by consensus.

'So we're all agreed on forming a new condominimum, then, with classic multiple ownership?' confirmed Grounsell.

'Yes,' replied Smelt with a grin, 'but I don't think we'll be keeping the condoms to a real minimum!'

From each to each were reflected meaningfully relevant smiles.

'Anyway, I've got too much else to do,' added Smelt, 'there are the texts from the Orijin to decrypt, an investigation into GoD and religions, the WitcheS to be kept under control ...' He stopped and hesitated for a breath or two and began to look even more serious.

'I've been talking to Mycroft' Smelt continued, 'and there are many other specialist matters I need to study. Most important is the ZygoSplit which has affected *all* the recent events. I must find the precise meaning of the word and of the meaning of its effect.'

'ZygoSplit?' repeated Smelta.

'Yes, in Mycroft's words, it is *the* Controlling Paradox. We *must* look it up in the Lexikern to understand the grave consequences of its significance.'

'I can ingest the words of the message,' said Smelta, 'but I find the potential interpretation rather less appetising.'

'Oh,' added Smelt with the planet on his shoulders, 'and numerous other tasks must I study, including the subjugation of the under-WizardS, not yet created; the cataloguing and testing of spells; more study of the Orijin itself which I gather the Gobblings know rather more about than they have yet admitted, having been its curator for hundreds of millennia and, of course, the total re-organisation of the upside-down Ozzilland.'

He was watched in silent awe by the assemblage; a respect merited by his meteoric elevation from, as it were, submarine to satellite.

Smelt looked at the others and laughed in embarrassed confusion. He dropped his head into his hands and asked rhetorically, 'Oh, GoD, what should I do first?'

The smile of a runcible pussy began to appear in front of him; a voice said, 'You called?'

End of the Precursors

Squeithian Lexikern

An Encyclopaedic Lexicon for Netherwear

IMPORTANT HISTORICAL NOTE:

Squeith is more correctly written as Σqueith using the olde form of the letter 's', because of the curious mathematical nature of the planet and all that therein is. However, as most modern literates (readers) are not (wholly literate, that is), then the terminal 's' has also been adopted in a larger form ('S') for initial and median use.

A Lexikern is from lex - word and kern - a term used by olde fashioned Caxtons (printers) to define the slight overlapping of some letters, like A and V for improved visual effect; 'i' is an olde fashioned conjunction, meaning 'and'. Therefore, when lots of words are listed together where their meanings tend to overlap, we now have a *LEXIKERN*.

~a *suff.* the suffix given to a herd leader - the chief female of a herd. *e.g.* ***Polit46a*** is the herd leader of Polit46 and ***Smelta*** is Smelt's herd leader.

Agreement, The *n.* a contract made about one hundred and two cycles ago between Triseps and Gobblings following the Ozzilland rookanga scare. The Agreement has seven tenets and forty seven clauses. The Seven Tenets are listed below (*for the rules on counting to seven, see 7 in Arithmates' Addendum*):

0   Neither Triseps nor Gobblings have any rights over the territory or property of the other.

1   There should be no contact between Triseps and Gobblings except in dire emergency.

2   That Trisep leaders should not admit the existence of the Gobblings or The Agreement to ordinary Triseps.

3   That publicity about any contact should be suppressed or dismissed as ridiculous.

4   That Gobblings would not make excessive or unnecessary visits to the surface or colonise the surface or otherwise interfere with Triseps or their space.

5   That both Gobblings and Triseps agreed to remain warless for all time so long as each keep to the contract in every word.

6   That Triseps would warn Gobblings of any impending disaster such as potential collision with a giant meteor or major wars between our own countries.

7   If any Triseps should accidentally fall down any of their temporary holes, then they would not be returned.

Agwgwlland   *n.*   *(pron. argoogookland)* A country Sunsetward of Squeith with areas called unpronounceable things like Ffordd Llwydd, Gwyllyddiân and Welks. Lots of alps. Lots of valleys. Triseps bred there are mostly either miners or teachers. The Polewarders of Agwgwlland have their own secret language that nobody else understands and male choirs infamous all over the planet. They are also famous for playing with their odd-shaped balls, a game which they are particularly good at, particularly when compared to the useless frogs! See *Welks.*

aisle *n.* a corridor of land in the midst of surrounding water.

aka *n. pron: ay-kay-ay* a second or subsequent name for a Trisep, place or object. It was once an acronym for something-or-other, but nobody remembers what. ***Example:*** dingdong aka callall was an expensive device enabling daughters to have long and expensive chats to their boyfriends when they are only next-door.

Alexigram Dingdong *n.* see *Dingdong, Alexigram.*

Alit *p.p. vb.* Shorter than *alighted.*

Allysp Rings *n.* An Antipoleward coastal town, now at the bottom of Ozzilland, which used to be somewhere in the middle and a bit more obscure. Discovered when Allysp *(cf)*, the famous expeditor discovered a Ferrikross *(cf)* of Faerie-rings *(cf)* and endlessly chased-up other Triseps for their theories.

alp *n. pron: alp* a very high hill; any hill over 1000 hites high. See also *Etnavolc* and *magmablast.*

Alp-Etnavolc *n.* See *Etnavolc.*

Alp-Ever-rest *n.* See *Ever-rest.*

Amorics *n. pron: amorix* a large continent, capital: Launder (where the washing's done), where the Triseps think they own the world, unlike Squeithians, who really do own the world. All the planet's worst diseases were seen here first, including Feminism, Faerie Contaigen, Granny Abuse, Mother-in-lorr Naggits, Second - Head - Collapse - Syndrome, Husband-beating, Feminism, and many others. Called the Amorics because of the amorous nature of the original inhabitants, who, after thousands of cycles of occupation were mostly beaten up and killed by the incomers so that they could declare Freedom Of Land Ownership, movement and speech and create a constitution giving equal rights to everybody except its original natives who they kept in reserve. Its inhabitants chew Coker Tree Gum *(cf)* and drink Coker sap from little metal containers. *Precedent:* Lynkern. *Deputy Precedent:* Effdeearr.

Anerak *n.* large town Sunsetwards of Selondre where there are twaks that enable the Anerakians to play with their snake sandwiches. See *twain* for full definition.

Anerakian *n.* a resident of Anerak. All such wear lots of badges, pebble glasses and semi-official looking flat hats. They carry a bag bearing the legend, GWR, which means *husband* in a local language of the Welks area of Agwgwlland. See *twain* for full definition.

Anerak Preservation Centre *n.* the place where twains and other related vintage transport memorabilia are stationed. See *twain* for full definition.

Angelicus Underground Transit Station *n.* an olde-fashioned tube railway station in the Poleward part of Selondre, the Squeithian capital. Notable and famed for its lifts which only work about once a week and its spiral staircase with 192 steps.

Ånjap *n.* the largest aisle-land of the Nipoff Archipelago. A strange little country on exactly the opposite side of the world from Squeith. Triseps from Ånjap could copy anything and usually improve on it, too. The country had a strange language of its own, impossible for outsiders, and many weird religious rituals. They also had Emperors who were worshipped like the GodS, even when they were dead. The upper classes had their own special poetic form called trirhythmic-septaline *(cf)*. When they were unhappy, they would go round cutting out their own stomachs for some weird reason. **Ånjapese** *n.,* their language. *adj.* of Ånjap. See also *Nipoff.*

Anticrime, Minister for *n.* Currently Lorranordå *(cf)*. This is the position in the government for the person who ensures the termination of things like self-deceasement, burglaristic activities and the like. Sadly, the only crimes he has not been able to overcome are the crimes against ordinary people and general corruption of a marauding band of half-wits called the 'West Mercia Constabulary'.

Antipole *n.* a country at the bottom of the planet, exactly opposite Pole. A bit cold. Nearest country is Ozzilland; except for a small pair of aisles in the New Seas called New Seaslland *(cf)* and an irrelevant one called Scotaisle *(cf)*.

Antipoleward *adj.* towards (or moving towards) the bottom of the planet, one of the four cardinal directions on Eqinox, the others being, *Poleward, Sunriseward,* and *Sunsetward.*

antipolular *adj.* pointing in the opposite direction from its original orientation; can also mean pointing towards the Antipole, the bottom of the planet; see *Antipoleward.* E.g. the moovacar became antipolular *means* it turned round.

anti-sound *n., vb.* a sound emitted (for example, by a callall during confidential calls) to stop a confidential conversation being overheard. Also used to silence noisy machines before the invention of silent nanotechnology.

Arbor-Orijinal *n.* a member of the original native tribe of Tree-Triseps of Ozzilland *(cf)*. There are a few left, but they have long since lost their magical capabilities and now make most of their money by exploiting the cave-paintings bequeathed by their ancestors. Their magic remained locked-up, accumulating in the mortal remains of their ancestors ready to explode.

Arena, The *n.* the sporting area where major sporting events contests are held, enabling Triseps to show off their physical capabilities in all kinds of areas. Sports used to be performed naked against each other, but are now performed normally and against a ticker.

arithmate *n.* one of a breed of very clever Triseps who know a great deal about very little, and in particular, they know everything about nothing and nothing about everything. To explain more precisely, they know all about the number zero and a lot about other *real* numbers except infinity (© Philosophers), about which they know absolutely nothing as infinity (© Philosophers) is the copyright property of philosophers. Because they never talk to people, some say that arithmates should integrate more.

arjibargy, arjibargying *vb.* to discuss and debate with some vigour, often with armies, like a band of marauding Triseps once did over the Forklland Aisles *(cf)*, during the reign of St. Thatch *(cf)*.

armcowch *n.* a more-than-usually comfortable cowch with three rests for arms. Very special older ones are made from the skins of dead critters, known as levva.

auspicator *n.* that which is or appears to cause the initiation of a more extensive sign or omen [*fr. n.* **auspice,** an omen] *P.S. why are you looking this up here? it should be a real word and in **every** Lexikern!*

Authorised Version *n.* The Old and New Promisings make up The Folius *(cf)* and have been translated into many versions, the most revered of which is the Authorised Version ordered by the infallible St. Thatch, the founder of the Thatcherfactorismoptimists Party *(cf)*. This is one of the translations of The Folius used by Jowver's Evidencers *(cf)*.

autobridge *n.* see hoverfloat autobridge.

Autocensus *n.* a large government computer which in theory keeps track of everything and everyone. In practise, it misses out on a great deal and except for population totals it usually has a significant error factor when providing a statistic. Another problem with the Autocensus is that its answers vary according to how much it has been massaged recently by visiting politicians; it then provides *massaged statistics.*

autodiary *n.* a device that tells Triseps where they should be and when. It will even tell moovacars where to go and where to be when expected. It will also make confirmation callalls to other diaries and readjust appointments to suit everyone. It will also take notes and expand them to a full speech. Quite useful, really.

autoerotic nanogroove *n.* method of reproducing the latest music style that most young Triseps like to dance to, in all-round multiphonic omnisound although their dancing is not so much a dance as a prelude to mating rituals. This type of tone sequencing has the effect of increasing the libido, hence the name.

autofollowing holocam *n.* a flying holocam which automatically tracks and follows its subject, transmitting its picture back to the nearest portoffice. Developed by ENN *(cf)* engineers and exclusive to them. Brilliant, simple and very effective. Annoys some public figures who get upset about being interminably followed by a machine! See *holocam.*

autogenerate *n.* something made specially to be experimented upon, usually a specially designed critter *(cf)* of one species or another. The important thing about it is that it has no brain and therefore does not feel pain, so is ideal for all sorts of weird medical and other experiments.

autostack **1** *n.* an automatic moovacar park. **2** *n.* a pile of Triseps in orgy formation. **3** *vb.* the act of parking a moovacar. **4** *vb.* piling a series of Triseps, one upon the next in orgy formation.

automed *n.* a complete doctor. The machine checks for any problems whatsoever, diagnoses those it finds and provides the correct medicine with any special instructions. The machine knows about every medical emergency that has ever befallen Triseps. It even knows about predicted conditions that have never yet occurred. Very occasionally, automeds have to check with external data to verify a condition, but not often. Automeds have never found a condition that they could not cure. Until now.

autosuk *n.* a silent device which hovers around cleaning continuously, all and every day and night, taking energy from the air to operate and making harmless atmospheric water vapour from any dust or rubbish it discovers.

autotranslator *n.* a moody little device for translating, almost simultaneously, any language into any other. They just sort of hang around in public places and spring into action when needed and if it feels like it, so long as somebody says, 'Eh?' One minor problem with the device is that sometimes it decides to speak phonetically (yes, it does!).

Azorrics *n.* one of the best ghotiing areas of Eqinox, once fought over in a battle between Sammowa and Eislland. See also *ghoti.*

bail battering *n.* a game where balls are aimed at bails and deflected by others if possible. The purpose of the game is to win temporary custody of the ashen remains of a pair of pre-flamed bails stored for some weird and forgotten reason in a beautiful gelt urn. It makes sense to Squeithian Triseps at least, although frogs, Triseps of the Amorics and social workers were never intelligent enough to understand it.

Bailey *n.* the designer of the original hoverfloat autobridge *(cf).* As you can tell from his name, his job was to bail out ferries crossing a river. He found this so boring (nearly as boring as being an actuary in fact), that he designed the first non-hovering, floating autobridge. This was so successful, especially for the Defenss that he retired on the profits and instead of bailing out ferries, started bailing out the poor. *(fr. O. Sq. bale-out = to remove)*

Ballam *n.* an area Antipoleward of the Squeithian capital of Selondre where bridies *(cf)* are common and which is now famous for having been the homeland of brainless Sharens *(cf),* who were developed there (and in the case of Sharens, 'developed' is the right word). Some call Ballam the gateway to the Antipoleward. See *Sinn.*

barber *n.* see *Riffs of Morøkka.*

bassinette *n.* a small bassin. A bassin was used in the old days for pushing elderly Triseps. Bassinettes are used for baby Triseps.

beefburgher *n.* a strange sort of instant meal made of a processed and cooked cereal compound and ground-up critter, invented by a Kelt *(cf)* called Mac-something-or-other. So called because the burghers of his town loved it to start with but then started to beef about what they claimed to be its rotten contents. They were wrong of course.

Belcanto *n.* a famous and very temperamental opera performer who makes a noise a bit like Cher-ants *(cf).* Some Triseps who claim to be intellectual call it singing. Actually, the intellectuals are really those whose friends are in receipt of Government Arts Funding.

berp *n.* the noise made by a callall *(cf)* when it wants to be answered or by a provisions hatch when it has finished making your order.

besom *n.* a special type of moovacar used by thaumaturges *(cf)* or WitcheS *(cf)*. These besoms, which are more sort of ridden than driven, are arranged in threes, in a seven-sided triangle and can fire twigs to kill in the direction of the bobble or tassel on the driver's hat. See *WitcH.*

Big Dick *n.* See *Makkaan.*

bleat *n.* something indefinable that is sent out through the air, in various frequencies, to e-commenters, hence EBC *(cf)*.

blonde *n.* a type of multi-coloured hair that is attractive to everyone who sees it, regardless of normal preference. See *brainless* and *Sharen.*

Blood *n.* a bright yellow substance, the same colour as a blush, which is inside Triseps and passes pure energy from one part of their bodies to another.

Bodgitt *n.* a builder who is particularly famous and is used for all of the more important building jobs. He sometimes gets it nearly right. **Bodgitta** *n.* Bodgitt's herd leader and naturally the only wife of his herd interested in her husband, the others being nominal wives.

brainless *adj.* a definition of Sharen *(cf)* and of social workers. See also *blonde.*

breath *n.* a short period of time; the time taken to take on a breath of air. Time is counted in breaths.

breaths *pl. n. slang* mamaglans, a term uthed by young girlth who lithp.

bridies *n.* ladies usually found in the street, or on street corners, to be more precise. Professionals in their own right, they stop passing males in their moovacars and ask them if they are interested in 'a bit of fun, luvvy'. Sharens *(cf)* have now fully replaced bridies (according to government statistics, which have a habit of showing what we are being told to believe rather than reflecting reality).

buttalact *n.* an edible thixotropic gel, made by shaking lact, the post-natal discharge from the mamaglans of certain large critters. Useful for spreading on dorolls *(cf)*, crispy surfaced soft, white baked yeast and flour mixture.

Caesust *n.* the sixth month of the year, named after an old emperor.

Calept *n.* a popular alcoholic beverage, indescribable because it is like nothing else in the entire universe.

Caleptic hi-ball *n.* a cocktail made using Calept and other weird substances (some of which are technically illegal, but only if they are manufactured manually; if made automatically by the provisions hatch *(cf)* then they cannot be deemed illegal as nobody is responsible for their minting.)

callall *n.* a communicating device, being an advanced form of the one invented by a Trisep called Alexigram Dingdong *(cf)*. Also *vb.,* to callall. When another Trisep callalls you, it berps to let you know it wants to be answered. See also *anti-sound.* See also *over-cipher.* Some older Triseps like Mycroft *(cf)* still refer to the callall as *the dingdong contraption.*

callallcode *n.* A code used to callall a particular Trisep. It can be switched into or out of the system as required.

cam *n.* picture taking device. See also *holo-cam.*

Cantor *n.* an antilogician of some repute, having started his life as a normal, boring arithmate *(cf)* (mathematician).

Carehedd *n.* the boss of the Multicare vehicle. Trained in all aspects of fire fighting, traffic control, policing and medical work.

casponite *n.* An incredibly attractive white rock, from which elgins *(cf)* used to be made.

Cate'aeddy *n.* pronounced kate-aid-ee. This is the name of the Chief EBC ENN Reporter. She seems to be most at home reporting on difficult things like wars, but there haven't been many of those recently. She is also famous for writing her two autobiographies showing her life of war reporting, *What Cate'aeddy Did* and *What Cate'aeddy Did Next.*

chequemate *interj.* a call made at the successful conclusion of a game of Financial Monopoly *(cf)* when the king and therefore all the money has been captured. **2** *n.* the game position necessitating making the call. Traditionally, the loser gives the winner a cheque. Also as *vb.* to place someone in a position where they cannot escape - either physically or metaphorically.

Cher-ant *n.* a noisy type of ant that makes a silly noise. Some lesser intelligences like frogs and social workers call it singing.

Chi Nar Mao *n.* Precedent of the Walled country of Faience, where the yellow Triseps live. Chi Nar Mao means Rod of Iron in Faience dialect, and that is how he rules.

chiver *n. see jam-chiver.*

ciphers *n.* codes, of course. What else?

circular reference - See *reference, circular.*

clarridge *n. (usu. as pl. ~s)* a segment of an extremely comfortable vintage air-conditioned, fully restauranted mini-hotel on wheels. The clarridges are organised into segments like snakes, which are pulled and pushed along twaks by twains, pairs of

pressure-vapour engines *(cf)* placed one at each end. See *twain* for full definition.

clump *n.* collective noun for a group of Triseps. *v.t.* to meet together. The word was minted when a Trisep defined himself as *a-lump*; when there were two Triseps, there would be a *b-lump* and three or more would be a *c-lump* or clump.

coitalising *vb.* practising replication techniques.

Coker tree *n.* a huge tree, which grows to over one thousand hites. Particularly famous for its sap which comes out as gum. Everyone in the Amorics chews Coker Tree Gum and drinks Coker sap which, for some unknown reason, Triseps like to drink out of the little metal containers used to transport it.

commenter *n.* a private, closed circuit version of the public e-commenter.

commenter, infobox *n.* a holoquadrant of an e-commenter showing written details of what is being shown, such as a speaker's biography, a news item's location, or an actor's personal private life.

compass mendips *n.* being complete with one's elgins, so to speak. The sort of Triseps who are not wholly compass mendips are those who give you false directions when you ask the way. They do so for the fun of watching you trek off in the wrong direction with the certain knowledge that you will never meet again. This is a game played by all students at one time or another. The term was minted by a clump of students who sent all passing trekkers to the Alp-Mendips during rag-week, causing major traffic jams there for weeks.

computer *n.* a machine that can do less than most Triseps give it credit for, although it can do more than it used to. Like computers all over the universe, really. Recognised for being stupid, but not quite as stupid as social workers or frogs.

computerese *n.* a special language used for talking to computers. Normal words, really, but some Triseps think that they have to put on a special voice as though the computer is deaf. **I said, some Triseps think that they ...** 'eh, what? who spoke?' Oh, never mind!

condominimum *n.* a cosmopolitan place ruled by various outside agencies, like governments and members of the Triseptokatholicus Order, where condoms are, for one reason or another, kept to a minimum.

Contaigen *n.* an illness as opposed to Faerie Contaigen or The Contaigen, which is a particularly nasty illness.

Contaigenee *n.* any miserable wretch of a Trisep who is suffering from the Contaigen and is under the unfortunate care of Profmed.

Convention *n.* pron: *con-ven-shun*. A meeting of Triseps, usually on a specialist subject. Hence *vb. Conventioning.*

Conventionium *n.* pron.: *con-ven-tee-own-ee-um*. A gigantic hall in Selondre, the Squeithian capital. It is elastically expandable or contractible to hold as few or as many delegates as necessary for a particular Convention.

Con-Vinci *n.* A famous historical Trisep, famous for proving that the planet was a vexal septiquadecahedron and not a sphere. He used to be called of-Vinci, but St. Thatch, infallible leader of the Thatcherfactorism-optimists Party thought that he was trying to con everyone, so ordered that he be renamed.

Convinciing Geometry *n.* Special kind of geometry which enabled Con-Vinci to prove that Eqinox was a vexal septiquadecahedron and not a sphere. Discovered or invented, depending how you look at it, by Con-Vinci *(cf)*.

corn-seed scrunchies *n.* see *scrunchies.*

coronglay *n.* a musical instrument not dissimilar to the Squeithian trumpet and creating an equally appalling squalling drawl.

cowch *n.* a special seat designed exclusively for the awkwardly structured Trisep.

cowch spud *n. a* Trisep who spends his/her entire life on a cowch doing absolutely nothing but watching the e-commenter and changing channels with a psycho-trigger hairclip *(fr. cowch + lisp-S + pud because they only eat puddings).*

criss-cross *vb.* not dissimilar to being cross-crissed, but the opposite, really.

critter *n.* any living quadruped other than Triseps, who are different because they have Soles *(cf),* are intelligent (even on the Green Aisle) and laugh at jokes. In the old days they used to be eaten and the post-natal discharge from their mamaglans was added to dried leaves and hot water to make lactinfuse. Since nanomachines, real critters are now only eaten by members of the Necropol Club and a few obscure sub-tribes, like social workers, who refuse to conform to civilisation. Also prized for their skins, which makes levva *(cf).*

Croll *n.* the first town in Poleward Faience where all the male Triseps disappeared for an unexplained reason.

Cronus *n.* a mythological GoD, whose name first appeared in ancient Greasy. Rhea's brother. They were renowned for their incestuous behaviour. Often used as an expletive, as in *Cronus! I need a geeantee* or *Cronus and Rhea! I fancy Sharen.*

cycle *n.* a seven year period on Eqinox. The second sun is the same distance as the first sun once every seven years. When this happens, all sorts of strange things happen to tides, sex drives, females and reproductive organs. Some refer to cycles as *period cycles.*

Dåagøn Häzs ice cream *n.* very tasty cold stuff, originally made in the Amorics, but where the name pretends that it comes from Fjordlland *(cf)*, even though it very definitely does not and even the silly shaped characters are not recognised in Fjordlland.

Dagoba *n.* a place that holds the relics of GoD; the shrine built at Eden Garden.

Dalli *n.* a unit of currency. 47 Dallis to the Lama. The expression, *one dalli short of a lama* means the same as *losing one's elgins.* See also *elgin.*

Dark Elves *n.* a member of a tribe of Gobblings resident in the Underplanet beneath Sammowa and Ozzilland. One of the Seven Tribes. Their special characteristics are their tanned bodies and creepy-crawly stance, even though they loll on only two legs. Their language is called Elfin B.

deceasement *vi.* having become deceased, permanently. End of story. The verb, in this case, is very much intransitive.

decession *vb.* the criminal act of performing unnecessary self-administered premature deceasement. Killing oneself was once considered such a serious offence that offenders who succeeded were hanged to make sure and those who failed were hanged for trying until somebody realised that this was a bit like offering a job in a ghoti and chip shop to cure obesity. It is still a serious crime, but the punishment is now to be kept alive and cured by the automed.

decryption *vb.* disentangling ciphers. What else?

Defenss *n.* The clump *(cf)* of armed soldier Triseps who are always prepared to help in any emergency, whether on land or sea or in the air. They used to fight wars, but there aren't many of those these days.

Degenerate State *n.* the state of the Parthenon, from which Qontûm was determined. See also *Parthenon, Qontûm,* and *Infinity (© Philosophers).* See also the Arithmates' Addendum for *Infinity (© Philosophers).*

Delius Myth *n.* a set of recipes for combined music which can be good if it is not performed by Cher-ants *(cf);* a good story and some nice food. Sometimes Triseps will take the Delius with the food but without the Myth (story) or the food without the music, but a far better dinner party is created when you combine the Delius and the Myth for a good triple recipe.

Deteriorations *n.* the fifth folio of the Pentatouch in the Old Promisings *(cf)*, written by one of the sages touched by GoD. Nobody bothers to read it these days except the religiots, so most of us don't really know what is in it, but everybody talks about it. This one is about the lorrs given to the Triseps and how they deteriorated once they started ignoring the lorrs. Sad, really.

Dick *n.* See *Makkaan.*

Dingdong, Alexigram *n.* The inventor of what we now call the callall *(cf)*, except that in those days, of course, the device was rather simpler and operated in sound only. It is said that he discovered it when he called to his assistant in the next room, "Solder" (that was his name: *Solder*), "Solder, come here, I want you."

Dirwan *n.* a Trisep who upset the religiots by suggesting that Triseps evolved from lower critter forms, and that *they* evolved from even lower forms still. His *Theory of Evolvement* was almost right, but it did cause a great upheaval in philosophical thinking. The religiots said that his theories went against Genetics *(cf)*.

disensconced *vb.* interrupted, especially when in what might be called a *sporting position.* A bit like throwing a bucket of water over two dogs, really.

Domesday *n.* a special day when everyone was counted - once - for the chronicle of a religious work called Numerology, the fourth folio of the Old Promisings of The Folius. Details are lost as to why this day was so important, but it was something to do with a dome being built - the records mention a Green WitcH in the East End, but it was all so transitory that nobody any longer remembers anything about it. One other reference is to that of a big "White Hephalump" but nobody understands that reference either. See also *Numerology.*

Domesday Records *n.* another name for the folio of Numerology *(cf).*

~dort *suff.* the suffix given to female offspring during the building and learning cycles, cycles one and two. *e.g.* Polit46dort is the female offspring of Polit46.

dorolls *n.* crispy surfaced, soft white baked yeast and flour mixture, ideal for eating with a thin spreading of buttalact *(cf).*

Doughnut *n.* A toroid by any other name, of course.

Dundy *n.* An Ozzilland crocodile hunter whose main claim to fame was his competence arising directly out of his apparent (but not actual) incompetence. Famed in the History Records for being the first out of the hole with Mycroft after the liberation of Ozzilland by Mycroft and Quax. Despite his apparent yokelistic character, he was a brilliant arithmate *(cf).*

earshot *n.* the range of sound *usu. pref. by* **within**. being close enough to a sound to be able to hear it with ears, which in the case of Triseps is a fixed distance of forty-seven times seven lengths.

EBC *n.* Eqinox Bleating Centre. Planet Five's broadcasting Network, bleating all kinds of messages, programmes, etc. over kappa-waves.

eck, ecks *n., adj.* one of a set of four symbols used to denote a grotty Ozzilland drink. see *four-ecks.*

e-commenter *n.* holographic vide-receiver for the public network. A number of pictures are displayed simultaneously because brains can take in a great deal more than the details of just a single picture. The pictures are divided into holoquadrants because it was realised long ago, that the brain is better occupied seeing several scenes at once, or even several different plays. See *commenter, infobox.*

Eden Garden *n.* mentioned in the folio of Genetics as being the first place in the entire universe where GoD created life. Also the new name given to Squelchpool. Unfortunately, everyone liked the sound of Squelchpool so much that they carried on using it.

Effdeearr *n.* Deputy Precedent of the Amorics *(cf)*, under Lynkern *(cf).*

Eislland *n.* a country which was devastated by Sammowa in the Great Western Wars over ghotiing rights in the Azorrics, when an atom-splitting molotov was, as it were, *sent* to them.

Eisllandgate *n.* the name given to a major cover-up following suggestions that the entrance or *gate* to Eislland *(cf)* had been abruptly and corruptly moved by magic.

Elfin B *n.* the language of the Dark Elves of Sammowa & Ozzilland. The only Trisep who can speak this is Mycroft.

elginfunction *n.* the uncertain characteristic of the Degenerate State of the Parthenon, from which the base definition of the various Qontûm theories were calculated (or rather, guessed at, initially). See also *Infinity (© Philosophers)* in the Arithmates' Addendum.

elgins *n. usually pl.* little spherical rocks named after a Trisep who controversially took some from Greasy *(cf).* Used particularly by children and a few of the ultra-intelligent, who roll them at each other. To *lose one's elgins* means to be *out of one's bassinette*. See also *Dalli,* See also *Casponite.*

engrandisement, received *n.* kudos gained by accidental proxy, particularly from promotion of one kind or another, such as from a normal Trisep to a WizarD.

enholing *vb.* making a Σ shaped hole in something, usually a ticket to travel on a snake sandwich. See *twain* for full definition.

ENN *n.* Eqinox Nebulus News. A 24 hour, on the spot, news channel.

Freedoms for Religious Equality Amendment Kreed, F.R.E.A.K. *n.* exactly what it says it is, really, a Religiots' Charter. About three million words of bureaucratic nonsense which says, rather less precisely or concisely, the same as the title. Not worth looking up in a dictionary really. Basically, you can do what you want within a religion, so long as it doesn't affect others and is between consenting adults. The amendment amended an international treaty that said simply, *Every Trisep has the right to practise religion whenever and wherever desired.* But then, the bureaucrats must keep themselves busy somehow.

Equi-mail *n. pron: ee-male* an olde-fashioned written communication, sent on pulpleaves from anywhere on Eqinox to anywhere else. Used from the earliest recorded times (recorded on pulpleaves) Middle-Eons until the invention of computers, autodiaries, holograms, etc., and electronic stuff generally. Unfortunately, there is no record of how Triseps communicated before pulpleaves were invented because the earliest History Records were also kept on pulpleaves.

Equi-mailing *n., vb.* a batch of Equi-mail; to dispatch Equi-mail.

Equi-mailings *n.* the numerous writings from early GoD followers to others, found in the New Promisings *(cf)* of The Folius *(cf)* between the four GodspellS and the Folio of Revealment.

eqiquake *n. pron: ekwikwake* a quake of the surface of Eqinox. They happen here, too. No different. See also *geofault, geoplatelet.*

Eqinox *n. pron: ekwinoks* another name for Planet Five. Described by its inhabitants as the best planet they had ever visited, even though they wished they hadn't, and hadn't ever been elsewhere. Triseps are taught that it is spherical because that is easier to describe than its true shape of a *vexal septiquadecahedron (cf).* Mycroft *(cf)* once calculated that only one in 47^7 (506 623 120 463) planets would be this shape. The radius and the diameter (see vexal septiquadecahedron) of the planet are identical at 15463 kl (see *kl*). In theory, the population should be stable at one Trisep per quad, but this does not always work out in reality.

Esquimeaux *n. pron: es-kim-owes* a sub tribe of Gobblings who appear in the Antipole, wear critter skins and build little round houses made of ice. They freely offer their wives to keep visiting Triseps warm at night. See also *Pole-Esquimeaux.*

erection *n.* something that is put up, or erected, or rises up. In other words, a building - usually.

Etnavolc *n.* a particularly famous alp which is still being formed from magmablasts.

Evenden *n.* just another place. You don't need to know about this. Yet. Believe me, you **will** find out about it in years to come!

Ever-rest *n.* a particularly tall hill, or alp, which it is every Trisep's ambition to climb without any artificial aid. Tensing *(cf)* is an important exercise in preparation. When climbing it, you are for**ever-rest**ing, hence its name.

ex-cam *adv., adj.* without a cam or holocam present; a meeting taking place *ex-cam* takes place in secret. Like flammable and inflammable, ex-cam and in-camera *(literally, "in the darkness")* actually mean the same thing and not opposites!

Exercises *n.* the second folio of the Pentatouch in the Old Promisings *(cf)*, written by one of the five sages of old, who had been touched by GoD. A religious work. Only ever read by the religiots and other interested parties such as teachers. This folio was about the movement of the seven tribes of Yishrel over Planet Five; in other words, their exercises.

expeditor *n.* a Trisep who goes round on expeditions exploring and then (and this bit is important) chasing-up other Triseps for their theories. Allysp *(cf)* was one example.

extra-nuptial *n.* anything done outside normal nuptial arrangements. Sex, mostly.

facility, ~ies *both are sing. and plural. n.* unisex toilet and bathroom with clothes cleaning and repairing machine, personal valeting machine and general purpose provision facility. A smaller version is fitted to all moovacars. This is known as the mini-facility.

Faerie *n.* little biped, a member of a tribe of Gobblings resident in the Underplanet beneath the Amorics *(cf)*. One of the Seven Tribes. Their special characteristics are their large white wings, their gay clothes, gay actions and penchant for members of their own gender. A famous picture taken with an olde-fashioned cam shows a number of them dancing at the bottom of a young female Trisep's garden. See also *Gobblings.*

Faerie Contaigen *n.* a nasty form of the disease given by Faeries to anyone they kissed in the Amorics. Mended by the automeds - eventually.

Faerie-rings *n.* circles of very slightly raised ground around a place where Gobblings have or once had a hole from their underground homes to the surface.

Faience *n.* also known as **Walled Faience**. A country Sunriseward of Squeith, near Ånjap. Full of yellow Triseps and run with a rod of iron by Precedent Chi Nar Mao. Overrun by Trolls.

false-truthing 1 *n.* a statement which appears to be wholly true but is in fact somewhat economical with the realité. **2** *vb.* the act of prevaricating when fabricating a false allegory.

fantastic *adj.* wonderful and majorical, of course! What else?

Ferrikross *n.* an ancient lucky-charm in the form of an iron cross with legs, otherwise known as a quadric gammagram *(cf)*. Always spelled with a capital at start and end to keep evil spirits out of its name, like all lucky charms; otherwise the charm will produce an unfortunate but unspecified effect on the writer of its name.

Financial Monopoly *n.* a game where rents are paid on owned squares of a cheque board to stop the king being captured. When the winner captures the king and therefore all the money, he shouts chequemate *(cf)*.

Firebrand *n.* a gambling game played with some printed cards which some Triseps have become so upset about that they have killed others after claims of cheating. Named after a brand used to sort out fires and let in oxygen.

Fjordian *adj.* denoting or of Fjordlland; usually referring to the beautifully lilting accent and attractiveness of the Triseps living there.

Fjordlland *n.* a country with deep ravines inletting the ocean. The country is also renowned for its skiing and Dåagøn Häzs ice cream *(cf)* (which actually has nothing to do with it and was invented in the Amorics!)

Ffordd Llwydd *n.* a valley near Welks, with its own male choir. Famous for nothing else except an old fossilised tree mine, which primitive Triseps burned to keep themselves warm. See Welks.

flag *n.* a bit of coloured material or metal stuck up in the air that tells you what country or town you are in.

flatcam-pic *n.* pre-holographic still image of an object or scene. Early flatcampics were in sepia and white, but later they were in full spectra. X-ray versions imaging in the full x–ray spectra were developed, but never really caught on except in hospices, of course, where a pre-automed Quax would study them before laying bets on how long the patient would remain unpegged-out.

fobia *n.* a worry about something. Herd leader with milkman fobias are common!

Fobofobia *n.* irrationally being worried or frightened of being irrationally worried or afraid, of course.

folio *n.* set of olde-fashioned pulpleaves with designs printed on, providing information to those who have learnt to decipher or decrypt them. Also the individual parts of the religious work, The Folius *(cf)*.

Folius, The, *n.* the set of folios of the writings of those *'touched'* by GoD. Read almost exclusively by the religiots.

Forklland *n.* a tiny aisle in the Azorrics, where the ghotiing is good. Saved by St. Thatch from a band of marauding Triseps who were arjibargying about who should own it.

Four-ecks *n.* olde-fashioned alcoholic water drink made with Ozzi'opps (which only grow in Ozzilland), before the invention of nanomanufacture *(cf.)*. As tasteless as all such drinks and palatable only to Ozzillanders, who prefer to drink it so cold that the flavour is swamped by the iciness.

frenshorn *n.* a musical instrument not dissimilar to the Squeithian trumpet or coronglay and piercing an equally appalling squalling drawl. Don't ever buy one without the attachments, including a spare embouchure, which it needs if it is to function properly.

frisby *n.* also known as a flying sorcerer because of a myth that sorcerers were not so much Trisep-shaped but more, well, sort of frisby-shaped. Frisbies were originally children's toys; then they became adults' toys; then throwing them at each other became a national game. One unfortunate embadged Trisep from Anerak *(cf)* once suggested that the planet was shaped like a frisby and was being thrown between one GoD and another!

Gamma *n*. An olde-fashioned symbol for x-rays, looking like this: Γ.

gammagram *n*. any drawn device consisting of a number of olde-fashioned writing symbols called gammas in various patterns. See also: *Quadric Gammagram.*

gee *n*. sweet smelling transparent drink. See geeantee.

geeantee *n*. a drink made of a sweet smelling, transparent alcoholic drink, gee and a water, carbon dioxide and perfume tonic drink called tee.

gelt *n*. a soft and highly valued bright yellow shiny metallic element commonly used in jewellery. Now manufactured by midasnanos *(cf)*.

gender *adj*. One of the four sexes, male, herd leader, other female and the new gender, Sharen.

Genetics *n*. the first folio of the Pentatouch in the Old Promisings *(cf)*, written by one of the sages of old, who had been touched by GoD. A religious work. This one is about The Creation (see Dirwan).

Genetics, Natural *n*. see *Natural Genetics.*

gentletrisep *n*. polite form of address for a mature male Trisep.

geofault *n*. the line between two moving geoplatelets where eqiquakes *(cf)* occur.

geoplatelet *n*. one of the forty-seven surface plates which make up the structure of the planet, Eqinox *(cf)*. See also *vexal septiquadecahedron.*

Gerry *n*. a Trisep who is a builder, hence *v*. **Gerry-built.** ~a *n*. Gerry's first nuptialised partner; his herd leader. All of Gerry's buildings have a blue plaque stating, *Gerry Built* which stays on until long after the building unbuilds itself and self-demolishes shortly after completion.

ghoti *n*. pronounced *'f-i-sh'*. gh is 'f' as in enou*gh*. *o* is 'i' as in w*o*men, *ti* is 'sh' as in no*ti*on or sta*ti*on. The best flavoured ghotis are found swimming in the Azorrics. They are eaten raw in the Nipoff Archipelago. See also *Eislland* and *Sammowa.*

GoD *n*. the One, the Ultimate Being who is worshipped by those who are not intelligent enough to be able to work out a more logical answer. See also *HobB*. For some obscure reason now lost even to the religiots, the name of God should really be written in the special letters of the ancients, hence its proper written form: G°Δ, and some still do, but only pedants and serious religiots *(cf)*.

GodspelL n. any one of four folios of the New Promisings of The Folius. GodspellS tell the story of GoD's private sacrifice for his Triseps and of all the miraculous magic or 'spells' he can do, when he really wants to. See Also *Old Promisings, New Promisings, Authorised Version, The Folius.*

Gobbling *n*. any of a series of tribes of miniature human-being like critters but considerably more devious than we know how to be. The Seven Tribes of Gobblings are *(for details of how to count to seven, see 7 in the Arithmates' Addendum)*:

Tribe	Location
0 Hobbimps	Squeith
1 Dark Elves	Sammowa & Ozzilland
2 Faeries	Amorics
3 Kobolds	Yishrel
4 Lepperdcorns	Green Aisle
5 Sprites or Esquimeaux	Scotaisle & Antipole
6 Trolls	Walled Faience
7 Urchins	Zimgululland

All Gobbling tribes have the capability of performing motorphroyd *(cf)*. *This* enables them to travel freely underground by creating pipes. The pipes are built by mental activity alone.

Gobblingfobia *n*. a not surprisingly natural fear of Gobblings. This disease has become common among

Triseps, but has never been reported among Gobblings.

golejibbit *n.* the special post at the end of an area of grass where Welks *(cf)* played with their odd-shaped balls. Also a sign used by the Triseptokatholicus Order, who make the sign of the golejibbit by touching themselves on various parts of their body with various of their many appendages.

golesentry *n.* the Trisep who stops their odd-shaped balls going past the golejibbit *(cf)*.

GrandwizarD *n.* male Trisep who is the husband of seven wives and has seven daughters and whose father, grandfather, etc., also had seven daughters, back seven generations. Able to perform ultric-magic, which is much more fun than ordinary magic. A bit like the difference between sex and scratching your back head with your third arm, really. Always written with a capital at each end to keep out evil and because of the unspecified nasty things that will occur to the writer if written any other way.

Greasy *n.* Another country, somewhere else. Famous for its stories about Cronus and Rhea, and for supplying elgins to the rest of the world. Also famous for having funny writing. If you couldn't understand it, you would say, *it's all Greasy to me!*.

Great Western Wars *n.* took place about three hundred cycles ago. Started when a foreign power stole an olde-fashioned water-vapour powered railway engine, called the Great Western. During these wars, Sammowa dropped an atom-splitting molotov on Eislland, leaving nothing but a gigantic crater. Details are unclear and there must have been a cover-up because all the witnesses have since died, conveniently.

Green Aisle *n.* an aisle *(cf)* which is mostly green. Famous for stories about little green bipeds with pointed ears and magical powers which are spotted like lepperds and tell corny jokes; they call them Lepperdcorns. Also famous for the high viscosity of the brains of Triseps who live there. Also the *Traffic-Gestapo* have painted yellow lines everywhere which mean that you can't park at all. Where they paint double yellow lines, it means that you can't park there at all at all. Precedent is called Big Dick, or more correctly, Makkaan *(cf)*.

Grief Encounter *n.* a service of the automed where the bereaved or confused are counselled. This often takes place in the hospivoid *(cf)* of a Multicare *(cf)*.

Grounsell *n.* The Minister for Ground Works for the Eqinox Government

growable cable *n.* a rope with fast nanomachines which enabled it to grow. A bit like a spider's web, really.

ha-ha *n.* an invisible ditch to stop critters being in the wrong place. Trouble is, you tend to fall into it if you don't look where you are going, so everyone laughs, hence its name.

hams *n.* amateurs. Particularly applied to amateurs using olde-fashioned wire-less communicators to talk with each other. GoD alone knows why they do it when they have perfectly good callalls these days.

Hawker *n.* see Stephen.

Hawking, Stephen the *n.* see Stephen.

headstead *n.* an often ornately carved frame placed at the head of a sleeping cowch. Made out of multicoloured woods and usually handmade, they have a special significance in that every Trisep retains a mental image of the headstead of the sleeping cowch on which he or she was conceived.

Helvetica *n.* a country with high mountains and lots of snow. Neutral in wars and famous for its lakes and skiing holidays.

Helvetica War Crimes Treaty *n.* a pact stopping any unfair Defenss action. Punishment for the perpetrator of a Type One War Crime is being kept alive in permanent excruciating pain for not less than five lifetimes. A typical clause reads: *Any Defenss or any other personnel who kill or injure with intent to kill any other where the injured party is unarmed and can be captured and there is no immediate danger to the former shall be guilty of a Type One War Crime.* The treaty also describes the penalty: *Punishment for the perpetrator of a Type One War Crime is to be kept alive in permanent excruciating pain for one whole lifetime on each count to a maximum of one thousand lifetimes. On completion of the sentence, pain shall be increased very slowly until the prisoner dies in screaming agony.* This punishment has only ever been carried out once: on a ruffian of the first order called Herrhess.

Helvetican Defenss knife *n.* a very useful tool issued free to every member of the Helvetican Defenss forces as an advertising ploy and subsequently sold at vast profit Eqinox-wide as being something special, which of course it wasn't.

hemisphere *n.* half a sphere. This can be hollow, like the hemispheric cave of Qontûm city.

Heptember *n.* the seventh month of the year, between Caesust and Octember. The Hepts of Heptember (the seventh day of the seventh month) is a particularly special and magical date, on which strange unexplainable events often occur.

hepts *n.* the seventh day before the ides *(cf)* of the month, a very special day. More important, even, than the ides themselves. This replaces the olde-fashioned nones which were the ninth day before the ides.

Heralds, Seven *n.* see *Precursors, Seven.*

herd *n.* the name given to the clump *(cf)* of wives of a male Trisep. Each male is allocated wives in his birth year, according to the ratio of males to females that year.

herd leader *n.* first nuptialised partner. The only female partner who plays any worthwhile part or is of any consequence, really.

Herrhess *n.* a famous war criminal who ordered the killing of lots of Triseps. Under the Helvetican War Crimes Treaty *(cf)*, he was sentenced to the maximum of one thousand lifetimes of being kept alive in permanent excruciating pain, but this was eventually commuted to six hundred and twenty lifetimes as a matter of leniency.

History Record *n.* the permanent record made by an archivist. Every important event must be recorded for the History Record preferably live, but if not, then as soon as possible afterwards. This record takes priority over all other forms of news gathering.

hite *n.* what vertical measures are measured in. One hite is equivalent to the height of a Trisep. The ratio of hite to length *(cf)* is 1.6180339 but nobody can remember why. There must be a reason.

HobB *n.* Another name for The Evil One, believed to be all powerful, like GoD *(cf)*, by the religiots, the thaumaturges *(cf)* and the WitcheS *(cf)* alike. As with the name of GoD, ancient symbols are used for the name of HobB, The Evil One, but it is now only written as H°þß by extremists.

Hobbimp *n.* a member of a tribe of Gobblings resident in the Underplanet beneath Squeith. One of the Seven Tribes. Thought to be evil at heart, like HobB, The Evil One, they contrive a pretence of pleasantness to outsiders, usually, while being exceptionally vicious and vile to their mates and demonstrating a new definition of honesty and truth, exactly like the author's ex-wife, really, who also has a terminal case of Naggits *(cf)*. Their special characteristics are their translucent bodies, linguistic capability and ability to communicate with each other by Phroydian thought-transference. Like all Gobblings, they are capable of motorphroyd *(cf)*.

hogg *n.* a fat critter cut up into rashers and eaten (when dead) by Triseps. Also used for medical experiments. The meat is particularly nice when fried and eaten with a fried Ovum.

hoggupines *n. pron: hog-you-pines* another possible silly name for Triseps, coined because of their genetic nearness to hoggs and their pine-yellow blood colour.

Hospice *n.* a place where the most difficult to treat illnesses or accidents are treated in a ward. These places are now extinct except for the one at Selondre which is kept for real emergencies. All medical problems are now treated by automeds *(cf)*.

hospice *vb.* to place a Trisep in a hospice.

hospivoid *n.* the hospice section of the Multicare vehicle. Fully equipped to perform any operation or other healing function, automatically. Trisep doctors haven't been needed for several hundred years now, since computers and robots took over the function. Until now.

holocam *n.* a holographic vide-camera with exact positional sound recording facility. No, it was not hollow.

holocommenter *n.* a sort of television set, only holographic.

holofolio *n.* an olde-fashioned pulpleaf folio, complete with words and pictures and turnable pages, shown in a holoquadrant. Except it isn't, of course, it's entirely computer-generated!

holographic *adj.* of holography. Moving images and sounds of things that make you feel as though you are actually there, even when you know that you are not.

holomap *n.* a three-dimensional holographic map, such as is found in the weather holoquadrant *(cf)* of an e-commenter *(cf)*.

holoquadrant *n.* a holographic picture. One of a series of such pictures available to viewers of the e-commenter.

holotechnology *n.* all of the general technology surrounding holography.

holo-video-manual *n.* a holographic training video, for example for auto-lasers used in the Defenss forces.

Holy Sprite *n.* a translation by Smelta meaning *Wholly Spirit (cf)*.

hoverfloat autobridge *n.* a piece of Defenss equipment designed to bridge water, a ravine or other gap, temporarily. It hovers. If something fails, it will float.

husband *n.* a male herd leader. According to females, the true definition is "a bad thing"

hydrogen *n.* a basic atom, from which other atoms can be nanomanufactured.

hydrotrophic conversion *n.* the growth or manufacture of anything from water. Expression used to describe the conversion of one substance into another. See also *nanotechnology*.

Hypocrites *n. pron: Hip-ok-rit-ees* a politician of an earlier eon after whom the Hypocritic Oath *(cf)* was named because he swore to himself that he would *engender negative precision* and *ensure that the truth was never a casualty of excessive exuberance,* especially in terms of *denial of the obvious* or *admission of the ridiculous.*

Hypocritic Oath *n.* an allegiance vow sworn against the cross of the golejibbit by all politicians. In principle, it ensures that the politician will always ensure that the truth is used as economically as possible and that, whenever possible, they will practise the art of false-truthing *(cf)* or prevaricating when fabricating a false allegory, as it is sometimes described. Named after Hypocrites, a politician of an earlier generation who minted such phrases as *economical with the honesty of the allegory* and *false truthing (cf).*

ice-cream cone *n.* an un-truncated, truncated cone, used for holding ice-cream before you eat it. If you didn't know that, I feel sorry for your childhood.

ides *n.* the middle day of the month, when ideas traditionally flow forth. Ides is a corruption of *ideas* from before written material was standardised in the Middle-Eons.

Idi Dada, Ah Meen *n.* Precedent of Zimgululland *(cf).* Speaks Pijin *(cf).* Urgently in need of a Phroydtest due to advanced brain fever.

implanting *vb.* putting one thing inside another, such as putting soldiernanos into an existing building and then impregnating new, differently programmed nanomachines to change the design. A bit like sex or gardening, really.

impune *vb.* making a statement that implies a threat without actually saying so, e.g. *"you will regret swearing at me!"* impuned the judge.

infinity (© Philosophers) *n.* this may not be defined because the philosophers own the copyright on it, causing great problems for arithmates and others using mathematics. See *Infinity (© Philosophers)* in the Arithmates' Addendum. The writer of this Lexikern was unable to wrest permission for publication of its meaning in case the arithmates got hold of it and started using it contrary to Lorranordå's regulatory parameters. Whenever the word is written, it must by lorr always show the copyright attribution appended.

infobox *n.* a blob of information displayed on the bottom of an e-commenter. This shows all sorts of extra information like who the reporter is, where the programme is coming from, how many Triseps are watching, any technical information on what is being discussed, views of the viewers, etc. A very useful facility.

intertwingle *vb.* to embrace in an excruciatingly beautiful cuddle, so serene and perfect and spiritual and physical that mere words of a Lexikern could not possibly describe it. So we won't. **~d** *adj.* the act of being so embraced.

I-smeller, I-smeller *interjection* an exclamation of triumph on discovering or solving something. I-smeller is the antilogic of you-reeker. [*Fr.* old Greasy: *I've found the smelly used bath-water.*]

isometric *adj.* as opposed to orthographic. A way of projecting a hologram so that it looks as if you are looking down on the object from one corner.

jam-chiver *n.* a spine-chilling shiver which bounces back and forth from one head to the other in waves, through the spine. So called because the wave occasionally jams and needs to be shaken free.

Jowver *n.* The name of GoD in the folio of Genetics *(cf)*. One of the names used in The Folius. See *Jowver's Evidencers.*

Jowver's Evidencers *n., pl.* a religious sect who believe that everything that happens portends the end of the planet. Followers spend their time knocking on doors and warning Triseps of the coming end of the planet. They are to be avoided if possible. A useful tip to get rid of them is to tell them that you are a member of the Triseptokatholicus Order *(cf)*, and make the sign of the golejibbit, even if you are not. As well as the Authorised Version *(cf)*, they have their own strange and not quite correct translation of The Folius *(cf)*.

Jumbo *n.* nickname for Sqoddie747, who was rather overweight and was subject to a considerable overhang.

jumbo *n. slang* kappa-length or kl, equal to 747 lengths.

kappa-wave *n.* waves which permit transmission of data, including holographic images. See also *EBC.*

kappa-wave blockaging *n.* interference with communication waves between callalls, bleating commenters, etc.

Kelt *n.* any tight-fisted Trisep living Poleward of a line defined more by history than any real reason. Famed for inventing things, having their own lorrs, keeping even more money than they earn and having an accent which means that you have to ask them to repeat everything three times.

Keltik Septagram *n.* a true seven pointed star made of genuine elgins from the Parthenon. When placed in certain places, such as the Antipole, this is one of the most powerful conversion tools known to Trisep. Normally only used by WizardS of higher orders at times of life-threatening emergency. First seen on jewellery made by ancient Kelts.

kl *n. abbr.* kappa-length or 747 lengths. Sometimes known as a jumbo. In Ozzilland, they are called Ozzikays.

Kobold *n.* a member of a tribe of Gobblings resident in the Underplanet beneath Yishrel and surrounding countries. One of the Seven Tribes. Their special characteristics are their multi-coloured clown-like clothes.

Kernal *n.* the senior Defenss Trisep, who is in charge of the Sqoddies.

Kraye943 *n.* Squeith's largest and most powerful computer. Used for working out the most complex mathematical and scientific problems. Some idiot once asked it to analyse the number 42 because a passing hitchhiker said it was important, and it came up with the answer, six times nine; this baffled the whole of Squeith for a time and it was ages before anyone (Mycroft, actually) realised that it was working in base 13 *(see Mycroft)*!

lact *n.* the post-natal discharge from the mamaglans of certain critters. See also *lactinfuse, buttalact.*

lactinfuse *n.* before the invention of nanomaking, lactinfuse was a drink made by drying the leaf of certain aromatic shrubs and adding boiling water. Most Triseps also added lact, the post-natal discharge from the mamaglans of certain critters.

Lama *n.* unit of currency equal to 47 Dallis.

Launder *n.* Capital of the Amorics and seat of government; the place where you get the washing done. *Pop. 47⁴ (4879681)* See also *Septagon.*

length *n.* a horizontal unit of measurement equal to one length of a Trisep. The ratio of hite *(cf)* to length is 1.6180339 but nobody knows why. See *kl, hite.*

Lepperdcorn *n.* a type of green, pointed eared Gobbling that lives in the Green Aisle. So called because they laugh like the spotted lepperd and tell really bad, corny jokes.

levva *n.* the skin of a dead critter *(cf)*. When dried and processed (which includes treating it with bodily waste products, but we won't talk about that), it can be used for high-quality armcowches, shoes, belts, red braces for firemen, and all sorts of other goodies. Of course, the best is Wopian, made in Wopia *(cf)*.

lexikern *n.* a book listing the kerning together of letters to form a lex or word, a list of such words. **The Lexikern** - the Ultimate List of all words, now useless because the Autotranslator does all the work for you. *Fr. lex,* word + *i,* of + *kern* overlap.

lexis *n.* the part of a Trisep's brain that deals with syntax and semantics (words and grammar, etc.). It's just slightly off to the left at the top, if you really needed to know.

linkdoor *n.* a clip which extends from the side of a moovacar to connect it to another vehicle, enabling personnel interchange whilst in flight.

lorr *n.* any rule made by the Eqinox Government which must be obeyed. More specifically, any regulatory parameter definitively specified by *Lorranordå (cf).*

Lorranordå *n.* Minister responsible for good behaviour, or *that which must be obeyed* in the Eqinox Government.

Lorranordåa *n.* Lorranordå's herd leader. She makes the lorrs for him. He calls her, *She who must be obeyed.*

Lovel *n. usu. pl.* a member of a tribe of religiots or GoD lovers whose activities and lorrs *(cf)* became the basis for lorrs across the planet. Lorranordå, the Minister for lorrs in the Eqinox Government acknowledges the historical part played by the Lovels in the formation of those lorrs through their folio, Loveliness *(cf).*

Loveliness *n.* The third folio of the Pentatouch in the Old Promisings *(cf),* written by one of the sages of old, who had been *touched* by GoD. A religious work. This one is about the Loveliness of the GoD and also about the loveliness of the Lovels, a clump *(cf)* of devout but fanatical GoD lovers. It also defines the complex and precise lorrs which must be obeyed if GoD is to be satisfied, including sacrifices of critters and murderers, although it stops short of the older and more widespread pagan practice of sacrificing pre-copulate daughters.

Luke-Warm War, the *n.* the not quite war between the various tribes of Gobblings and the Triseps when they each thought that the other was responsible for the disappearance of Ozzilland and the Ozzilanders who lived there, as well as the Dark Elves living in the caverns beneath.

Lynkern *n.* Precedent of the Amorics and a living legend. He was famous for his Emancipation Proclamation to abolish the last slavery on the planet. He was so popular that he was resurrected by his people three days after he was assassinated.

M *n. abbr.* Mycroft *(cf).*

MacDonald Ranges *n.* a range of alps in the middle of Ozzilland that were once near (well, fairly near!) to Allysp Rings. The range of alps were so called because of their remarkable similarity to a beefburgher *(cf).*

MacNün-Polepengus *n.* see *Nün-Polepengu.*

Maecenas *n. (pron. my-key-nus)* Chief Scientist and Scientific

Historian to the Eqinox Government. In his more junior days, he was Chief Scientist to the small state of Roame.

Magicknot Line *n. (pron. majin-owe)* any line, such as that found on the edge of the Ozzilland geoplatelets where a strange knotting effect occurs as a brain or callall signal crosses it. The autotranslator calls it a *marjin-out-line,* which may explain its etymology.

magmablast *n., vb.* a spewing of magma into the air from a hole in the ground. Sometimes *alps (cf)* such as *Etnavolc (cf)* are made this way.

Makkaan *n.* Precedent of the Green Aisle *(cf).* So called because he can, although most Triseps on the Aisle can't and are offended by the name of those like Makkaan who can. Also known as Big Dick because that was the name on a spanner he used when little to dismantle things like tractors.

male morning-after pill *see* Morning-After Pill for Men.

mamaglans *n.* the female appendage producing lact, a post-natal discharge.

Marjinowline *n.* the autotranslator's term for the Magicknot Line *(cf).* Sometimes it prefers to speak phonetically.

Mensa *n.* the Mental Exercises and Neural Stimulation Association. This bunch, weird to a Trisep, claimed to be slightly cleverer than average and founded the inter-being intelligence contest on the grounds that the ultimate in non-volatile war must surely be pure mental activity, battling wit against wit, this being preferable to real war. It usually ended in one hitting the other for making it with her/his husband/herd leader.

micro-neutron gun *n.* a very tiny weapon that fired deadly rays. As in all planets, the history of weapons was that each generation became smaller and deadlier. This was no bigger than a badge and was triggered by brainwaves from the psycho-trigger hairclip.

microphone *n.* a very little one-way callall that needs to be attached to a normal callall to be any use at all.

midasnano *n.* a the freely available, specially designed nanomachine, which will not only make gelt but will completely manufacture an article in gelt. Later versions also manufacture coloured crystals inset into the gelt, making jewellery to your own design.

midcoat *n.* a jacket that goes round the middle of a Trisep. Triseps are notoriously difficult to dress because of their shape and tailors of old were considered to be a cut above everyone else.

Middle-Eons *n.* a period of history when not much is known about, between the ancient times and the old times.

minarettes *n.* small minars, minarets. A minar is a giant tower.

molotov *n.* a device which makes a big bang, ranging from tiny ones that will blow off a finger to giant atom-splitting molotovs that will destroy a whole country.

moovacar *n.* a device for taking between one and eight Triseps from one place to another. There is a space like a dashboard which provides a holographic three-dimensional map which tells the trekker *(cf)* what the time is and how long to the destination. Various types include cargo-carrying versions and non-sleeping short-hop, farming, etc. In order to trek one, you need enough intelligence to be able to give it the name of your required destination. It will do the rest for you. Almost everyone is intelligent enough to use it; except social workers, that is.

Morning-After Pill for Men *n.* Probably the most effective form of contraception in the universe. Curiously, no-one has ever figured out how it works, because if the man does not take it post-coitally, the woman gets pregnant. It is possible that some medical WizardrY *(cf)* is involved here.

Morøkka *n.* see *Riffs of Morøkka.*

Mother-in-lorr Naggits *n.* a common form of the particularly nasty and sometimes vicious syndrome of Naggits *(cf)*. This is often referred to as 'that female condition'. Men do not suffer from this, but they do suffer from equally nasty diseases. See *Naggits* for full definition.

motorphroyd *adj., vb.* the capability of moving or transforming things by mental activity alone. All Gobblings have this ability and can, for example, create pipes through solid ground and then reconstitute the original, at whim. The capability can also be learnt by WitcheS and WizardS. See also *Phroydtest.*

Multicare *n.* a complete disaster recovery machine for all kinds of rescue and recovery. When Multicares first flew and had separate pods for each function, they made a lot of noise and were dubbed 'Thunderbirds', but everybody thought this was a silly name, so it didn't stick.

Muzzeltoff *adj.* a good old expression used by Yishrelis and meaning, basically, 'good luck' or 'good health'. Nice word, isn't it?

Mycroft *n.* the most intelligent Trisep and greatest polyglot on Eqinox. Mycroft, often known just as **M**, controls Squeithian intelligence and can solve many problems that even the most advanced computers cannot, including social, legal, logic and mathematical problems.

Publicly, he is only known for helping his brother, Sherlock, solve the most heinous crimes and for smoking netherwear in his pipe. It was Mycroft who discovered that 42 being six times nine was in fact in base 13 *(see Kraye943)*. Mycroft had one brother, Sherlock, who was a great detective, but usually high on illegal substances, making him more of a heroin than a hero. He can speak all sorts of useful languages, like Sammowan, Elfin B, Gobbling, Esquimeaux and Nipoffese.

Mycroftese *n.* A curious form of Squeithian terminology spoken only by Mycroft and intelligible only in parts by the most intelligent on the planet. Rarely understandable by one individual in full.

Myth *n.* a jolly good story. See *Delius Myth.*

Naggits *n.* a rather nasty disease of the female of the species. The worst cases are confined to mothers-in-lorr, but herd-leaders sometimes catch it as well. The disease causes shouting and screaming, often not just at people but also at saucepans, windows, kettles and anything else in range. Sufferers are not those with the disease, but the others around them, particularly husbands. The disease used to be cured in the Middle Eons by iron torture instruments called bridles; however, bridles never worked, so tongues were removed. These days, automeds use the Phroydtest to check and remove the condition. Bad cases still require the removal of the tongue, however. Some queer sort of males have suggested that the disease will be permanently cured within a generation by killing all females at birth, but this seems a bit too drastic to everyone else.

nanobuilt *adj.* manufactured using nanomachines. Usually refers to large structures such as buildings that would have been manufactured 'on-site' where they would stay.

nanogroove *n.* part of a device for making a strange set of noises at various frequencies which those with appropriately attuned ears call music. See *autoerotic nanogroove.*

nanomachines *n.* machines used to make things. Since the invention of machines which work at atomic level which modify one substance into another (mostly making things from water in the atmosphere or recycling them back to water), nanomachines have manufactured anything required at the whim of a Trisep. Computers control these.

nanomade, nanomanufactured *adj.* nanobuilt. Usually refers to smaller things that would formerly have been made in a factory and transported to you.

nanomanufacture *vb.* to make by nanomachines.

nanostructure *n.* the way something is made at microscopic level. also *biol.* the triple septihelix ribena-acid from which all life forms on the planet - and by extension it is assumed in the entire universe - are constructed.

Nanotech329 *n.* one of hundreds of technicians working with nanomachines. This is number 329. Why mention him? Well, he's a bit more vociferous than average, and because of his number being a special multiple and therefore having special magic properties, he's somewhat brighter than average.

nanotechnology *n.* the whole science surrounding nanomachines. Now quite well developed, but there were a lot of teething troubles initially, form which some after-effects are still being felt.

nanowave *n.* a special type of nanomachine which makes hot food. Found in homes, moovacars and any other places where Triseps might like to eat from time to time.

narcolexic attack *n.* talking in the sleep, usually only done accidentally, such as when sleeping with the wife and calling her Sharen. Occasionally, the attack will take the form of a magic poem, but only by WitcheS or WizardS or those destined to become such, but who do not yet fulfil all the criteria.

Natural Genetics *n.* the science of reproductive viability evaluation and the study of the obscure phenomenon whereby all second and subsequent children of a male are females, unless the first male needs to be replaced for some reason, such as premature deceasement. Nobody has worked out why this happens, but it does have the effect of keeping the number of families or 'herds' constant, even though the number of females varies according to the current level of elicit extra-nuptial replication activities.

necro-vaporation *n.* a term minted by Cate'aeddy, EBC's ENN Chief Reporter to describe the way that black Trolls decomposed and just melted into the ground beneath them after their death by being shot and killed with twigs from the seven-sided triple besoms of thaumas and WitcheS.

Necropol Club *n.* the last reserve of male Triseps, prohibited to females. Mycroft lives there and says that his vital brain activity is not interrupted by the constant screechings of old women of all ages and every gender. Full of levva armcowches and organised by the silent and efficient Steward. So called because it was legendarily *the* Club for necrotic (dead or retired) politicians.

netherlight *n.* light at the bottom of the x-ray spectrum. X-rays have different colours at different frequencies just like visible light.

Netherlight is at the bottom (or low-frequency end of the range, just like red in the rainbow, really.

netherwear *n.* clothing worn immediately next to the skin of the nether regions. Most Triseps wear disposable ones, these days, that are made by nanomanufacture. Olde-fashioned washable ones are used once then smouldered and inhaled by Mycroft in his pipe.

New Promisings *n.* The new religious writings written shortly after the time of the invention of a game played with odd-shaped balls using golejibbits *(cf)*. There are four *GodspellS (cf)* which claim to tell the truth about GoD, lots of Equi-mailings and the famous *Folio of Revealment* which tells what the future holds for all Triseps in a frighteningly graphic way. Unfortunately, it is written in an allegorical style only understood by GoD, so it isn't much use even though some (like *Jowver's Evidencers, cf*) insist that they alone understand it. The Old Promisings and the New Promisings together comprise The Folius.

New Seas *n.* an area of sea between Antipole and Ozzilland at the bottom of Eqinox. New Seaslland *(cf)* is on the Sunriseward *(cf)* edge.

New Seaslland *n.* a small double aisle country not quite in a direct line between Antipole and Ozzilland. Main produce before nanotechnology was a thixotropic gel called buttalact *(cf)* made by shaking lact, the post-natal discharge from the mamaglans of certain critters.

Nipoff Archipelago *n.* a group of aisle-lands Poleward of Ozzilland and on the opposite side of the world to Squeith. Main language Nipoffese. Population: one thousand, three hundred and fifty-eight Triseps to the quad. Main aisle: Ånjap.

nogozone *n.* an area around a Defenss installation (or anywhere else, really) where all movement is prohibited and anyone or thing violating the restriction will be destroyed instantly.

Nostril-Dame, Old Mother *n.* a one-time secular seer or prophet, condemned by the religiots as being a follower of HobB *(cf)*. She wrote her prophecies in *The Septuries,* being forty-seven folios, each of forty-seven trirhythmic-septalines *(cf)*.

nucleic nanostructure *n., adj.* the basis of how everything is made at sub-atomic level.

Number of the HobB *n.* it is stated in the Folio of Revealment *(cf)* of The Folius *(cf)* that this number *'shall be upon us and shall be upon the forehead of every one of us and shall be upon the hand of every one of us and shall be upon us between our navels. And that number shall not be written by any Trisep lest he be struck down. And the Number of the HobB is Seven Hundred and Seventy Six plus One and that Number shall not be writ by word or by digit or spoke by any but by HobB himself."* Many religiots claim that they can see the Number in the skin furrows of individuals. Sceptics say that you can find any pattern in the skin furrows if you look hard enough. You pays your Lamas, as it were, and you takes your choice!

Numerology *n.* the fifth folio of the Pentatouch in the Old Promisings *(cf)* of The Folius, written by one of the five sages of old, who had been touched by GoD. A religious work. This one is about the numbers of Triseps who followed GoD throughout the generations. They did not bother to count wives or slaves or the GoD-forsaking majority, though. Also known as Domesday Records because they counted everyone and their status on a

24

special day called Domesday - something about a long forgotten dome being built in a place called the East End, and something to do with a Green WitcH, but most of the details are lost because it was all so transitory. See also *Domesday.*

nün *n.* a black and white female member of a religious sect, in particular the Triseptokatholicus Order *(cf).* There are a large number of nüns in the Green Aisle *(cf).* Nüns live in Tonsurages *(cf)* (surrounded by trees and with a skating rink in the middle) and always seem to walk around in pairs; a whole series of letters to an olde-fashioned daily chronicle called The Thundering Temporra once discussed how to split the nün pair by walking between them; for example by distracting them both at the same time in opposite directions and then sidling round between them.

nün-polepengu *n.* a black and white sort of flying ghoti that stands upright and lives at the Antipole *(cf).* So called because they vaguely resemble nüns *(cf)* of the Triseptokatholicus Order *(cf),* both in their appearance and their herding instincts as well as their predisposition to walking round in pairs. One day, a thoughtful Trisep introduced some to the Pole as well; these were soon eaten by bears, who cooked them and ate them between slices of bun, calling them MacNün-Polepengus *(cf).* Eventually, they all settled down and lived together, the nün-polepengus catching fish for the bears and the bears acting as minders and warding off other predators.

October *n.* the eighth month of the year, as you would expect from the name.

Old Mother Nostril-Dame *n.* see *Nostril-Dame, Old Mother.*

Old Promisings *n.* The original five folios of the Pentatouch *(cf)* now supplemented by the sensible, poetic, prophetic, historic and sometimes plain ridiculous scribblings of religiots or those who have a claim to be interested. The Old Promisings and the New Promisings together comprise The Folius. See also *New Promisings, The Folius.*

Omeg *n.* the sacred river. Sacred because it was known to be near the original source of life on the planet. Omeg, the name, because we all know that 'Omega' is start and finish in all things.

oracular delusion *n.* a sound which does not exist in reality but only appears to exist due to some unexplained phenomenon.

orgy *n.* like all orgies, great fun. See also: *extra-nuptial, autostack, autoerotic nanogroove, Sharen.*

Orijin *n.* the sphere that was found in a shallow pit in the squelches of Squelchpool. It was found when scientists were looking for the origin of all life forms, hence its name. From the markings, it had obviously come from Planet Three of another solar system, although the star map seemed a bit too symmetrical for comfort. The star map only showed fifty stars in a regular pattern in one corner of a rectangle with lots of horizontal lines on it. One joker suggested that it resembled a flag, but no-one took her seriously; it was obviously a map of a different part of the universe.

out-takes *n.* a break-away faction, particularly of soldiers. A bit like outlorrs, really, but 'taken out' rather than being outside the lorr.

over-cipher *n.* encrypted callall that cannot be overheard by those listening-in, or even by any interception.

Ovum *n.* a female gamete. Some species produce these with a thin outer crust made of stone and large enough to eat. Particularly nice when boiled in water for three minutes. Also very tasty when fried and eaten with sliced rashers of hogg *(cf)*.

Oxford Dictionary with Pictures *n.* A folio discovered in the Orijin in which were three pictures of God, or the Wholly Spirit (not to be confused with holy sprite. One picture was of an old being with a beard, sitting on clouds, one was of a younger being with only two legs, only two arms and only one head tied and nailed to a golejibbit and the third was a bottle of a light brown fluid labelled *Bells*.

Ozzikays *n.* a unit of length equivalent to 747 lengths. Used only in Ozzilland, but nobody can remember why they were called kays in the first place. See *kl.*

Ozzilland *n.* a large, flat, hot country, renowned for its curious wildlife, in particular the hopping rookanga *(cf)*. Everything in Ozzilland is upside down. They write upside down and some Triseps even stand on their heads. Funny place, really; even the language is a bit blurred and funny. Perhaps the Triseps are strange because most of them are descended from ex-convicts who colonised Ozzilland about 500 cycles ago. Allysp Rings *(cf)* is one of the main towns, now coastal. The continent was originally the home of the Arbor-Orijinals *(cf)* and is made up of seven geoplatelets which seem to want to move round from time to time. Total area: 229 345 007 quads. Pop. 823543.

Ozzillandese *n.* an obscure dialect only found in Ozzilland. Thought to be derived from very old prison slang because the inhabitants of that land are all descended from transplanted convicts.

Ozzi'opps *n.* a plant which grew only in Ozzilland which was used to make four-ecks, a vile tasting alcoholic water drink palatable only to antipodals.

Ozzipolit23 *n.* A leading politician in Ozzilland - not even half way to a full vote!

Ozzipolit7 *n.* Ozzilland's ambassador to the Convention.

Ozziqontûm *n.* the capital Underplanet city for Dark Elves beneath central Ozzilland. As all relating to Qontûm, there is always a doubt as to the probability of its being in one particular place or moving to another at any one time.

Parthenon *n.* an old building in ancient Greasy made of elgins. The elginfunction defined the Degenerate State of the place as a significant bearing on Qontûm, but it is so complex that we ought to leave it there at this stage. See also *Elgins, Qontûm, Infinity (© Philosophers)* and the *Arithmates' Addendum.*

peeka *n.* the circle squaring number. The ratio between diameter of a circle and its circumference. Roughly equivalent to root 47 divided by root 7 when plotted acentricly.

Pentatouch *n.* the five original folios of the sages who claimed to have been touched by GoD. These were called Genetics, Exercises, Loveliness, Numerology and Deteriorations (*cf:* each folio). These are the first five books of the Old Promisings of *The Folius*. See also *Old Promisings* and *New Promisings.*

people *n.* don't know this word. Must be talking about dioptic bipeds from another planet.

period cycles *n.* see *cycle.*

Philosophical Denial of Wisdom *n.* a branch of philosophy defined by the Dark Elf, Sophist *(cf)* as Structured Antiwisdom *(cf for full definition).* The real reason that the subject existed was because Sophist, the

Dark Elf who invented the subject, wanted a lot of riches and kudos from his intentionally obfuscatious publications and lectures.

Phroyd *n.* a famous Trisep who studied Triseps who were out of their Bassinettes. According to Phroyd, all Eqinoxian brain disorders could be traced back to a rude comment made shortly after birth when mothers would traditionally say, *I'm fed up with changing this damned baby.*

Phroydtest *n.* an automed test and cure for brain disorders of Triseps. Named after a famous Trisep several hundred cycles ago. See also *motorphroyd, Phroyd.*

Pijin *n.* a language spoken by Triseps of Zimgululland, from where slaves were taken in the Bad Old Days. This language is sometimes translated by the autotranslator, depending on its mood and whether it is asked to do so.

pinnacle *n.* a point, like the end of a needle, but always at the top; usually!

pipe *n.* a long hollow tube with a mouthpiece at one end and a container for burning old leaves or (in the case of Mycroft) netherwear at the other. The most famous pipe is smoked by Mycroft *(cf)* who uses it to blow smoke-rings and the most intricate designs of whatever obscure topic he is currently mulling over.

Planet Five *n.* the fifth planet from the Sun. See Eqinox.

plumbumic balloon *n.* a variant of a lightweight child's toy which went against all of its original design principles. Designed by a heavyweight sanitation technician, Plumbum, his device usually had the effect of falling about Triseps' ears and making sizeable dents in the desired effect of any contributory comment from a joke at one extreme, to a seriously placed debating statement at the other.

Poetlore *n.* in Sammowa, Poetlore is the mythology of the country, set down in rhyming couplets.

Pole *n.* a country at the top of the planet, exactly opposite Antipole *(cf).* A bit cold there, really.

Pole-Esquimeaux *n.* Esquimeaux *(cf)* who live in the Pole region at the top of the planet. Not much different from normal Esquimeaux who live at the Antipole at the bottom of the planet.

Poleward *adj.* towards the top of the planet, one of the four cardinal directions on Eqinox, the others being, Antipoleward, Sunriseward, and Sunsetward.

Pontipwl Front Row *n.* see Welks.

Police *n.* these Triseps have differing functions depending on your personal preference for crime or honesty. In theory, they used to have something to do with lorr enforcement but in practise they found that their position helped them perform more corruptly.

Polit23 *n.* Another obfuscating politician, not even half way to a full vote.

Polit46 *n.* An ordinary politician, as his name suggests. He was elected Squeithian Precedent after his predecessor was killed by a falling meteorite. It didn't just kill him - or he could have been re-cloned - but he was totally burnt up and destroyed. Unfortunately, he was more interested in his own power than in his constituents. But then, aren't most politicians?

portoffice *n.* a portable office in a flying vehicle. Most organisations have given up using fixed offices for portoffices where Triseps really *must* be together for some reason. Most Triseps work from home these days and arrange work around their social life.

Precedent *n.* the Trisep who is the leader, currently Polit46; so called because he precedes or goes before all others during his term. *Adj. precedential.*

Precursors, Seven *n.* also known as the Seven Heralds. the factors governing the sudden rotation and apparent disappearance of Ozzilland. They were as follows (*for the rules on counting to seven, see 7 in Arithmates' Addendum*):

0 the Qontûm probability factor; the event probability remains stable at seven in forty-seven to the power of forty-seven but there seemed to be a natural but undefined understanding that this would occur at the right time to coincide with the other precursors.

1 All planets and both suns in the solar system were in precise alignment, creating massive magnetic and gravitational stresses.

2 It was exactly 329 cycles since the last WizarD suffered a dysfunctional cognitive response (deceasement).

3 Residual magic building itself up to its own crescendo, as it will do if left to its own devices, just had to explode

4 Geoplatelets gyring to reach their own Eqinox.

5 Predictions of the End-Times from the Folio of Revealment, the last book of the New Promisings; also the secular prophets and seers.

6 Ozzilland now has a population of precisely 7 to the power of seven, or 823 543 Triseps, if you follow the traditional counting method set out in Numerology, the fifth folio of the Pentatouch of the Old Promisings.

7 The sudden and necessary movement of the magic into the new WizardS, like Smelt.

If you don't understand the numbers, and there are many who don't, check the *Arithmates' Addendum.*

pressure-vapour engine *n.* an olde-fashioned machine used for pumping water. Wheeled versions ran on twaks, like twams, and were called twains because they operated in pairs, sandwiching snakes of seven or more comfortable, air-conditioned, fully restaureanted, high class hotels on wheels called clarridges. See *Anerak.* See *twain* for full definition.

professors *n.* Triseps who profess to know more than others and sometimes do.

Profgeol *n.* the Professor of Geology.

Profmed *n.* the Professor of Medicine, of course.

Profsiens *n.* the Professor of science, also called Thermos *(cf).* See also *Thermos-Dynamism, lorrs of.*

proteañ *n.* goodness; life giving food for cells. Energy giving food for cells.

provisions hatch *n.* a box in moovacars, theatres, stadia, Conventionia, etc., with a nanomaker inside. Anything can be ordered from it - mostly used for alcoholic drinks and other sustenance. There is a hole to place a finger in so that the computer knows when you are talking to it and not to yourself and a door which opens into a void where anything you have asked for is manufactured and presented to you. This is also where you deposit your waste for recycling back to water vapour (although it retains a permanent memory of everything destroyed so that it can be reconstituted if you make a mistake).

psycho-trigger hairclip *n.* see micro-neutron gun.

pulpleaves *n.* flattened tree-pulp used with writing as an olde-fashioned form of data storage and transmission.

Purple Air Space *n.* the amount of space required for safety reasons around a precedent's moovacar. The same space is specified as being the minimum when carrying dangerous loads such as atom-splitting molotovs. Rarely requested now that moovacars have so many safety features.

Putout *n.* a fireman, of course. Each Multicare vehicle had a number of specialist helpers. Putout1, Putout2 and Putout3 were fire-fighters.

Qontûm *n.* an underground city of Gobblings, so called because its characteristics and location are probably defined under the rules of the Qontûm Theory, an idea of Thermos proved by a Trisep called Stephen the Hawker *(cf)*. See also *Infinity (© Philosophers)* in the Arithmates' Addendum, which explains why there is an uncertain problem about any sensible definition of the word. For a full, true and accurate definition, see *ZygoSplit*.

Qontûm State *n.* the country where the Gobblings live, which itself conforms to certain rules. See also *Infinity (© Philosophers)* in the Arithmates' Addendum.

Quad *n.* an area of land equivalent to forty-seven lengths *(cf)* long by forty-seven hites *(cf)* wide.

quadric digammagram *n. arch.* a symbol similar to the Quadric Gammagram but using the much more ancient digamma instead. The digamma is known only to those Greasy scholars who study pre-classical Greasy. This entry is here for passing interest only, it isn't mentioned elsewhere, so I don't really know why we bothered mentioning it, but perhaps you can write to us if you know better.

quadric gammagram *n.* a drawn device consisting of four olde-fashioned writing symbols called gammas, ranged round a centre point; the resultant symbol is a cross with legs. The symbol and evidence of power for Gobblings. It was later discovered that far away on Planet Three of another solar system, the same symbol was used by a band of marauding ruffians called the Third Reich. These ruffians were nothing to do with barbers (see *Riffs of Morøkka*).

Quag *n.* a wet patch which it is not recommended that you lie in. Quags range from damp patches in the ground to large ponds where swanns *(cf)* used to swim.

quax *n. pron. quacks* a doctor, ducky.

Quax *n.* a particular doctor: current leader of the Gobblings. To be more precise, leader of the Hobbimps, but the Hobbimps tend to lead the rest of the Gobblings, so their leader is leader over all the Underplanet ... but not everybody knows that ...

reference, circular - See *circular reference*.

religiot *n.* any fundamentalist, over-the-top member of a religious order, such as Jowver's Evidencers *(cf)* or the Triseptokatholicus Order *(cf)* or even one of the hundreds of independent religious groups. [*contraction from:* religious idiot]

Revealment, Folio of, *n.* The last folio of the New Promisings *(cf)* and The Folius, following the GodspellS and the Equi-mailings. There are a lot of details about the End Times as well as warnings to groups trying to set up as churches. This volume is perhaps most famous of all for the bits concerning the Number of the HobB *(cf)* which is 776+1 *(see Arithmates' Addendum for full definition)*.

Rhea *n.* a mythological GoD, whose name first appeared in ancient

Greasy. Cronus' sister. They were renowned for their incestuous behaviour. for usage, see Cronus.

Riffs of Morøkka *n.* a tribe of dark coloured Triseps who are all barbers. Traditionally, they arrive at Defenss bases and cut the hair of Sqoddies before they go into battle. Barbers can always be recognised by their red and white striped moovacars.

Rodjacook *n.* An investigative reporter of some note for ENN. He always asked lots of questions to people who ignored him, kept walking and locked themselves in rooms to get away from him. Inference of guilt was always generated without actual evidential retort.

rookanga *n.* a very jumpy native critter of Ozzilland, famous for its special hop. Very tasty to Gobblings.

rotolift *n.* a device like a big wheel which will take you to any one of a number of locations on the same or other floors of a building.

runcible pussy *n.* a pussy conjured purely from imagination, or by magic, which has a reality level somewhere above non-existent but below actuality.

St. Thatch *n.* See Thatch, St.

Sammowa *n.* a country involved in the Great Western Wars. Sammowa destroyed Eislland by sending an atom-splitting molotov. This was all because of an argument over ghotiing rights in the Azorrics. Located slightly Poleward of Ozzilland. See also *Poetlore*.

Sammowanese *n.* language used by Triseps of Sammowa. Ordinary Squeithian words are used, but in a strange order which nobody has yet found a logical or grammatical sequence for, even though there very definitely is one. See if you can find it.

Sammowapolit7 *n.* the Sammowan ambassador to the Convention. Sammowa's leading politician.

sappachine *n.* made by the Ånjaps these days, but invented by a Trisep called, of all things, Joseph Cyril Bamford, whose initials are used to this day to identify the non-Defenss versions. Not needed much since nanobuilding began, although they will do some jobs faster, particularly if you want the earth to move.

Scotaisle *n.* a tiny, once barren landmass just Poleward of Antipole in the general direction of Ozzilland.

scrunchies or **corn-seed scrunchies** *n.* a common food taken to break the fast of the morning, 'breakfast' as the meal is commonly called. Usually eaten covered in lact, the post-natal discharge of critter mamaglans, and a sweetener. Toroidal in shape, they are also screwed up and used to tie young females' hair.

Secret-Session 1. *n.* the period of time when a meeting convenes ex-cam, or in secret so that its discussions are not publicised. **2.** *vb.* to so meet. Usually applied to major political or war-time meetings when politicians and senior Defenss Staff do not want the general public to be aware of their deliberations or conclusions.

Selondre *n.* was the Squeithian capital and seat of government, where all the best facilities, Selondre Hospice, etc. are housed. *Pop: 47^3 (103823)*. However, most Triseps preferred to live outside it, so it is more of a museum city now. There were some useful special facilities, such as optional clump *(cf)* training at the University, the Hospice, etc., although even that now only had about six patients who had extremely rare, hard to conquer problems.

septagon *n.* a seven-sided object (*fr.* old Greasy, *Septic,* the seven-sided waste droppings of Trisep WitcheS.)

Septagon, The *n.* the government building in Launder *(cf)*, capital of the Amorics, where Precedent Lynkern lives and works with his assistant, Deputy Effdeearr.

Septagram *n.* see *Keltik Septagram.*

septallion *n.* a large group of Defenss personnel. Usually but not always led by one level seven officer with seven level six officers and seven at each level down to ordinary able-Sqoddies.

septic *n.* a dropping from a WitcH, which is a seven-sided square. These are stored in tanks called septic tanks.

septic tank *n.* a seven-sided tank used for storing septics, the seven-sided droppings from WitcheS.

septiquadecahedron *n.* the shape of a forty-seven sided solid object with flat sides. See also *Convinciing Geometry,* vexal *septiquadecahedron.*

Septuped *n.* a being with seven legs (not pedals). Actually, it isn't; it has four legs and three arms. See also *Trisep.*

Septuries *n.* A work written by Old Mother Nostril-Dame, a secular mystic visionary who nevertheless held strong and strange religious views and who wrote forty-seven folios, each of forty-seven trirhythmic-septalines *(cf)*. Some believed that this work accurately predicted the future, but it seemed HobbisH strange that all such predictions were seen and proved in retrospect and none of his predictions were ever exposed and accurately explained prior to an event occurring.

seven *n.* a very special magic number. See 7 in *Arithmates' Addendum.*

Seven Heralds *n.* see *Precursors, Seven.*

Seven Precursors *n.* see *Precursors, Seven.*

Seven Tenets *n.* see *Agreement, The.*

Sharen *n.* a new gender of bridies *(cf)* developed in Ballam *(cf)*, with multiple two-way genitalia which could satisfy up to twenty Triseps at once. Specially designed to be blonde *(cf)* at one end, dark the other and naturally brainless, her various sizes of mamaglans satisfied all preferences. 'Sharen' is the noun form derived from the verb, *to share.* Sharen is the only way of satisfying the dream of being surrounded by genitalia of one's personal preference; that's why everybody wants one, but nobody admits to wanting one. Also sometimes referred to as the brainless bridies of Ballam.

Shealar *n.* a carelessly derogatory term of address for female Triseps in Ozzilland. By unfortunate coincidence, the word is identical to a Hobbimp word that means *infected brothel inmate.*

Sherlock *n.* a Trisep famed only for being the brother of Mycroft *(cf)* or M, the most intelligent head and Head of Intelligence on Eqinox. Also famous in his own right for solving a few crimes and usually being high on illegal substances, making him more of a heroin than a hero.

shush button *n.* Stops the other Trisep hearing you making rude comments during a callall.

shushcallall *n.* a callall made using *anti-sound (cf)* so that only the two parties involved can actually be heard.

sidle, sidling *vb.* Moving by hoof. When Triseps move, they do so semi-sideways.

Sinn *n.* Family name of two particular Triseps, Madame and Cardinal. Madame Sinn was a famous bridie *(cf)* of Ballam, notorious for her medium-class brothel-keeping activities but Cardinal Sinn was a Saint of the Antipoleward Amorics so that the good and evil in the family would remain in balance (as it always must).

sleeping cowch *n.* a cowch designed for night use. These are always double to enable pairs of Triseps to practise replication techniques.

Smelt *n.* a Trisep who smelts - a particular one. He works with iron and gelt and makes all sorts of interesting ornaments for a living, but seems to have his fingers in many other pies. A sort of a politician, on the quiet! **~a** *n.* Smelt's first wife. His herd leader.

smile-shaped *n., adj.* the shape of a smile. This is often used to describe the gap between a builder's midcoat and his rear trousers, where his bottom was partly visible. This is a sort of uniform for builders.

soldiernanos *n.* special nanomachines designed to fight other nanomachines. They are VERY carefully designed so that when they have killed the right number of other nanomachines, they self-destruct before they take over the whole planet. Also useful for seeking and destroying contamination in the ground.

~son *suff.* the suffix given to male offspring during the building and learning cycles, cycles one and two. *e.g.* Polit46son is the male offspring of Polit46.

Sole *n.* the un-evidenced secret spirit on which life is theoretically based. According to the religiots, Everyone's Sole is owned either by GoD or by HobB and you will have a place either in GoD's Haven (Called Heaven) or in HobB's Hellole. *Etym.:* Sole is so called because it is the part of you that is directly under GoD's foot.

Sophist *n.* Precedent of the Dark Elves located beneath Ozzilland. Professionally a (or, as he would tell you, *the*) teacher of *Philosophical Denial of Wisdom (cf)* to all Gobblings. He has also written many folios on *Structured Antiwisdom (cf)*. His knowledge of the subject can be matched only by Mycroft.

spec *n.* a transparent container used for drinking, made from silica. In other words, a glass. A pair of specs would be a pair of glasses; got it?

spectra *n.* more than one spectrum. Usually used to refer to the differing spectra seen by ordinary and x-ray eyes.

spectrum *n.* the complete range of frequencies visible to the ordinary or x-ray eyes of Triseps.

Speed-Routes *n.* olde-fashioned roads. These were the ultimate in surface road engineering, linking everywhere to everywhere else and enabling more Triseps to go further than they needed more quickly than they really needed to. Before hydrotrophic nanotechnology was invented, they were used for moving vast quantities of goods from one place to another and back to their origin before being sold.

spellbound *n., adj.* tied up with witchcraft. Also means confounded and amazed by something beyond understanding, like a female Trisep.

spirating *n., adj., vb.* an activity which tests the endurance of Triseps, who rotate until they collapse. They call it dancing and it is done to the sound of the latest autoerotic nanogroove.

spire, spiring *vb.* go round in a circle, to rotate.

Sprite *n.* a member of a tribe of Gobblings resident in the Underplanet beneath Scotaisle and Antipole. One of the Seven Tribes. Their special characteristics are their white clothes, dance-like movements and jolly little faces.

spunj-squelch *n.* an artificial ground surface placed around tall buildings to stop self-destructive Triseps like Vittler jumping off and killing themselves, thus committing the crime of decession. As a result, incidents of committing decession dropped dramatically.

Sqoddie *n.* any one of a number of Defenss personnel subordinate to the Kernal. Sqoddies are at seven levels; Level Zero being the lowest and Level Seven being the highest. Levels one, two, three, four, five and six are various intermediate levels of Defenss *(cf)* hierarchy. All seven levels are subject to Defenss discipline.

Sqoddie747 *n.* a senior level seven Sqoddie who was responsible for the first checks into the lost Ozzilland. Nickname: Jumbo, due to his excessive beer-belly.

squelch *n.* a wet area of soil and water mixture. This mud is very dangerous because anyone who steps into it will probably be sucked in and killed. If this happens, they are left there and this becomes their grave. A quag *(cf)*.

Squelchpool *n.* the area of squelches adjacent to Omeg, the Sacred River.

Stephen *n. pron: stee-ven* a brilliant Trisep who had all sorts of weird notions which turned out to be right, mostly. He went round hawking his ideas until someone bought them and ended up being called Stephen the Hawker. See *Qontûm*. He was also quite famous for writing the popular science book, *Qontûm State Has Moved Here, Probably,* and *Qontûm: the Probability of Uncertainty* as well as for having a robotic tone to his voice which is irresistible to all the ladies.

Structured Antiwisdom *n., vb., adj.* That logic which, when applied to that which is impossible, makes it plausible; when applied to the implausible, makes it feasible; when applied to the unfeasible, makes it viable. The art or act of plausibility of the unfeasible by means of false logic. The topic of many books by Sophist *(cf)*, Precedent of the Dark Elves of the Underplanet beneath Ozzilland.

sub-atomic picocode *n.* information stored in a space smaller than an atom. When it was discovered that there were many parts to the atom, it was used to store data. Every atom can contain the entire data of the universe, if properly stored. The problem is that if they get lost, nobody can find them.

sub-conscientious *n.* the state of being *unconsciously painstakingly and diligently honest and capable.* Sometimes, it is said that when HobB *(cf)* gets hold of the sub-conscientious, a fellow's Sole *(cf)* will become *unconsciously painstakingly and diligently evil and destructive.*

sub-particle *n.* a part of a particle, defined down to something smaller than atoms.

sub-structure *n.* a smaller part of a superordinate structure.

sulphur-carbon *n.* a ghastly mixture of chemicals, being mostly sulphur and carbon. Surprisingly good when hot for sustaining microbes.

Summit *n.* a meeting of very senior delegates, whether Triseps or Gobblings.

Sunrise *n.* widdershins or anti-temporra direction. One of the four cardinal directions on Eqinox, the others being Poleward, Antipoleward, and Sunset. Hence: *adj.* **Sunriseward.**

Sunset *n.* Temporra-wise. One of the four cardinal directions on Eqinox, the others being Poleward,

Antipoleward, and Sunrise. Hence: *adj.* **Sunsetward.**

swanns *n.* an extinct bird that used to sit on quags. Famous for the songs they sang before they died. Perhaps the most famous swann-song was not irrelevant, it was about a hippopotamus, a very bold hippopotamus who wallowed in mud, mud, glorious mud!

Sigmata *n. pron: sig-ma-ter* **1** (more correctly: Σigmata) the ancient sign of the professional arithmate *(cf)*, Σ, which becomes emblazoned on their foreheads, palms and feet unexpectedly during the night, often bleeding from time to time. Some religious Triseps (see *Religiots*) believe that those with the Sigmata can perform miracles, usually because *real* numbers baffle them and they don't seem to understand mathematics beyond the simple sequence of positive integers (0 *[although some don't count 0 because you can have as many of them as you like and they still add up to nothing!]*, 1, 2, 3, 4, 0, 5, 6, 7, etc.). Also, the shape of the sign of Σ itself. **2** The sign is also used in arithmetic by genuine arithmates and helps them sum up their arguments.

Squeith *n. pron: skwithe* A not very large but vitally important country, where Triseps consider themselves too important to mix with other nationalities. The original white ones (like Mycroft) are particularly arrogant and have rigid ventral labia affecting their speech and they often refuse to mix with the other pigments, calling them names (although the pigments do the same as much, if not more, to the whites).

Squeithian *adj.* of Squeith. Also the international language of Triseps.

tee *n.* water, carbon dioxide and perfume. See *geeantee.*

Temporra, The Thundering *n.* an olde-fashioned daily chronicle, famous for the mailings written to it and its daily cryptic interlocking word puzzle.

Tensing *n.* a famous Alp-Ever-rest climber, guide and carrier of goodies, whose exercise routine helps all subsequent climbers. Hence all climbers now practise Tensing Exercises.

Thatch, St. *n.* Infallible leader of the Thatcherfactorismoptimists Party. Her pronouncements were almost holy and as frequently writ as publishers were willing to pay her; and nobody ever dared admit that they were wrong for fear of being branded wet, the most vile insult. In the eyes of many Triseps, she was on a level with the GodS and her behaviour proved, according to Phroyd, that she thought herself to be one.

Thatched Charm *n.* the smarmy artificial charm put on by a politician when hoping to con others into believing that he is genuine. Named after St. Thatch *(cf).*

Thatcherfactorismoptimists *n. pronunciation is not suggested as this was the problem with the name in the first place - but sometimes abbreviated to "the old farts".* a political party once led by St. Thatch that became extinct mostly because of its ridiculously long and unpronounceable name. See *Thatched Charm, Authorised Version.*

thauma *n. abbr.* thaumaturge *(cf).*

Thaumaturge *n. pron: thorm-a-terj* another name for a mother-in-lorr after she has become a miracle-worker by not nagging for seven days and seven nights. Nevertheless, mothers-in-lorr only become thaumas at times of the gravest world crises. All mothers-in-lorr are involved in covens and have graduated from driving moovacars to driving besoms. One in forty seven becomes a WitcH who can perform big spells that really work. Ordinary Thaumaturges can only perform minor miracles, like making things disappear at inconvenient times. It takes a WitcH to make them reappear. Thaumas can be recognised by the white, pointed bobble hat.

The Agreement *n.* see *Agreement, The.*

Thermos *n.* another name for Profsiens who worked out the universal lorrs of Thermos-Dynamism *(cf).* He also invented a device which was so clever that it kept hot things hot and cold things cold, but most people could not use it because they found that it did not work when two cups of coffee and two ice-creams were placed inside it together.

Thermos-Dynamism, lorrs of *n.* Thermos worked out the universal lorrs that say **(Lorr 1)** that to get energy, you need to eat, which is the same as to work, and you must work to eat; also that you can't create heat out of coldness unless you're a social worker when your coldness makes everyone else hot under the collar. He also used his herd leader and mother-in-lorr to prove that **(Lorr 2)** the more pressure you put on her, the more hot air she produces, so **(Lorr 3)** without the heat of the mother-in-law, you stay out in the cold. He also said **(Lorr 4)** that heat is passed (like wind) by convention (conventionally, the way it has always been done); by irradiation (by x-ray); or by seduction (sexually transmitted heat, also known as thermo-coupling). However, the so-called **Zeroth Lorr** says that if a hot couple are balanced when in a ménage-à-trois, then they will not become unbalanced when they are with each other, although Phroyd has other views.

thirty-breaths-to-landing warning ping *n.* a warning message from a moovacar, thirty breaths before landing, giving the trekker *(cf)* a chance to prepare for landing.

Thundering Temporra, The *n.* see Temporra, The Thundering.

tonsurage *n.* a home for nüns, particularly those of the Triseptokatholicus Order. So called because trees are grown round the edges and there is a skating rink in the middle for their religious observances. Tends to be full of females dressed up and pretending to look like nün-polepengus.

Tournäment Square *n.* a square in Walled Faience, where historic uprisings by the Triseps against the government have traditionally taken place. So called because of these tournäments between the revolting peasant students and giant military machines, where many thousands of student Triseps have died under their massive tracks. Traditionally, foreign reporters will flock to Tournäment Square to report the country's more relevant historical happenings.

Traffic-Gestapo *n.* Triseps who like wearing uniforms and taping expensive little bits of paper to moovacars parked where they don't want them to be. See also *Green Aisle.*

Treaty, The *n.* see **Helvetica War Crimes Treaty.**

trek *vb.* to drive as a passenger or instigator to move in a moovacar.

trekker *n.* one who goes as a passenger or instigator to move in a moovacar. The one who treks.

trinoculars *n.* noculars specially designed for the three eyes of Triseps, with an x-ray enhancer for their third eye.

Trioptic *adj.* with two light-spectrum eyes and one x-ray-spectrum eye, like each head of a Trisep. There have been arguments in the past about whether Triseps should really be called Hexipeds because of the six eyes of both heads, but others pointed out that you might just as well called them Yellow-blushing hoggupines because of the genetic nearness to hoggs *(cf)* except for the blood colour.

triple septihelix ribena-acid *n.* the molecular nanostructure from which all life-forms on the planet, and presumably in the universe, are made.

trirhythmic-septaline *n.* a Nipoffese form of poetry beloved of the upper classes from Ånjap. The poetry takes the form of three rhyming words in the first four lines and four rhyming words in the last three lines; seven lines in total. The extra line zero is usually omitted unless you are a WizarD, except for Old Mother Nostril-Dame *(cf)*. There are many other complex rules, too, but these are enough to get you started!

Trisep *n.* a normal shortform for Trioptic Septuped, so called because they have three independent eyes, four legs and three arms. They are the only intelligent beings on Squeith ... or at least, they used to think that they were!

Trisepitarian help *n., adj.* Special help provided by one or more Trisep for other Triseps. Remember, Triseps are Triseps, and Humans are Humans. To spell it out, a Triseps is not a Human or they would have been so called!

Triseptokatholicus Order *n.* a sect of religiots, hated by the Jowver's Evidencers. The Order use a slightly different translation of The Folius from others. The Order has a large number of nüns *(cf)* in the Green Aisle.

Troll *n.* a member of a tribe of Gobblings resident in the Underplanet beneath Walled Faience *(cf)*. One of the seven tribes. Their special characteristics are their black, pointed faces, long, dangling arms, a penchant for bananas and lots of long, dark hair.

turtle *v. past perfect:* **turtled** to roll (usually unintentionally) *exhaust* over *mamaglans*, as it were until one ends up upside-down on the floor somewhere. The usual response when watching is, "you should be in a circus" or "I missed it first time, can you do it again." That request is always refused due to pain.

twain *n.* sometimes called a snake sandwich. A twain is so called because olde-fashioned pressure-vapour engines operate in pairs, twin power units sandwiching a snake of seven or more very comfortable, air-conditioned, fully restaurated hotels on wheels, called clarridges. Every Anerakian *(cf)* owns a forty-seventh part of a clarridge or engine and works on it every spare breath to keep it going. When they have visitors to their Preservation Centres, Anerakians like to show off their driving skills and their badges and to tell you all about their *gaijes, sanding valves* and *ghoti plates,* all of which no non-Anerakian is permitted (or wants) to understand. Others wear uniforms and enjoy enholing tickets when visitors come, as well as wearing a uniform to guard the snake from non-payers, vandals and unhappy elements, like rain and fire.

twak *n.* what a twain wuns on, according to Anerakians *(cf)*. See *twain* for full definition.

tyddly-wynks *n.* A silly game played by supposedly intelligent Triseps, particularly members of Mensa *(cf)*. In principle, they push little green edible balls that grow ten to a pod (called decapods) along the floor with their nose and ping them into a miniature chamber pot by wynking their eyelids to which they have attached little counters.

ultric-bionic analysis *n.* a full analysis of every atom within a sample, defining its biostatus and biofunction.

ultric-proteañ *n.* super-goodness; very high quality life giving food for cells. Like proteañ but containing much more energy-giving goodness.

unbuild *vb.* the act of removing a building. In particular, the act of reconstituting a hole so that the compressed sides re-form the original material. Hence, **unbuilt** *adj.* Nothing to do with Gerry *(cf)* whose buildings (which always have a blue plaque saying *"Gerry Built"*), become unbuilt of their own accord in a self-demolition process.

Underplanet *n.* the numerous layers of Eqinox below the surface, where the Gobblings live. Divided roughly into the same countries as the surface because they do not live under the oceans. Each country has its own tribe of Gobblings and some have sub-tribes. The main seven layers of the Underplanet house and feed the Gobblings, but the bottom two layers are only used for farming because of the higher temperature, being closer to the magma layer. In certain areas of high land, they also build their cities up to five layers higher; the exceptionally tall Alp-Ever-rest has seven extra layers inside.

Urchin *n.* a member of a tribe of Gobblings resident in the Underplanet beneath Zimgululland *(cf).* One of the seven tribes. Their special characteristics are their black hair knotted into thousands of tiny plaits and their strange dialect, similar to that of the Triseps on the surface above.

vexal *adj.* having a curved outer surface like that of a much larger sphere; convex so that the radius and diameter are equal, like certain coins.

vexal septiquadecahedron *n.* the shape of a forty-seven sided solid object with vexal (convex-curved) sides so that the radius is identical to the diameter, making the diameter constant, exactly like the 23.5 dalli coin *(cf in Arithmates' Addendum).* See also *septiquadecahedron.* See also *Eqinox,* which is this shape. See also *Convinciing Geometry, geoplatelets.*

Vinci *n.* See *Con-Vinci.*

vipertree *n.* a very large, self-defending tree, whose leaves exude a lethally venomous sap. This, when mixed with saliva from any tribe of Gobbling will cause the deadly symptoms of the Contaigen when it touches a Trisep, for example, by way of a wet kiss. The tree is deadly to Triseps, but adored by all of the Gobbling tribes, who visit the surface mainly to eat it. That's not a problem, so long as they don't kiss you afterwards!

Vittler *n.* a depressed Trisep who provides equipment and stores for the Defenss forces, if he really has to. He would rather spend his time trying to modify the various weapons to kill himself - always unsuccessfully because they are all double-safety designed not to kill their operators.

vittles *n. always plural* any supply or supplies from the Defenss stores. If it is a weapon, don't trust it because it may have been modified by Vittler to shoot the operator and if it is an automed, he will have tried to modify it to perform deceasement rather than curing your illness!

voodoo mind-malaise magic *n., vb.* a form of magic performed by certain primitive Trisep clumps who prefer to live in wild forests rather than joining civilisation.

Walled Faience *n.* See *Faience.*

Welks *n.* a mining region of Agwgwlland, with dreadful male choirs, where the Triseps are little and dark and hairy and enjoy playing with their odd-shaped balls, a game which they are unusually good at. The Pontipwl Front Row is particularly famous, but no-one can remember why.

Wholly Spirit *n.* translated by Smelt to be **Holy Sprite**. A bottle of **W. S.** One of the three images of GoD discovered in the Lexikern in the Orijin. Obviously it meant that GoD had completely livened up (or sprite-ened) Planet Three from where the Orijin came. Holy Sprite or Wholly Spirit was obviously that planet's equivalent of the Orijin. Not to be confused with Sprite *(cf)*.

WitcH *n.* a senior thaumaturge who can perform big spells that really work. Triseps don't really like talking about WitcherY, except those who are, who do. A WitcH can easily be distinguished by her droppings called septics *(cf)*, so called because they are seven-sided cubes. A WitcH can also be distinguished by her black pointed hat with a tassel on. If the tassel ever jumps up three times and points at you, you would be safer to read yourself the last riot-acts or perform some sort of disappearing trick. In certain circumstances, an ex-wife will become a WitcH.

WitcherY *n.* the capability of doing things by magic. It really is quite surprising what can be done by WitcherY. It isn't talked about much and most Triseps won't even admit its existence to each other. See *Thaumaturge.*

WizarD *n. pl.:* **WizardS** a male Trisep who is the husband of seven wives and has seven daughters and whose father also had seven daughters and whose grandfather also had seven daughters. Able to perform magic, a bit better than ordinary WitcheS. A capital at each end, of course, to keep out the devil!

Wopia *n.* the boot-shaped country best known for its high grade levva *(cf)* developed, as might be expected, to make boots. They got the idea from the shape of their own country. Wopia has two types of underworld, but that's another story.

Wordsmyth *n.* a Trisep who writes fiction in poetry and other myths using his vast knowledge of words.

writtentime *n.* The time it took to write this book, being exactly 31 days in January and February of 1996. This is opposed to the four further years it took to fail to find anyone stupid enough to publish it, mostly returning it with the comment, "it is too complex" *(which translates as: "I am too thick to understand it")* or in many cases, returning it *without even opening it,* let alone reading it …

Year *n.* One Eqinox of the sun. A second Eqinox occurs once every periodic cycle *(cf)* of seven years, when the second sun appears and plays havoc with reproduction cycles.

Year-of-the-Decapod *n.* Every year has a name. Numbers are only used for cycles and within each seven year cycle, the years are named after various vegetables.

Yellow Cross Organisation of Helvetica a clump *(cf)* of Triseps dedicated to Trisepitarian aid. Not much use these days, but effective in the old days of wars and strife. The flag is a reversal of the Helvetican flag, being a yellow cross (the colour of blood) on a black background.

Yippy *n.* nickname of Yishrelprecedent, the Precedent of Yishrel.

Yishrel *n.* a country from where the seven tribes originate. Actually, they trampled all around the world getting exercised before they threw out some squatters and returned to their homeland after several thousand years. See also *Exercises (the second book of the Old Promisings of The Folius).*

Yodle Valley *n.* a place in Helvetica where Cher-ants make silly noises.

Zimgululland *n.* a country of dark coloured Triseps, formerly a source for slaves in the bad old days, located in the band of hot equatorial jungle-squelches. They speak in a language called *Pijin (cf).* The Precedent is called *Idi Dada, Ah Meen (cf).*

ZygoSplit *n.* a set of differential and paradoxically diametric antitheses found on Eqinox as modified by the *Netherwear Influence.* As a further direct result of magic and infinity (© Philosophers) characteristics (and by the way it should be mentioned here at the end of the book), there is a problem: the word Qontûm itself, whether on its own or combined with other words such as State, Theory, Mechanics, Leap, Field Theory, Efficiency, Electronics, Ozzi~ Number, Statistics, Elginfunctions *(cf)* (as in elgins from the Parthenon, where the Degenerate State of the place was defined) has, as a word, its own Uncertainty Value such that its meaning may move at any one time according to the Probable Forces then acting upon it: probably; thus Qontûm Efficiency not only defines Qontûm as an Uncertain Number, but even radiates doubts about its own accuracy of definition. For more information, we recommend that you read Stephen's *Qontûm: the Probability of Uncertainty* and *Qontûm Has Moved Here, Probably.*

Arithmates' Addendum to Lexikern

0 Zero. This number, when added to any other set of numbers leaves the number unchanged. However many you have, they still add up to nothing. The same works for lists. Therefore, if you wish to count (say) seven objects but you have more, you actuallyy count as follows: 0,0,0,0,1,2,3,4,5,6,7. Also, in the olden days, Triseps would add a letter when inserting, for instance, a house in a street, but now you can add a house after house number three, call it 0 instead of (say) 3A and keep the same number of houses as there were to start with, thus: 0,1,2,3,0,4,5,6 etc. In that road with two zeroes, there are, of course, six houses. See also *7* and *Gobblings*.

1.6180339... the ratio of hite *(cf)* to length *(cf)* of a Trisep. Nobody knows why it is this ratio, but some Triseps think this must be an important magic number. It is likely to turn out that there is a probability that it is. Probably, that is.

2 The root of many of the more difficult problems - or rather, the root of it is!

7 a magic number, secondary only to 47. Dunno why it is a magic number, but there are often seven of things, numbered zero, one, two, three, four, five, six and seven. Of course, the item numbered zero represents nothing, so zero to seven is one to seven plus zero, which equals seven, of course. If you understand that, then you are up among the best of the professional arithmates.

23.5 dalli coin *n.* As there are 47 dallis to the lama, this represents 50% of one of the main units of currency. The important aspect of this coin is that, like the planet, its radius is the same as its diameter, giving it seven sides but a constant diameter. A 9.4 dalli (20%) coin has similar characteristics.

42 a special number equal to six times nine. See *Kraye943* and *Mycroft* if you can't work out why.

47 the magic number, which seems to crop up in the most unexpected places. Sometimes combined with pi, root two, etc. to form other semi-magic numbers.

There is a very good reason why 47 is so important, isn't there?

329 another exact multiple which seems to crop up all over the place. Nanotech329 is an example. It was also exactly 329 cycles since the last WizarD suffered a dysfunctional cognitive response (deceasement).

463.871407... another one of those curious numbers which is exactly divisible by forty-seven. This is the length of the pipe from Squelchpool to Qontûm-under-Squeith. If you have problems with this number, think of 47 blackbirds baked in a square pi, or something like that.

776+1 *n.* The *Number of HobB (cf for full definition)* with which every Trisep will be marked during the End Times and which, it is said in the Folio of Revealment, will herald the last days before which GoD will require Himself to return to Eqinox and recover its GodlinesS for himself. The number itself may never be written or spoken in any form, but by HobB himself.

2209 a round number that keeps appearing. It's one of those nice sort of round numbers that's a bit special, like 47, 53, 8192 and √2. It seems to appear all over the place, a bit too regularly for comfort.

3123.998... this is the diameter of the hemisphere of Qontûm under Squeith in lengths. Of course, this number is an exact multiple of forty-seven. If you still can't work it out, remember that there might be a second route to discovering the answer!

4747 an interesting number used for special purposes, such as to define the clearance distance around a flying moovacar when granted purple air space

108 241 quads of Ozzilland were demanded by the Gobblings in their first negotiations for using that land. The number is something to do with squared-up magic numbers, although why this amount of land was required is a best-kept Gobbling secret.

823 543 Triseps lived in Ozzilland at the time of its disappearance. Fascinating coincidence, that, because it is a magic power of a magic number, but that is just stating the obvious.

229 345 007 quads is the size of Ozzilland itself. Like all relevant numbers on Eqinox, it is of great interest, being an exact multiple of 47.

506 623 120 463 a very big number. This is the probability factor of a planet being a vexal septiquadecahedron like Eqinox. Actually, you will find that it is quite an interesting number, if you play with it.

E = $\sum \Pi \circledR^3$ *formula* the formula defining the shape of Planet 5, Eqinox. A common sight on Trisep students' tee-shirts, even though only a few actually understand it. The shape is, of course, a vexal septiquadecahedron *(cf)*, but if you don't understand that, it doesn't really matter because all it means to us is that it was a constant diameter but not spherical. If you still don't understand, ask an arithmate, mate.

∞ Infinity (© Philosophers) the only thing arithmates are permitted to know about infinity (© Philosophers) is that it is some sort of special large number, because the philosophers own the copyright on it. As a direct result, mathematics, physics and virtually all other sciences take on a wholly different perspective than elsewhere in the universe. Not in alphabetical order, perhaps, but wouldn't you expect to find infinity (© Philosophers) at and beyond the end, even of a Lexikern?

One philosopher pointed out that Triseps have four legs and three arms and because, *"even that is odd"* and the only even and odd number is infinity, therefore Triseps are infinitely definable or put another way, are definable as infinity.

End of the Squeithian Lexikern

A Seven Question Quiz:

First see the definition of 'seven' in the Lexikern (Arithmates' Addendum).

0 Find 47 words that are 'portmanteau' words - made up of more than one word to mean something slightly different. *E.g. pulpleaves, sub-conscientious, singing Cher-ants, Trisepitarian (equivalent to humanitarian but for Triseps).*

1 Find 47 examples of invented words and expressions (most of which were designed to be obvious), *e.g. Narcolexic attack, autofollowing holocam*

2 Find 47 examples of literary references *e.g. Omeg (reference Alph the sacred river? - Coleridge, 1816); Mycroft (Sherlock Holmes' brother?); hephalump (and Christopher Robin?); 'Three treadless tyres, an old felt hat, oil drums, a lorry load of tar blocks, and of course, a broken bedstead there.' (quote from Michael Flanders of Flanders & Swann fame).*

3 Find 47 examples of references to real current or historical people or groups. *E.g. Maecenas; Stephen, who goes round hawking his ideas on Qontûm until someone buys them; or the Yellow Cross Organisation of Helvetica (their blood is yellow) - this equates to the Red Cross Organisation of Geneva although of course, Helvetia means Switzerland, but* **Helvetica** *is actually a typeface!*

4 Find 47 examples of fascinating or obscure usage, *e.g. Squelch for bog-lands, coitalising for lovemaking.*

5 Find 47 examples of word puns, *e.g. grief encounter; oracular delusion; I-smeller instead of eureka (you reek eh?).*

6 Write your own trirhythmic-septaline poem.

7 Check the *Lexikern* and write to the author c/o the publisher correcting any faulty definitions (or any other typos!). All initial letters are answered. Please give an e-mail address if you have one.

Netherwear - *The Blurb*

The sphere of the Orijin containing an Oxford Dictionary was travelling for several million light years before landing with all the gentle precision of a meteor into Squelchpool Moor and creating a new lifeform, Triseps.

On this planet, you can get a black belt in Marital *(sic)* Arts, depending on the quality of your extra-nuptial replication practise; politicians swear the Hypocritic Oath, ensuring that the truth is employed as economically as possible and Arithmates get Sigmata (Σ) emblazoned on their foreheads but cannot use infinity (∞) because the philosophers hold the copyright on it.

Find out more about this strange planet with a new language and new verse forms; where nanomanufacturing makes everything; where everybody's name reflects their job, from Bodgitt the builder and Quax the doctor to Lynkern the Precedent (who leads by doing everything first); where Sharens (from the verb *to share*) from Ballam share *everything* … and not forgetting Stephen, who goes round *hawking* his theories on Qontûm until someone buys them - and Cate'aeddy who reports everything with an autofollowing holocam.

Find out about the Green Aisle - a corridor of land in the sea - with Lepperdcorns that are spotted like leopards and tell really corny jokes. And Ozzilland - upside down in several different planes all at the same time, where Allysp the expeditor (who expedited expeditions) found the rings and founded a settlement called Allysp Rings.

While you're at it, learn the new verse form of the trirhythmic-septaline with poetry minted during a narcolexic fit (sleep talking!) - or was it just an oracular delusion?

It's all so much fun and there's so much new to learn, you'll just *have* to read the book! If you don't, the autotranslator (with a mind of its own) will probably start telling the story anyway …

Finally, before you criticise a spelling, always check it in the comprehensive 700 word *'Lexikern',* listing the kerning of words …

Also available from Blotterpress

Available from Amazon or direct from www.BlotterPress.com:

ISBN	Title	By
978-0-9571944-0-3	The Penny Book Millionaire (Paperback)	Chris Stedman
978-0-9571944-1-0	The Penny Book Millionaire (Kindle eBook)	Chris Stedman
978-0-9571944-2-7	The Cedars' Influence (Paperback)	Chris Stedman
978-0-9571944-3-4	The Cedars' Influence (Kindle eBook)	Chris Stedman
978-0-9571944-4-1	Netherwear (Paperback)	Chris Stedman
978-0-9571944-5-8	Netherwear (Kindle eBook)	Chris Stedman
978-0-9571944-6-5	2012 Joke Book (Paperback)	Chris Stedman

Available in PDF format from www.BlotterPress.com (without ISBNs):
The Penny Book Millionaire
Netherwear
2000 Joke Book
The Cedars' Influence